AGAINST THE MACHINE: *LUDDITES*

ESSENTIAL PROSE SERIES 177

Canada

Guernica Editions Inc. acknowledges the support of the Canada Council for the Arts and the Ontario Arts Council. The Ontario Arts Council is an agency of the Government of Ontario.

We acknowledge the financial support of the Government of Canada.

AGAINST THE MACHINE: *LUDDITES*

Brian Van Norman

TORONTO • BUFFALO • LANCASTER (U.K.)
2020

Michael Mirolla, editor
David Moratto, interior and cover design
Front cover Image: Diane Eastham and Made by Photo Lab
Guernica Editions Inc.
1569 Heritage Way, Oakville, (ON), Canada L6M 2Z7
2250 Military Road, Tonawanda, N.Y. 14150-6000 U.S.A.
www.guernicaeditions.com

Distributors:
Independent Publishers Group (IPG)
600 North Pulaski Road, Chicago IL 60624
University of Toronto Press Distribution,
5201 Dufferin Street, Toronto (ON), Canada M3H 5T8
Gazelle Book Services, White Cross Mills
High Town, Lancaster LA1 4XS U.K.

First edition.
Printed in Canada.

Legal Deposit—First Quarter
Library of Congress Catalog Card Number: 2019946620
Library and Archives Canada Cataloguing in Publication
Title: Against the machine : Luddites / Brian Van Norman.
Names: Van Norman, Brian, author.
Series: Essential prose series ; 177.
Description: Series statement: Essential prose series ; 177
Identifiers: Canadiana (print) 20190162481 | Canadiana (ebook) 2019016249X | ISBN 9781771834797 (softcover) | ISBN 9781771834803 (EPUB) | ISBN 9781771834810 (Kindle)
Classification: LCC PS8643. A557 A64 2020 | DDC C813/.6—dc23

For Alan, and as ever, for Susan

~

1812

YORKSHIRE
North Riding
West Riding
East Riding
PENNINES
North York Moors
Yorkshire Dales
Yorkshire Wolds
Bowland
Craven
Ainsty
Holderness
Mickleton
Redcar
Middlesbrough
Bowes
Whitby
Richmond
Northallerton
Scarborough
Sedbergh
Pickering
Thirsk
Helmsley
Filey
Filey Bay
Ingleton
Malton
Norton
Flamborough Head
Bridlington
Bridlington Bay
Ripon
Driffield
Slaidburn
Harrogate
York
Skipton
Beverley
Bradford
Leeds
Selby
Halifax
Huddersfield
Wakefield
Goole
Hull
Spurn Head
Saddleworth
Barnsley
Doncaster
Rotherham
Sheffield
Bawtry

PROLOGUE

Antsey, Leicestershire

IT WAS SNOWING indoors.

It was big, white tufts floating inside the mill with the rumble of the waterwheel and clacking of the looms. It was the clamour of mechanical parts and curses of the overmen strapping at terrified children who picked the loose pieces of wool from beneath clattering machines. It was the stench of grease, sweat and carded *woollen*. And the heat; the heat that made a man faint away after fourteen hours at his machine. And now some fool had dropped a bale and the wooly fibres twirled around the shop like snowflakes. Big flakes, the like he'd seen on days of deep winter with the air fresh and clean. And as it floated down the fleece snarled the machines. Workers muttered in fleecy snow as they lost time and money to the unnatural blizzard.

It was this which broke him.

"'Tain't natural," Ned said. He was a tall, well-muscled boy, dressed in tattered fustian stained with the sweat of his toil. Despite his fourteen years his face was swarthy, like a man's face, brought on by long days of mill work. And now as he flustered over his stocking frame, clearing the fleece, cursing the heat, he recalled better days before the *enclosures* when he was a true boy out on the *weld* with a flock of sheep and his collie, Spot. The weather sported around him: big, bosomy clouds sweeping the horizon shadowing grass so green just after the rain and a breeze which coddled him like a mother.

His mother now dead, his sister carding wool, his father an overman flush with his power had forced the boy into the mill to drudge through each day from dark to dark, sunlight now just a memory, a pewter colour seeping through narrow windows high up on the sandstone block walls.

"'Tis the *brass* we need!" his father said, his big voice always too loud. "Now your mother's gone and the farm's taken off there's no other way. Dost understand, lad? Stop your tears! The dog was old and no use t' us now. I've found a place for you in the mill. You'll do this or go for a soldier. I'll not feed you nor your sister without your help!"

But the fleece has cloyed into the warp and each moment his machine is stopped no *brass* will be made. His fingers plucked at the threads like those of an enraged harpist. It took too much time to unclog the machine and with each passing moment his rage stewed and boiled.

Oatcake for breakfast in the dark, then hard black bread and water while standing at his frame for his lunch, then the repetitive hours of shuttle-knit-shuttle-knit and the roasting heat and the stink of lanolin and the clamour and shake and now this; this prigging, prinking, pulling with his fingers at warp threads.

"Dammit!" he spat, shoving two bloody fingers into his mouth, sucking blood, tasting salt.

"Boy!" the overman snarled. "Get that frame going!"

Ned glared past his shoulder at the man, now advancing, his thick strap dangling from his belt, hand straying toward it: a threat of a beating.

"'Tis clogged! I was fixing it!" Ned shouted.

"Then stop standing about and get back t' work!"

"Aye! I'm trying!"

"Now!"

Then at it again, this time with his other hand; blood in the cloth means no coin. He picked the last of the snow dream away and was left with an unsettling maze of threads. He tried a knit: clatter, bang ... and all crooked.

"Shite!" Now he must pull the errant weft out. More time lost.

"Do it!" the overman bellowed.

The machine would not submit. He'd gone under and over it, searching out the snag but could not find it; the overman bawling abuse all the while. He knew he was in for the strap the moment he emerged from beneath the frame. But there, in the detritus of discarded wool beneath the machine, was the hammer. A sledge so big the men had a name for it: *Enoch*. Made in the smithy of Enoch Taylor. Ned's pastor had told him once the name meant *wisdom* from something in the Bible, but he knew it was named after Enoch Taylor. It didn't matter now. He would not submit to a beating. He grasped the hammer and crawled out to face the overman. The strap was already loosed. It swung in the overman's calloused hand all leathery shine, thick with anticipation.

"You'll not touch me," he said, shifting the maul into both hands, holding it chest high.

"Set that down!" the overman ordered, but with a quaver in his voice.

"I'll not do a thing 'til that strap's gone!"

"If that maul ain't put down now I'll have you up t' the *Maister* and cast out of the mill!"

"'Tis nowt t' me. I'll not take a beating."

"You'll take what I give!" The overman's voice was too shrill. It brought the mill to silence. The fleece snow was gone by then, replaced by the normal thickness of dust as though they all lived inside a cloud. From somewhere off by the looms a girl's voice cried out: "That's the way, Ned! Give him the business!"

And that helped him; cracked him even more.

He recognized then that the overman was actually smaller than him. Now it came clear what had made the man seem larger: his power. All that size shrank before Ned as he hefted the hammer. The man retreated a step, just enough. A laugh tittered throughout the mill, growing.

The overman's eyes shifted left and right. He had lost his power and, bereft of it, had no idea what to do next. For a moment the two of them stood facing off: boy to man, hammer to strap, for now Ned too found he had no recourse. He tried to think of some action, some words which would settle the thing. Already it had gone too far.

Then the overman glanced past him. Ned knew, even before he heard, what was coming.

"Edward Ludlam, what would you be up to? No good, I see!"

The voice of his father, overman father, rang out harsh in the still of the silence and dust.

That voice pushed a weakness into Ned's arms and lowered the hammer. There was no response to this man who possessed such a weight. It ran back all the years of childhood commands which were never contended.

"Turn about and look at me!" And Ned turned.

Thomas Ludlam was a hard man: thick, muscled, dark, eyes like stone. If he'd ever been kind Ned could not recall it. What he could remember was cuffs and kicks in the hard school of his father's creation. And the way his mother would shrink when Thomas entered the cottage, his presence filling the single room crowding out all else as his family waited, pensive, for his mood. Sporadically he might be in good spirits, usually brought on by drink, but he could turn sour abruptly. If his wife was too slow bringing food to the table, or Ned unfinished his chores, or his sister too carefree with her kittens, there would be costs. And just now that mood was a thunderhead as he faced down his son in the maw of the mill where everyone feared him.

"You'd challenge an overman, child?" he said, ensuring his deep voice was loud enough to surmount the rumble of the waterwheel.

"The frame was clogged. 'Twas all that fleece! I'll not take a beating for something that weren't my fault!" Ned said. Too loud, a mistake.

"Talk t' me like that one more time and you'll be in for a true thrashing!" His hands curled into huge fists. The fists looked like rocks. Ned knew what they could do.

"Father, I didn't mean this t' happen!"

Tears welled in the boy's eyes.

"I'm overman here," his father roared, "and this man as well! You'll yield up that maul and give way t' your punishment!"

"'Twas the machine, da! Not me!"

"Did you not think t' square your heddles, boy?" his father said sarcastically. Ned lowered his head. The tears dripped black on his fustian blouse, turning to mud in the blouse's dirt. He had not thought of that fix, an obvious thing, but the snow and the noise and the very day had conspired against him. Now his father thought him a simpleton.

Breaking him.

And just then peering down through his tears past the rags of his clothes past the head of the hammer he looked further into himself. He remembered his father kicking the kittens, slapping his mother, killing his dog, thinking him simple, and *that*, finally, with everything else, shattered anything left of the boy. In an instant a man looked up into the eyes of his overman. Father no longer.

"Square my heddles, Sir? No, Sir. But now just let me do it for you."

And with that he let the hammer head drop, feeling the shaft run through his calloused hands until it had reached its end and the huge iron head thumped the floor. Then he swung it: a huge arc up, around, over his shoulder and smashed into the delicate heddles of the frame. The frame exploded in splinters, and he hit it again, then again, revelling in the destruction. Threads of wool fluttered out like banners of victory with each crushing blow.

His father came at him.

The hammer came up.

"Stay back! Touch me and I'll have Enoch on you!"

And, wonder of wonders, his father retreated; confused by the boy become man become hooligan he too found no answer to what happened next. Ned strolled past the first overman, who also did nothing, to the next stocking frame.

"And how about this one? Can I square up the heddles?"

And again he smashed. Splinters everywhere. Then another. Then he moved on toward the doorway down the long hall of the mill. No one blocked his path. No one came after him. As he passed each machine he would swing and smash and leave shards in his wake. As he neared the thick oak door he heard cheers, and turning, saw them all clapping.

And back down the walkway, between the machines, the walkway littered with fragments of his rebellion, he saw his father standing there: broken too.

He opened the door and walked through it.
Outside.
Into the sunshine: golden green, warm and free.
No one in Antsey ever saw him again.

News of this incident spread as does all unusual news. And after a time, when it became less unusual, when machines were sabotaged or mills burned, and people fought their masters' greed so as not to starve, they would jokingly say: *"Ned Lud did tha'!"*

And later: *Luddites*.

1

A PENNINE FOG crawled down from the moors on a January night in the year 1812. It was a cold fog, filled with the icy moisture of what men in those parts called *moor grime*. It was a thick fog, sluggishly flowing its way down the vales of the countryside, drowning them in its coils. Through the West Riding in Yorkshire it moved over Marsden, Haworth, Huddersfield and Halifax, reaching as far east as Bradford. It smothered the land like a hoary blanket and concealed every movement within its grey realm; even certain men tramping through slushy snow toward John Wood's cropping shop and a meeting with their destinies.

They were hardened men whom hard times had brought to this place. There had been massive change since the century's turn. Farmers and shepherds driven from common lands by the Enclosures Act. Then in 1811 torrential rains had ruined the harvest and caused starvation. More pertinent, there had been a plunge in production of *woollen*, the material made from combed, long-fibred wool which, when woven and finished, made the hardiest cloth in the world.

Bonaparte's war suppressed English trade in Europe. Parliament struck back with Orders in Council forbidding trade with *any* nation with French connections. Then the Americans entered the fray against England, stopping another market.

To keep their fast waning trade, the mill owners sought technological answers. They began to employ machines to do the work of men: *gig-mills, knitting frames, power looms* and *shear frames*, all driven by water from streams in north England's vales. So families who had spent generations working the wool lost their livelihoods and fell into penury.

Finally, men banded together to stop the hopelessness. The wet, fustian clothed group, surreptitiously knocking on John Wood's door in the dark of night in the thick of fog, was one such desperate band.

They entered Wood's small cropping shop: a medieval mix of stone, wood and leaded glass panes. There was a table at one end and some stools but most of the shop consisted of *woollens* stretched on frames with nary a glint of new age mechanicals. John Wood possessed too small an operation and too little ready money for machines. Yet he coveted them. This night would see his opening strategy. Wood was lean, middle aged and balding. Yet it was his eyes which told the tale of the man: sharp grey orbs constantly moving, behind which an observant person might discern a calculating mind.

The first in was Thomas Smith. A portly young fellow, his freckled skin glistened from the fog's dampness. He removed his soaking hat beneath which a dirty blond mop of hair tumbled into his hazel eyes. He was a simple fellow, a follower.

William Thorpe, next, was older: a huge man who could reach up and touch the rafters of Wood's shop. He was brawny and strong and possessed a barrel chest, the result of his love of good ales. He was illiterate, as were most souls of the West Riding, but he was no man's fool. And no man ever dared fool with him.

Behind him came Benjamin Walker, as opposite Thorpe as a man could be. Somewhat gawky in look, Walker was a weaver. He was thin; not in a womanish way yet still delicate from his careful weaving. Ben Walker was cautious. In a world of bigger, bluff men he had to be; though he did not have to like it. Instead he used gossip and rumour to achieve his goals.

The fourth of the group was the man John Wood had most wanted at this meeting. George Mellor was but twenty-two years old yet possessed experience beyond his years and an almost carnal charisma. He was striking: sparkling diamond eyes within a firm face, high cheek bones and a solid chin, hair close curling and auburn in colour. He was also John Wood's step-son and had only just returned from his merchant voyages, to Russia and other foreign ports, within the past two years. Still, since that time he had swiftly advanced to *journeyman cropper.*

The build of his body showed shearing's effects: He was sculpted and strapping; for to crop the *woollen* a man had to control a fifty pound metal shear, then push the huge, sharp blades together so deftly as to remove miniscule flaws in the nap of the wool and turn it to smooth, fine *worsted.* It was a highly skilled trade requiring delicacy and strength and George Mellor was one of its best.

Mellor's father had disappeared from Huddersfield long years past leaving his family penniless. So the lad had had to make his own way, taking ship as a cabin boy advancing to sailor for seven years, until he'd returned to find his mother, Mathilda, remarried to Wood. Wood and Mellor had grown to respect each other.

If there was to be a leader in his secret campaign, John Wood knew it would be George Mellor: a young man who had learned to read and write, a youth who had seen obscure parts of the world, a fellow who tolerated no edicts and felt no inferiority toward the titled and wealthy. His magnetism would make others trust him. And he in turn trusted John Wood.

Wood was counting on it.

Wood placed a pewter jug and cups before them on the table. The smell of the shop, damp lanolin and old wood, comforted them as they drank their ale. Wood commenced the meeting.

"I've taken the liberty of inviting some guests. I think you'll agree 'tis a wise choice." His West Riding accent was prominent though unnoticed by his peers. It may have sounded to an outsider as ludicrous, even rustic, but the men who spoke it knew it marked them as Yorkshiremen, known for their business acumen and hard work.

"Who are they?" Walker half stood, seeming ready to flee.

"Sit down, Ben!" Mellor said, laughing. "You'll be pissing your britches before you know it."

There was no love lost between Walker and Mellor, for Walker loved a local girl named Jilly Banforth. Unfortunately, she'd made it clear she preferred the lusty George Mellor.

"Dost believe me a careless man?" Wood said, chuckling. "Here they are!"

From the shadows stepped a man and woman affluently dressed. Mellor stood quickly to greet them.

"John! Mary! 'Tis good to see you."

"It is, George," the man replied, "and our thanks to you, Mr. Wood, for your invitation."

His accent was different from the others: more refined; that of an educated man, one from more southerly parts of England. His face was handsome: eyes hazel, hair a light, thinning blonde. He wore tight pantaloons with riding boots, eschewing the *woollen* stockings and rough breeches of the poorer men. With his greatcoat undone, there was a glimpse of a fashionable jacket and short waistcoat beneath and, quite notably, the white linen *stock* of the clergy.

"Aye, John, 'tis good you're here," Wood said. "Brothers, you all know Curate Buckworth and his wife, Mary."

In the hallowed tangles of the Church of England there existed, as in all bureaucracies, a distinct set of seniorities. John Buckworth's place was to serve as Curate of Dewsbury, a small situation at the edge of the West Riding under the auspices of the Very Reverend Hammond Roberson, Vicar in charge of the Parish. Roberson performed that office with a certain prejudice against common people and was not loved for his work, whereas John Buckworth was esteemed for his caring nature.

Buckworth, born in the town of Gravesend of a moderately wealthy tea trade family, was a second son and as with most second sons who would not inherit the family business, was sent off to school to make something of himself. He chose the clergy, by far the most obvious course for, with a suitable position and the proper marriage, John could become a man of substance.

Buckworth possessed a slim, well proportioned frame which attracted those of the female sex from amongst his parishioners; never a bad thing. Eventually he'd met and married the lovely, accomplished Mary Taylor; daughter of a Nottingham mill owner.

Mary Buckworth was dressed in a *redingote* of deep forest green. Beneath were a plum jacket, muslin dress and a tailored chemisette. The usual calfskin gloves and fashionable turban completed her ensemble. Mary was a woman accustomed to fashion. She was the daughter of a wealthy, devoted father who had wished to see her advance beyond his own mercantile world. So marriage to a man with potential to rise in the Church was the perfect answer. It was also the answer to other, more troublesome elements: in particular, Mary's rebellious nature.

A brief interlude with a Captain Hollingsworth when she was sixteen had ascertained her passionate character though, fortunately, the thing had been nipped in the bud without scandal. But Calvin Taylor had recognized the unfortunate spirit his daughter possessed and had married her off with an attractive dowry to the young Curate Buckworth.

John Buckworth loved his wife to distraction. Not only was she physically beautiful with unsettling green eyes beneath honey locks, she possessed a perfect pale complexion and a figure simultaneously petite yet full. If her lips were a hint too sensuous and flashing eyes too fervid, those elements John overlooked. More significantly to him, his Mary possessed an intelligence which consistently helped him create both sermons and texts far beyond his own talents.

"Now then, John," Wood said, "you've brought your ... what do you call it?"

"A manifesto," Buckworth said, withdrawing a document from his coat.

"Mr. Wood," Thomas Smith said, "watch your voice, Sir! What about Special Constables? They could be lurking!"

"Nonsense!" Mellor replied. "We're as safe in this shop as in the fields, and a damn sight warmer." He glanced quickly toward Mary. "Please excuse a rough cropper's tongue, Mrs. Buckworth."

"You need not concern yourself, Mr. Mellor," she said, smiling. "You recall my father once owned a mill. I am accustomed to workmen's jargon."

Mary's accent was also markedly more refined than all but her husband's with just the soft click of Nottingham in a few of its consonants.

"But where are the others, Mr. Wood? John said this was an important meeting."

"They keep vigil at Cartwright's mill," Will Thorpe said.

"But why?" Mary asked.

"They await the coming of ..."

"Cartwright has ordered machines," Mellor said, finishing the thought, accompanied by grumbles around the table. "He's bringing in shear frames. So men stand outside his mill in protest."

As the others muttered, Thorpe turned to Mary.

"Are ye staying here, ma'am, for the meeting?"

"Yes, of course," she said, a trifle confused.

"What's the trouble, Will?" Wood asked.

It took a moment for Thorpe to respond. He had carefully measured his words.

"I see no sense in a woman joining this business. 'Tis the work of men; a brotherhood! Women have no understanding of this."

"Ah, but this one does, Mr. Thorpe," John Buckworth said. "We both see the way the world is going. Had Mary's father not sold his business he would now be facing ruin. Believe me, Sir, we know a new order must be advocated."

"But a woman ... " Thorpe could not find his way from that path.

"Will," Mellor said, "we need these good people and more like 'em! They're educated. We ain't. They can make the pamphlets we'll need t' spread our word t' the public."

"But *you* can write," Thorpe said.

"Not like these two," Mellor said.

"Can we get t' the business, George?" Walker said.

"Right then," Mellor said, smiling. "To business!"

2

"I HAVE THE newspaper: the *Leeds Mercury*."

George Mellor spread a broadsheet on the table.

"Is that one edited by Edward Baines?" Mary asked. Clearly she knew of the newspaperman and his liberal reputation. Clearly as well, from the tone of her voice, she agreed with his views.

"Aye!" Mellor replied. "He's followed events quite some time now!"

"He's also somewhat of a radical, George," Buckworth said.

"Just look here!" Mellor raised his voice in excitement. "They smash the machines that beggar them! The Nottingham lads are showing them soldiers a bit of real sport!"

"So it's come to that," Buckworth said. He picked up the broadsheet, angling the page toward the lantern's dim light.

"Soldiers?" Walker said, again nervous.

"It says they've hundreds organized there." Buckworth closed the paper. "The least we can do is support them. We must publish my manifesto!"

"More words," Thorpe replied.

"You're right, Will," John Wood said. He did not want his stratagems going astray. "I believe in your words, Curate Buckworth. And that's the true business here! You, Sir!"

Buckworth was taken aback.

"I don't understand ... "

Mary placed a hand on his arm, Mellor subtly moved to Buckworth's other flank.

"John," Mrs. Buckworth said quietly, "listen carefully now."

"Join us, man!" Wood said, enthused; his plan depended upon his next words. "'Tis time for action! You must become one of the brothers, one of Gen'ral Ludd's followers!"

If ever a man bore the look of a cornered animal, John Buckworth did in that moment. His eyes skimmed quickly from Wood to his wife, then to Mellor. He spoke in a halting manner.

"Luddites? You intend … vandalism then?"

"Were you not safe with your money, friend," Thorpe said, looming across the table, "you'd see things a different way."

Mellor placed his hand on Buckworth's shoulder, the curate's wife tightening her grip on the other side.

"You must examine … both sides … before you stoop to violence," Buckworth said, stuttering, then regained his confidence. "These machines might become a blessing for you if society were different. There is an international economy which reaches far beyond our Yorkshire. These machines will allow us to join that economy, increase our trade. The machinery itself is not evil. Think how efficiently it works, how it does the most arduous part of a workman's task!"

"It takes our jobs! Leaves us nowt but beggary," Walker replied.

"If the owners would recognize people's needs," Buckworth said, "surely the situation would improve."

"If? If?" Thorpe thundered. "What's the use of your sermons t' starving men? If the *maisters* would do as you say, well, it would be better we all know! But they won't! What do they care about us when they make their *brass* a bit faster?"

"The course of the Luddites is not negotiation," Buckworth said, "but confrontation. Violence is no remedy."

"Aye, but it makes 'em sit up and take notice!" Thorpe shouted.

"The Luddite plan will never succeed. We need reform, Mr. Thorpe, not revolt!"

"Reform? Bah!" Walker said.

"But would it not be better to lay these matters before the owners and reason with them?"

"Reason with 'em? Reason with stones I say, for their hearts be hard as flint!" Thorpe said. "The only chap who can reason with them is *Enoch*!"

Thorpe raised a huge sledge hammer from a line of tools beside him, the head weighing thirty pounds. This maul had a storied history; forged by Enoch Taylor when he'd been a mere blacksmith, now he owned a manufactory. Now he made the cast-iron shear frames which would put yet more men out of work.

"Enoch hath made 'em," Thorpe recited, "and Enoch shall break 'em!"

It was a powerful, ironic statement and popular rallying cry.

"This chap," Thorpe said, "is the best reasoner I know! When he breaks them machines in a hundred pieces, then the *maisters* will understand!"

"But the country needs money, Mr. Thorpe," Buckworth said, remaining calm. "Bonaparte has cut our markets and now the Americans look to do the same. Am I not correct in this, Mr. Wood? If you could, would you not purchase machines?"

The shift took John Wood by surprise. This was treacherous ground.

"I've no wish t' put men out of work. And I've heard shear frames do a poor job of finishing. I've no use for machines that cheapen my product." Wood shifted the focus away from himself. "George Mellor, what say you?"

"Say you'll join us, John!" Mellor squeezed Buckworth's shoulder in a friendly fashion, then looked to Mary. "What does your wife say? Mary?"

"My husband is a man who abhors violence," Mary responded. "I know his feelings but, forgive me John dear, your arguments have fallen short."

Buckworth registered shock as an expected ally turned defector. For a moment he found he could not speak, then stuttered a brief: " ... destroying machines?"

"As symbols of injustice, John," Mary said boldly. "You have said yourself in your manifesto there must be a focal point."

"My manifesto — " Buckworth said, trying to regain his footing.

" — will be ignored, if there is not some reason to hear it," Mary exclaimed. With his logic gone, his arguments in tatters, John Buckworth collapsed beneath her will.

"My wife is a wise woman. I ... I shall join you. My head tells me you are wrong but my dear wife shows me the way."

"You'll take the Oath?" Mellor said.

"The Oath is illegal. Taking it means imprisonment, or transportation."

Buckworth glanced again to Mary for her approval. It came in the smallest nod of consent.

"I will take the Oath." Buckworth spoke more assuredly, his way cast for him, yet with no idea where it would lead.

"The book, Thomas!" Mellor turned to Smith who produced a tattered Bible. Mellor placed Buckworth's right hand upon it and into his left thrust a soiled, much used parchment. "Then read the Oath, John, and swear."

Buckworth read the Oath, its ink smudged from many hands grasping the parchment, the parchment itself stiff and curling. He read carefully, as he would any writ, though he noted how it was oddly composed. He stopped and stuttered two or three times as he tried to comprehend the style of a barely literate hand.

The Oath read, and Buckworth recited:

> *"I of my own free will and A Coard declare and solemly sware that I will never reveal to aney ... Person or Persons aney thing that may lead to discovery of the same ... Either in or by word sign or action as may lead to aney Discovery under the Penelty of being sent out of this World by the first Brother that May Meet me ... Further more I do sware that I will Punish by death aney trator or trators ... should there aney arise up amongst us I will persue with unseaceing vengeance, should he fly to the verge of Nature. I will be gust true sober and faithful in all my deailings with all my Brothers So help me GOD to keep this my Oath Invoilated ... Amen."*

Buckworth finished, his *Amen* almost a prayer of regret, when Wood took the Bible from him and said: "Now you're *twisted in* as we call it. One of us, Curate Buckworth."

Buckworth faced Mellor blankly as the latter smiled.

"Now our business done, we'll be off t' the Shears Inn up the road for a jar of celebration! Well done, John Buckworth!"

"T' the pub!" Thomas Smith said. Yet amidst the noise Buckworth paused.

"I would join you, Sirs, but must see my wife home first."

"No John!" George Mellor said. "'Tis your night! I'll see your wife home then join the revels later!"

"Mary?" Buckworth turned to her, his eyes a question to which she responded with a wonderful smile, her green eyes becoming sea soft, securing her husband's acquiescence.

"I am proud of you, dearest," she said. "This night is your night. You must be its centre as you are mine."

"Off now, all of you!" Mellor instructed. "Upend a tankard or two. I'll join you soon!"

With his commands the men boisterously donned their coats and hats anticipating the Shears. It took little time to disperse and walk the two miles to bring them their *bitters*. Buckworth found himself relishing the walk even if the road was slushy, even if fog concealed all around him.

In the shop, the men gone, their shouts and laughter dissipated in the distance, George Mellor closed and barred the door. He turned to look at Mary. Seconds passed with his look and Mary, trembling slightly, turned away from him. The intensity of their mood made her loosen her jacket collar with quivering fingers.

"Well, it's ... best we go home ... " she said softly.

Mellor took a step toward her.

"Mary ... " he said, hesitant as well.

She turned to him, her face revealing a confusion of love, lust, longing and guilt. He swept her into his arms, she welcoming the embrace, and they kissed long and hungrily. His hand began to move over her, brushing her breast, pushing her hips closer to him. She returned his passion but as he began to tug at her laces she broke away.

"George, please, not here. Any of them might return."

"That will not happen, dearest," Mellor said, smiling.

He tried again to draw her into his arms but she resisted.

"No, George."

"In God's name, Mary, I need you now."

"Then walk me home. It will be safe there."

"In your husband's house?"

"Why not? We've manipulated him, George. Against his will he's joined you."

"We agreed it would be good for the movement as John Wood advised … "

"I cannot take the chance of being discovered."

"Aye," he said, "you're ashamed of me."

"We've been over this, George. I love my husband but he is … not you. Since the moment I met you in father's shop, you just off a ship looking for work. Even when he told you he was selling and could not hire you, you didn't wilt or slink away. I felt your power even then. And that is why I am yours, why those men are yours, why my husband is yours now too."

She had turned him, his bitterness disappearing as a smile crossed his face. He grasped her and lifted her off the floor spinning her around like a weightless doll.

"Mary … Mary … you're a wondrous woman!"

She laughed as she spun.

"George, put me down!"

"Aye, I will, but you must promise me one thing."

"Oh? And what would that be?" She smiled, straightening her outfit. As quickly as he'd become jovial, George Mellor altered: his voice full of worry.

"I'll need your help in this, Mary. 'Tis a frightening thing t' lead men yet they seem t' expect it. I'm a dolt, dear Mary."

"You are a born leader, George Mellor, despite your humble place. You shall be a great man one day soon."

Once again, with her words, his mood shifted. He grinned.

"And you'll be mine!"

"But now, see me home," she said gently, her eyes an uninhibited jade. "We'll walk quickly. In my bed I'll have some of that power of yours!"

"In your husband's bed," he said bitterly, but she shook him from his mood with a look, a touch, and a few simple words.

"Tonight it is yours, and mine, together. Hurry now ... where is your coat?"

As the two departed they extinguished the lantern. From an alcove which lead to his office John Wood moved through the dark. He too was smiling. The night had brought all he'd wanted. The inclusion of the curate and his manifesto would offer endorsement to his designs and young George Mellor had taken the lead to become the spearhead of his plans. In order to stay afloat, Wood planned to sabotage his wealthy competitors. The curate, the cropper, the wife and mistress ... they would become his arsenal.

But where they would take him when he set them loose, and the consequences arising, he could not possibly realize.

3

ANOTHER MEETING OF a much different nature took place a week later, not far down the valley. This gathering occurred within the substantial mansion of Magistrate Joseph Radcliffe and his new, young wife, Fanny. Milnsbridge House was a neo-classical building of multiple rooms and high ceilings set in the midst of cultured gardens.

Instead of ragged young men the attendees arrived on horseback or in carriages and wore double breasted frock coats, tall slightly conical top hats and riding boots over buff trousers. The women present were adorned in Empire silhouette, high-wasted dresses inspired by the tastes of the Regency. They wore bonnets and long white gloves as well.

Where a single lantern had lit John Wood's shop, Milnsbridge House was illuminated by expensive wax candles flickering from candelabra or seated securely in wall sconces. Fires burned in the hearths. And in Radcliffe's library fine wines were served to the gentlemen while, in Fanny's drawing room, maids provided tea and cakes for the ladies.

This meeting had been convened by Radcliffe, Parish magistrate and master of Milnsbridge House; a rich man becoming richer each day. A somewhat diminutive, portly man with white mutton chop whiskers flanking his round, Punch-like face, Radcliffe belied his grandfatherly looks with a potent ambition.

Hammond Roberson, Church of England, sat behind an oak table amidst the glow of leather bindings lining Radcliffe's library shelves. As Vicar for the West Riding and ambitious a man as Radcliffe, he represented the true, Anglican Church and a societal place with the parish's Tory wealthy. His own wealth, obtained through marriage with his dear Phoebe, recently deceased, gave Roberson a great deal in common with Radcliffe. For Roberson too was an older man, though more charismatic with his broad shoulders, hawk-like head and large girth. The two men had become principals of their community: the one as a secular magistrate, the other as vicar to the affluent.

Seated with them was Major James Gordon, commander of the recently arrived Yeomanry imported to assist special constables appointed by Radcliffe. Together these forces would protect the region's mills and owners from the growing vandalism which had started in Nottingham. The three chaired this meeting of manufacturers who lounged about the library.

Major Gordon was a strapping man, tall and lean, resplendent in scarlet, though a missing left arm explained the reason for this particular command. Secretly, Gordon wished for a place in the real war on the Continent. Instead, he'd spent the evening listening to the snivelling voice of John Lloyd, solicitor aspiring to barrister, who stood beside the three men at the table. Lloyd had not been offered a chair.

He was, however, much more significant than his superiors deigned to admit. His bleached face, pale eyes, mousy hair and receding chin gave him the air of a stupid man. He was anything but. Acting as their legal assistant, he was capable of anything to advance himself and would prove so eventually to all and sundry. Beneath his humble demeanour, the grey solicitor was ruthless, cunning and completely self-serving.

At the moment he submitted to Gordon a slip of paper covered by semi-literate scrawl.

> *We Hear in Formed that you got Shearing me sheens and if you don't Pull them Down in a forgot Nights Time We will pull them Down for you Wee will you Dam infernal Dog. And Bee four Almighty God we will pull down all the Mills that heave Heany Shearing me Shens in We will cut out Hall your Damd Hearts as*

Do Keep them and We mill meock the rest Heat them or else We will Searve them the Seam. Yers for General Lud

"And you laid hands on this ... where?" Gordon glanced at Lloyd.

"It was in Liversedge, a hotbed of troubles," he replied, his north country accent tamed by years of stern self-instruction. "Mr. Henry Parr" — he gestured — "that tall man there in the corner, grey coat, received this a fortnight past."

"Mr. Parr," Gordon said, raising his voice, "might you tell me in what manner this message was presented you?"

"It was not presented at all," Parr replied. "It was found tacked to a doorway at my mill."

"Aye," another, much larger man wearing brown *worsted* said, rising from his chair, his face ruddy from wine or perhaps the heat of the fire. "These bastards strike in the night then run off. Myself have had tools stolen from Ottiwells!"

"And you, Sir, are?" Gordon asked.

"This is," Radcliffe said, gesturing, "Mr. William Horsfall, manager of the Ottiwells mill. He is one of our strongest supporters against these criminals; indeed, a leading member of our *Committee for the Suppression of the Outrages*."

"This has gone on far too long, Sir!" Horsfall's voice was as big and harsh as the man. Everything about him: military-style moustache, six foot solidity and iron grey eyes bespoke a brutal, unapologetic personality. "These past months have seen machine breaking in Lancashire, Nottinghamshire and Cheshire. It shall not happen here in Yorkshire if I have my way and indeed, gentlemen, it appears our government seems to agree!"

"And how is that, Mr. Horsfall?" Roberson asked.

He was answered by the slippery, smug tones of Lloyd.

"Parliament has recently passed a motion declaring the act of breaking machines will result in a sentence of death."

"Aye, and good for them! Machine wreckers are cowards!" Horsfall shouted. "Before this is done, I'll ride up to my saddle girth in Luddite blood!"

"Oh, I don't think it need go that far, Mr. Horsfall," Gordon said. "We have plenty of men to act on your behalf."

"And what do they do?" Horsfall said fiercely. "Your soldiers draw their pay and are billeted among our people. They eat our food, drink our ale, and sit!"

"And you as well should sit, Sir!" Magistrate Radcliffe had had enough. The meeting was threatening to slip from his control; not something he would abide. Horsfall, red faced, began to argue then thought better and sat down, taking a swallow of wine as he did.

"And this?" Gordon had ignored Horsfall's bellowing and already referred to another crumple of paper, holding it up for Lloyd to see.

> *Ned Lud Gives Notic, to the Coperation,*
>
> *If the Coperation does not take means to Call A Meeting with the Hoseiars about the prices Being—Droped Ned will assemble 20000 Menn together in a few Days and will Destroy the town in Spite of the Soldiers ...*

"But twenty thousand men? This is simply not credible." Gordon's words brought another owner to his feet.

"Then what of this?" he cried, striding forward forcing a paper directly into the Major's hand. "I'm a Huddersfield man and I received this three nights ago! This is not the same group of fools as wrote those others! Go on, Sir, read it aloud for all to hear!"

Gordon handed the sheet to Lloyd who, smiling momentarily at this recognition, held forth with a voice that, even when he tried to project, came out in a kind of conspiratorial rasp.

> *Sir,*
>
> *Information has just been given in that you are a holder of those detestable Shearing Frames, and I was desired by my men to write to you and give you fair warning to pull them down, and for that purpose I desire that you will understand I am now writing to you. You will take notice that if they are not taken down by the end of next week I shall attach one of my Lieutenants*

with at least 300 men to destroy them, and furthermore take notice that if you give us the trouble of coming so far we will increase your misfortunes by burning your Buildings down to ashes, and if you have the impudence to fire at any of my Men they have orders to Murder you and burn all your Housing ...

By the General of the Army of Redressers,
Ned Ludd, Clerk.

"Luddites!" someone shouted as Lloyd finished. The room burst into a cacophony of lamentation. There were cries of: "They've an army!" Others repeated the common rumour: "They've been seen on the moors, marching and training!"

Then another man stood waving a parchment above his head. It took Radcliffe some time to bring the gathering to order by removing a book from a shelf and hammering it upon the table. Gordon waited for quiet, then said: "And you, Sir, have something to add?"

"I do," the man said, resplendent in a hunter green frock coat with shining brass buttons. He appeared a pragmatic character.

"For those of you who do not know me, my name is Cartwright ... William Cartwright, of Rawfolds Mill north of here. I have a thriving business and am in the process of importing *shear frames* from the Taylors' ironworks. I'll be bringing them in as soon as Enoch Taylor confirms their completion. My plans were never made public yet only yesterday, nailed to a pillar of Huddersfield Cloth Hall, one of my people found this."

He raised the parchment. It was quite large; the lettering prominent.

"If I may, I shall read from it," Cartwright said.

"Please do," Radcliffe said.

Cartwright read:

All Croppers, Weavers & Public at large:

Generous Countrymen. You are requested to come forward with Arms and help the Redressers to redress their Wrongs and shake off the hateful Yoke of a Silly Old Man and his Son, even more silly and their Rogueish Ministers, all Nobles and Tyrants must be brought down. Come let us follow the Noble Example of the brave Citizens of Paris who in sight of 30,000 Tyrant Redcoats brought A Tyrant to the Ground. By so doing you will be best aiming at your own interest. Above 40,000 Heroes are ready to break out, to crush the old Goverment and establish a new one.

Apply to General Ludd Commander of the Army of Redressers.

"This refers, gentlemen," Cartwright said, "to the Taylors as 'a silly old man and his son,' to ourselves as, how do they put it ... '*all* Nobles and Tyrants' and goes on to proclaim French Jacobin ravings of revolution!"

"This is outrageous!" Horsfall bellowed.

"It is treason!" Radcliffe shouted.

Gordon waited for the room to settle. He signalled Cartwright forward and relieved him of the parchment. When the noise had dissipated, he spoke in even tones: "More significant, gentlemen, this pronouncement and the previous one have the mark of the literate about them."

"And the two pieces are the most recent," Radcliffe said.

"Both, it seems, within the past week," Roberson answered.

"And both with the moniker of *Ludd*," Gordon said.

"That is precisely what I find troubling," Cartwright said, "this *Ludd*, who now seems a General, and further references to an 'army of redressers'."

"This has the feel of revolution," Radcliffe said, "particularly the reference to *citizens of Paris*."

"As you mentioned, my dear Radcliffe," Roberson said, placing a hand on the magistrate's forearm, "it contains the smell of Jacobinism. Add that to this war with Bonaparte and I believe, Major Gordon, we are facing something dire. More than Mr. Lloyd's assessment of what he termed: *workers dissent*."

"I said nay ... no ... such thing!" Lloyd said. It was the best he could do, taxing his naturally conspiratorial voice to its full; challenging his language instruction as well.

"Had I known of these last two specimens my deductions would have been very different." He glared at Roberson, who was not his actual employer. He would never have done so with Radcliffe.

"A dangerous state," Cartwright said. "Indeed this war with old Boney has reduced the cloth trade to tatters. Our only redress is more efficient production. Yet the common people cannot fathom it. They only know they are being replaced by machines. I, for one, have given donations to needy former workers. Perhaps you gentlemen should consider the same."

"But not all of us have your kind of *brass*," a voice said from the back.

"Who made that remark?" Radcliffe stood, neck craning in search of the offender.

"John Wood, Sir," came the reply as Wood rose from his place. Even in his very best, his clothing was no match for most of those present. This caught Gordon's attention.

"You are a mill owner, Sir?" he asked.

"Aye," Wood said, "of Longroyd Bridge. 'Tis a small shop measured with most here, but I own it free and clear."

"Sit down, Wood!" Horsfall rose. "This convention is meant for significant owners. And Cartwright,"—he turned abruptly—"I am not in the habit of giving away what little profit I presently make to beggars who would rob me!"

"Mr. Horsfall," Reverend Roberson said, "it is the part of the Church to deliver community charity. Still, gentlemen, I must prevail upon you for increased support of our Church."

"Tithing is not an easy thing when our economy is a shambles!" Horsfall said.

"And what, Sir," Roberson said, "do you propose?"

"The Army," Cartwright said. "These are troubled times, Reverend. We are faced with threats of revolt. Major Gordon, I request a portion of your troops be sent to guard my mill. Rawfolds is quite some distance from your quarters thus my need for a permanent watch. I shall accept the cost of necessities, bed and board. What say you?"

It was Gordon's turn to hold forth. Everyone in the room was tense, many standing, brought to a state of dread by their anxious discussion.

A proposal had been launched. Gordon, who had found himself in far more precarious situations during his military career than facing this mass of country gentlemen, was taciturn as he responded.

"Gentlemen, let us take our seats. I am aware of the state of affairs in the West Riding. As you know, General Maitland at Buxton through Colonel Campbell at Leeds, has directed the Yeomanry to garrison your towns. I have a mere four hundred men. Until tonight I had thought that sufficient. I see the sense in Mr. Cartwright's request but there is a military principle here which I must not ignore: that to divide one's force is to squander its power. Should I spread my few men further afield guarding each and every mill, their usefulness would be nil."

"As I said, Major," Horsfall said, "your men can do nothing."

Gordon ignored the outburst.

"I intend to provide Mr. Cartwright, and *only* Mr. Cartwright at present, with five men as a guard. I shall use local men of the Cumberland militia. They should suffice. Radcliffe, does this tactic satisfy you?"

"It does. I believe, Major Gordon, and gentlemen, we have found the beginnings of an answer to the threats. Have we any other business?"

The room again burst into a cacophony. Radcliffe hammered once more with his book. The room settled.

"Seeing no other business at this time, I suggest we partake of the company of our ladies who have so patiently awaited our presence in the drawing room. Gentlemen, the servants shall show you the way. I declare this meeting concluded!"

"But not," Vicar Roberson said, "without a closing prayer, I think you'll agree."

The men bowed their heads as the Vicar found his voice.

Ambition had been satisfied.

4

A MUCH DIFFERENT ATMOSPHERE existed in the drawing room while the men were about their affairs in the library. With its high windows and polished parquet floors the room was intended to exemplify the importance of Magistrate Radcliffe through its neo-classical style of design, copied from the famed Sheraton.

Scattered through the room were Mayhew chairs upholstered in pale cerise offsetting the pastel green of the walls. A few small rosewood tables were laden with tea trays and platters of lemon cakes. As it was evening, the room was illuminated by a chandelier brightly reflecting its candles and a busy fire within a marble hearth shot through with pink. It was a fashionable room proffering the hospitality of the house.

Several owners had brought their wives. The women had found their places in small groups about the drawing room. There was seldom a chance for this kind of social gathering as so many lived in communities far from the others. So this opportunity was not to be put aside lightly. Indeed, while the gentlemen held their meeting, their ladies indulged in a general gossip on the state of affairs far beyond the world of business in the much more significant realm of society. Fanny Radcliffe, through her marriage to the magistrate, had assumed a singular social significance in this tacit caste system. It showed in her confidence and sense of fashion. Her Empire style dress was a subdued floral pattern in sable and *blanche* befitting a wealthy matron, though this particular matron was a mere twenty-two years old. She was a blonde, blue eyed, Derbyshire girl who loved the social whirl. As far as anyone knew she was a merchant's daughter selected by old Radcliffe as a kind of trophy wife and if she was a trifle prideful, that touch of arrogance was to be indulged in one so fortunate.

Her best friend was Curate Patrick Bronte's wife, Maria. She was as attractive as Fanny though in a more buxom manner. The two young ladies had found mutual companionship in what they both considered a backwater, soon to be vacated through their husbands' exertions. York was a dream they both held dear; London a social paradise beyond dreams.

They too were community leaders. The other women had fashioned themselves after Fanny and Maria, wearing restrained though stylish winter garb, in varieties of pattern and material. Though the season had muted the colours of their clothing, their jewelry, white gloves and reticules made up for any lack of sparkle.

Elizabeth Cartwright, for instance, was quite happy to be present, so isolated was she in far Rawfolds. So too were Eleanor Foster and Julia Fairhead, both included within Fanny's fold. The older more affluent women, of whom there were four, stayed in their own group headed by Mrs. Anita Cooke, wife of a wealthy northern mill owner. This faction was friendly though somewhat distressed at the younger ladies' exuberance. Still, these groups could cross between their respective castes without the least comment or disapproving look from others.

For there was a third set of ladies present who could never aspire to the glories of the more wealthy women. These were the wives of the lesser owners with their small mills and *draperies*. Mathilda Wood was one of this group. She had looked forward to this night simply to see how the other half lived: to tour Milnsbridge House, enjoy the respect of mannered servants, taste pure tea from china cups, and eat sweet cakes made from the finest flour.

She sat with two others, Ann Brooke and Alma Grimes, in their best finery; knowing they appeared drab to the others. Her husband had insisted she come when he normally would have denied her. She wondered what his motives were. She felt self-conscious as she sipped her tea.

The youngest group, and Fanny, were in fine fettle.

"Where is Mary Buckworth tonight?" Fanny queried. "Your husband is here, Maria. I wonder Vicar Roberson did not insist upon Curate Buckworth at the men's conference?"

"Apparently John caught a cold last week tramping through snow to meet a family of his parishioners," Maria replied.

"Does your Patrick do the same?" Fanny asked, using the husband's familiar name speaking as she was to her dearest friend.

"Not so much as he would like," Maria answered. "But then Clifton contains a somewhat better class of people than Dewsbury. Poverty can be so difficult."

"I assume," Elizabeth said, "you've heard of the threats issued against our husbands?"

"Oh, Joseph doesn't trouble me with those kinds of things," Fanny said, smiling. "He likes to keep business and family life separate."

"William is nearly beside himself with worry," Elizabeth said, her face revealing the story of her feelings. "He has ordered cropping machines and there have been warnings."

"Isn't that what this business is about tonight?" Maria said.

"I'm sure I don't know." Fanny glanced around the room, gesturing to a maid. "More tea?"

"Patrick tells me in Lancashire and Nottingham some violence has occurred."

"Do you think there will be trouble here?" Fanny said, then nodded toward a maid.

"I fear so," Elizabeth answered.

"Ma'am?" the maid said.

"Perhaps more tea, Sally," Fanny ordered. "And have Betty look 'round the other ladies to see if they might need something."

"Tea right away, ma'am. I'll pour myself. The ladies in the corner have done with their cakes. Should I bring more?"

Fanny glanced past the prosperous Cooke group toward the three women in the corner. Her pretty mouth pouted into a frown. She did not like these women invading her home. Now they had finished their cakes so quickly, like the rustics they were.

"Our tea first, Sally, and as to the pastries let us leave some for the men. I think our ladies in the corner look quite stout enough. Have Betty take them more tea, however. Lord, I do hope they don't drop a teacup."

"I'll see t' it, ma'am," Sally replied, turning her head to conceal the frown on her face. She needed this work in these hard times even if this pompous child was her mistress.

"I shall insist to Joseph this not happen again," Fanny muttered.

"My husband received a rather distressing, threatening note," Elizabeth said.

"I wish we could just stop speaking of this," Maria said. "It is ruining my evening."

"Of course," Elizabeth responded.

"There must be other topics?"

"I'm sure." Elizabeth held her composure.

She could not afford Fanny's displeasure.

Her husband, William Cartwright, was an unusual man. He had brought Elizabeth to the Spen Valley shortly after the turn of the century. Cartwright had rented the mill at Rawfolds. While most owners were content to work their mills in traditional ways, Cartwright had decided to specialize in cloth finishing on a much larger scale. He began using a new method of work called the *factory system*, where his workers' lives were controlled by his scheduling.

Elizabeth tried to accompany William each Tuesday on his visits to Huddersfield's Cloth Hall, during which time she would take tea with Fanny. Fanny, of course, was indulged by her wealthy, much older husband to the point of being spoiled. And so Elizabeth found herself with the cream of local society: sharing whispered confidences, conferring subtle judgments, following the flow of gossip Fanny and friends so relished. Yet even as she ingratiated herself, she felt sympathy for Mathilda Wood.

The mood in the room shut out the less affluent ladies as effectively as a physical wall. All simply divided into their factions. Yet despite the societal walls, there was a common thread. Even in the group comprising Mathilda Wood, Ann Brooke and Alma Grimes there was alarmed conversation regarding threats from the Luddites.

"But these Ludds would not attack such a small place as ours, would they?" Alma asked.

"Of course not," Ann replied. "My husband said 'tis the fact'ry mills they're after."

"My John," Mathilda said, "has told me these Luddites are croppers."

"He knows them?" Alma exclaimed.

"No, but my John's close with his workmen and hears them talk."

"I've heard nothing," Alma replied. "And you should listen t' me, Mathilda, that kind of talk might bring trouble upon your man should some of these little ladies hear it. They're quick t' tell a tale whether 'tis true or not."

"Best keep it t' ourselves." Mathilda poured her milk. "Let the fluttering birds chirp away."

At that moment a miniscule spaniel entered the drawing room. Commonly known as a *King Charles*, the dog was Fanny's endeavour to align herself with the nobility; many of whom kept similar dogs. It possessed short legs, long black and tan fur, and a pug face framed by floppy ears. Clearly it was accustomed to the run of the house as it galloped through the room, ears afly, into the arms of a felicitous Fanny. It devoured a piece of cake from her hand. When the cake fell to the floor the dog followed, taking in every morsel. Fanny and Maria laughed, clapping their hands. Fanny called the dog 'Milly' and continued a mantra of: "Good Milly, sweet Milly, my little Milly," enamoured of the creature and oblivious to the looks from women who thought the dog a self-indulgence.

After more cake, the dog dashed around the room from dress to dress pawing at this one, sniffing at that, even accepting small morsels from reticent hands. There were "oohs" and "aahs" from the gathering until the creature found itself at the feet of Mathilda Wood. Mrs. Wood possessed little love for dogs that did no work, so when the bitch clawed at her hemline a swift kick to the chops resulted in a doggy yelp and an equally outraged shriek from Fanny.

The dog quickly scuttled out of the room. Before she reached the double doorway a servant had scooped up the toy spaniel and carried it off with piercing instructions from Fanny as to its care. Then Mrs. Joseph Radcliffe, magistrate's wife however young she might be, turned on the older woman like a mother protecting her child.

"I will thank you, Mrs ... What is your name? Wood, yes. You have been invited into my home, by my husband incidentally and not by me ... I will thank you to learn to behave as a lady. Little Milly was doing no harm ..."

"The dog was tearing my hem!" Mathilda replied, not a lick of fear in her voice.

"I warn you ... Mrs. Wood ... once again, you are a guest in my home. Should you take advantage, I shall have you removed."

"My husband's here at the meeting!"

Fanny grew red in the face and began to quiver. Her friends feared a faint. But Fanny summoned her youthful resources.

"You are not a lady, Mrs. Wood," she said, with as much contempt as she could muster. There was grim silence among the others. After a moment Mathilda stood, gathered her belongings and faced the young woman.

"I'll take my leave then," she said calmly. "If you'll have one of your lackeys tell my husband, I'll be at the front door."

And just as she finished, the men began to enter the room still discussing the matters occasioned by their conference. The men had been looking forward to the more social aspect of the evening but as they entered they noticed the tension. Fanny literally ran to her husband in tears. They conferred quietly as Radcliffe sought to calm her. Other men joined their wives. Mathilda met John Wood in the doorway and taking his arm turned him to face her. After a few seconds he, in turn, offered an offended visage to the gathering then wordlessly the two departed.

From William, however, it became clear to Elizabeth Cartwright that she would be preparing for five redcoat guards. She was pleased enough her husband had succeeded in his plan to protect Rawfolds, yet it made her think of others' agendas.

Elizabeth pondered how someone like John and Mathilda Wood would defend their small holding. She observed the ominous single-armed presence of Major Gordon and what it meant. And she marvelled that Fanny Radcliffe could possibly take any satisfaction from the old goat to whom she was married.

Indeed, in the very near future, Radcliffe would come to exhibit a mercilessness no one would have expected while the vacuous Hammond Roberson would become as misanthropic as ever a man of the cloth could be. Elizabeth's own unusual husband, against his will yet true to his form, would become a hero; though not to her. And ultimately, though she could not have known it then, she would lose all love for her husband and leave him.

5

POWERED BY THE Spen's current, Rawfolds Mill, William Cartwright's domain, bulked itself alongside the river. Four stories of stout sandstone gave it a tawny aspect in the sunlight. Its shutters and doors were painted black. Block-like in appearance, weather worn in aspect, it was an impressive structure: its main building more than a hundred feet long. It possessed two smaller buildings as well: two white painted cottages offering a gentler look. One of them was home to William and Elizabeth, the second served a more mundane office.

The second cottage was a kind of overseer's station with a few rough tables and stools. With a water pump it served as a room where the men might eat their food away from the noise and grime of the mill. Cartwright was not a cruel man. He worked his men hard but offered them a respect they returned because of such thoughtfulness as the cottage. Of course there was dissent. These were hard times and with the times came the discharge of men and increased workload for those remaining.

Though it was winter, on this particular day the sun was out. It warmed the south cottage wall. Two workhands and a young apprentice had hauled three stools from the shed and sat in the sun with their mid-day meals. Each of them wore customary clothing: thick woven shirts with thicker breeches and *woollen* stockings. They had set aside their leather work aprons, strung now over a barrow leaning against the white wall. Their shoes were simple clogs, their vests old felt.

"'Tis lovely in the sun here," Thomas Smith said, taking a drink from his tankard.

"Aye," Benjamin Walker said, his mood foul, not matching the warmth of the day, "and a short time t' eat your meal, Tom. That God-rotted mill bell will soon be sounding. Then 'tis back t' the *shite*."

"Better work than no work, Walker; better half a loaf than none."

"Bread! Why thou'rt rich, man! You have bread? For me 'tis but oatcake."

"Me as well, Ben. Oatcake."

"I give you oatcake, the staff of life!"

Walker hefted his oatcake aloft in his fist then noticed the apprentice concealing his food. It was enough for Walker to investigate. The apprentice was a hefty lad, larger than the thin, wiry Walker despite his youth. He had a pleasant round face and bowl cut black hair. He was twelve.

"And what would you be nibbling on, you young *shite*?" Walker advanced on the boy. The boy tried to rise but stumbled and dropped the cheese he'd been hiding. He quickly grabbed it up before Walker had the chance. Dirt or no dirt, it was food.

"Now what's this?" Walker grew shifty. "Cheese? Why the young bastard has cheese and won't share with us! Here now, lad, give us a taste."

"'Tis mine!" the boy shouted.

"'And where would the likes of you lay hands on a hunk of cheese such as that, Jamie Dean? Lifted from somewhere?"

"And what if I did?"

"Why that's a hanging offence, boy." Walker smiled, but there was malice behind it.

"'Tis but a small chunk, Mr. Walker."

"No matter, lad. I'm obliged by the law t' report you. Unless ..."

"What?" Jamie Dean asked.

"Share out the cheese, there's a good lad," Walker said as he reached around the boy's back. Startled, young Dean used his right hand to punch Walker's stomach. It was not a hard punch, simply a reflex, but its force bent Ben Walker over. The boy stepped back, not knowing what to do next. Walker, his hands clutching his stomach, glared at the boy with hard eyes.

"Jesus *shite*, Smith, the egg has a wallop! Why you cursed young fiend! You need a horsewhip, Jamie Dean!"

Walker chased him around the shed, the boy running from fear of his words more than the man himself, Walker slowing after only one course. On his second pass, Smith grasped the boy's arm and ducked a wild swing by a fist full of cheese.

"Easy now, lad, 'tis all in fun," Smith said, laughing. "You've beaten poor Walker. Sit down and eat up. Such a hardy young son as you'll keep bullies away. Ain't I right there, Walker?"

Walker had collapsed on a stool, winded from the blow and the chase.

"Pass the ale. I'll have that at least!"

Smith gave Walker the tankard, shrugged, and was about to bite into a dried apple when his face lit with his winning smile. A poor man, apparent from his tattered clothing and discomfited stoop, had rounded the corner of the shed.

"Sam Lodge!" Smith exclaimed. "A sight for sore eyes. There's no work here, Sam, if you're looking." Lodge was a burly man, round shouldered and thick, but his face was wasted from hunger and strain, his stance humble, his voice a defeated flatness. Lodge had seen very hard times and they'd told their tale upon him.

"'It ain't for that I came, Tom. George Mellor asked me t' meet him here."

"And us as well so says Smith," Walker said. "But where is the man, Tom? We've short time enough 'til the bell."

"He said he'd be here," Smith replied. "George'll be good to his word."

"Aye t' that," Lodge said.

"How fares the family, Sam?" Smith asked.

"Not good, Tom. We've some food from good-hearted people. We find the rest in fields and forest. My wife, bless her soul, tries t' make for the best."

"Can we offer something? Oatcake? 'Tis good today; my woman has outdone herself."

"I thank you." Lodge looked up and, taking the oatcake, quickly put it in a pocket. "For my children."

"Here, Sam." Smith proffered his dried apple. "Some fruit for your wife."

"And a quaff of ale for yourself, man. You must keep your strength." Walker passed the ale.

"I don't know what t' say. My thanks, lads."

"'Tis no shame, Sam, t' be out of work. 'Tis happening daily; more and more gone."

"Aye," Walker said, "and high time we done something about it!"

"Mr. Lodge?" Jamie Dean spoke quietly. "I've some cheese. Your babies would like it."

Lodge accepted the cheese. Tears filled his eyes.

"Has it come t' this?" he said.

Smith threw an arm around Lodge's hunched shoulders.

"Easy now, Sam. We all do our part."

"Mr. Walker." The apprentice pointed toward the mill pond shore. "He's here."

The men turned to watch George Mellor make his way across the dam from the fields beyond. He easily vaulted the dam gate and walked up toward the four. As he came closer he smiled. He had strong, even teeth: unusual in most men. Poor diet seemed to have done George Mellor no harm.

As he approached, a wave to go with his smile, the sun illumined his eyes. They were uncommon eyes for any man; perhaps Viking blood, many speculated. His eyes caught the sun like cut diamonds.

"Lads! 'Tis good t' find you here!" Mellor greeted them, then stepped forward to shake hands with Lodge. "And you in particular, Sam!"

"You've come about the Movement?" Walker asked.

"Aye."

"But we've jobs, George." Smith said. "You've made threats about breaking the new machines when they come. We don't want trouble. We want t' work!"

"Aye, Tom, but there's many can't walk through that mill door yonder," Mellor replied. "Lodge here for one and soon, if these *maisters* get their way, it'll be the rest."

"Listen t' him, lads," Ben Walker said. It was always smart to be on Mellor's good side. Though he disliked the man he could never show it. Too many others, to Walker's exasperation, seemed to like Mellor very much.

"It ain't the machines themselves, lads, but they're the mark of the *maisters'* greed. And that's why we must smash 'em!"

"I've a family t' feed," Smith said. With his father crippled from years digging peat and his mother with his four siblings, Thomas Smith was the only bread winner in his household. Since the night of the meeting at John Wood's shop his mind had changed several times regarding his intention to join the Luddites.

"Shut your gob, man," Walker said. "George is a stout brother. You've said so yourself. He'll not lead us astray."

"The Movement's growing, Tom," Mellor said. "There's croppers, weavers, even stocking men out of Nottingham. Why you know yourself we've educated people with us now."

Mellor turned to Jamie Dean. He smiled down at the lad.

"Would you join, boy? Would you make a mark for yourself?"

"I would, Mr. Mellor," the boy said. He may have been a mere apprentice, but George Mellor's words had made him feel significant. It was something Mellor did well.

"Brave lad." Mellor clapped a hand on his shoulder.

"My friend Johnny Booth, he told me how the *maisters* crush us."

"The pastor's son?" Mellor asked. "From the Wesley Church?"

"Aye, that's him. He has school learning and wants change 'round here. Him and me talk about it."

"He's your age?"

"No, Mr. Mellor. He's older and soon t' go south for school."

"I'll remember him, Jamie, and thank you for telling me," Mellor said thoughtfully, then turned to the others. "Now, I've forty men promised this day, t' come t' the meeting next week and take the Oath."

"But I heard the *maisters* have asked for soldiers. And I've heard Cartwright was one of 'em. What then, George?" Walker's cowardly streak once more got the best of him.

"There's thousands around here sympathize with our cause. We know the land we were born in. We'll be wherever the soldiers ain't; disappeared in the homes of the loyal and true."

"But we've work," Smith said. Mellor rounded on him, impatient with his bleating.

"You know Cartwright here and Horsfall at Ottiwells Mill are bringing in shear frames? Horsfall's place is beside Taylor's ironworks so we can do nothing there, but Cartwright's making plans t' bring them over the moor by waggons. And then?"

Smith nodded, intimidated by Mellor's charisma.

"You'll be cast out, Thomas, like poor Sam here. Your job gone. Can you doubt it?"

"Well I'm in then!" Walker said.

"Me as well," Smith said.

"And me!" Jamie Dean said.

"And what says Sam Lodge?" Mellor turned. "Of any here, you should know best."

Lodge did not answer at first. His eyes gazed down at the ground.

"They're good words, George. But I must look t' my family first."

"We'll help you, man. The brotherhood takes care of its own!"

"I'll ponder it. I'll ask the wife ..."

"Your woman speaks for you?" Walker said, always ready to exhibit his superiority.

"No," Mellor said. "I want no man who's not sure. But know this, Sam, if you're not with us, you're against us."

The mill bell began its quick, sharp clangor just then, disrupting the conversation.

"The bell, lads. Time ..." Smith said, setting out for the door. Young Dean did not follow.

"I'll go right now and find my maul!" he shouted. Mellor stopped him.

"No, lad! This ain't the time. We must be organized."

"Aye, as you say, Mr. Mellor ..."

"Call me George, Jamie. You may be a lad but today you've proven yourself a man."

Walker and Smith turned then and walked up the cinder path, the boy following, leaving Lodge and Mellor alone in the sun. The two stood in silence watching them go, then Lodge shrugged his shoulders, turned and began to walk down the riverbank. Mellor quickly caught up, taking his arm in a firm, friendly grip.

"Sam, before I leave I've something for you. Here, take it, a shilling."

The coin gleamed in the sun as Mellor opened his hand.

"No, George, 'tis too much."

"'Tis from a good woman; a rich woman who helps others. Take it, Sam, please."

"How can I thank you, George? How can I repay it?"

"No need of repayment, Sam. One friend t' another is all. I was lucky t' meet this woman and once she heard of your troubles, she insisted."

"Still I'll not promise t' come t' the meeting," Lodge said.

"I know that, Sam. But I hope you will."

"I want t' come. I've nowt left ..."

There is a history of privation in the West Riding. Every man, woman and child living there has known it since time immemorial. The climate is harsh and inconstant. The land is stony allowing few crops. It is mostly oats and root vegetables which must last through the winter. The wind seems to ever blow as a whiff, a zephyr, a breeze, a gust, a gale, a storm, or a maelstrom.

Life in the West Riding means isolation: small hamlets set down in valleys, single farms so far from others connected often only by tracks. The moors these paths cross are predatory though they seem innocent enough; beautiful even. Hawthorne in early May appears before leaves in the valleys below. After that come primrose, then bluebells colouring the turf in their tiny blooms. Later, in summer, foxglove rises in mauve ladders and heather begins to turn cloudy purple. By fall what was once an easy walk is turned to a trek blocked by thick tufts of bracken.

The moors are so often quiet and peaceful with fresh water running down *cloughs* and ravines, with the waving white flowers of *bog cotton* or thick amethyst of heather beckoning the traveller to sit and rest. One sits and listens to the flitting of pipets through the air and the whistle of curlews flying over their nests. Flocks of starlings whir overhead.

With the stone walls of sheep folds and the rough rock shelters the shepherds use ... one begins to think himself safe. But then the mist falls and obscures everything and the traveller turns about, not knowing which way to move. For to go one uncertain way a man stands the chance of stepping in muck concealed beneath turf, sinking deeper and deeper, just gone, disappeared in a bog. Or if he stands still the cold fog chills his bones until he simply lies down to rest and never again rises up. Or when the storms come, the gales with strength enough to lift a man bodily over a cliff to the long fall and crunch of death at the bottom ... no, the moors are not so innocent.

And if nature's predation were not enough, the West Riding has known its share of human disgrace: the violence of plunder, rapine and slavery at one time or another down through millennia. So many have felt the boot of the master on their necks or the grasp of contending armies while they try to live their lives through tax and toil. And now another change has come to this place in the form of machines and something from outside has pushed itself in. Change has brought misery and poverty.

How could there not be revolt?

6

ZEBULON STIRK, LEAD carter and proprietor of Stirk Haulage, was worried about the coming dark up on Hartshead Moor. He was making the Rawfolds Mill delivery for William Cartwright but the trip had become something of a trial. It had been hard going for his four big waggons since their departure from Taylors' iron works. They had set out in the dark of the early morning and now with dusk they were yet on the snow covered moor, their destination still some miles away.

They were carrying *shear frames:* two huge cropping machines broken down into their parts to be transported. The Taylors had invented these massive mechanisms by attaching several pairs of cropper's shears to a wooden beam frame across which would stretch a roll of *woollen*. Then a massive rotating cylinder would take up the material and move it under one fixed blade of the shears while the other blade was automatically opened and closed by a cam shaft driven by a water wheel. One of these new inventions could crop in eighteen hours what a skilled cropper, using hand shears, took more than eight days to do.

So these new machines, Stirk knew, were causing trouble. Cartwright had insisted the parts not be taken on obvious routes for fear of discovery by Ludd's men: outlaws, Stirk had been told. So Zebulon Stirk, against his will but for additional money, had charted a course away from the turnpikes. He'd found what he thought were the best tracks up through Hartshead Moor away from any towns, hamlets or farms.

And that had become the problem. His four waggons, each hauled by two mammoth Black Horses, Stirk's best, found the rough roadways dangerous. The moor tracks were snow covered and icy. They'd had two broken wheels that day; each one an hour's work to replace. Then the roads had developed steep grades. The horses, each pair handled by an accomplished carter, had slipped and slid along these trails despite their winter-spiked shoes and were close to exhaustion. Stirk felt lucky no horse had lamed itself. They were expensive animals, the best at the work required of them, but these loads and this ground were proving too much.

And it was growing dark.

Night on the *fells* was not a welcome thought to Zebulon Stirk. The weather was dangerous in the uplands and there were, because of the secretive route, no shelters nearby.

"Aye. What of this now, what's best?" Stirk said, peering at a track wending down the steep side of *clough*. They must take this way to get off the high moor. He leaned back, shouting to his waiting drivers: "Each man should get down from his waggon and lead his horses. One slip and it's over the edge. Mighty steep."

Stirk buttoned his leather coat to the neck for warmth. He was a solid man, just like his horses, and as big and gentle. He possessed a large, rather equine head with a nose which stood forward proudly above his slightly protruding teeth. He'd been at this work for years and those years had given him rough, ruddy skin from hours in the wind.

Stirk knew the risks. He also knew the technique to take his train down the *clough*. That knowledge did not make it less dangerous. It was a narrow way and could easily pitch a cart over the bluff, dragging horses and drivers to their deaths. He gave his apprentice the reins and climbed down from the waggon box striding forward to his horses. He was not the kind of man to place another in a danger which he himself was not willing to share.

He started down the steep trail, carefully gentling the huge mares, their shoulders as high as his head, their proud heads towering above him. The waggon's brake squealed alarmingly but Stirk kept on. He walked beside his 'Daisy,' the smartest and best of the brood, and held her harness tightly soothing both she and her partner, 'Flora.' Despite one or two heart wrenching moments, hooves slipping on ice or the crack of a wheel rim in a rut, he made the descent before dark, his other waggons following.

After half an hour's rest he urged his men onward along the valley track which followed the stream, flat and even ground now. The train set out at a walk, each man leading his team through the dark. Then the weather descended upon them in an icy mist. He had expected that, but there are worse things than weather Zeb Stirk was about to discover. They'd been walking only another half hour when he heard scuffling noises.

An icy snowball flew out of the fog and smacked into Daisy, making her rear up and snort, nearly pulling him off his feet. Stirk cursed. Then a cluster of snowballs came flying in, and pieces of frozen turf, hitting the waggons, the horses, the men. He heard taunts and curses.

But the last thing Zebulon Stirk expected was the appearance of devils. Apparitions rose from the ridges above him, revealed by gaps in the fog, and floated along hillocks on his flank. He turned to look back to find his whole train of waggons attacked. Peering forward again he urged his girls into a quickstep, himself running beside them, the turves still flying, the voices still wailing. Then on the roadway in front of him a frightening black figure loomed. It fired a pistol into the air.

In the fog, in the vale, in the dark, the sound was like a cannon. The horses panicked. For a moment Stirk panicked too as he felt himself lifted off his feet by Daisy's rearing. Once more on solid ground he readied himself to prevent her from bolting. But she had stopped of her own accord, as fearful of the figure in front of them as was Zebulon Stirk. He was not a religious man, but prayers began streaming from him as he caught sight of the fiends around him.

Their faces were black as charcoal and the dark with the mist made them singular shadows. Every one wore a hat of some type to conceal the hair beneath. Stirk realized they were men, not devils, though some dressed in women's attire to add to his confusion. Others wore masks, their eyes gleaming white above the cloth folds. While some carried knouts, the knobbed bludgeons thick and deadly, others bore mauls or sledge hammers, and he noticed fearfully four or five pistols in hand, the guns' iron glinting in the glimmer.

Stirk knew he was finished. There had to be thirty. There was no way past them and no retreat. They seemed organized. None broke rank, no one spoke after Stirk had been halted.

"Who are you?" Stirk questioned, his voice high and strained. The man took a frightening step forward. He wore a black and red mask and Stirk could see now as the man closed on him a face blackened with charcoal that made his eyes almost diamond shards. Extraordinary eyes. Hard, glittering eyes in a massive man who towered over Stirk.

"The brotherhood of General Ludd!"

"Christ Almighty," Stirk said. "Luddites!"

The leader moved closer. His jewel eyes bored into poor Stirk who could feel warm piss running down his legs.

"We'll take a look in your waggon, driver. We'll see what we see." The man's voice rose to a command: "Number Two, take Six and Seven and tell me what's in the waggon!"

Immediately the figures moved. As they passed Stirk he noted one of them, dressed as a woman, was even bigger than the leader: a virtual giant. Stirk felt genuine fear for his life. These men meant business. That business had been anticipated and its avoidance planned by Stirk and Cartwright. Yet these Luddites had somehow discovered them.

"How many more waggons with you?" the leader smashed through Stirk's thoughts with his question. There was no point in lying.

"Three more, Sir. Just back of me."

"No more up top?"

"None. Surely you must know that."

"Number Three, Four an' Five." The masked leader briefly turned away from Stirk. "Take four men each and bring up the waggons. Bring the drivers here t' join their friend. Or are you the overman?"

"Aye, I'm the lead carter. This be my business. I suppose that means you'll kill me."

Stirk received no answer other than a gloved hand on his arm. He was turned around to face his waggon. The three men were in the waggon now, inspecting each part, large or small.

"Aye, they're shear frames alright," the man called Number Two shouted. "You were right, Geo ... Number One! 'Tis Cartwright's cropping machines."

The man jumped down from the waggon, ran pell-mell toward Stirk and struck him with his knout. Had Stirk not brought up his arm in defense he would have been dead from a smashed skull. As it was his arm cracked at the wrist. He cried out, twisted, and fell to the ground. He tried to close in upon himself anticipating more blows, then heard the leader curse his assailant.

"Damn you, Two! We'll have none of that! I told you before!"

"But this is the overman!"

"No!" Stirk screamed. "I'm no overman! Just a carter doing the work I was paid for!"

"Cropping shears, though none such as I've ever seen." The leader took a long look into the waggon's box then turned to Stirk. "What's your name, carter?"

"Name's Zeb Stirk. I've a business out of Huddersfield. My wrist ..." he sobbed, the pain powerful.

"You should feel ashamed, Stirk. Your work here takes other men out of work."

"My work is haulage. I don't ask the purpose. Christ, my wrist's broke."

"Number Two, find a man who knows t' set a bone."

"Why would I help him?" Number Two answered. He was a small man, one whom in ordinary circumstance Stirk knew he could easily better.

"Because I gave you an order! Move!" The leader said.

The small man ducked away.

"My thanks, Sir," Stirk said to him.

"Our business is with the machines, not you."

He turned to the rest of Stirk's men, brought forward and held by the outlaws.

"You'll be bound together for the night, but we'll let someone know of your whereabouts by morning."

"What of my horses?" Stirk had to ask; the great beasts were his lifeline.

"They're yours so you'll keep 'em; but your waggons are t' be put t' the torch along with the frames they're holding."

The horses were led off. By this time men swarmed the waggons. Ohers threw parts down from the boxes, iron thumping onto the frozen turf. More men used their sledges to smash their way through the waggons' cargoes. The destruction became a frenzy, the sounds of the hammers crashing on iron echoed around the misty valley. Soon the waggons themselves illuminated, the flames licking upward until they were four huge, hot bonfires in the dank night.

A man came to help Stirk with his wrist.

Stirk's apprentice had tried to run. He was brought in bleeding. He'd been roughed up. The big leader dispatched other men to care for his wounds, then took the original group aside. While the hauliers were tied together both the boy and Stirk were attended away from the rest, closer to the cluster of Luddites now in the midst of an argument. Stirk could not help but hear.

"I told you, no roughness!" The leader, it seemed, was barely holding his wrath under control. The men who had beaten the apprentice seemed confused.

"But Walker told us t' teach 'em a lesson ..." one of them said.

"No names, you fool! We're not after men. 'Tis the machines we wanted."

"But they were delivering the machines, George!" another man said. Stirk heard him clearly.

"I told you, no names! Are you daft, man?" the leader said, then turned to the one named Walker.

"Number Two, come here!"

The man moved slowly. He *is* a coward, Stirk thought.

"Fool!" The leader grasped the small man by his collar. Stirk could not hear the next words but he could feel their intensity. In spite of himself he felt a strange sympathy for the coward being chastened. All Stirk heard finally was a rasping: "Now get out of my sight. Go on. Make sure the horses are tied securely."

Once released, the little man hurried past Stirk. His eyes flashed anger now he was away from the threat and he muttered: "By the Jesus, Mellor, I'll not have you treat me that way."

He had not even noticed Stirk through his fury. But Stirk had heard two names this night. Should his attackers learn of his knowledge he would be a dead man, he knew. So he began to moan. It was not difficult, his broken wrist egged him on. If he was making noise then the leader would think he'd heard nothing at all.

Zeb Stirk was not a stupid man. He suffered himself to be tied with his men in the cold dark of Hartshead Moor knowing he would be safe in the morning, knowing so long as he breathed no word of the names he'd heard this night, he would remain safe. He would be questioned, he knew. His story would match that of his men: Luddites had attacked the train, burned the waggons, then drifted into the night fog like phantoms, unknown and unnamed. For should he let slip any inkling, the men who had found out his clandestine route from Marsden to Rawfolds would as easily learn of his tattling.

And they would kill him.

It would be some time before he heard those names again. It would be a long time before he set aside his fear, stepped forward, and used his knowledge against them. By then they would be not mere outlaws, but murderers.

7

EARLY FEBRUARY, GREY twilight seeped through the windows of John Buckworth's home in Dewsbury. Nearby the Church, the curate's house was a compact residence built of sandstone, its slate roof much darker. It was a typical middle class home. The steps to the white front door were flanked by a few evergreen bushes. The front door opened onto a hallway on either side of which were the dining room and the parlour, steps led to the upstairs bedrooms.

The existence of a parlour room in one's house was a mark of social status. It was evidence the owner had risen above the majority who lived in but one or two rooms. The parlour was where the larger world encountered the private sphere of middle class life; the curate's visage was presented to the public here in the best room of the home.

It was not a formal drawing room such as Milnsbridge possessed, but a much smaller, most pleasant living room. Normally the Buckworths' parlour would have been a trim, tidy place: burgundy walls hung with a paintings from Mary's father's collection, one or two mahogany tables with candle lamps and other bric-a-brac displayed, comfortable upholstered chairs, a delicate fire screen fronting the flickers of the stone fireplace and a fine *turkey* carpet on the floor. At that moment, however, it did not have the look of trim at all.

Scattered through the room were reams of paper covering chairs, tables, even the calico cat which slept peacefully beneath a small mound of folio, though one green eye occasionally opened to be sure of the state of affairs in the room. For the room was a bustle of business: Mary and John sat at separate tables, quill pens in hand, ink pots open, sand for blotting in small glass jars at their sides. Both of them bore ink stains on their writing fingers.

Mary wore a lilac morning dress with high neck and long sleeves, quite devoid of decoration. Covering her head was a linen *mob cap*, typical 'at home' undress, though stylish nonetheless. Over her shoulders was a simple *India* shawl. She wore somewhat worn satin slippers. Her husband was coatless, his white linen shirt and grey *woollen* breeches were accented by light coloured stockings. He wore no shoes nor his curate's stock at present.

Both inhabitants were in high colour not so much from the fire as from the fire within, for they worked together on a project dear to them both. At the moment Buckworth, standing by the window to catch the last rays of light, had just finished reading a completed manuscript. He brandished the document with self-assurance.

"Yes, this is excellent, Mary. Very good! I'm sure the owners will listen to this."

Mary glanced up from writing her copy. She smiled.

"It is a strong and clear manifesto, John, as only your skills could create."

"But not without more than a little assistance from you, my love."

"I merely altered a few of your words, to offer a sharper meaning."

Buckworth walked from the window to Mary's table placing a hand on her shoulder. They had shared many evenings such as this.

"Now if only George Mellor can be convinced," Buckworth said earnestly.

"His priority is pamphlets, my dear," Mary said. "The ones we produced a fortnight ago have had some effect; or so I've been told through the gossip chain."

"Indeed, it appears the owners are confounded to find how the pamphlets altered in style."

"It was great fun though, wasn't it, dear, to pretend to those errors?"

"Were the business not so serious I'd have burst a button laughing!"

"We must be careful, John," Mary said, tone changing. "George will want more and we should not produce too much. That would bring a further determination to discover the author."

Buckworth reached behind her and pulled his chair beside Mary's. He sat heavily, a sudden shift in his mood apparent.

"I know, dearest. But George Mellor is a persuasive man, an intriguing man. For all his lack of education he has bettered himself as no one I've ever met. Taught himself to read, you know. But of course, I recall you tutoring him so often over the past few months. Still, he has a strange power. I am worried he'll try to change my writings to suit himself."

As he spoke Mary rose to turn away from her husband, crossing to the fire, keeping her face concealed. Her voice when she responded sounded ever so slightly constricted. Buckworth himself missed his wife's emotion within the thrall of his own.

"How is your tea, dear?" she said.

"Oh fine, fine ... Mary?" His tone changed again.

"One moment while I pour ..."

"Mary ... I've wanted to speak with you about Mellor."

Had he been looking he would have seen her back straighten and a splash of tea miss the cup she was holding. She glanced over her shoulder but Buckworth was gazing out the window.

"What do you mean, John?"

"I've noticed you speaking more often with him."

"I still teach him his letters. And as you said, he is an intriguing man. Oh, he is of low station but he has a quick mind and a strong commitment. I find him rather a ... passionate man, dedicated to justice, I mean."

Mary came to the table with his tea cup. As she set it down Buckworth placed his hand upon hers. His face was a mask of concern.

"I feel I should warn you about him, my love."

"Heavens, why?" she replied, clutching her cup, lifting to take a concealing sip.

"Mary, that passion you speak of, that power in the man ... is dangerous."

"I don't understand ..."

"Oh, I don't for a moment believe him nefarious. His honesty is renowned as is the commitment you speak of. Why he has recruited scores of men to the cause. His character is, well, magnetic. But he is an impatient man, Mary. He wants confrontation. A rising ..."

"Perhaps he should have been a soldier," she replied.

"Why yes." Her thought kindled something within her husband. "He *is* a soldier in his own mind, serving this General Ludd whoever that might be. But Mary, you must mind yourself around George. I'm afraid he will use you somehow to influence me. He is capable, I believe, of any action to further his cause."

Her husband was far too close to the mark for Mary's comfort. She set down her cup.

"Of course I'll take care, love. But why talk of this now?"

Buckworth's intensity grew. His voice lowered.

"There has been a confrontation, Mary, and there shall be more. Not even this manifesto will stop them. Apparently William Cartwright tried to bring his machine parts by waggon across Hartshead moor. It was supposed to have been done secretly, but somehow George discovered the plan. He and his men attacked the waggons."

"Yes," Mary replied, unguarded for the moment by her concern.

"Do you know of this?" Buckworth questioned. "How could ..."

Swiftly Mary recovered, fortunate to have a quick mind beyond her naïve husband's.

"I suspected it, John. After the night of your swearing in I was sure something else had been arranged. On our walk home George ... Mr. Mellor, spoke of it. There were hints of a plan though until this moment I hadn't comprehended what he meant."

She lied as though her life depended upon it for indeed it did. Not a trace of her intimacy with Mellor must ever be suspect or all would be chaos. She might be a passionate woman but she remained a clever one. The lisp of lightness in her voice convinced Buckworth that nothing more than an exchange of words had taken place.

"I feel such a fool, Mary, telling you these things when your own mind is so capable. I apologize for thinking so little of you, my dear."

Those words made Mary feel such remorse that she kissed him lightly on his forehead as a mother might her child.

"John?"

"Yes?"

"You must take great care yourself as well. This is a dangerous business. Oh, I wish I had not been there to sway you to the Oath. But John, I could not help it."

"Don't worry over me, my love." Buckworth's tenor deepened, a sense of masculinity brought on by her words. "I'll not let George Mellor use me. But I must have him approve this manifesto. Perhaps I'll speak to his step-father. George seems to listen to him. This," he said, brandishing once again the inked paper, "is the answer, Mary. Reason, not confrontation, shall win the day. This is, after all, the age of reason and we must make our way beyond violence. George will agree to this, surely."

"I am sure he will," Mary said, not feeling sure at all.

—

Down in the *clough* between Steel Head Lane and Penny Hill another cottage squatted low and rough beside a dog path bridge crossing the stream behind it. In the February twilight the watercourse steamed from the cold, wafting up silver-white threads to lap at the building's base. The square structure was comprised of stone and earth in an unsure amalgam of both. It rose only to the height of a tall man. Its roof was made of turf while a coarse fieldstone chimney tottered up one wall. A cracked wooden door on leather hinges with a leather hand-pull served as its entrance and one window, covered with stretched sheepskin, peered out the back toward the stream. This was the home of the Lodge family.

No parlours here, the place consisted of only one room: polished dung floor, rough-hewn table and benches, a low fireplace emitting smoking peat, and straw mattresses on four low cribs for sleeping. Some pegs were hammered into the wall holding the occupants' few articles of clothing. A cow's hide hung across one corner behind which lay a narrow bed and a tattered paper silhouette of a woman's face, to serve as art, on the wall. A rag rug made of canvas with bits of fabric sewn upon it created a touch of colour. Hanging on the fire hob was a cook pot containing a cloth of *pease* pudding. The cloth held barely enough for two, yet six lived here.

The interior of the hut was lit with rush torches: the rushes collected from stream banks then cut when still green and dipped in mutton fat. They smoked with an unpleasant odour but offered the only available light. They illumined the large eyes of four thin children dressed in tatters, watching their mother and father in turmoil. More and more often it happened. It frightened the children for they could see with their dark, wise eyes that, though their parents loved each other, the stress of privation was telling.

Their parents faced each other across the room's rough table. The table was half-set with chipped earthenware and six wooden spoons sat bundled together at one corner. The battle had begun suddenly, before the spoons had been placed by their bowls. The children's mother stood by the table holding a wooden ladle. She was dressed in a dark, soiled skirt which dragged on the floor. It might once have been blue but now was only a muted black. She wore a man's wool shirt. It too had seen better days.

Bonnie Lodge was a big boned woman reduced now to a shade of herself through hunger and hardship. Her once brilliant red hair had gone grey with worry, her hands were callused from menial work and her eyes had been dulled from poverty. She was a young woman, perhaps thirty, though she looked twenty years older.

She faced her husband, Sam, in his rough breeches and sheepskin coat, his feet clad in clogs, standing helplessly near the door. His burly body was hunched with concern and as usual his eyes gazed down at the floor. She had stopped him from leaving just when he'd worked himself into a state strong enough to actually do so. And now Bonnie had taken that instant and shredded it in the sharp clip of her voice.

Finally he found the courage to raise his eyes to meet hers.

"But I must go, Bonnie! 'Tis a call out for the meeting tomorrow night!"

"Just sit down, Sam Lodge! You're not t' go t' any meeting with the likes of them men!"

"George Mellor's shilling kept us for weeks. Now the *brass* be out. I'll not live like this!"

"And dost suppose I like it any the more? 'Tis God's will. We'll get on."

"Aye, scratching from pillar t' post, begging of others! I've my pride, Bonnie!"

She raised the ladle, pointing it across the table at him like a wand which would somehow transform him back to the gentle soul she had married.

"Pride? And where will your pride take you with them outlaws? Gaol or transport, or worse! You've babes here by the fire, Sam. Look at them. With you gone what'll become of them? 'Tis that Mellor put you up t' this!"

"I owe the man, Bonnie."

Her voice rose to match the waft of the ladle. She would not allow her man to be played for a fool. She knew she must be harsh.

"Aye. The money. And where would the likes of George Mellor come across that kind of *brass*? 'Tis Luddite coin for sure! It was meant t' make you feel beholding."

"'Twas a gift!" Lodge shouted. "He said it had nowt t' do with the Movement!"

"Then treat it so. George is a good man, but he's in deep with them machine breakers."

"They've done nowt wrong!"

"The Oath is wrong! It ain't legal! And what happened on Hartshead Moor last week? Four waggons burned. Who done that, Sam? The *Boggarts* of the Mist?

"Don't be simple, woman."

Instead of answering him, Bonnie turned to her children. She knelt in front of them, their eyes anxious. She touched each one, the boys on the shoulder, her single daughter on her face. Each of them looked to her for some answer, but she had only a warning.

"My sprogs, you must listen careful now. Your da' and me are talking of something you can't tell anyone. Understand? You must keep silent or we'll have trouble. Hear me?"

The children said nothing but she saw they understood. Bonnie Lodge sighed, steeled herself and turned back to her husband. She walked slowly around the table, stood beside him, took his big hand in hers and tried reason.

"Sam … what can I say t' make you understand?"

"I'll … I'll not take the Oath," he said. She had settled him a little. The warning to his children had made him cautious as well. "I've made up my mind t' that."

"It won't happen that way, Sam. You'll go t' the meeting and they'll expect something from you. Can't you see? I don't want you going t' that meeting."

It was then Sam Lodge looked into his wife's eyes. He had not arrived at his decision carelessly. When he spoke his voice was strong and his hand held hers just that bit more tightly.

"Listen, Bonnie. For a year now I've taken the charity of men who have little enough themselves. 'Tis not only George Mellor. 'Tis all the men. They look on me with pity. Can't you understand what that does t' me? I want t' be a man again. I have to do this, Bonnie. For the life of me, I must!"

After a moment Bonnie backed away. She held Sam at arms' length, her eyes moving up and down his figure. Then she shrugged and spoke, her voice a whisper.

"Oh Sam … 'tis just I fear for you. No telling what they'll all come to and you with 'em if you're not careful."

"I'll take care, Bonnie. I know my duty t' you and the children."

"Go then, Sam. I'll not stand in your way."

"I love you, lass."

"I know."

It was just turning dark when Sam took up his stick and left the cottage. He had a long way to go. The meeting was called for the Shears Inn at Liversedge; miles of hiking across the moors. He was troubled. Both his wife's reluctance to let him go, coupled with news of Hartshead Moor, gnawed at him. Lodge could not comprehend why George Mellor would summon a gathering so soon after such an attack. It was bound to attract special constables. He shrugged. Whatever it was it couldn't be helped. With stick in hand he set out up toward Sowood Green knowing he had a long travel ahead. He had no idea how long that travel would be. It would take him to places he'd never dreamed. It would take him halfway around the globe. Never to return.

8

THE SHEARS WAS a two-storied edifice standing upon the brow of the hill on the Halifax Road near the centre of Liversedge. John Jackson's cropping shop was up the road at Quilla Lane and Rawfolds Mill just across Hartshead Moor only two miles away. This proximity and its reputed good ale led to the Shears having earned its place as a rendezvous for *woollen* workers.

As news of the Rawfolds frames passed and men told of Cartwright's vow to replace them, more took to coming into the Shears. It became a place for dissatisfied men: out of work, out of patience, even outlaws. The presence of open fields at the rear made for an easy escape in the event of local militia appearing.

It was a cozy place downstairs: a series of small rooms each with a few tables and chairs. The second story, however, was made up of three larger rooms. From the top of the stairway which ran up to the middle room, a man could see into the others through their wide doorways: making the upstairs a kind of hall. It was here men took to meeting, out of earshot of the landlord James Lister, a sheriff's officer who, despite his rank, seemed ignorant of the weighty matters debated upstairs. A publican such as he, no matter what his official title, earned a great deal from these second floor meetings; too much to turn them away.

The top rooms were crowded. The bar maids were forced to lift jugs above their heads as they threaded their way through men standing and sitting, talking and proffering their tankards for refills. Pipe smoke blued the air, the air itself a mix of tobacco and sweat and beer. The warmth of so many bodies required no need of the fireplaces even in February.

At first the meeting was jovial. As the beer took hold Benjamin Walker announced he would sing a ditty before the business got underway. Standing upon a table, so as to be seen and heard by all, he started in. Despite his slight size, Walker had a fine voice which carried in a bright tenor throughout the rooms. He revelled in the attention. He did, for an instant, glance down toward George Mellor who stood with John Wood and a stranger who had come in the dark, just to be sure they were smiling. Then he sang ...

Come Cropper lads of high renown
Who like t' drink strong ale that's brown
And strike each haughty tyrant down
With hatchet, pike and gun!

At the end of the verse John Hirst, Bob Whitwam and Jonas Crowther, sitting at the table, joined in for the chorus with cups held high, swaying them back and forth at Walker's knees.

Oh the Cropper lads for me,
Gallant lads they be!
With lusty stroke
The shear frames broke.
The Cropper lads for me!

Walker took up from the three voices with more confidence, in his element.

What though the Specials still advance
And troopers lightly round us prance,
Us Cropper lads still lead the dance
With hatchet, pike and gun.

Then the chorus was raised by more men stomping their feet to the hard rhythm all workmen know, gradually all three rooms joining in.

Oh the Cropper lads for me,
Gallant lads they be!
With lusty stroke
The shear frames broke.
The Cropper lads for me!

Now others sang the verses along with Walker, drowning his tenor beneath their voices, making him feel diminished and angry. Still, he kept singing. There was little he could do in the face of such solidarity. The rooms sang the two final verses together ...

And when at night, when all is still
And the moon is hid behind yon hill,
We still advance t' do our will
With hatchet, pike and gun.

Great Enoch still shall lead our van
Stop him who dare, stop him who can.
Step forward, every gallant man
With hatchet, pike and gun.

And finished with the chorus.

Amidst cheers and calls for more ale these men were cocky. They had done a thing they were proud of, a thing which had reverberated throughout the West Riding. More ale was served.

John Wood leaned close to his step-son to be heard above the clamour of the rooms.

"Best begin now, George, or you'll have no one t' listen."

"I will, John. And my thanks for bringing Mr. Kentworthy."

"'Tis for the good of the men's morale. You must keep that up, lad, or they'll fade away."

George Mellor nodded. He banged his pewter tankard, empty now, against the table from which Ben Walker had just descended. Mellor, despite his encouraging smile to Walker, had thought the song too overt so soon after Hartshead and too much for even James Lister below, who had to have heard it. He despised Walker's need for attention. Still, the man had accomplished something on that table. He'd brought the others together, into a solidarity. Mellor's clanging tankard finally produced a near silence. He himself then mounted the table.

"I'm calling this meeting t' order now! Pay attention, lads! A captain of General Ludd has come t' give us news and help us devise our plans. I give you Mr. Joseph Kentworthy, of Nottingham!"

Mellor stepped down to the cheers and applause of the men, replaced by Kentworthy who had to be assisted on to the tabletop by Will Thorpe. Kentworthy was an unlikely revolutionary: rotund, ruddy, nearly ball-like in appearance. His shock of white hair and broad snowy beard, his neat *worsted* suit, his florid face with its milky eyes and rubicund nose and his high pitched, almost womanish voice were rare to the toughened brothers of the West Riding. Still he was an important man. He took Luddism further afield than almost any other, risking his life in so doing.

Kentworthy made his living dealing in second-hand wool cards and thus had legitimate reason for travelling from district to district without suspicion. His occupation provided an ideal cover. If his travels allowed a few small perks — complimentary food, wine, ale and beds from those to whom he ministered, and those perks had created the corpulent individual under whom the solid table now groaned, well, that was the business of insurrection. Applause subsided to respectful quiet.

Which was exactly what Kentworthy did not wish. He'd wanted them in the mood he'd just felt. He'd wanted them stoked to the point of imprudence. He'd wanted them angry and reckless. He had wanted these men to heed him and then do what he needed them to be doing ... creating mayhem in the West Riding.

"Good evening, lads!" he shouted in his shrill falsetto, his Nottingham accent ... an outsider. The men acknowledged him. Not jovial enough.

"I thank you. First, let me say looking 'round this room I'm glad to see so many present. Mr. Mellor here tells me you're brave men all!"

The cheers from the men encouraged Kentworthy but still, he needed more.

"Well and good, for 'tis a hazardous game we play, we know full well. But have we not been driven to it? Curse the machines and curse the men who make and use them!"

The applause and cheers grew stronger.

"The fire's stoked, lads! I've much to tell you! Through Nottinghamshire, Lancashire, Derbyshire, Cheshire and now of course, Yorkshire, our Movement is growing! We've hundreds of weapons collected and strong arms to use them! In Middleton, Burton's mill was attacked! Our men driven off but we came back again and did her in! In Stockport an evil man name of Goodwin had his house set afire. At Horbury the Thompson mill was attacked. Of course we all know what's happened not far from here!"

That got the crowd's ego just as he'd known it would, a simple sly reference to their own deeds amidst the list of others. They knew they were not alone now, that others had taken up the cause, and so would be ready for his next words.

"Your Magistrate Radcliffe has formed special constables. The government has sent soldiers. They should be fighting old Boney in Spain! They fear us, lads, for the Movement grows every day! The Parliament's passed a law, lads!"

Sudden silence, as he knew would happen as well. He let his words sink in.

"Your own Parliament has made it death to smash a machine! They never once think we do this to keep our families from starvation. It's our lives for their lives; they think so little of us. So we must show them we'll not be cowed. I've two orders of business this night. The first, George Mellor has told me of your own deeds. A good beginning, but you've seen from my news bigger things must be done. First you'll need targets."

At this George Mellor, nudged by John Wood, weighed in. Standing on a chair, his size brought his head to the same level as Kentworthy's.

"That's simple," Mellor said loud enough for all. "There's two *maisters* here must be taken in hand. I mean Cartwright of Rawfolds and Horsfall of Ottiwells. Most of us know how those two brag, day on day, what they'll do with Luddites. We've sent warnings t' both and then Hartshead Moor. The only reply from Cartwright was t' place soldiers t' guard his mill! I think 'tis time he's had his lesson!"

The men shouted their agreement in an uproar of approval.

"Why that's excellent," Kentworthy said to Mellor, "high profile man?"

"Aye, that's sure! We'll not rest until Cartwright is done for."

Shouts of approval echoed around the rooms. Once they had died down George Mellor was disturbed by a lamb-like voice just below and behind him.

"George? Mr. Kentworthy?" the voice said.

"In a bit, John," Mellor returned, annoyed. Fortunately, anything further was drowned out by Kentworthy's own high pitch.

"That brings me to the second order of business," he said. "There's one thing hinders us. We've not so many guns as I should like. If we're to go at a mill with soldiers inside we'll want something besides a few mauls and hatchets."

"Where do we get 'em?" Walker asked.

"Hunting guns, man! Every big house has them. If they'll not give them up, take them!"

Mellor turned on Kentworthy, his eyes diamond shards, the way they flashed when he grew emotional. Kentworthy almost backed off the table so stunned was he by those eyes.

"From our own people? That's what you want?" Mellor said icily.

"For the Movement!" Kentworthy said. "You must learn to use fear as a tool. You must become hard men for only hard men'll stay the course!"

"But this is wrong! It's completely wrong." John Buckworth finally found a chance to intercede, the crowd quiet just then.

"Who is this?" Kentworthy asked.

"Curate John Buckworth, Sir," Mellor answered.

"Well what's the problem, Curate? You don't agree with our plan?"

"Mr. Kentworthy, with all respect, Sir, your plan is immoral."

"Look you ..." John Wood took a step from the background but found himself too late to prevent Buckworth's objection.

"These men are not soldiers, Sir, and yet you want them to fight against soldiers. Now you tell them to turn on their own, make their neighbours fear them! There's no need for this. As we've seen, the Movement in other parts of the country has brought attention to our plight. It is time to use reason here in the West Riding; negotiation ..."

"Nonsense!" John Wood shouted, still trying to bring things back on track. But Buckworth had hit his form.

"I have here a manifesto! A declaration of our rights and needs! The owners are not fools. They want no riot or vandalism. They will read this and listen to us!"

"What of Cartwright?" Wood asked.

Men muttered.

"He feels threatened. The owners face the loss of their markets. If we speak in language they understand I'm sure they'll see changes must be made ..."

"'Tis greed is all they understand!" Will Thorpe shouted. "They'll not listen!"

"Easy now, gents!" Kentworthy shifted tactics again. "'Tis certain, Curate, you've not studied this clearly. In order for the Movement to grow we must show our strength! Then these *reasonable* men you speak of will fear us and learn to listen. Why man, when the time to negotiate comes we'll be able to dictate the changes. 'Tis down with the *maisters* and parasite nobles who've lived off our sweat for a thousand years!"

He had them again. Beneath the cheers of approval and thumping of tankards on tables the rest of the argument was lost to all but George Mellor and Will Thorpe nearby.

"You speak of revolution," Buckworth said.

"I speak of liberation!"

"And have the French anything to do with you?"

"You bastard, you call me a traitor?"

"John, remember your Oath," Mellor said. "This man comes from General Ludd."

"And who is this General Ludd we hear of? Is this fat Jacobin truly his agent?"

"You've had your say!" Will Thorpe grasped the clergyman by the collars and placed him none too gently in a chair. Kentworthy quickly smiled a beaming, sweating, rubicund smile and employed a healthy dose of patronization. He'd noticed Buckworth's accent and knew the man was not local. It was simple to damage his stature.

"Enough, lads! Enough. This *southern* curate and me will speak further," he said, then turned to look down on his adversary. "Better minds than yours have plotted this course. It would do you good to listen."

John Wood knew there must be no conflict. With an urgent nudge from Wood, George Mellor spoke. He addressed the room cutting the meeting short.

"Alright lads, we've laid our course. Mr. Kentworthy has leagues t' travel this night. We'll do our planning on Cartwright next week. You'll hear from the usual sources! Drink up, lads! 'Tis time we were home!"

Kentworthy was helped from his tabletop by Thorpe then escorted quickly down stairs and outdoors by Wood. With things apparently settled most men began to leave. A few remained for further ale. Some had pressed a tankard upon George Mellor when he spotted Sam Lodge at the top of the stairs. Quickly he broke through his brace of supporters and advanced on Lodge, taking his hand in a welcoming grip. He knew how far Lodge had walked to get here.

"Sam, you've come!"

"I fear I'm late, George."

"'Tis no matter, lad. The best news of all is you've come!"

"I'll not take the Oath. I've promised Bonnie."

"That's not a good sign, Sam."

"I'll run errands, carry messages, be by your side. I'm a loyal man, George, but I've given my word t' my wife."

Mellor perceived the man was close to cracking. He possessed that rare quality of sensing the natures of others. It was a skill he retained yet was ignorant of it: the way an untested athlete has little idea of his powers until called upon to prove them. He placed an arm around the burly man's shoulders.

"Easy now, Sam. I believe you. You'll be my right hand. There's a place for all in the Brotherhood. But no meetings, lad, not without the Oath. None will know your part."

"I know, but at least *you'll* know I'm still a man."

"We'll drink on it, Sam. Belinda! Two tankards of best brown if you please!"

Belinda Starkey smiled as she poured the ale, and just as she left for further service, winked a violet eye at Mellor.

Filled with a sense of his mission launched, George Mellor departed the Shears long past closing. He set off at his usual brisk pace to make Longroyd Bridge with enough time to catch a few winks before work in the morning.

The carriage, parked in a side street, caught his attention just by its presence. He'd been careful with his drink, as he always was, and was no less sharp than normal. It was late in the night and here was a carriage, horses harnessed, driver atop his high seat, simply waiting in the street. Mellor began to consider special constables then put the thought aside. Had there been specials prowling nearby the Shears they would have raided the place.

He ignored the carriage and strode down the Halifax Road until hearing the "Walk on!" of the driver, the jingle of harness and clip-clop of hooves. He searched for a way to escape. Two cottages sat side by side on the slope of the hill with a grassy lane between them. Quickly he ducked between the homes then, unseen by the carriage driver, ran hard down the lane and turned back uphill. The carriage's passengers would expect him to continue his original direction.

In a flash he had circled the upper house and, peering around its corner, saw the carriage stopped at the laneway. Silently he sneaked to the back, then waited for it to move on. When it did he hoisted himself on the rear, his weight disguised by the forward pull of the horses. The vehicle continued down the hill slowly, clearly searching. Placing an ear to the cloth covered rear quarter he listened for conversation. He needed to know who he might face.

He heard only one man's voice, several times, instructing the driver. At the base of the hill the voice called for a return up the hill. As the carriage turned Mellor leaped off the mudguard and cutting the inside radius, grasped the handle of the carriage door and was quickly up and in, facing the lone inhabitant, ready for a weapon.

Nothing more than an older man faced him: a thin man, well dressed, prominent nose and mouth, his eyes set wide and, at that moment, wide open with surprise. Then, he smiled. It was a winning smile and George Mellor relaxed. This man was clearly no foe. His voice was an agreeable baritone, his attitude apparently guileless.

"You are George Mellor," he said, after touching his chest near his heart. "I see you are all I've heard about. I've nearly had a conniption!"

"Aye? And why's that, Sir. You've been speaking with someone about me?"

"I have. I'm sorry. My name is Thomas Ellis. I am a weaving mill owner."

"I see. And what would a *maister* have t' say t' me?"

"Please don't judge me by my occupation, Mr. Mellor. I do not judge you this night."

"You were at the Shears?"

"Downstairs. Close enough to the staircase to hear some of the chat, and most certainly that song. You had quite a chorus up there with you."

"Why does that interest you?"

"Let us say I came from a different station than the one I now occupy. As you might tell from my speech, I am no Yorkshireman. I came here to make something of myself in the cloth industry and did so in Nottingham: first hosiery, then cotton. But I have not lost my roots; though I might be in favour of new machines I don't much admire the way the unemployed have been treated. Some might term me a Jacobin, but I have no interest in revolution. Perhaps, you would call me an idealist."

"I've another like you in my ranks, Mr. Ellis. He wants negotiation. That won't work. Do you see, Mr. Ellis, the need t' grab the *maisters'* attention?"

"I do see that, yes."

"Then you're not the idealist you said you were."

"I suppose not. The only way to draw Parliament's attention to the plight of the jobless is through shock. It seems, from what I overheard, you have plans in that direction."

"Aye. Parliament has upped the stakes with their law. Seems they've no common sense in this matter. What difference now between killing a machine and killing its owner?"

"That, I hope, is where you shall draw a line. I heard this night of Rawfolds Mill. I heard too Mr. Kentworthy's advice: steal hunting guns from folk who have them. He is wrong and, might I add, a dangerous man, Mr. Mellor."

"Still, if we're t' go at the mill and there be soldiers, we must have guns."

"And I am prepared to assist you with that."

Ellis reached into his pocket and withdrew a bundle of notes, handing them to Mellor. Mellor quickly flipped through them, counting, eyes widening as he realized what he held.

"There must be fifty quid here!" he exclaimed.

"Use it for the poor, Mr. Mellor, but use it as well to purchase weapons ... not many, for that will draw attention, but enough to equip a small squadron. Should it come to pass, you shall need force against force. I do not recommend it, but I understand it could happen."

"Why do this?" Mellor asked.

"I am a supporter, but must remain a silent partner in your affairs. I am also an advocate for *Parliamentary reform*. The country needs governmental restructuring. The Parliament, you may know, is corrupt ... rotten boroughs and such ... controlled by men who care for little more than lining their pockets. I hope you might see past your West Riding here and look toward the greater vision. Do you think that a possibility?"

"I want t' make a difference," Mellor said, thoughts of Mary's advice on his mind.

"Then I think, from what I know of you, Sir, you shall. Now, we've been long enough together. It is late and I fear we might attract attention. Please use the funds as I ask and, should the need arise, contact me for help but only in direst circumstances."

He proffered his card and opened the door. As he stepped down, George Mellor turned to look once again at his strange new ally. Thomas Ellis had given him hope. Mellor had never considered Parliamentary reform. Yet it seemed a very good idea. He would ask Mary.

By the time the carriage had pulled away he realized he'd forgotten to thank the man. As much as he wanted, and though he would try, George Mellor would never see him again.

9

By March it had begun. Small actions but noticeable. Shear frames smashed at Golcar, more destroyed in Linthwaite, Hoylehouse, and Honley. A mill belonging to a Mr. Vickerman, commonly known for his mistreatment of workers, had had its machines set afire during which Vickerman's own household was invaded and his furniture brought out to feed the flames. The assaults were made by organized bands who roughed up anyone foolish enough to get in their way and were adamant and efficient in wrecking machines.

There were tales of men late at night on the moors drilling and training. Officials began to worry. No one had been killed yet, though many thought it but a matter of time. It was one thing to fight two wars: against Napoleon in Spain and against the Americans across the Atlantic, but this was a different kind of conflict. This had the look of a war within, a civil war mouldering in the populace, fermenting into something frightening. But who were its leaders? It seemed the vandals stayed hidden among the people who, either for fear of retaliation or other nefarious reasons, offered authorities no information.

—

Thus, Radcliffe convened another meeting, this one of a much different sort from the January assembly. Reverend Roberson was invited and Major Gordon as well. Now, however, there were two younger men ... John Lloyd, of course, Radcliffe's rising *eminence gris* and Captain Francis Raynes, commander of the Stirlingshire militia regiment, just arrived from Scotland.

They met in the library once more. A fire blazed in its hearth. Reports from informants, owners' complaints, maps of the area, pencils for notations, cups of coffee and a few remaining crumbs of pound cake littered the table.

The conference had not been an amicable one. Cravats dangled askew, eyes hung heavy, tempers grew short. People these men knew as friends lived now in dread brought on by increasing attacks and rumours. None of them was comfortable at what was being perceived as their failure. Lloyd was speaking.

" ... with this latest offense," he said, "a reward of one hundred guineas posted for the Prince Regent's head!"

"Nailed up at the Huddersfield Cloth Hall! How could they do such a thing? Imagine, threatening a Royal!" Radcliffe said.

" ... and the current threat received by Magistrate Radcliffe himself ..." Lloyd said.

"You've had a threat?" Roberson turned to Radcliffe.

"Indeed." The round face stared balefully across the table. "Delivered by paper wrapped 'round a rock and thrown through my kitchen window."

"How dare they!" Roberson said.

"When did this happen?" Major Gordon asked.

"Just this morning."

"Could this person have known of our meeting?"

"Have you no spies here at all, Major Gordon?" Roberson asked.

"Paid locals," Gordon said, "who tend to tell what I wish to hear."

"Perhaps you could be more persuasive, Lloyd," Radcliffe said.

"I am not sure Mr. Lloyd's methods attain more knowledge than my money gets," Gordon said. "Torment rarely finds truth, Mr. Lloyd."

"Leave that to me," Radcliffe said.

"It hardly conforms to *habeas corpus*, Radcliffe," Gordon said.

"I know the law, Major, and have no need of you to remind me! Where is your vaunted militia? Can you not have your men more ready?"

"In fact, Reverend, that is the very reason for Captain Raynes' presence today. His Stirlingshire regiment is mostly cavalry. Captain?"

"Thank ye, sir!" Raynes stood and unfolded a map. He was a strapping young Scot, loyal to the bone. He considered himself a gentleman rather than some beastly Highlander. He possessed red-gold hair, deep blue eyes, the square jaw of an athlete, and the intense ambition of a young man brought up in all the correct English schools. Most traces of his Scots' heritage had been erased. Perhaps a slight slip in accent might occasionally embarrass him but other than that he was ready to play a hero's part. His voice was a clipped, military tenor.

"As ye'll see, gentlemen, we hae much territory to protect. As we've noted wi' the infantry and even the Second Dragoons, by waiting in place we'll not catch the culprits. I hae an idea, Sirs, I hope ye'll find convincing."

"Get on with it, Raynes," Gordon said.

"Gentlemen, I propose flying squadrons of cavalry patrolling the countryside in the night. We'll appear anywhere: one night perhaps in Marsden or up on the moors 'round about, the next may find us in Huddersfield's streets and the next up near Dewsbury. The point, Sirs, is mobility. Thus far we've played the Luddites' game. React, chase and lose. We must manoeuvre, gentlemen, keep them on the defensive, stop up their plans with uncertainty."

Raynes stood tall as he finished, excited at the possibilities. The others simply sat silent, stunned by the captain's confidence. All but Lloyd were older men quite unaccustomed to youthful vigour. It took a moment until they responded.

"Why Captain, that's brilliant!" Roberson said.

"Indeed!" Radcliffe said. "And to add to their effectiveness I shall institute a Watch and Ward program throughout the West Riding!"

"Might I suggest something, Magistrate," John Lloyd said, not prepared to become *second fiddle*. "I have another possibility which might strongly support Captain Raynes' efforts."

"You can sit down, Raynes," Gordon said. "I believe you've made your case."

Raynes did so, sitting as straight as though at attention.

"Indeed," Lloyd said. "The Captain's flying squadrons can respond much more quickly than our present arrangements permit. May I offer that their effectiveness might be burgeoned by information provided to them in advance?"

"I've made that point, Lloyd," Gordon said. "Paid locals are not to be trusted."

"I could not agree more, Major Gordon. But when I was in Cheshire, I took it upon myself to assume the guise of a travelling tinker in order to gain information from that region's populace. I wish to place myself, gentlemen, in the same disposition here."

"Of what possible use would that be, Lloyd?" Radcliffe said, scoffing. The man was becoming a trifle too striving, forgetting his place as an assistant.

"Sir, though I am no local, a tinker is required everywhere. I *do* have some skills in the trade. And while I make my mends, I shall have my ears open for any chatter providing intelligence to Captain Raynes. Thus we have two operations working apart, yet co-operating."

Lloyd knew his bleached face, reedy eyes, and weak chin formed a visage easily forgotten. He could effortlessly pass through the villages of the West Riding. He would spend time among ordinary people, never part of them, never rightly remembered. He would scrutinize locals in search of rebellious talk.

"You realise the risk if you are caught by these criminals?"

"I do, Sir."

"Of course you'll want to be paid more," Radcliffe said.

"Not at all, Sir. Expenses perhaps, but the only remuneration I request is the offer of a prosecuting solicitor's position. I wish to indict those men whom we, that is Captain Raynes, will apprehend."

John Lloyd was an ambitious man. Eventually the criminals would be caught and then Lloyd would call in his markers to be appointed prosecutor. And that appointment would in turn lead to a far more significant position than the one which he currently tolerated.

"I'm not sure I like your tone, Mr. Lloyd," Radcliffe responded. "What you suggest is not often offered a man of your station."

"I shall be risking my life, Sir," Lloyd said, a slight catch of breath enhancing his meaning. "I merely ask for recompense within your power to bestow."

"Well, gentlemen, this afternoon has crafted considerable progress regarding our tactics," Reverend Roberson said. "Flying columns, Watch and Ward, and a spy in the midst of the enemy." The conflict between Radcliffe and Lloyd postponed, he was ready to move on with his day. "I shall be off. Church business to attend."

As Roberson stood, he collected two pistols he had taken to wearing openly so that even his congregation should recognize his resolve in this matter.

The officers departed quickly. Radcliffe stayed the Reverend with an offer of sherry. John Lloyd simply left by the servants' entrance and walked to Milnsbridge. In his rented room he unwrapped bits of worn, ragged clothing and the tinker's tools he had brought from Cheshire. He then arranged for the purchase of a mule and a two-wheeled covered van. Finally, he wrote and posted a short letter to one Mr. M'Donald. He prepared to submerge into an existence he had once known well and had very much wished not to know again; but ambition urged him on. He would be Raynes' spy. He would be Radcliffe's revenge. He would be justice against these despicable Luddites.

—

April arrived gently: In the forests the elm, oak, and lovely horse chestnut began to bud, beneath which grew sheets of anemones, wood violet and primrose. The plaintive notes of plovers wafted over the moors and woodland birds: Nuthatch, thrush, and chaffinch flitted through the soft air.

But this was no ordinary spring. This spring marked the amplified aggression of Luddites. The Movement was growing. One early April night its force was revealed in a quite unusual manner.

Just east of Huddersfield lay Thomas Atkinson's Bradley Mills, a mere mile from the Cloth Hall, the centre of the *woollen* industry. That soft spring evening, starry and bright, numbers of men gathered along the roads leading to Bradley Mills. They were disguised in strange clothing, their masked faces concealed further with charcoal blacking. They bore hatchets, pikes, and huge hammers. They formed up slowly in increasing numbers not as a mob but in orderly dispositions. They marched toward the village.

People in houses nearby the road doused their lights and stared out between curtains at the passing strangers. None had seen anything like this before. The men marched without speaking but nothing could silence the tramp of their boots on the stony road. When they approached Bradley Mills, the buildings' dark stone hunched against the night sky, the troop formed a line facing it. If there had been defenders they'd long run off. Yet nothing happened.

It appeared the marchers awaited something. Their discipline was impressive. And then up Nab Hill far to the east the sky shattered with white sprays of rockets rising. There was a cheer from the men. One of them, a huge man, stepped forward and lit a torch. Others with hammers smashed the mill door, each taking a symbolic turn. The wood was thick but it splintered quickly beneath the pound of swinging iron. The big man watched, then was joined by another, smaller individual.

"Seems 'tis going alright," Thomas Smith said, glancing up to look at the blackened face of his friend Will Thorpe. "The rockets'll trick the soldiers away."

"Aye, that's true."

"Why so many men?"

"'Tis part of George's plan, Tom. *Maister* Atkinson has a love for machines the same as Horsfall and Cartwright. We send a message this night. And if we're t' take Rawfolds we must practise. We need t' know how t' move men, how t' control 'em, how t' make 'em into one force."

"'Tis simple now with no guards, Will. And if this is George's plan, where's he? I've not seen him all this night."

"He wants others t' take command. Get 'em accustomed t' leading large groups. That's why I'm here. Wait now ..."

With that Thorpe stepped forward and held the torch high for all to see then waved it from side to side. At his signal two more groups from each end of the line moved toward the mills' side doors and found entrance there. Sounds of hammers on wood and then metal and breaking glass filled the night. Thorpe brought forward Curate Buckworth and young Johnny Booth. Thorpe looked down at them.

"You'll go on in now, you two, and nail your papers t' the wall inside the doorway."

"It's a manifesto, Mr. Thorpe," the youth said.

He seemed amused at the big man's ignorance. Johnny Booth was proud of himself. He had a bright future ahead. He was enrolled already in school in the south and impatiently awaiting departure. In the meantime his social conscience was enhanced, as was his reputation, by contact with Buckworth and the Luddites.

"I don't care what you call the thing. Do as planned; what George told you."

Buckworth tugged at Booth's sleeve and the two quickly entered. Several men looked askance at them. They did not comprehend these cerebral actions, manifestos and such, knowing only to smash machines was their message; any other being superfluous.

Buckworth and Booth soon came out and Thorpe was about to raise his torch to provide the signal to retreat when he heard an unusual sound. Others too heard it, though only a few former military men understood its meaning. One older fellow joined Thorpe.

"Can you hear that, Number One?" he cried in panic.

"Aye? What's the problem?" Thorpe asked.

"We must get the men out of here now!"

"Why?"

"Tis horses, man! Cavalry!"

By then it was too late. From the east, riding hard, came the jingling, rumbling sound of cavalry. In the moonlight the men could make out mounted soldiers. Some of the throng broke and ran while others milled about in confusion. Thorpe had forgotten to post sentinels up the roads and so Captain Raynes' tactics had come to fruition. It was Raynes himself who led the patrol.

He had split his force sending a third up Nab Hill to capture the men perpetrating the rockets deception and led the rest to Bradley Mills, informed he should do so by John Lloyd the day previous. He had expected a small force of louts. With only twenty sabres at his back he realized he could not fight fifty men no matter how untrained they were.

His stuttering moment of bewilderment changed everything. The crowd of men, seeing cavalry, scattered like chaff in a wind. They split and ran, many across the mill stream into the forest beyond. Others took heel toward the village and its narrow ways. The men in the mills were the last to attempt an escape. Raynes had finally gathered his thoughts and led a sortie to the nearest end of one building. Between the building and the cavalry's horses, several raiders were trapped. Yet Raynes' men seemed not to know what to do with these unarmed rustics. Then a small group surrounding Thorpe raised muskets and fired a volley.

Two soldiers were wounded. The broadside had issued from untrained, panicked men. Still, it had had the effect of jarring the confidence of the troops. As the soldiers aided their wounded, the trapped raiders once more entered the mill and escaped out the other end. Thorpe's group of shooters dispersed in the dark.

Raynes was left with no prisoners and two wounded men who, though they would recover, would stain his enterprise with the stigma of failure. He had had no idea from Lloyd, who had not known himself, just how large would be the force that night at Bradley Mills.

The action led to changes. Raynes and Gordon, in later planning, created supporting patrols. Thorpe's error of not guarding his flanks was remedied. Lessons were learned that night of Bradley Mills. Both sides would be more prepared the next time. And the next time would lead to killing.

Lessons were learned.

10

JOHN BUCKWORTH'S RECTORY was across the cemetery grounds from his church in Dewsbury. Though the church itself fronted the road, the more easily for the congregation to meet their carriages, the house itself was somewhat isolated. Set amid placid elms and concealed from the public church yard by a blackthorn hedge, a single gated gap in the hedgerow admitted one to a pleasant lawn, dotted by the first spurts of azalea and sprays of primrose.

On this starry evening every window was dark but one on the second story. The bedroom of John and Mary Buckworth was occupied by Mary, in a white cotton night dress currently rucked up above her waist as she curled on the bed alongside a nude George Mellor. In the lamp light she admired his splendid musculature, the smoothness of his flesh, his auburn curls and the sparkle in his eyes. Mellor lay in a sated sprawl beside her, her lovely head with its honey hair resting upon his arm. He turned to her and her green eyes went emerald to match the glow of his diamonds.

"Uhmm. George, again please ..." she murmured.

"No, Mary dear, you've taken my power away. I must rest."

She pretended to pout then became engrossed with the object hanging from a leather band resting between his pectorals. Mary was unclear why this miniature hammer, only two inches long and made of pewter, was important to Mellor. It was a simple thing; so simple she knew it had to have meaning.

"George? Why do you wear that tiny hammer?"

"'Tis special t' me, Mary. More, since the Movement started."

"It's a Luddite sign? A symbol of rank?"

"No, dear. 'Tis special only t' me. It was given me when I was a boy. I frittered my time in a blacksmith shop when my mum and me lived in Marsden."

"I thought you'd always lived in Huddersfield."

"No. When my da' run off my mum got a place cleaning house for a man and his son, neither had wives. In those days while my mum worked in the house I tried t' make extra *brass* by cleaning the shop. The father took a shine t' me and made me this."

Mellor fingered the tiny hammer.

"It wasn't long before mum found a better place back in Huddersfield and then I went off t' sea. But this little maul has great meaning now. It was Enoch Taylor himself gave me this, a miniature of the sledges him and his son James made in that shop."

"So it is a symbol after all!"

"Aye, we're enemies now though he doesn't know it. Still, you like this wee hammer? Here then." He removed the thong from his neck and pressed it into Mary's hand. "A present from me, a symbol of our future."

"Oh, I couldn't accept it, George. John would notice."

"Just tell him it came from the market in town. John's *twisted in* Mary. He'll know its meaning. You might keep it close t' your heart."

"Yes. Yes, I'll keep it and keep you near me."

"I love you, Mary."

"I know, dearest," Mary whispered as she placed the necklace over her head, tucked safely inside the bosom of her night gown.

"Do you want some tea?" she asked.

"Aye, now that's a wondrous notion."

She slid out of bed, allowing her hem to fall over her legs and down to her feet as she crossed the room to fetch the lamp.

"I'll have to take the light with me if I'm to make it safely," she said. To which he laughed and when she demanded to know why he paused before he spoke.

"'Tis just so suddenly you're transformed. Again the curate's practical wife ..."

"Oh, not so practical as that, my lad," she said, returning to the bedside to kiss him passionately. The kiss lasted longer than expected. George Mellor found his strength returning in a tumescent rush.

"Dear Mary," he said, stopping, "'tis the change you make from one t' the other. I don't know how t' keep up with you."

"It seems you keep up very well, my love."

"But a dish of tea would bide me well."

"Very well," she said, scowling and then laughing. "Pull on your breeches and come to the kitchen. With Annie gone we'll have to stir the fire."

"Where's she this night?"

"Off visiting her mother. I told her she mustn't ignore her familial duties."

"Did she not find that strange?" George said, chuckling.

"Well I had to tell her something. How often do we have this chance? A real bed in a warm place and time to enjoy ourselves."

"Aye, that's true."

With George mostly clothed and Mary having donned her dressing gown, the two descended the stairs to the kitchen at the back of the house. George continued outside to relieve himself while Mary made tea. When he returned she saw him leaning against the doorjamb."

"And what are you up to?" she said, smiling.

"I was thinking again," he said, "how you alter yourself one moment t' the next."

"And am I so different from you, George?" Her mind was challenged now, as her body and heart had been upstairs.

"I don't know ..."

"With me you are warm and passionate. Yet when I see you among your men I hardly recognize you."

He frowned, then sat at the kitchen table. She had struck a chord she had not meant, yet the thought had weighed on her mind for weeks.

"The Movement's got bigger now," he said flatly, clearly unwilling to discuss the subject. It was just the kind of challenge which made Mary Buckworth's blood rise.

"You can't see what's happening?"

"Now, Mary ..."

"Don't patronize me," she said, frowning. "Your men are bullying people, George."

"I've tried t' stop it. I can't control them all."

The conversation had, unsought, become a debate. This kind of thing occurred often between them, their young minds as questing as their bodies. Mary brought the tea to the table while Mellor fetched cups as they continued.

"But that is my point. If they can't be controlled, they must be stopped. You have criminals now in your ranks, George, and these raids give them license."

"'Tis your husband speaking now, Mary, through you! He's sore because his manifesto was scorned when he tried locking horns with Kentworthy. Don't bring your husband into this."

"Why not? It's his house. And it is *me* speaking, not John!"

"Then I'll take my leave."

Mellor moved to the door. His hat and jacket were hung on a peg.

"George, please, don't act this way."

"I'll take no more mention of John Buckworth," he said, despite himself.

"There isn't much choice, George. I'm married," she said, regretting her words.

"Leave him!" Mellor said, his face so close to hers he could have kissed her. She pulled away, trying to bring reason back. Her voice softened. She half turned, floundering in the midst of the complexity of what she felt she must say.

"You like John, don't you?"

"Aye, I do. His heart's in the right place."

"I admire him, George. And I love him ... oh, not the way I feel for you but he is a good, gentle man. It's bad enough to cuckhold him without bringing him public shame."

"Dost think it worse t' lie t' the man? Lord, Mary, when are we going t' be honest?"

"Can't you see what it would do to him, and for that matter you and me, if I left him? Society would castigate us!"

"Cast ...?"

"Rebuke, punish, destroy us with gossip!"

"Then damn society, Mary!"

"George, your language ..."

"What's society done for me? Why do you think I'm doing this now, lass? I've had enough is why! The Movement's going t' change things. 'Tis then I'll come for you, Mary, and no one will give a care!"

"I thought you were fighting change. This sounds like you want just to replace certain things with the things you want for yourself."

She had taken him to where he was unaccustomed. She could not have known it, being young and full of her own opinions. That moment brought him to an emotion he had not known was within him. His response came in a rush with barely time to breathe between thoughts.

"No man can stop change! 'Tis impossible. Time's like a stream, Mary, and us in our little boats float upon it and follow its current. Aye, we can paddle a while upstream, fighting the way, but soon we tire and take our rest, then the current pulls us along again. What I'm trying t' do is smooth the waters for them who come after. The *maisters* must see, with our people starving, with each man locked in his place, with no place t' go but gaol or transportation ... they must change things, or let things change them! For neither can they stop time!"

"Now *you* sound like John," Mary said softly.

"I know I do! He's educated and I listen t' him. But we're at odds, him and me. He believes he can reason with greed. I know better. The *maisters* don't want change. The only way t' make 'em see things is by killing their commerce!"

This strange and uncommon turn of phrase from the man she thought she knew so well struck Mary as a clapper strikes the bell. In that moment she might have actually left her husband despite her qualms. But that did not happen, for at the summit of her thoughts came a knock on the kitchen door.

Mary felt her blood go cold as she considered the ramifications: the curate's wife and the cropper; it sounded like a filthy joke. Now discovered, now about to be exposed, she thought of the whispers, the laughter, the turn of heads as she envisioned in that instant being cast from society. She shivered as she went to a window and, plucking at the curtain, noted the burly bodies of working men gathered in her yard, and one giant at the door.

Knocking.

Mellor signalled to her to hide herself while he went to the door. She stepped into the darkened pantry. She heard the door open, Mellor's voice with another deeper voice responding. The door shut. Then he was there, in the pantry, with her.

"I must leave, Mary. There was trouble at Bradley Mills this night. Some soldiers came across our men ..."

"Bradley Mills? John said today he was going there!"

"Aye. He wanted t' put up his manifesto as a warning t' the *maisters*."

"Oh, God, I thought it was church business."

"He's not hurt. Thorpe would have told me."

She grew suddenly cold.

"How did Thorpe know you were here?"

"As I said, Mary, I must stay atop things. The men must know how t' reach me and this night was important. I should've been with them, but I couldn't stay away from you."

"With my husband gone, you mean; likely upon your orders."

"No, Mary ..."

"This is my home!"

"I'd no choice!

"This will come out. Someone will speak of it. Did you think of that? What will they think? God, what will they think?"

"They know nowt. I'll say I was awaiting John ..."

"At night? And what if John had come here with them?"

"Thorpe wouldn't let that happen. He kept a good eye on John t' protect him."

"You had Thorpe minding my husband so you could be here with me?"

"It was t' protect him. I promised when he was *twisted in* I'd not put him in danger."

"You promised *me* you wouldn't let John get involved in the raids!"

"He wanted t' go! How am I t' stop him?"

"By being a leader!"

"That's not fair!"

She did not answer him. She was finished talking. She knew then despite her love for him, and her admiration, something had given way inside her. Despite his words of self-doubt she saw now George Mellor was indeed capable of dangerous things. His words this night, his powerful words describing what he was attempting, rang clear. He had left her no choice while making his own.

"Get out of here, George. Don't come back."

"Mary, I've told you ..."

"This was our secret, George. You've betrayed it. You and I are finished."

"I love you, Mary ..."

"You've decided what is most important to you."

"What do you want from me?"

"Get out! Go with your bloody Luddites! But you mark my words, George Mellor, you'll die if you keep on with this!"

Mellor, furious, slammed the door behind him and pulled on his jacket against the night cold. He joined Thorpe and the others. He walked with them toward Huddersfield, careful to stay clear of Bradley Mills. They went south instead across Cockley Hill making sure they were far from roads travelled by special constables and now, according to Thorpe, cavalry. When he heard the story, George Mellor acknowledged this new response. It did not bode well for his plans against Cartwright.

But when he was alone again, he once more thought of Mary and the way they had left things. He knew her enough to know he could not return: both the circumstances and her willful nature would prevent him. He was but twenty-two years old. That night he shed tears for the woman he loved. Once every while he would reach for his precious *Enoch* and not finding it, knew where it lay, or at least hoped it did.

It did.

Following his retreat Mary too had realized the consequence of her anger and wished she could take back the things she had said. For she too was young, merely a girl though a woman grown and the wife of a curate. She too lay abed that night, after her husband had returned home aglow with the triumph of posting his platform. She had half listened to him though luckily he'd brought young Booth and the two paid no heed to her listlessness. But when it was dark in the bed in the room in the house where she felt she did not belong, she clasped Mellor's charm in her hand and thought of him, missing him, terrified by her own final words to the man she loved.

11

HUDDERSFIELD WAS AN old town, though not actually a town at all, for its terrain was owned by the Ramsden family on retainer from the Crown. It was said to have derived its name from Oder, or Hudder, the first Saxon who'd settled there a thousand years past. Its situation on the high road from Manchester to Leeds, the number of farms upon the surrounding moors, and an abundant supply of water-power ensured copious cloth production since the early seventeenth century.

The product of Huddersfield and adjacent villages was, of course, principally *woollen* consisting of broad and narrow cloths: serge, kerseymeres, cords, and even a variety of fancy goods, such as shawls and waistcoats whose fabrics were composed of worsted or cotton. Huddersfield had competed with the surrounding boroughs for its share of revenues for two hundred years but the town's masters had possessed aspirations far beyond their peers. So in 1765 a commodious cloth hall had been erected for the merchants at Huddersfield by Sir John Ramsden. Fifteen years later it was enlarged by his son.

By 1812 the Cloth Hall was an imposing edifice. Topped by a cupola clock tower soaring above the brick face with its showy white accents, the actual structure was circular and two stories high. Being three hundred yards in circumference, the building had a diametrical avenue one story high which divided the interior into two semicircles: the one side into shops, and the other into open stalls. Inside gathered hundreds of merchants and manufacturers each market day. Their clothes were a rainbow of colours and their various top hats and *rehoboams* bobbed up and down with their movements as they bent to feel the fabrics. The place smelled of lanolin, stone and tobacco. The noise of bargaining reverberated in strident echoes throughout the hall. The haggling was fierce.

At first glance the Cloth Hall seemed a madhouse as men rushed from shop to stall in search of the best fabrics. Yet sales were conducted through strict regulations prescribed by the Hall's governing body. The doors were opened at eight in the morning and closed at half-past twelve, ending the purchasing part of the day. They once again opened at three in the afternoon for the transfer of cloth. This was a much more orderly scene with bales being loaded upon pack horses for trips along tracks across the moors, though some merchants with more ample funds employed waggons which set out upon the toll roads toward Leeds, York, Manchester and Sheffield. And just this year, the Huddersfield Narrow Canal had been opened to move stock from the market to Marsden, then beneath Standedge Moor by a three mile tunnel to Diggle's boat locks, and on to the Portland Basin and Manchester; an expensive but far more efficient method.

Outside the Cloth Hall many traders had had warehouses erected resulting in more merchants' emporiums. This outdoor market-place formed an expansive square at the front of the Hall's Georgian façade. Here, surrounded by prosperous houses and shops, luxuries were traded and on every Tuesday, Huddersfield Market Day, the square was bustling with energy.

"It is as I've told you, gentlemen, nowhere is anyone safe from them!" William Cartwright said, finishing his homily to the gathered few. He was joined by Atkinson, a pale-faced ascetic man in appearance. It had been his Bradley's Mills saved just in time by Raynes' cavalry.

"And it seems the authorities are unable to prevent them!"

He spoke angrily.

"Not true, Atkinson," Magistrate Radcliffe responded. "Captain Raynes halted the destruction of your shop in the face of overwhelming numbers."

"And to what end?" Henry Parr of Marsden asked. "Not one man captured! Not one of the criminals shot or sabered! The horses actually did more damage than the Luddites!"

"And where is Raynes, by the by?" William Horsfall asked. "The captain was to be here today was he not, Radcliffe, to explain his actions?"

Joseph Radcliffe was furious. With Lloyd packed off to accomplish his infiltrations, with no Hammond Roberson there to defend him, and without his lovely young wife to deflect the reproach, Radcliffe's authority was called into question.

"I tell you this, gentlemen ... though security prevents me from revealing the extent of our measures, we are making progress."

"What about more troops?" Cartwright asked.

"You have yours," Radcliffe answered.

"But five of them to guard the entire of Rawfolds! Insufficient, Sir. And none of the other owners have been issued any soldiers at all!"

"You were personally threatened and your frames shipment destroyed last month."

"My wife is beside herself with terror anticipating an attack."

"And you think mine is not?" Radcliffe's voice raised half an octave. "I've had threats in the form of stones through my windows. I myself have been fired upon only last week on the Halifax Road. Troops are coming, I assure you. I'll not let this state of affairs continue."

"Indeed," Atkinson said, "I have here the latest *Leeds Mercury*. This report states, and I quote: '*Leeds and Huddersfield have, with their military patrols, piquet's, etc. assumed rather the appearance of Garrison towns than the peaceful abodes of Trade and Industry.*'"

"Those words are Edward Baines', a radical! You note he belittles our attempts at order. My suspicion tells me he is one of them!"

"Oh hardly," Parr said, "He's a newspaperman doing his job."

"That may be so," Horsfall replied, "but he speaks of towns, not the countryside. Where are the soldiers for Marsden, or Linthwaite? We are too far away for quick response."

"General Maitland has written me personally. More troops shall arrive ..."

"It is not the towns suffering these attacks, Radcliffe."

"I will tell you this," Radcliffe said, his voice crackling with ire. "Major Gordon has cavalry squadrons patrolling each night through the West Riding."

"We've seen what they were capable of at my mills," Atkinson said, derisively. "And where in heaven's name is that damned Raynes?"

"I have a man out risking his life," Radcliffe said, "for information. I cannot reveal his name but will tell you, Atkinson, it was his intelligence which led Raynes to your mill."

"Obviously it wasn't worth much. When Raynes appeared with a mere twenty men ..."

"You all know until that raid none of us suspected a band of that size coming together."

"And they *were* organized," Atkinson said. "I saw it myself. Orderly, almost military in conduct. I think something huge is brewing out there, yet we have no inkling."

"Gentlemen, you might thank me for having organized the Watch and Ward but I note you feel otherwise. I shall take a turn about the Hall."

Radcliffe abruptly departed the group, wending his way through stacks of cloth and crowds of men in the midst of business. Still, as he passed he was acknowledged with a tip of a hat, a slight bow, or from lesser men a tug at their forelocks. Despite the dispute with the mill owners he was an important man.

"What of Raynes?" Horsfall shouted above the ruckus of the hall. Radcliffe half turned, his smooth face cut with wrathful furrows, then deigned to ignore the man by continuing on his way. He was seething inside. Nothing was more important to him than his dignity and standing as magistrate. Yet both had been mocked this day. He found he increasingly disliked the devious Lloyd. He doubted Lloyd's motives, loathed his scheming for advancement and was unnerved in the presence of those pale, reptilian eyes.

Raynes was another kettle of fish. Raynes was a military man to the hilt and held no doubts regarding his duty. And while he might quibble at Radcliffe's belief regarding the interrogation of captives he followed his orders as instructed. John Lloyd too, Radcliffe admitted, followed his new directions with gusto; indeed, the man seemed to enjoy acts of torture. In his mind Radcliffe knew his procedures were not *precisely* legal, but there was indeed something significant brewing in the West Riding. As he exited the Cloth Hall into the crowded throng of the marketplace, he too wondered what had become of Raynes who had not appeared as promised.

—

Captain Francis Raynes was at that moment being admired in the mid-day sun at the corner of Westgate and Market Square just in front of The George Inn. He was being observed through the windows of Mrs. Dobson's tea room by Fanny Radcliffe and her friend Maria Bronte, as they sat at a table sampling the widow Dobson's savouries and fine tea. While business men gathered in the Cloth Hall, their families, who often accompanied them to town, spent their own time in the shops and food emporiums mostly around the square. Mrs. Dobson's room was a popular and exclusive place where those with wealth could find solace from the crowd; thus the presence of Fanny and Maria.

They gazed upon a Scottish god of war: from his thigh high riding boots through his dove grey *overalls* to his fine scarlet jacket with gold tasseled epaulets and the grey with gold *shako* perched like a crown upon his head. The two ladies giggled as they regarded each other over white linen and near empty teacups.

"He is impressive, is he not?" Maria commented, quite aware of her partner's blush.

"Indeed Maria. If only we might talk with him. I've heard from my husband he has new strategies regarding Luddites."

"Oh?" Maria said. "I wonder what those might be."

"If we could but ask him," Fanny said, casting her gaze through the window.

Raynes was a beautiful man, thought Maria, and though she was entertained by his good looks her young friend was positively enraptured. The reason of course was clear. Poor Fanny was wed to a much older man. Maria doubted the girl had ever known a young man's touch.

Maria's own husband, Patrick, was youthful and attractive, if a trifle untamed. He had a man's sense of his sexuality yet possessed unique views against those values commonly held regarding women as inferior beings. Maria, seeing Fanny bereft of a good marriage's adornments, felt she owed her friend the chance to grasp her dreams if but for an afternoon.

"Perhaps we should finish our tea and take a stroll across the street," she said.

"Oh, I couldn't be so bold," Fanny said, flushing. "I've only been introduced to him once."

"You are a modern woman," Maria said. "A paragon of your society. Look at it this way ... you are simply deigning to recognize one of your husband's deputies."

"Oh? Yes. Yes! That is the answer of course! Oh, Maria, let us go before he departs."

The two women rose, Fanny leaving the necessary upon the table, and exited Mrs. Dobson's establishment. The cobbled street was chaotic: the rumble of waggons, the shouts of hawkers, the speed of horses and commotion of a crowded plaza making it difficult for two women to navigate. It took a moment for them to work up the courage to cross the roadway but before they could their heads were turned by a familiar voice.

"Ho, dear wife!" Curate Bronte appeared at their side. Despite his religious vocation, he was dressed in flamboyant fashion: a royal blue jacket with outsized white cravat, buff trousers rather than conservative breeches fitting tightly over half boots of brown leather.

"I've been looking all over the square for you. I've someone I'd like you to meet. Where the devil have you been, dearest?"

"At tea in Mrs. Dobson's."

"I should have known," Bronte said, smiling. "And I beg pardon, Mrs. Radcliffe, I've yet to greet you this day." He bowed, doffing his black beaver top hat.

"And I you," Fanny responded with a curtsy. "You are well, Curate Bronte?"

"In excellent form, madam," he said, grinning.

"Patrick," Maria said, "we were about to cross the way to meet Captain Raynes. You see him there at The George? Fanny is acquainted with him."

"Only slightly," Fanny said.

"But he is precisely my reason for finding you, my dear," Bronte said. "The captain and I have just shared an ale and I told him he must meet my wife. He himself is married, you know."

"Oh," Fanny said.

"But his Anne is not with him, ladies, as this is a military assignment. He would, I am sure, welcome the company of two lovely ladies such as yourselves. Let us cross."

Holding up his hand, Bronte led the ladies into the teeming street, ensuring traffic halted before them. Raynes noticed them coming, for obvious reasons.

Maria was dressed in spring lavender, Empire style bosom, with matching douillette and bonnet in purple while Fanny, the wealthier of the two, was a vision in rose floral chintz beneath a new-style mauve *Spencer* jacket and matching satin high hat, a garnish of pink flowers lining its brim. Raynes' eyes opened just a little wider as he beheld her blond curls and blue eyes and the lines of her figure so artfully portrayed by her attire.

And with his turn toward them, the April sun glinting upon his uniform's silver buttons, Fanny noted his dark eyes and lighted hair as he swept off his shako and bowed deeply. Fanny felt an unfamiliar and uneasy twinge in places she thought she should not be feeling. That sweeping turn, that intense bow, and the very nature of Fanny's confidence was blown away as leaves in the wind.

Once only, long years past, had she felt anything at all similar and that had been for a brawny stable boy at her father's business. The mood had brought her distressing dreams and listless days until her governess had become sharp with her, conferring with her father regarding her ennui. She'd had no idea what their conversation had entailed, only that she was to be sent off to London for *finishing* as her father had called it.

In London there were balls and banquets, card parties and garden gatherings as she was introduced to society. And when she'd returned home and that same stable boy had held open her chaise door, she'd barely noticed him as she stepped down. Four years later a marriage was made for Fanny to Magistrate Joseph Radcliffe. Unfortunately he was not the man she had dreamed of; indeed, he was old and soft and smelled musty. She did her duty in the marital bed but felt nothing and nothing, that is no child, came of it. But she lived a pampered life, her whims indulged by a paternal husband who treated her as a kind of prize but paid no heed to her deeper needs, those needs expressing themselves currently within the aura of the exalted Raynes.

Still, despite her feelings she quickly remembered her manners and curtsied, just lightly, just enough to impress upon him her superior quality. Yet what she truly wished was to walk with this shining officer over windblown, sunny moors in a never ending intimacy ... until she was poked in the ribs by her friend and returned from her reverie.

"Captain Raynes has just told us his stratagem of night rides to find and destroy these Luddites," Maria said. "Did you not heed him, Fanny? Is it not a marvelous concept?"

A knight! That was it. And she a damsel restrained by an ancient wizard. If only he could rescue her. And they would ride off, she wrapped in his arms upon his snowy charger, ever south, beyond England's shores to a land where dreams are made.

"Mrs. Radcliffe, are ye well?"

"Yes," she said. "Yes, I am sorry. I could not help but notice your youth for such a position as Captain, Sir."

"Aye, well I thank ye, madam. It took quite a sum to purchase my commission but I hope to put it to very good use.

"I'm told," Curate Bronte said, "Major Gordon thinks a great deal of you, Raynes. You've done well!"

"I wish, Sir, I could serve with our forces in Spain rather than here. Still, I hae my duty and hae noted right here in this district the potential for a revolt, likely imported from France."

"Oh, I'd not be so sure of that," Bronte said. "That was an entire country after all ..."

"Which began wi' Paris and a few provinces." Raynes' soft dark eyes hardened to glossy stone. Fanny loved the way his eyes became so fervent. "And led eventually to old Boney. No, Curate, this uprising must end."

"But no one has died," Maria said. "You believe matters so dire?"

For just an instant Fanny wanted to turn and slap sense into her friend. How dare she oppose the brilliant captain!

"Yet," Raynes said, "the way they carry on seems to foreshadow something larger and wi' reinforcements arriving, we'll soon come to blows."

"My husband has been fired upon," Fanny said. "And men have looked askance at me for no reason."

"Ye see then," Raynes said, stepping a heartbeat closer, "my point. A magistrate simply about his work, his lovely wife insulted, himself threatened and nearly shot; this is what we face, Mrs. Bronte. This is the worst of enemies: our own people gone astray."

His words swept over her like a tide. The sound of his manly voice gave her shivers. She was inexorably attracted to him. Without thinking she placed her gloved hand upon his arm. His own hand's warmth touched hers through the silk as he took her on his forearm while she stood beside him.

"Perhaps we might stroll to the river," she said, "the four of us, I mean."

"Why of course, Mrs. Radcliffe," Raynes replied, affected himself by her touch and her beauty. His own dear Anne was such a plain woman with none of the style of this cherub on his arm. His feelings shifted from martial to melodious as they took their first steps, turning the corner at The George Inn and walking, with the Brontes in tow, down Westgate toward the river.

They spoke then of finer things: of clothing and puppies and swans and just then the way the river glittered in the sunlight. They laughed together as a clumsy barrowman tipped his load trying to manoeuvre past them. Sometimes they were silent, thinking secret thoughts as they stood on the stony arch above the river. Their thoughts were of each other though neither dared say, dared look too long, touch too often, be anything other than what each pretended: genteel friends on a polite promenade.

Yet she had heard his martial plans and marvelled at his courage. And he had glanced into deep pools of blue and come away stricken with emotion. She had felt cords of muscle as she'd held his forearm and wondered what it would be like to feel those arms embrace her. He had heard her musical laughter and thought how different she was from his dour Anne. And finally, upon the Brontes' warning that it was growing late, they had gazed at each other and allowed their emotions full expression as each came away from that moment very much altered.

As Raynes departed on his way to his night ride, his thoughts, for once, did not dwell upon the future but the immediate past. And the woman who strolled back up to the Cloth Hall to meet her formidable husband for the first time in her marriage thought, not of her position, but of what might have been.

12

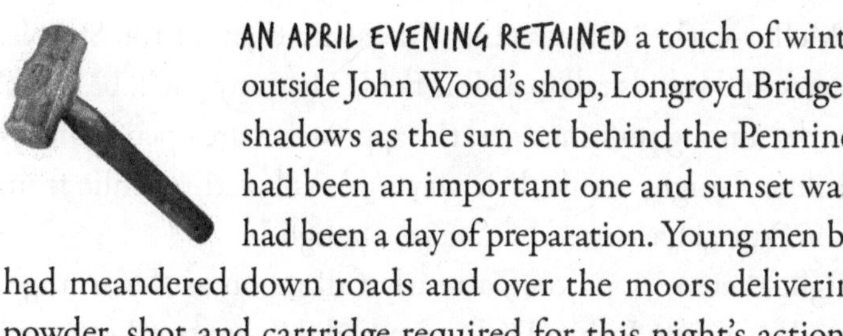

AN APRIL EVENING RETAINED a touch of winter cold. Just outside John Wood's shop, Longroyd Bridge cast lengthy shadows as the sun set behind the Pennines. This day had been an important one and sunset was a signal. It had been a day of preparation. Young men bearing sacks had meandered down roads and over the moors delivering the gunpowder, shot and cartridge required for this night's action. For it was this night which would show the owners, indeed the entire West Riding, just what the Luddite Movement could accomplish.

George Mellor was tense and preoccupied. The past month of assaults had been his work: his preparation. Yet as he stepped outside John Wood's shop, bundled for the cold and armed with a brace of pistols, he realized just how much of his plans had been accomplished through the mind of his step-father. Organizing couriers, gathering weapons, assembling his forces, even the idea of men using numbers beneath their disguises had somehow not seemed entirely his own. Always there was the whisper of Wood, the subtle glance, the slap on the back when young George had finally understood.

Yet John Wood had decided not to accompany them this night when a Luddite force would gather. The scale was remarkable. Men would arrive from Huddersfield and all down the Colne Valley, from Honley and along the Holme, from tiny places like Brighouse and Elland

and Dewsbury and larger ones like Wakefield and even as far off as Leeds. Perhaps a hundred men who, with the dying light, would be leaving their homes bearing weapons and hammers to reach their meeting place. They would rendezvous at a place called the *Dumb Steeple*.

And yet John Wood would not come.

The gaunt obelisk was known to all and to all it had meaning. A millstone grit column, twenty-six feet high, topped by a ball-shaped finial, some believed the name a corruption of the phrase *doom steeple*, so called as it once had marked the boundary of Kirklees Priory, within which doomed men could claim sanctuary from secular law. Other, simpler men knew the name: "*Because it says nowt*!" Whatever the beliefs, that particular place had also been John Wood's notion, thought Mellor. He remembered the two of them over tankards of ale, Wood answering Mellor with: "If it was me, I'd gather them at the Steeple. 'Tis a landmark and stands tall in a clear field. That way you'll be able t' keep some order among your men and the approaches are open countryside so no soldiers might sneak their way in. 'Tis but three mile from Rawfolds, son. You'll have need of a moon though."

This night there *was* a moon, a nearly full moon as the arrangements proceeded. Young Joshua Dickinson had shown up at Longroyd and delivered ammunition. He'd travelled all day from place to place to end here. He now stood with the men who would be Mellor's lieutenants: big Will Thorpe leading the hammer and axe men, Tom Smith the company of pistols, George Rigg to be chief of the musket men, Sam Lodge to run messages and Ben Walker, complaining as usual, to bring up the rear with the men who would throw rocks at the windows, creating a diversion.

Still, John Wood would not come.

"It would be for nowt," Wood said as he ushered Mellor out the doorway, "as I've told you. I'm a *maister*, though a low one. It wouldn't do for such as me t' march with the men."

George Mellor wished he could see past those eyes and into the mind which so subtly had guided him. He was nervous; petrified really. He was no leader, no General. And yet he found himself now departing upon a campaign to become just that. He had wanted his stepfather along to help solve the inevitable crises which could occur once the action began.

"But there'll be other small *maisters* there, da'! Thomas Brook from Lockwood, for one! He's no different from you."

"Still and all," Wood said, "this kind of work ain't for old men like me. Now get yourself gone, George, and make me proud!" And with that the small troop had set off down the lane toward Huddersfield accompanied by more complaints from Walker.

"What's that man doing here, George?" he said, pointing a finger at Sam Lodge. "He's not one of us. Never took the Oath. I don't like a man who could be a snake in the grass."

"I'll say this once, Walker. You know the man and know too why he won't take the Oath. But he's loyal. He'll run my orders from place t' place this night. He's doing this t' prove he's no coward. If you don't like it you can stay behind."

Mellor's sudden strictness took Walker by surprise. Once again he'd found himself on the wrong side of the man, those glittering eyes piercing him. As quickly as a finger plucks a string Walker changed his tune, trying again to be accepted by the man he loathed, yet feared.

"You know me, George," he said softly, "just watching out for troubles."

"Seems you make more than you find," Mellor replied, then turned his back and walked down the path to the road, Walker meekly following.

John Wood watched the group depart. He smiled in satisfaction. His son was his weapon in an economic war few realized was transpiring. John Wood had grasped it early on; had understood its complexity and worked to enhance his position by using others as proxies to curtail rich owners and provide himself the chance to compete. He watched his step-son cross Longroyd Bridge then turned back to his cottage with thoughts to comfort his wife who would be anxious for her son. George was the lad Wood had always wanted: strong, smart, ambitious ... and now on his way to make history.

The plan was clear. They would divide whatever sized force gathered at the Dumb Steeple into companies of men carrying muskets, pistols, axes or hammers. Every man would be disguised and numbered off. They would march across Hartshead Moor in the dark to avoid attracting Raynes' patrols in order to reach Rawfolds mill. Sam Hartley, a former worker for Cartwright, would be their guide to help them get close enough to surprise and subdue any sentries. Then before an alarm was raised a diversion would protect the men who were to advance and break down the mill's door. Rocks thrown from all angles would smash every window in the place. Other men would use muskets to reply to gunfire from the building. They would use companies of pistoliers to attack and enter the mill. Then they would destroy its contents and disperse before Raynes arrived. George Mellor would lead his amateur warriors with the knowledge he'd gained from his previous raids, coupled with John Wood's elusive instruction.

He was uneasy. As they greeted more men who joined their march, Mellor went over the plans as they walked. Finally, crossing the Calder River, he gave up his worry as a useless exercise.

He thought then of Mary Buckworth, seeing her as the fury who'd told him to leave her house. He began to wonder what she would be about now when supper was finished, the maid clearing up, John in his library toiling on Luddite missives.

He looked up then from his thoughtfulness and glimpsed the Dumb Steeple lit dully by one or two torches; a beacon. He realized they might also present his enemies a clue and told Joshua to run forward to have the torches extinguished. With that hasty process, that rapid decision, he emptied his mind of the Buckworths. He now had more pressing issues. He had to become a leader of men, a General of untrained proletarian warriors.

—

At nine o'clock they reached the Dumb Steeple to find a meagre few gathered around it.

George Mellor stepped up to the obelisk and delivered his orders.

"While we wait, we must ready ourselves. We'll need lookouts down where the field starts. They'll direct the men in and give warning should they hear soldiers. Johnny Booth, you organize Joshua, Jamie and the other young lads. Send them out t' the field's edges. I need outliers t' cover my flanks, fleet of foot so each can come with a warning if needed."

The boys quickly did as instructed, surprising Mellor with their discipline.

"Will Thorpe, Thomas Smith, George Rigg, Ben Walker ... each stand off a way from the Steeple so those coming in will join your companies. John Hirst and James Haigh, study each man and depending on what they carry send 'em t' the proper leader: Thorpe the hammers and axes, Walker the unarmed men, Rigg the muskets, Smith with pistols. Make them line up. Each must wear his hat and mask. Make sure each blacks his face then give them their numbers!"

By ten o'clock more had begun to arrive some carrying mauls and axes, some with weapons, even long pikes from the old days. Soon there were seventy by John Hirst's count, then in a half hour more than a hundred. They came in disguises. Each man had charcoaled his face. Every one wore a hat, for in those days to be without one was regarded as odd, and the hats helped conceal the colours of their hair. Around midnight Ben Walker ran up and told Mellor there were three hundred men.

"I've not seen the Leeds men," Mellor said.

"They must be coming from the north! If we leave now we'll meet them at Rawfolds!" Sam Hartley shouted. "'Tis time t' be off, George!"

The companies set off in good order. They marched along moor tracks with Hartley to guide. The moon was a fine luminosity, the weather fair, the ground rough but these men were accustomed to that.

It was three miles to Rawfolds Mill.

They passed through the hamlet of Hightown perched above the Spen Valley. Cottages were darkened for the night but if a man looked carefully he could glimpse certain twitches at window curtains. They trudged through Hightown. The sound of so many feet on the road made a marvellous pound. Curate Bronte's abode was nearby but if he heard them he kept his head down ... men on their way to a reckoning.

William Cartwright was asleep in his counting house, a few paces from the mill. His trusted men now slept on cots made up in the mill as did the five soldiers placed on the floor above the main door. When the time came, as Cartwright knew it must, he had organized them so trained men would load muskets for the soldiers, thus maximizing their firepower. But he had done more. He had taken some pride in showing off his defenses to friends and contemporaries. Even Captain Raynes had offered praise.

Most obviously, at the mill gateway Cartwright had posted two sentries. Next, the great doors of the mill had been studded with iron and given a drop bar of solid oak. The first floor's windows had been boarded from the inside up to the height where even a man standing on another's shoulders could gain no entry. The flagstones of the upper floor had been re-designed to be raised by pulleys making walls to shield defenders as they fired down on the mill's yard. Should the attackers somehow break through the entrance, the stairway itself was protected by iron spiked rollers which could be shoved down the stairs, crushing and shredding those foolish enough to attempt the climb. At the top of the stairs, as a final measure, tubs of vitriol stood ready to be tipped and so burn the aggressors with sulfuric acid. Finally, on the roof of the mill, four stories up, the call-to-work bell was manned; an alarm loud enough to be heard miles away and meant to be rung throughout an attack, thus bringing reinforcements.

Elizabeth Cartwright had grasped the need for defensive measures but she considered spiked rollers and vitriol barbaric. Indeed, she'd begun to question her marriage to a husband who had become a man she'd never thought existed. It had once all been well with them. William was gentlemanly in his habits. Yet as time passed Elizabeth found she had less in common with her husband. She had recognized her husband's harsh design regarding machines and attempted to ameliorate events by organizing aid for those he'd put out of work.

Cartwright had accepted her charitable acts at first but it wasn't long until he realized his competitive edge would be lost and ambition thwarted unless he could make more money. It made him a different man. More callous. Less loving. He'd stopped her assistance to the unemployed.

Eventually he'd left the cottage the two had shared as man and wife and debarked to his counting house. He had blamed the bleak economic times and had had it re-furnished. As it became his citadel's headquarters Elizabeth hardly ever saw him. She retreated to her cottage and scarcely left it. She spent days thinking of her place in the order of things. She recognized she did not belong here. Yet the scandal of divorce disputed her thoughts.

Elizabeth too was asleep that night of April eleventh in her cottage. It was the heavy barking of her husband's mastiff which awakened her to the horrors of the night.

13

THEY STOOD QUIETLY among trees facing the mill, all dark within. The size of the building subdued them as it hulked beside the millstream. The outbuildings' rooftops could be glimpsed above the thick hedge which formed a kind of wall and made a gateway twenty yards from the mill door.

It was a fortress.

Mellor took up a position in an outcrop opposite the entry. Behind him formed his companies, nearby his commanders. He spoke to Will Thorpe.

"I don't like the Leeds men not being here."

"'Tis a long way, George. They'll be trying."

"Too late now. What's this?"

At first when he saw a figure amidst the shadows of trees, Mellor took hold of his pistols, ready to draw and fire. Then appearing in the moonlight stood the slight shape of Curate John Buckworth. Clearly, he had been waiting. He held a copy of his manifesto.

"Why are you here, John?" Mellor said. "I've forbidden you the raids."

"I thought this time, George, since it would be so extensive, I should be here."

"Why were you not at the Steeple then?"

"What steeple? Heavens you have so many men here. Where did they come from?"

"Where did *you* come from?" Mellor's question came in a growl. "How did you discover our plans?"

"One of the boys, a messenger you sent out today, is part of my choir. I naturally asked him what he was about and he told me. I came to Rawfolds straight from Dewsbury. I know nothing of any steeple."

"Did you see any men on the roads from Leeds?" Thorpe asked.

"I'm sorry. Only a few local men gathering, but they left the road in a group and set off over Hartshead Moor. Is the steeple there?"

"Don't mind that now," Mellor said. "You'll keep behind me!"

"Yes. But how can I help?"

"You must do as you're told, John. Stay safe."

Mellor turned away as a group of men hustled up to them from the mill. They held two captives. Hartley stepped forward.

"These men guarded the entry, Number One," Hartley said, careful to keep to numbered identities. "They were asleep and we got their guns. Can you believe it? Blunderbusses! Cartwright means business."

"Stay with me," Mellor replied signifying Hartley then gave orders to another man: "You'll take them back into the woods. Take two men with you. Gag and tie them."

The man tried to lead the others away when suddenly Walker stepped forward shoving one of the prisoners to the ground.

"Albert Stiles! I know you, you traitor!" Walker threatened to kick the man.

"You stupid bastard! I'll have none of your bluster this night!" Mellor shouted.

That brief bark and glitter of eyes backed Walker away. When the captives were taken off Mellor turned to Sam Lodge.

"Sam, get back there and tell every man the prisoners ain't t' be harmed. 'Tis machines we're after this night, not men. Not unless they fight us."

"And what of Cartwright? Ain't he t' get his lesson?" Walker said, embarrassed by his chastisement.

"You've been playing a mite rough, Ben Walker, of late. I want no more. I'm ordering you t' pass the word. When we get inside the mill there's t' be no assault on any man except t' quell him."

"I'm no messenger!" Walker said. "You have Lodge for that!"

"And he's away with a message this moment, so now I'm telling you! Move man, and when you're done join your company and get your men ready."

"Throwing rocks? What's the good of that?"

Mellor took a frightening step closer to Walker. It was Walker's turn to cower.

"Don't waste my time."

Mellor dismissed him then turned to Thorpe.

"How many with us?" Mellor asked Thorpe.

"I think near two hundred. Walker says three."

"He's wrong. Where in hell are the Leeds men? They'd make us a hundred more."

"They don't know the local roads. Raynes' men will be about as well. No telling what's happened. Look George," — Thorpe grasped his friend's arms — "we can do this."

Suddenly the howl of a dog split the night. It continued barking from somewhere inside the mill yard. The hedge concealed it. Its barking would awaken the mill's inhabitants.

"Smith, take Hartley t' guide you; find that dog and shoot it!"

"Aye!"

The dog's yowling jolted Cartwright awake. It was not his animal's normal sound but a longer, rougher baying at something it could not recognize. Cartwright knew in that instant the time he'd anticipated had come. He jumped out of bed, pulled on his boots, grabbed a musket and ran across the yard.

Hammering on the door he was let inside through a small louvered portal set into the large one. Once inside, Cartwright climbed the stairs to find his men and the soldiers awakened as well, each in various states of dress: some with nightcaps still on their heads, others their breeches beneath bed gowns, the soldiers more dressed than the others. They were accustomed to alarms.

"To the windows, all of you!" Cartwright commanded, each order stuttered out in a rapid discharge. "Loaders to your musket stacks. Start loading now! Pull up the floor stones as well!"

He turned to the window. Outside was moonlit. He glimpsed two dark shapes creeping along the hedge toward his mastiff's kennel.

"You out there!" he bellowed. "I warn you now you are trespassing! I've soldiers of the Cumberland Militia along with other stout lads and none of us will give up this mill to vandals!"

His reply was the spit-fire of a musket and the shadows became, in that flash, two men. The dog yelped as it died. Cartwright cursed, aimed his own musket and fired at the men in his yard. There was a cry. He saw one of the shadows fall. The other scrambled out the gateway.

"So that's to be the way, is it? Well, we've your answer Luddites!"

From the roof the bell began ringing. The clanging would bring reinforcements but meanwhile Cartwright had no idea what he was facing. Then suddenly, to a muffled command, torches were lit in the woods across from his mill; torches in a line that told him he faced an army. He had thirteen men.

"Jesus save us," one of them said.

—

"Christ, that bell!" Mellor said. Torches illuminated him now, torches surrounding him so his men could see him clearly.

"It'll bring Raynes," Thorpe said.

"Sam!" Mellor turned to his friend. "Quick now. You must get to Walker. He's to start throwing stones! Break the windows! Make a diversion! Go now!"

"And me?" Thorpe asked.

"We must hurry, Will. That bell ..."

Tom Smith returned. He was shaking.

"They shot Hartley!" he cried, his voice shaking, as though he could not believe it. "I couldn't go back t' get him. He's bad, George. Lying trapped near the gateway!"

Then the mill bell stopped.

—

"What's happened? Where's the bell?" Cartwright shouted. His answer came in a moment. An apprentice appeared on the steps from the upper floors.

"The bell's broke!" he cried. "The pull snapped. We was pulling too hard, me and Alf!"

"Find more rope! Fix the pull, you fool! We need Raynes here!"

Then came sounds of glass smashing all around them as scores of stones found the mill's windows. The din was surreal. It seemed as though Luddites had found their way in like rats through each undefended cleft.

"Sir," the Cumberland corporal said, "they'll be coming."

—

Mellor heard the jangle of glass from inside his ring of torches. In a voice as powerful as any commander he summoned his force.

"That's our diversion! For General Ludd, men! Muskets make ready. Cover the men going through the gate. Thorpe! Take your men and deliver me down that door!"

Multiple cheers sent them forward: hammer and axe men to the front, musket men just behind. Their torches advanced toward the gateway then through it.

—

It was Cartwright's turn. He thundered down at them: "I give you final warning! Stay back from my door!"

—

Mellor shouted a reply from the gateway: "This is for the men you've put t' beggary with your machines! Smash that door, lads!"

The twenty with hammers began taking turns slamming on the door. The ring of metal on metal resounded as they struck iron studs in the wood.

"Door's ironed!" Thorpe cried. "The hammers won't do it!"

"Axes then!" Mellor shouted and the order was followed, other men with axes finding gaps between studs but there was so much iron one miss and a blade would warp against the black knobs that speckled the door.

—

"Prepare!" Cartwright ordered and muskets passed hands in the room above the door. Then the unexpected occurred. One soldier refused his gun, turned to Cartwright and simply stood there, his face distorted by his defiance.

"Mr. Cartwright, Sir, I'll not shoot them men!"

"You've been ordered! Corporal, order this man to shoot!"

"You heard him, Shepherd, take up your firearm!"

"No, Corporal. I'm done with this. 'Tis my own brother could be out there."

The man left his window, backing away. He stood near the fireplace and would not budge. Cartwright now had five loaders, five shooters including himself and two apprentices frantically working at the roof bell.

It would have to do.

"Aim below us on the door! We have to drive that bunch back first! Ready?"

His answer was grim silence. These men knew what they were about to do.

"Shoot!"

The volley came from only five guns but they were enough. The sound of the muskets nearly deafened the men in the room. The loaders handed over the next batch of guns for a second volley and it too exploded, filling the room with grey smoke. Cartwright could hear screams from below and gritted his teeth. They were about to fire again when a different volley answered theirs from the hedge line, more muskets than they, but the balls smashed through the glass ricocheting off stone and did them no harm.

George Rigg's untrained musket men's weak reply.

—

At the door below it was different. Several had been wounded. Some badly.

"Thorpe left the door momentarily. He carried an injured man over his shoulder as any normal man would a child, stopping at the entry, setting the man gently down, then looking at Mellor with tears in his eyes.

"God's teeth, George, they're shooting at us."

"God damn their souls! Are you wounded Haigh?"

"Aye. Arm wound. 'Tis bad but Hartley's only just alive. Shot in the chest."

"I'm going back t' that door," Thorpe said. Suddenly young Johnny Booth appeared, hammer in hand, the head of it almost too heavy for him to hold.

"I'll go with you," he said.

"You're too young, lad," Thorpe replied. "Don't waste your life."

"No man should stand aside when there's murder! Lead on, Mr. Thorpe! My friend Jamie Dean's up there and I mean to join him!"

The bell began clanging again. Once again a barrage of fire flamed out from the mill. Johnny Booth never made it that far.

—

Their attack had become a confusion of fire; a cacophony of explosions. The brutal efficiency of the shot from above had staggered them: poor wounded souls crawling back toward the gate, others lying in the dirt screaming from pain. It shattered what discipline they had achieved. Men began peeling off, running for the woods.

Mellor felt powerless to do anything, stymied as he was by the noise, the dust, the shouts and wailing; the men he could see now deserting his ranks. A force of impassioned men had been turned by the deeds of professionals into a terrified rabble. He had never faced anything like this. He found himself a helpless child. He was afraid, yet more angered than frightened, of slaughter. He leaned down to speak with Hartley.

"Hartley, can you hear me?"

"Aye," Hartley said weakly, then coughed blood.

"What can we do for you?"

"'Tis all up with me, George," Hartley murmured. "I need the curate now."

Buckworth went to one knee and began a prayer for Hartley.

"We must leave here, George," Sam Lodge said, "before they kill us all!"

Instead Mellor ran into the yard to the fallen Johnny Booth. The boy had taken a ball just above the knee, the lead slug had nearly torn his leg off.

"Johnny, I'll take you back t' safety."

He lifted the boy and carried him but the boy screamed and begged to be set down.

"Sir, just leave me. Please!"

With blood on his hands and fury in his brain George Mellor did the only thing left to him ... fight.

"Give me Booth's hammer, Buckworth. I'll finish this!"

"You can't, George. Those men are trained soldiers!" Buckworth grabbed at Mellor's sleeve, trying to take his friend back to the gateway's safety.

"Leave off, Curate! What men go with me?"

"Me!" Smith shouted. "I'll get the pistol men t' back us."

"And me, the bastards!" Rigg shouted furiously, grabbing an axe.

"Me as well, by your side," Sam Lodge said firmly.

"Sam, you're not a sworn man. You should leave here," Buckworth said, grasping his arm. Amidst the tumult he was at a loss. All of these people were supposed to be Christian.

"It ain't enough t' let us starve, Curate. Now they kill us like dogs! No man can walk away from this."

"No quarter, lads!" Mellor screamed. "We'll pay them back with their own *brass*!"

They began to run to the door where only a few were left. Buckworth remained to help Hartley when young Joshua Dickinson ran up to him.

"Sir! Curate Buckworth!" The boy pointed up toward the hills. "They're coming!"

"Who? The Leeds men?"

"No, Sir! Soldiers! We heard horses not half a league away!"

"Listen, son. Find some men and take Hartley off."

"I can't move, Curate. Christ, it hurts." Hartley coughed; blood dribbled down his chin.

"Alright, Sam. I'll stay with you. Joshua, run into the yard and tell Mr. Mellor ..."

He did not finish. He twisted and fell, his hand clasped to his back. Joshua ran inside to fetch Mellor. When they returned Mellor dropped to the ground beside Buckworth. His hands felt for a wound. The hands came away bloody. Even then in the moonlight Mellor could see Buckworth's face pale as death. Still, with an effort, the curate whispered.

"Cavalry ... coming."

Thorpe and Smith had now reached the gateway as the rest of their men ran toward the woods. Thomas Brook, the mill owner who had joined them, stopped beside them.

"Raynes is coming," he said, his eyes round with panic. "Follow me, George. I know a path around the mill pond!"

"How far away are the soldiers?"

"Not far," young Joshua said.

"We have t' leave," Thorpe said, his voice profound sorrow.

"Aye," Mellor said, gathering the remains of his self-control. He held Buckworth in his arms. "Order all men away! Take the high moor tracks. Raynes can't follow you there. Go on now, Will. Thomas, go with him."

"What of you?" Smith replied.

"I'm taking John home."

"Christ, man, there's soldiers coming!" Thorpe shouted.

"I'll make it."

"You'll be caught."

"I've a duty t' this man. Now get out of here and take the rest with you!"

Three hundred windows had been shattered. One hundred and forty shots fired. The entire encounter took but twenty minutes of confusion, blood, terror and courage and now it was done. Once again George Mellor felt helpless. He wondered how soldiers maintained their detachment in battle. He wondered how any General could do what he was supposed to in the midst of such turmoil. But more than all of this came an underlying feeling Mellor had never before sensed in himself. He could not believe men would kill for possessions. He could not conceive of an owner using a force to murder men to protect machines. He sensed John Wood had tried to prepare him but no one could be prepared for butchery.

In that instant George Mellor changed.

—

For a few moments they were alone in the silence. Of the wounded only Hartley, young Booth and Buckworth remained, the rest having either helped themselves off or, receiving help, had retreated. Mellor picked up the slight form of Buckworth and set off toward the rear of the mill to follow the stream into the trees. He was stopped by a sopping Thomas Brook, drenched from head to foot. He had lost his hat and his straw coloured hair stood out like a light in the night.

"What's happened t' you?" Mellor said.

"I was running and fell into the pond. My hat's gone. If they find my hat they'll know it's mine. I'll be arrested. George, you've got t' help me find my hat!"

"I've another task. I must take Buckworth home. He can't be discovered here."

"But my hat ..."

"Likely sunk. Come with me. We'll stop by a house and get you another."

"Then let me help with the curate."

Before they could continue hooves pounding on the road drove them into deep brush. Peering out Mellor expected Raynes yet instead found Vicar Roberson, his huge girth and hawk's face unmistakable. He held two pistols aloft as he pulled up by the gate. The troop of cavalry reined in behind him, carbines ready. Mellor found it strange that Reverend Hammond Roberson should be commanding a troop of cavalry. A man of God armed ... it fit this hellish night. His voice now filled the dark beneath the waning moon.

"Cartwright? Are you in there? It's Hammond Roberson with reinforcements!"

"What took you so long?"

"We heard your bell, then it stopped. We'd stood down, then we heard it again. You told us that bell would ring through an attack!"

"The bell pull broke ..."

"Eh?"

"Never mind. I've two apprentices will answer for their folly."

"Where is the enemy? I see two on the ground."

"There were hundreds!"

"Where?"

"Here!"

"And only two left?"

"I'm coming down," Cartwright shouted.

"Dammit!" Roberson said. "I'd wanted to engage those sinners myself!"

Mellor and Brook had heard enough. They took Buckworth away. They kept to the trees, heading up toward the top of the ridge to Primrose Hill Farm. The Naylors lived there. Sympathizers. Mellor knew he could borrow both a barrow to cart poor Buckworth, and a hat for Thomas Brook so he would not stand out from other men.

He knew Raynes would soon arrive at the mill with his company of Queen's Bays. Raynes would not bluster like Roberson. He would search far and wide for any man out this night. In a topsy-turvy world of mayhem, armed vicars and dying curates, of simple men driven to desperation then driven away by slaughter, anything could happen.

Indeed it was happening within George Mellor. He could feel his emotions draining from him, as the blood drained from John Buckworth.

—

With the barrow borrowed from the Naylors and after a welcomed drink of water, Mellor discovered Ben Walker cowering not far from the house. He came out of the dark like a ghost.

"George," he mumbled, still in shock, "what happened back there? I had my men smash the windows. I did as ordered."

"The difference is we came for machines, they came for blood."

"But I thought you had a plan." Walker could hardly contain his self-satisfaction.

"I should have had more than one plan but I'm no General, Ben, as you know. Now we've other problems. Brook lost his hat. I tried for a decent one here at Naylor's but she gave him this busted straw thing. It was all she had. It looks suspicious."

"Won't his own hat be found? People know his hat," Walker said.

"Aye. 'Tis likely. Both of you must get up t' the high moors. Find your way t' Brook's mill. Once there, you'll be safe."

"What about you?" Brook asked. "That barrow's heavy."

Mellor, pushing the barrow, refused any help. This, he knew, was on him alone. He sent Walker and Brook away then set off by back ways toward Dewsbury and the encounter he dreaded. He'd only gone half a league or so when Buckworth awakened. Mellor let down the barrow holds and knelt by the wounded man.

"John, you're with me?"

"Yes. I ... Where is the moon?" His voice was weak, barely audible. Mellor leaned closer, touching Buckworth's hand.

"Waned now. Gone."

"I cannot feel anything, George. Why can't I ..."

"Easy now, John. You were hit in the back. Just rest. I'll take you home."

"But ... soldiers?"

"You'll be safe."

"I think I shall die."

"Don't think that. Think of Mary. You'll see her soon, and the sunrise."

"A new day ..."

"Aye," Mellor muttered. "'Tis that."

"What happened, George?"

"I thought they were men like us."

"Give them my manifesto ..."

"Aye. I'll give 'em something they won't soon forget." The words were bitter. They came from the soul of a bewildered man.

"I'm so tired. Please ... George ..."

"Aye John?"

"Take care of Mary."

"Oh, Christ ..."

Curate John Buckworth died a while later. He died without benefit of holy rites. He died in a barrow bumping along pushed by a man who with each step was draining himself of humanity.

So he might replace all feelings with one.

Rage.

14

WILLIAM CARTWRIGHT EXITED his mill via the louvered door, much splintered but still intact, and made his way through the chaos of broken glass, smashed tools and abandoned weapons littering the yard. He reached the two men lying in pools of blood at Roberson's feet, peering down at them as though they were animals. His soldiers remained upstairs: two cleaning muskets, two others guarding the mutineer. The five workers who'd acted as loaders and the two apprentices came down behind him, curious as to what mayhem had wrought. They brought lanterns. Their glow lit the yard making strange, shadowed angles of the detritus strewn on the ground and, in the light, Cartwright saw the two wounded men.

"Why you're Sam Hartley. I recognize you. You worked for me, you bastard."

"Who are your leaders?" Roberson asked. "Where have they gone?"

"Water ..." was all Hartley could manage.

"You'll have none until you've provided answers," the Reverend said. Roberson was in furious form. He reached out a foot and tapped at the splintered leg of Johnny Booth. The boy screamed in agony.

"I know you as well," Roberson said. "You are the lad to be sent up to school, are you not? Yet you waste your chance and your life with felons."

"A mere boy," Cartwright said. "They use children against me." He blithely ignored his own two apprentices who now stood, eyes agape, at the horror before them. Behind them two workers noted what was happening and after a quiet conference, returned to the mill.

Roberson was about to resume his interrogation when he was abruptly interrupted.

"What in heaven's name are you doing there?" a woman's voice rang out of the dark. Elizabeth Cartwright had made her way from her nearby cottage. Through the fray she had witnessed little more than running shadows and the flares of musket fire from her window but she had heard the agonies of wounded men and the curses of others and just now, crossing the yard, had seen enough to turn her stomach. She glared at Roberson as she would a mad dog.

"You call yourself a man of God?"

"Get back to your cottage, wife!" Cartwright said. "This was insurrection!"

"These men must be cared for."

"These are Luddite lawbreakers!"

Yet even as he spoke his two workers, men who had loaded his guns, returned from of the mill. One knelt and gave the wounded men water mixed with wine to help quell their pain while the other placed stones beneath their heads to serve as pillows. Elizabeth knelt beside them.

"What are you doing, woman?" Cartwright's harsh voice split the air. "I told you get back to your cottage. Do so now or I'll see you carried there!"

She looked up at him, her eyes stones, then slowly stood and retreated. She would remain for days in her cottage. Elizabeth knew she had reached the end of what once had been her dream, now turned nightmare, with William Cartwright.

—

Roberson was questioning the two wounded men when Raynes appeared with his dragoons. He reined to a halt by the ring of lanterns surrounding the party of victors and victims. His horse was lathered from the hard ride. His squadron had heard the bell from far off but when it had stopped they'd done much the same as Roberson's group: stood down until they'd heard it peeling again.

"Late once again, Captain?" Roberson said.

"It appears we all were," Raynes replied coolly as he observed the remains of the fight. "Mr. Cartwright, how might I assist you?"

"Sergeant!" Roberson said, ignoring Raynes. "Send a man to Magistrate Radcliffe. We shall take these two up to the Yew Tree Inn. We'll keep them there. Have some men take down these doors. We'll use them as litters."

"But ye'll not be going t' the Yew Tree," Raynes said.

"Is that so?" Roberson said.

"It is, Sir. That Inn is too close to this place and people will gather once they hear what's happened. You recall Radcliffe's instructions to isolate prisoners?" Raynes turned his back on the vicar and issued his own set of orders.

"Sergeant! These men are to go to Robertown to the Star Inn. That is twelve miles from Huddersfield along the road south from here. These dragoons will accompany ye. Post them as guards outside the Inn. Be sure ye do, Sergeant; these are the first Luddite raiders we've caught and ye won't know who might hae followed ye."

"Aye, Captain. I'll see it done."

"There's more. Ye'll find a man there, a tinker. His name is Mr. Lloyd. Shut these two criminals up with him. None else, mind. And guard the doors. No one, other than myself or the magistrate is to see these men. I will take the vicar's cavalry and scour the countryside; see if we might flush out a few more."

Roberson approached the captain alongside Cartwright. Cartwright seemed to have become less belligerent since the altercation with his wife. The stress of the attack and the shock of that twenty minutes had drained him. Roberson, who had seen no action, was his usual blustering self.

"Captain, I command this company under the purview of Watch and Ward!" Roberson said. "How dare you interfere?"

"Vicar Roberson." Raynes moved close to the big man and in a near whisper, though loud enough for Cartwright to hear, made himself clear: "Ye are a civilian and no matter how important ye think ye might be, this is a military matter. Should ye choose ye hae my permission to accompany the dragoons, Sir. They may hae use of your consecrated skills should either of these men die on the way. Otherwise dinna trouble me with your protests. The Sergeant is now in command. And Mr. Cartwright," — he turned and faced the mill owner — "I shall wish a word wi' ye in a moment. Judging from what I see here ye've had quite a night. I'd like a description of what happened and, might I add, Sir, ye're to be congratulated upon your defense."

Raynes smiled. Cartwright preened. Roberson fumed.

And two humans suffered at their feet.

—

The Star was a building of some distinction in Robertown. A coaching inn, it stood just across from the Huddersfield Turnpike toll-house. It was a large structure constructed in Elizabethan style: a gateway into a walled courtyard, stables to one side, the inn itself filling the other two sides of the square. It was perfect for security. Indeed it was Major Gordon who had suggested it serve as a headquarters for Raynes and the newly arrived dragoons. It would suit Lloyd as well for those times when he returned to report his investigations. The Star was busy enough for Lloyd to pass unnoticed in his tinker disguise.

It had other advantages as well. The inn possessed an interior warren of multiple hallways and staircases. On its second level it was divided into groups of isolated compartments. To reach one section from another, a man would have to take himself downstairs to the public room then up another stairway to arrive where he wanted. The rooms put aside for the prisoners were far down a long hall with rooms on each side, all now tenanted by dragoons.

Upon their dawn arrival no one but servants were awake. Despite his instructions, Roberson took command again. He found John Lloyd in his room, waited for him to dress, then followed him up to the prisoners' compartment. All seemed to go well until they reached the hallway where Roberson was stopped by the sergeant. The sergeant was a man who understood rank and for civilians who lacked it, he had little respect.

"I'm sorry, Vicar, I received orders from Captain Raynes just who was allowed t' see the prisoners. You ain't on that list."

John Lloyd might not have been the most impressive man with his diminutive stature and conspiratorial voice; but he was an astute manipulator. He swiftly sized up the situation realizing that Roberson and Raynes had somehow crossed swords. Yet he knew Roberson and Radcliffe were close. A good word from the vicar might benefit his advancement. He also knew Radcliffe had, thinking Lloyd a grasping social climber, taken a dislike to him. He realized he could resolve both matters at this very moment, beginning with the vicar.

"I too am sorry, Sergeant, but I shall have need of Vicar Roberson. A man with the reverend's stature shall compel the prisoners to tell the truth. What man on his way to his Maker would think otherwise?"

"Those ain't my orders, Mr. Lloyd."

"I'm rather sure you were not expecting last night to be given this type of command, were you? I would rather not mention to Captain Raynes that you hampered an interrogation."

The words, delivered in an offhand manner yet threatening so much beneath, took the sergeant with such force he hesitated for only an instant before stepping aside.

"Aye, Mr. Lloyd. I've no understanding of these matters. You are the man in charge, so I'm told by Captain Raynes. Vicar Roberson, I hope you understand I just did as ordered."

"Quite alright, Sergeant." A mollified Roberson smiled generously. He glanced sideways at Lloyd and left the sergeant in his wake. At the end of the hall, just before they passed through the door to the waiting prisoners, Lloyd plucked at his sleeve and the two men stopped.

"Who are they and how badly injured?" Lloyd asked.

"Enough that this young scholar, Booth, has half his leg off. He won't see tomorrow."

"Then we'll begin with him."

"The other's name is Hartley. I'd like you to know, Lloyd, I appreciate my inclusion."

"Could it have been any other way?" Lloyd said, putting his hand on the door and turning the knob while glancing back at the sergeant. "Sergeant, please bring me the company's surgeon. Tell him he'll need his tools."

"Aye, Sir," the sergeant replied, relieved to find he had not angered this little man who possessed such power. He went himself in search of the surgeon.

In the room both Booth and Hartley lay shackled upon separate beds, both unwashed and stinking of blood and urine. Roberson retrieved a handkerchief from his pocket and held it to his nose. Lloyd seemed comfortable despite the gore. Young Booth had suffered from loss of blood and was barely conscious. Still blacked with charcoal, his face was streaked from his tears. Lloyd immediately went to his bedside.

"Now then young man, it seems you've paid a price for this night. How bad are we then?"

Lloyd only slightly turned Booth's ankle, jostling the leg just a little yet causing the boy to shriek with pain.

"Yes, I see," Lloyd said calmly following the lad's pleas for mercy. He was unaffected by Booth's agony and the snarl of threat emanating from Hartley.

"You'll leave the boy alone, you bastard!"

"Ah, Hartley." Lloyd turned to the man as though noticing him for just the first time. "I shall come to you. And we'll have this lad fixed up quick as you like when the surgeon arrives."

"Surgeon?" Booth heard through his pain.

"Of course, young, erm ... what is your first name?"

"Don't give him nothing"! Hartley said.

"We're going to take off that pesky leg," Lloyd said.

"You can't take my leg! Please, sir! What'll become of me?"

"You sound an educated lad. I've heard of one-legged scholars. If you co-operate who knows how far you might succeed in this world. Tell me, who taught you?"

Booth was too petrified to answer. The surgeon entered.

"Take a look," Lloyd said and stepped back to join Roberson by the door.

The surgeon examined Booth, then told the boy his leg must be removed.

"You can't!" the boy moaned, exhausted from agony.

"I'll just go back and get my herbs, and some rum ..."

"No." Lloyd said. "Off with the leg but nothing for pain."

"Surely, Sir." A faint whiff of Roberson's humanity finally emerged to reveal itself. "You see for yourself the boy is in pain ..."

Turning to face him, Lloyd's face was inches away when he whispered: "I require tidings for Magistrate Radcliffe. I follow his instruction. I'm sure you understand."

"Of course," Roberson replied, retreating inside his façade, more than a little intimidated by the smaller man's capability to threaten without seeming to.

"Now boy, what is your name again?"

"It's John! John Booth, Sir! Please, not my leg!"

"I'm afraid it must be removed as the surgeon says. Now that can happen quickly along with rum and herbs, or by a different manner. It was so easy to provide me your name. Let us have done with this quickly. What is the name of your Luddite leader?"

"Say nowt!" Hartley cried.

"The saw," Lloyd instructed the surgeon. "I shall require you to cut slowly."

"That is inhuman, Sir," the surgeon said bluntly. "He could die from shock."

"Then leave the room, Surgeon, and leave your bag."

The surgeon hesitated.

"Need I send a message to Major Gordon? I've given you an instruction. Obey it!"

The surgeon departed.

For half an hour tormented screams travelled the hallway reaching down the stairs of the Star. The building's thick walls could not hold them. Dogs barked in fear and men quailed with bewilderment. The screaming was almost unworldly. It would echo in the minds of those who heard it for the rest of their lives. It would be spoken of fearfully in markets, in pubs and parlours, in mills and mines for years after.

Three hours later Radcliffe arrived with his new bodyguards. There were ten of them. Threats against him had grown to menacing proportions, thus the additional special constables. He was met on the lower floor by Lloyd. The two retired to a corner. Lloyd was anxious, not troubled by what he had done to two humans in a room, but for another more personal reason. He had failed in his efforts and no matter what compliments Roberson might pay him, only one thing counted with Radcliffe: results.

"Well?" Radcliffe asked. "What did you find? Names? Places?"

"Nothing."

"What?"

"The boy died in the process. The man gave up nothing no matter what was applied. Even nitric acid."

"Impossible! Turn him over to me."

"He's dead as well."

"I was a fool to give you this responsibility!"

"Here is Vicar Roberson, Sir. He was in the room. He'll tell you how I tried."

But the Roberson who appeared from the bar, beaker of whisky in hand, was not the same militarist who had the night previous commanded militia, nor the same man who had entered the room at the Star. He seemed less the outsized character he so commonly projected, less the gentleman of influence, less sure of himself, less large. He was diminished, and haunted.

Radcliffe noticed immediately.

"Sit down, Hammond! You appear weak."

Roberson sat. For a moment he stared into his drink then stared at Lloyd, as though he had finally met the Satan he'd so often preached against in his church. He turned to Radcliffe.

"Do you know what he said to me?" he murmured. Radcliffe was forced to lean closer.

"Who said?"

"The boy."

"I can only imagine."

"After all he'd gone through ..."

"The boy?" Radcliffe reiterated.

"Yes. While Lloyd was with Hartley I tried to pray for the lad. But he awakened ..."

"Yes? Get on with it, Hammond. Don't stare at your drink."

"He said: 'Can you keep a secret?'"

"He gave you information?" Lloyd muttered apprehensively.

"I told him I could," Roberson continued, ignoring Lloyd. "I held his hand."

"And so?" Radcliffe queried.

"He said: 'So can I.'"

"Of what use is ..."

"Then he died," Roberson said.

"Why are you telling me this?" Radcliffe asked.

"You ... you instructed this man to use such methods?"

"You've been apprised of everything at each meeting!"

"Do you know this ... man, at all?" Roberson lifted a finger, vaguely pointing at Lloyd.

"Of course. What the devil is wrong with you, Hammond?"

Vicar Hammond Roberson replied by pulling both pistols from his pockets and setting them on the scarred wooden table. He put them down gently, then stood slowly, the way a crippled man might. When he spoke again he seemed overwhelmed.

"I can no longer be a part of this, Joseph. I ... I thought it the right thing but now I see I've ... overlooked my calling. I shall go home ... tend to my parish ... assist the needy. I shall build a school for young boys. Yes, on the land next my house at Healds Hall ... that most of all. A school. For young boys ...

"Hammond?"

"The least I can do. After this. Goodbye, Joseph."

Hammond Roberson, the uncompromising ambitious cleric, departed the Star a changed man. He remained in the Spen Valley for the rest of his life tending his parish, building a church on a knoll near his house, founding and managing a successful school for needy boys. Until the age of eighty-four he was a familiar figure who no longer limited his time to the wealthy; rather, he seemed to spend a great deal of it teaching at his school. Each time a boy graduated the vicar was there to hand him his certificate and shake his hand. It seemed only then was he truly happy. He died a humble man; a true Christian.

—

Immersed in lazy morning dreams Mary Buckworth lay upon her parlour sofa. She was fully clothed and covered by her deceased mother's quilt. It was warm and downy despite its age and so comfortable it had soothed her night vigil. She dwelt amid visions of George Mellor dressed as a gentleman. Her fingers unconsciously fondled the pewter hammer he'd given her the night she'd sent him away. She had worn it since that night, beneath her clothing, as a memento. Then the pounding began on her kitchen door. With a horrid rush she recalled her situation. She realized she'd waited all night for John. She rose quickly, hustled from parlour to kitchen and opened the wooden door.

George Mellor stood there with John in his arms. For an instant she was about to smile when her brain, still dozing, awoke of its own with the shock of seeing the two together. Then she saw their clothing was covered in crusted blood. Mellor's face was black, as were his clothes. John's face was so pale, so opposite Mellor's. Then she understood.

"Oh my God! John!"

"I'm so sorry, Mary. I don't ... he wasn't t' go in the yard. He was t' stay back in cover. Mary? He stood forward t' help a man who was down. They shot him. They shot him and Sam Hartley and young Johnny Booth and I don't know who else! I tried t' protect him, Mary, I ..."

She heard horses down the road. Only cavalry made that particular sound. Mellor looked to his right with a kind of exhausted panic. She opened the door to allow him through. As he did she said nothing, only watched him as he placed her dead husband upon the scullery table as gently as he might lay down a babe.

"Oh, Mary ... the Lord knows you don't want me here but it was the only place I could bring him. I had no choice, Mary. I'm so, so sorry ..."

She accepted this information without seeming to feel anything.

She registered facts. Her husband was dead, brought by her lover, her lover hunted by the authorities. Her husband lay on her kitchen table, his clothing was filthy with blackened blood, and her lover had brought him here. He too was bloodstained. She must prepare her husband for his funeral, she must dress in black, she must drape the house, make it ready for mourning ...

"I will bathe and dress him. You shall help me," she said mechanically. The shock of the moment had turned her practical, offering her a kind of shell. She needed, above all, protection.

"Mary ..." He went to her, tried to hold her. She twisted away. He was not protection. She turned to face him across the table where lay her dead husband.

"Don't ... don't touch me."

"Mary, I couldn't ... none expected what happened."

Mellor still suffered disbelief. He'd begun to parse the wild pandemonium of the raid: the bark of gunfire, the smell of powder, shapes of men twisting as they fell to the ground. It had been smoke and running and shouting and struggling to batter that door beneath lethal tongues of gunfire. He remembered the ring of hammers on iron. He saw Johnny Booth's leg blown half away. He was supposed to have been a leader and what had he done but send men and boys into slaughter? He recalled his own rage as he'd lost control. He had planned it all so carefully following John Wood's advice. No one had said it could turn to madness. No one had told him he could lose control. Then his thoughts were disturbed by the sound of her voice.

"I knew," she said. "I knew he was lying to me as he went out the door last night. I let him go, sent him to his death."

Her voice was so flat it sounded inhuman.

"They fired on us like we were cattle. They don't think we're even human. By God, Mary, what makes men like that? Human lives for machines?"

"John said you were thinking of Rawfolds mill. Is that what happened last night? You ordered your men to fight soldiers? What does that make you?"

"None were t' be hurt. I told my men! It was only t' be the shear frames! Who could imagine they'd take our lives t' spare their machines? It was only us little men tryin' t' get them t' listen. It wasn't t' be a war."

"John told you what it would come to. I'm sure that's why he went last night. He would have asked to give Cartwright his manifesto. I'm right, aren't I?"

"Aye, he did."

"He told me he was going to help a family. My husband's last words to me were a lie."

"Those men won't take his manifesto. Do you think these murderers will listen t' paper pleas? They killed your husband!"

"No. You have it wrong, George. I killed my husband ..."

"Mary, that's — "

" — And *you* killed him with me. We brought him to this. The ball may have been from a soldier's musket but we are the ones who placed him in its way."

"Mary, come sit."

He tried to lead her to a chair but again she shook him off.

"All he wanted was to publish his manifesto. All he tried to do was help resolve people's differences. And no one would listen. Especially me."

She turned to the body lying on the table. There were tears in her eyes.

"John. John dear, I have no words ..."

Mellor felt his presence intruding upon a sacred place. He moved toward the door.

"I'll leave. I'm sorry, Mary."

She turned on him then, her hand grasping the table for support. Her voice shook with grief and rage and love.

"No, George. You will pay your respects and bind your guilt with mine. You'll stay here today. There is no point in going out to be shot down yourself. There has been enough death."

Her words slapped him. Her words made him see a different world from the one he'd dreamed, the one he had tried so hard to make. Now a different George Mellor faced Mary Buckworth but this man's eyes turned from diamonds to agate in a face which had aged ten years.

"Enough death? No, Mary, not nearly enough. I'll help you, Mary. I'll stay this day and do my penance. 'Tis my fault this man has died. But when we bury him tonight, in his own graveyard, I'll be buried with him."

"Don't say that, George."

"It must be said, as it will be done."

His words, so wild and strange in a voice so hollow with rage brought Mary back to a kind of reason. She had to protect two men this day and the thought of what lay before her made her fierce.

"George, we can't bury him tonight. He cannot simply disappear. It cannot be known he was on that raid. I shall say he was taken ill. No, better, an accident. Chopping wood for the fire. I'll say he bled to death. No time for a doctor. Then you happened by. You were here last night. That is what we shall say and who is to say anything to the contrary?"

He was no longer listening. He was within his own shifting world. She recognized in that moment he was not as strong as she. She listened to his monologue as he paced the room, head down, thinking his absurd thoughts. She had no idea they would become real, no idea where his words would take him, or her for that matter; on a journey so perilous only one of them would survive.

"I've seen myself this night what is possible. The Movement's done, dear Mary. All over now from what it once was. Once it was about change. But it ain't truly about machines anymore, nor the *maisters'* greed, nor even the changes John wrote about. 'Tis what I should have seen long ago but was blinded by my da'. We're nowt t' them, Mary. The *maisters* might say they want change. Truly they only want things the same as they ever have been, with them in power and us doing their bidding. They talk of economy and that French blockade; they talk of progress, machines and the future; but when they do they talk of themselves. They don't think of us at all."

He had moved to the fireplace. On the mantle he placed his pistols, laying them on the smooth stone. He turned and looked at her and the light of his eyes had gone out. His voice was beginning to sound emotionless; more mechanism than man.

"What are you going to do?"

"Give them a taste of themselves."

"Not more violence, surely ..."

"What gets their attention, Mary? What's the one thing they understand?"

"George, please ..."

"Power is all they know. So when we bind up and bury John Buckworth we'll do the same with George Mellor. What remains of George Mellor will have no hope, no need, no feeling. But it will roll down upon them like thunder, shear them as cloth and use them as coal and melt them as iron. And in the end these bloody *maisters will* progress or they'll die. Once I told you I wanted t' come t' you as an equal, join my life with yours. I look at John Buckworth lying here now and know that could never be. So I make my choice in the presence of your husband's body, in the place with the woman I loved. I'll love no longer. I'll become what they've made me. A machine. I'll teach them the meaning of power ... through terror."

15

AS THE TALE of Rawfolds unfolded, it sharply divided the West Riding as nothing had since the Civil War against Charles the First ... a hundred and fifty years past. There were those who supported Cartwright's stand. They celebrated his victory over foolish croppers who thought to hold back the winds of change. For the owners clearly perceived the Crown and Parliament, along with Justice and the Military, to be in their camp. To cross them would lead to gaol, transportation or even hanging.

Then there were those whose hopes had been dashed by the crushing defeat. They became bitter and hardened. The Luddite Movement, though much reduced by desertion since Rawfolds, retained its reputation; its smaller numbers now peopled by desperate, dangerous bandits.

But there was a third, confused cluster of inhabitants who had not been a part of either camp and now had no idea which way to turn in these perilous times. Small owners, ordinary merchants, plain labourers and artisans lived in fear of both sides, never knowing which would take umbrage against them or try to enlist them into their ranks. Their West Riding had altered itself from what once had been cordial and homely, to a place of looming menace.

After Rawfolds tales passed quickly from mouth to mouth as rumour will. Then the rumours morphed into another, more ominous manifestation. Two days after the attack, Sam Hartley's body was transported to Halifax, his birthplace, for burial.

Major Gordon had read the reports from Raynes, from Curate Bronte, from Lloyd and Cartwright himself though, strangely, nothing at all from Vicar Roberson. So he had not heard stories of torture passing from mouth to mouth among ordinary people. From the lips of the Star Inn's servants, those tales travelled the roads. The stories portrayed a strange man who had arrived as a tinker and revealed himself a monster. Yet no one could describe him, so unmemorable were his looks. He was at once short, tall, plump, skeletal, with hair like this or that, or none at all, possessing a shambling animal gait or the ramrod march of a soldier. But what he had done in that room at the end of the corridor, the images of so much blood told by maids who later were given the job of cleaning of the room, was beyond the pale. The major had not heard those things. So the major thought all well in hand with the Luddites reeling from their defeat and thus made the decision to transport Sam Hartley's corpse along the Halifax road for burial. Ten Yeomanry soldiers and their sergeant were tasked with its accompaniment.

It began simply enough, the waggon loaded in the Star's courtyard, then turning out onto the road at a moderate pace moving west. The first signs of something unusual occurred when a cluster of people gathered just down the road from the inn. They did nothing overt but simply stood quietly to watch the waggon pass. As the procession continued more people appeared at the sides of the road, silent and staring. Halfway to Halifax the waggon's driver, John Armstrong, pulled up at a stream to water his horses. As he did so he signalled the sergeant to his side, concealing their deliberations behind the horses. He wanted no watchers observing him in league with the authorities.

"Dost note anything unusual, Sergeant Smyth?"

"Lot of people out today. You sound a mite strange, Mr. Armstrong."

"Are you not looking, man? Do you not see each person wears a white armband?"

"Sign of respect for the dead," Smyth replied. He had little time for men who spooked so quickly. These were country people, a gaggle of rustics no match for his soldiers. Still, Armstrong responded vociferously.

"These people don't even know Hartley! Don't you find it odd they'd stand as he passes?"

"I had orders t' march out from Huddersfield then escort you and the body to Halifax."

"Sergeant, are you not mindful of what happened two days ago?"

"I know of the fight at Cartwright's mill if that's what you mean."

"Have you no idea men died in that fight."

"Only the two."

"More, man, but carried off, so 'tis said. Not left for Raynes or Roberson."

"I'd no idea."

"This waggon's become something more t' these people. They're grieving their loss. They're banding together."

"You think something should be done?"

"I think you should send a rider back t' the Star. Have horsemen out here right quick."

"There've been no threats."

"That's what I mean."

"My men can handle this rabble."

"You've but ten and we're only halfway t' Halifax. Hartley *was born* in Halifax. What do you think we'll find there?"

Armstrong was correct. As they approached Halifax hundreds began to line the road. With each additional assemblage Armstrong, Smyth and the soldiers felt the weight of animosity settle upon them. Finally the sergeant halted the procession and had his men fix bayonets as a warning.

There was no need.

Not one person from the gathered masses showed any sign of aggression. But it was in the air, in their eyes, in the tramp of the boots of the two hundred men who began to follow directly behind, forming a parade for the fallen. In the churchyard the multitude stood silently as the body was buried, the local curate curtailing the funeral rites so fearful was he of the crowd. That evening Sergeant Smyth did indeed send a rider back to Major Gordon with an unsettling message.

—

Outside Huddersfield Gordon received the message, not at his usual residence, but at a place called Longley Old Hall. Colonel Campbell, his superior, had arrived from his own headquarters and was lodging as a guest of the Ramsden family. There were maps on deal tables and reports upon his desk. He had summoned his major and Magistrate Radcliffe. Alarm at the course of events had brought Campbell all the way from Leeds along with additional troops.

Colonel Charles Campbell was not a man who was flustered easily but the West Riding had unnerved him. He was a florid character, given to the hunt at every opportunity, his ruddy complexion proof enough of his hobby. Radcliffe remained seated as the colonel circled him, papers in hand, Gordon standing stiffly beside the desk. Campbell was a blunt man. He might have been a general had he not failed to find a way to quell that most human weakness, his temper.

"You mean to tell me, Magistrate, that the inquest into these men's deaths lasted a mere few minutes?" Campbell's voice was a growl.

"A jury of six returned a verdict of justifiable homicide," Radcliffe said. "These men were brigands, Colonel, who died in the course of committing their crimes."

"The assault upon this Cartwright's mill."

"Indeed."

"Just where would you find a jury at that time of morning?"

"They were lodgers at an inn. The Star at Robertown."

"Hmm," the Colonel said, "seems a touch convenient, Magistrate."

"You question my judgement, Colonel? Might I remind you the assault occurred within my jurisdiction?" Radcliffe's dry voice rasped his outraged reply.

"These two we're discussing did not die at the scene of the attack."

"Later, Sir, at the Star Inn."

"Interrogated by this Mr. Lloyd of yours, witnessed by a Vicar Roberson."

"Yes."

"This Lloyd prevented a surgeon from doing his duty if I am to understand correctly?"

"Mr. Lloyd was in the midst of accomplishing his own task. He was attempting to discover the identities of the captives' accomplices."

"By killing them? Where is this Roberson? He can clear this up, I'm sure."

"It seems he is indisposed, Colonel. The rigours of the night. He is not a young man."

"Yet he rode at the head of a troop of militia? A vicar?"

"He is resolved in his principles regarding these Luddites."

"I see. This Lloyd fellow is, I gather, somewhat irregular with his prisoners. I must say, Major Gordon. The methods you seem to have sanctioned here have the smell of an inquisition, what?"

"Colonel," Gordon said, "Captain Raynes concurs with such treatment of the rebels. It seems the only way to persuade them to give up what they know."

"Yet they did not do so."

"That is true, Sir."

"Indeed. What has happened, according to Sergeant Smyth's report, is increased sympathy for the brigands among the general populace. Lines of people along the roads? Hundreds at the funeral of a mere mill worker? I am not so sure your methods are quite as effective as you believe."

"Yes, Sir," came the obvious reply. It had not been a question.

"You seem to have many questions, and even more opinions, Colonel," Radcliffe said as he stood from his seat. "Your additional troops are welcome, Sir, but I have had enough of your queries." Radcliffe prepared to leave the room.

"Sit down, you arrogant bastard!" Campbell replied, blocking Radcliffe's exit with the size of his body. "We're not done with this yet!"

"I am not one of your soldiers, Sir, to be bullied!" Radcliffe replied, not an ounce cowed by the colonel's looming presence. They were interrupted by Gordon's interjection.

"There is still the matter of the other one. The boy ..."

Both were aware of the delicacies of Johnny Booth's interment. If a little known worker like Hartley from Halifax had brought out such a throng then a local lad, and potential scholar, could likely lead to massive demonstrations from Huddersfield's inhabitants. The two men restrained their animosity.

"That boy will make Huddersfield a powder keg," Radcliffe said.

"I've men enough for protection on the journey into town," Campbell said. "We'll quell any demonstration with a show of force."

"I doubt it, Sir," Gordon said. "It's likely a multitude will appear. I'm not sure you recognize the depth of division in the West Riding. Your soldiers will likely be firing upon women and children as well as men."

"I do as ordered by General Maitland. The last thing he wants is for something to stir the rabble into a unified force. Good heavens, man, I am not here in such strength for the joy of it!"

"About this burial." Gordon once again sought to resurrect the problem.

"You have an idea, Gordon?" Campbell said.

"I do, Sir."

"Well then, spit it out! We haven't much time."

"My thoughts, gentlemen, are not to curtail a demonstration but evade one."

"And how do you propose to accomplish that?" Radcliffe said.

"By moving the body tomorrow morning, very early, before anyone is awake."

"What about spies? Surely, Major, you know they'll be watching," Campbell said.

"First, Raynes' dragoons can be dispatched to sweep the countryside," Gordon replied. "He is very effective. Then we shall send three waggons in different directions: one east, the other two west toward Huddersfield forcing any observers Raynes does not catch to split their attentions. When the two heading for Huddersfield reach the town they shall again take different directions. All three waggons shall look as though they carry supplies but one will contain Booth's body."

"You don't presume to bury the boy in the dark? What of his family?" Radcliffe, concerned for his reputation, wanted nothing nefarious to stain it.

"We'll wait until sunrise. It shall be done before anyone is aware. I myself shall set up a cordon around the cemetery. As to the family, the boy was a rebel. I shall ask you, Sir, to send your Mr. Lloyd to remove any thoughts of public complaint from the minds of his family."

And so it was done: a sweep of the area by Raynes' night riders, then the sudden departure of waggons, two of them shifting direction at Huddersfield, brought young Booth to the cemetery without event. In the dark six soldiers quickly dug the grave. At sunrise the body was placed with minimal ceremony into the ground before any chance of a demonstration. And, of course, John Lloyd, knocking upon the Booth family's door at the same time, armed with writs and forms and, beneath his whispering voice, the veiled threats which would keep the family silent, had completed Gordon's plan.

Colonel Campbell departed later that morning. The troops he had brought with him remained. The towns were brimming with them. As reported by a correspondent of the *York Courant* sent to observe circumstances in the West Riding: "*Huddersfield wears the aspect of a town under military power night and day.*" The army had taken a firm grip against Luddites and their supporters. Those caught between felt safe and relieved.

They should not have.

16

A DAY AFTER John Booth's burial another funeral took place in Dewsbury. Parishioners gathered to say farewell to their deceased Curate Buckworth. He would be missed. Such a generous minister cut down in the prime of his life by, of all things, an accident! His widow, the lovely Mrs. Buckworth, was distraught; insisting upon only one day's visitation. The curate's casket was closed and placed in the hallowed space in front of his pulpit. It seemed the wound was deemed too terrible to be viewed. Hearts bled for the widow. The parishioners of Dewsbury did their best to help her through her dark hour but she seemed turned to stone after the interment; as if all life had left her as well.

—

Two days after Booth was laid to rest another event took place amidst the false peace following Rawfolds. The soldier who had refused to fire upon *his brothers* was brought before a court martial. Only the military attended along with a single civilian witness. William Cartwright's evidence was accepted without question. The private was found guilty and sentenced to three hundred lashes. The severity of the punishment took Cartwright by surprise, particularly when he was told what it actually meant.

"Death," Gordon said. The two men were in The George, a bottle between them, the strong drink most needed by Cartwright as Gordon explained what would happen. Around them the building bustled with afternoon lunches served beneath the dark beams of the smoke stained ceiling. It was noisy this time of day yet the two men could hear each other; the nattering voices creating a strange sense of privacy with their din. Yet even the bustle around them could not disguise Cartwright's pallid face.

"Still, why must the ... uh ... punishment happen at Rawfolds?" Cartwright asked. "My workers shall see it. Think of the effect it will have."

"It will not be done here in Huddersfield. That's certain. Colonel Campbell will not tolerate another mob. No, it's better to permit but a few witnesses: some of your labourers, enough to spread word of his punishment at the scene of his crime. The people of the West Riding need to develop a fear of the British Army. There's no better way I can think to accomplish it."

"But such a tortuous death it will create more sympathy, Gordon. Surely you've heard they know already what happened to Hartley and Booth."

"Oh, this is not simply for the people, Sir, but the soldier's comrades as well. One of their number has broken a code which cannot be ignored. Let me tell you something of the Army, Cartwright. Some of these men may yet see action in Europe. Most of these rankers who take the King's shilling, are those who can find no other work. Oh, there are some who think to defeat old Boney, but most are drunkards, dullards or criminals. They are but a tankard of grog away from mutiny themselves.

"A soldier's life is a hard one. Military life is a challenge for men of their ilk. Have you any idea how many steps it takes to load and fire muskets as a squadron? So much training is required before a soldier can serve in battle: drills must be strictly followed ... and punishments applied for the most minor of errors. It is what these men comprehend. They must learn to act as a unit and come to love it more than themselves. So when one of them, this Private Shepherd in particular, refuses to obey an order in battle, he must be punished in a way in which all other men will be cowed to the point of submission."

"But flogging a man with a cat o' nine tails? Three hundred lashes?" Cartwright re-iterated what he'd been told.

"It will not go so far. They are usually dead after a hundred."

"It is a cruel and prolonged death, Major."

"And necessary, as I've told you. If you feel so badly, Cartwright, I believe the man was under your orders when he refused to fight?"

"He was."

"Then you may appeal for mercy. Indeed, as his commander at the time you may stop the punishment completely. I suggest you finish your glass and on your way home think about it. I shall see you on the morrow with a full company to form square around the flogging."

The two parted company, Cartwright retrieving his horse from The George's stables for the journey home. And a pensive ride it was. Cartwright was convinced Rawfolds would suffer another assault. He had lived on the Continent, in Flanders, as a merchant in the linen trade. He'd watched as France fell under the sway of Napoleon and shifted from a rough republic to despotism. So Cartwright had left the Continent for England: to the one place which hadn't seen an invasion since 1066. From linen to *woollens* had been a minimal transformation, but with it had come his ideas on industry.

Deep in thought, Cartwright set out from Huddersfield toward home. By four o'clock the April sun was beginning to wane. He'd reached open countryside and headed his mare between hedgerows bordering the roadway. Some movement in the bushes disrupted his thoughts. He thought he saw a flash. In five seconds he was sure.

Two men leapt from the verges on either side of the road. Each man held a pistol and both wore masks and hats. They shouted at Cartwright to halt while aiming their guns at him. The suddenness of their appearance and violence of their shouts frightened his horse. The mare shied from side to side. The men bellowed again for him to dismount. He knew he was as dead man should he do so. Still his horse continued her broken sidestepping, her bucks and dodges to evade the two villains.

Their pistols barked, sharp within the confines of the hedgerows, loud and smoking, alarming his horse. She galloped out of control right past them, one of whom she bumped with her shoulder sending him spinning to the ground. Cartwright found himself free of the thugs, open road ahead. He spurred his mare to further speed, all previous reflection gone in the rush of adrenalin.

"Damn it to hell," he muttered as he rode. "I'll see Shepherd whipped to shreds. I'll show these fools what it is to try to murder me."

William Cartwright's tenacity and determination asserted themselves once again. All doubts had dissolved. He would hold what was his against whatever odds they dared bring against him. The grim defense of Rawfolds would continue. One tyrant had driven him from his home. No others would.

—

He said nothing to Elizabeth of what had happened on the road home. At any rate she was no longer speaking to him. But it had shaken him. This was a clear attempt at murder. Yet the next day, the day of Private Shepherd's punishment, another unexpected occurrence ensued to curb further Cartwright's self-confidence.

A company of the Cumberland Militia had marched the mutineer seven miles to Rawfolds. They had set out before dawn on their secretive route. Nothing untoward had occurred on the march. Yet at dawn, from his cottage William Cartwright witnessed the impossible. The court martial had been held in secret. The place of punishment kept concealed. The march begun so early it was thought no one would notice.

They had.

Scores of people materialized from the morning mists to stand on the hillside across from his mill. Again they wore white armbands. They were sullen and silent and watched the militia form square around the man who had been stripped to the waist and tied to a triangle of sergeants' halberds. An army surgeon stood nearby to assess sufficient life remained for the punishment to continue. Several drummers, each with *cat* in hand, would carry out the lashing in relays; the way it had always been done in the Army. Cartwright stood near Gordon and Raynes as they officiated.

The first lash snapped in the morning silence and as the cords bit into his flesh, Private Shepherd yelped a sound more of fear and surprise than of pain. Pain would come soon enough. The first taste was precipitous, and clearly too soft of touch for the officers.

"Drummer Walsh!" Captain Raynes hollered. "This is no game. Should ye presume to wield your *cat* so softly ye shall be next on the triangle."

The threat had its effect. Walsh took nine more lashes, hard and solid, and Shepherd's cries were no longer yelps but shrieks as his back turned bloody. Then the next drummer loosened his whips and swung: the bawls of agony echoing in the valley and up the hill to the silent watchers. The suffering travelled the other way as well, toward Cartwright's workers mending the mill. They had stopped to attend the anguish of a man who had declared himself their brother. And then, as the third drummer worked his lash, Cartwright felt the presence of his wife beside him. When she spoke to him it was in hard, low tones unheard by others.

"You are going to allow this barbarity?"

"Elizabeth. Now isn't the time."

"Indeed William, it is."

"The soldier must be punished. Neglect of duty."

"The man you speak of is one of *them*." She nodded toward the hillside. "Each time he screams they feel it. How many lashes?"

"Three hundred."

"So you mean to murder him. You'll create a martyr. Do you think your property will ever be safe?"

Her thoughts, so echoing those of his journey home and the murder attempt, distressed him. He knew every word she uttered was true, yet he could not give in to her. Her silence of the past days had had its effect. Love and respect was replaced by loathing on both sides.

"This is a military matter."

"And this is your property. You have every right to stop this."

"Surrender to them?" He nodded toward the hillside.

"Give them justice. We are law abiding citizens, William, or at least we were. You do not murder men to protect machines."

"Yet they would kill me. Just yesterday on the way home from Huddersfield. Two men with pistols fired upon me."

"You came from the court martial? What would you expect?"

"It was held in secret."

"Are you so naïve?"

"They could not have known."

"Yet look out there. It appears they do."

"Elizabeth, they tried to shoot me!"

"It was here so many of them fought. Did you think they'd forget?"

The fourth drummer took his place. Shepherd was weeping, his back a mass of bloody stripes. Someone at the mill allowed a glass pane to slip his grasp. It shattered on the ground, like glass lashes. For a moment no one moved. Then the drummer began.

"Stop this now, William, or live your life looking over your shoulder."

His determination, his anger and fear came together in one shuddering emotion brought about by her words. He could hardly move, his body paralyzed by comprehension. He could not speak, his throat dry and raw. He heard the lashes splash against bloody flesh. He heard the count of the sergeant. He saw the morning sun illuminate the suffering boy who'd been called a soldier. He smelled the boy's blood as it tainted the air.

"Enough!" Cartwright croaked, just loud enough for Gordon to hear.

"What is that, Sir?" the major responded.

It took a moment for Cartwright to gather his breath.

"Under my command this man disobeyed. He's been punished enough."

"This is a military matter, Mr. Cartwright," Raynes said; voice like iron.

"Nonetheless, this is my property. I deem it finished."

"You have nae power ..." Raynes said, then was touched on the sleeve by Gordon. A look passed between them. Raynes said nothing more.

"Take him down, Sergeant," Gordon ordered.

The drummers approached. Gently they freed their comrade. Tenderly they carried him to a waggon laying him in its bed on his stomach. The surgeon applied a salve. Then from the hillside Cartwright heard a strange sound. It was the sound of applause. It lasted barely a minute but he knew it meant something had changed. Elizabeth looked at him for an instant, a remnant of emotion upon her face, then she turned and walked back to her cottage.

He knew at that moment why he'd married her. He knew just as surely the marriage was over. Her final act as his wife had saved him. Now he was, if not a hero, then a champion at least of fairness. If a master could show himself merciful perhaps those against him would realize he was merely protecting his business.

17

ANOTHER NIGHT AND John Wood's shop showed a dim lantern light twinkling through its dusty glass. Grey-white *woollens* stretched across their frames. The mood was tense. Will Thorpe opened and closed his fists signifying his fury.

"Well what in the name of God happened?" Thorpe said.

"I told you, Will, we missed him," Walker said. "And why do we meet in this bloody shed? Why can't we be at the Shears?"

"You fools, I should give you the beating you both deserve."

"Where's Mellor? It was him sent us the orders."

"He'll be along, Walker, and best watch your tongue. He'll be plenty mad when he hears of this. How in hell could you *both* miss Cartwright? Tom, you could hit a hare on the run."

"A man's harder t' shoot," Smith replied softly. "Maybe you should try it yourself."

"His horse was skittish," a panicked Walker said. "We stopped him on the way through Bradley Wood like George told us, but the bloody beast kept spooking all over the road! We both shot at him but we missed. Christ, what'll Mellor do with us?"

"You both know the Oath!" Thorpe said.

"But we've done nowt!" Smith said. "We tried t' kill him. Done as ordered! We've not betrayed our Oath!"

"You can take that up with Mellor," the big man replied.

It drove Walker to a frenzy.

"For God's sake, Will, the Movement's a shambles! Patrols never let up! Men jailed just for looking suspicious! Why should Mellor punish us who stay loyal?"

"Who can tell," Smith said. "Since Rawfolds all's different. George just vanished this past fortnight. Gone. Where's he been, Will?"

"That's none of your concern."

"We don't see the man anymore," Walker said urgently. "We got our orders from a lad; a messenger! How do we know it ain't just you taking his place?"

"He's been t' Halifax if you want t' know! Been staying with old John Baines and his son, Zachariah. Them two got the knowledge for this kind of thing. George has been learning the proper ways t' bring the Movement back together."

"He sent us t' do murder, Will." Smith's tension cracked as he spoke.

"Shut your gob or I'll do it for you!"

"You're mouthing Mellor's words now, Thorpe." Walker backed away subtly as he retorted. "At least I think for myself."

"You'd do better not t' think, Walker ..." a voice said from the dark.

"Who's there?" Thorpe turned, pulling a pistol.

The voice was George Mellor's but it was changed. The brightness of a young man had disappeared leaving a tone at once harsh and cold, yet solid and quiet in its delivery. It was a strange voice, like an automaton whispering.

"George?" Smith said uncertainly.

"Best not think, Thomas. Better t' do. Remember that and all will be easier."

"I thought you were in Halifax. How come you're here?" Thorpe asked.

"Softly, Will. I go softly and hear what I need t' hear. I've heard a great many things this day. Like men too nervous t' kill a *maister*."

His words set Walker on a tirade of frightened remonstrance.

"We tried, George! I tell you we tried! But he'd not get down off his horse! And the horse was edgy! We shot at him, George! We tried t' follow our orders ..."

"Two of you and both did nowt t' block the road," came Mellor's cold, calm reply ... the threat implicit. "You left him a way t' escape. And dost know what the man did after that? He witnessed a soldier given the lash. One of them who fought us at the mill." Mellor revealed himself from the shadows, his face was hard, his eyes flat. "But this man wouldn't fire upon us. Said we were his brothers. For that he was t' get three hundred lashes. Cartwright watched the first bunch then stopped the punishment. The bastard's a hero now and all because the two of you failed!"

"We'll go at him again, George!" Thorpe said.

"Don't be a fool, Will. The man's no longer a proper target."

It was Thorpe's turn to grow cold. His voice rumbled with antagonism.

"What dost mean? He was the one ordered fire upon us! God's teeth, George, you yourself swore revenge on him!"

"I've talked with John Baines in Halifax," Mellor replied. "He said we can no longer feel revenge. 'Tis a weakness. We must choose our targets more carefully. Think only of what we gain with each one, not for ourselves but for the Movement."

"And you have some new target, I'm thinking," Thorpe said.

"Since Cartwright's mill men are leaving the Movement. We must get them back. And those who don't return ... well, they've taken the Oath. They know the consequences."

"You'd turn against your own?" Thomas Smith said.

"I've a way t' show we mean business. Our new target is Horsfall in six days."

"Aye, and about time too," Thorpe said. "He's the one crowing louder than ever and must be made an example!"

"'Tis murder again you're talking, George," Walker said.

"If we're not prepared t' kill as *they* do we might as well give up and starve. The country's ripe, lads. Now we must strike, bring people back, put fear in the hearts of the *maisters*!"

"What about Horsfall?" Smith said.

"When he makes his trip from the Cloth Hall next market day. Two couldn't do it with Cartwright so we'll see what four can do."

"Us four?" Smith said.

Mellor produced a gleaming, long barreled pistol unlike any the others had ever seen. Its stock was black polished wood, its barrel almost two feet in length. The metal work of its parts was curiously elaborate; even elegant. The others stared as he brandished it.

"What ... what kind of gun is that?" Walker said.

"From Russia. I got it long ago when I was at sea."

"No need of threats, George. We've stuck with you," Thorpe said.

"I know you for true, Will, but you other two listen close. Should either of you try t' run off before the deed is done I'll shoot him whichever it is. This gun won't miss I'm sure you can see. So when we go at Horsfall, Smith is t' stand with Thorpe, Walker with me. Am I clear?"

"Aye, George, very clear," Smith replied, struck to the quick by Mellor's coldness.

"Just do as I've told you."

"And let you do the thinking for us ..."

"That's right, Tom."

"You're inhuman, George," an unnerved Walker said. "You plan death like a farmer plans harvest."

"Aye. And you'll be my scythe, Walker. Remember that."

"Where'll we meet?" Thorpe said.

"Dungeon Wood. 'Tis a mere half mile from the turnpike that heads up Crosland Moor."

"You mean near Warrener's tavern, just by Milnsbridge?"

"'Tis the way he always takes home from market."

"But that's near Radcliffe's place!" Walker said. "He has soldiers there!"

"Aye. That's what I mean when I say we'll get their attention. This killing will be so near Radcliffe himself, he'll hear the guns fire. Now you three go on. I've a thing or two t' do here with my da'. I'll meet you after close of the Cloth Hall, next week. East side of the wood."

As the three departed George Mellor slid shut the bolt on the outer door but heard behind him the click of another latch, the door to John Wood's quarters. His step-father had been listening. Mellor took up the glimmering lantern and walked quickly to that door just in time to hear a chair scrape. When he entered he found his stepfather pretending to work by candle light: papers strewn about the table, pen in hand. Mellor sat opposite him.

For a while the two did not speak. Mellor looked carefully at the man who had once been his mentor. Wood looked older in candle light. His balding head with its grey hairs more fine and wispy in the soft light and his small, lean body, compared to Mellor's muscular bulk, made him seem almost frail. But it was his eyes George Mellor studied: grey, calculating orbs now shifting uncertainly beneath his step-son's stare.

John Wood was unnerved. This was not the lad he'd sent off to Cartwright's mill. He knew of the Rawfolds defeat but had not been there to witness it. He had worried about his step-son when George had not re-appeared from the raid. Yet instead of relief he now felt trepidation. He searched for words but could find none beneath that inflexible gaze. He dipped his pen and scratched some numbers on a column of his ledger.

"Where's mother?" Mellor said.

"Upstairs, abed. You know how late it is, lad?"

"Aye. I had some business needed done."

"The Movement?"

"Aye."

"And I wasn't invited?" Wood edged up his reaction hoping to quell what he knew was coming. But George would not take the bait. Instead, he continued in the flat, emotionless voice with which he'd begun.

"I've been gone a while since Rawfolds."

"We wondered if you'd been killed. You should have let your mother know at least."

"I had no chance. I had t' bury the dead. Then I took myself off t' Halifax t' get away from Raynes' hunters. I spent a week with John Baines. He doesn't think as you do, da'. He told me about a man named Tom Paine in America. That man's a thinker. He wrote a pamphlet called *The Rights Of Man*, defending the French need t' clean up their country, then another called *Common Sense* that told the Americans to leave England's rule. This Paine is a republican, da'. And John Baines thinks like him."

"I see."

"No, you don't. I learned from him, da'. Things I should have known before Rawfolds."

"I'm not sure what you mean, George."

"Rawfolds was a mistake."

"Oh, I wouldn't say that ..."

"Let me finish. I've been wrong on a lot of things this past while. I believed it was me leading the men but I've thought since and come t' know I was really only doing your bidding."

"Now son, don't say that ..."

"Oh, you were good. The first raids made sense; and bigger bands of men showed our power. But really, da', we had none. No power at all. Those men I led t' Rawfolds weren't ready for a real fight. They were croppers and weavers and plain, simple folk with no training. I ordered them t' go at soldiers. I still don't know how many died. It wasn't until after Rawfolds I began to see the truth of you."

Two weeks past George had been a boy, thought Wood. He was something else now.

"When you didn't come with us I thought it strange," he said. "It was all a kind of diversion, wasn't it? Us pointed at the big *maisters* who owned the machines, t' give you a leg up in business."

"Son, all I did was advise you."

"I've no more respect for you, da'."

"Now just one minute." Wood stood, giving himself a momentary advantage.

"You betrayed me, da'. You did what you had to do to make your life better and so tried to help my mum as well. So I hold no grudge. But I've come t' learn things from John Baines."

"I heard your plans ..."

"I thought you had. 'Tis why I'm here now."

"You're planning murder, George. Have you any idea where this'll take you?"

"'Tis the hangman anyway. Baines and others like him figure it best go at the *maisters*. If I die then I'll take some of them with me. It ain't no more about jobs, nor *brass*, nor machines, but killing those who killed us. I'm outside the law now, da'. I'm here t' say goodbye t' my mum, then I'm gone."

"Dost know they'll call you a rebel? Dost know they'll say you're a traitor? Go on back t' sea. You can't win John Baines' kind of war!"

"Yet maybe 'twill give a chance for those who come after me."

"And who'll come after? With you and all like you dead?"

"You think too small, da'. This won't end. The *maisters*, the government, all the rich men who want things the same; they won't change, nor will we if they keep us down. 'Tis a war, you're right, but not like others. Its armies are class against class."

Finished with Wood, George Mellor stood, then turned and climbed the stairs to his mother's bedroom. He had another parting to face with the woman who had loved him when he was a child. He was a child no longer.

This farewell would be hard, but not as hard as what would come after.

18

THE OWNERS KNEW they had achieved a victory at Rawfolds. On Tuesday, April 28, just after close of business at twelve noon that Market Day, the Cloth Hall at Huddersfield became the scene of a fete for William Cartwright. He had foreseen the attack, had defended his mill and had become a heroic symbol for all. Yet his defense had been costly. Almost all of his windows were smashed and needed replacement, not to mention the hammered and hacked remains of his door. The men in the Cloth Hall knew those costs and knew it could as easily have been one of them.

So at noon attendants from The George, laden with platters of veal pies, plates of duck, barrels of beer and cider, a cornucopia of vegetables and all the sweets and cakes possible, made their ways across Market Square to the Cloth Hall. A small dais, decorated with red and white bunting, served as the stage for the tribute due Cartwright.

There were two hundred well-dressed men in the Cloth Hall that midday, their laughter and talk echoing through its passages, their victorious humour creating a mood of triumph which filled the hall with pride. A fiddler had been hired, the notes of his strings floating high above the clamour and hum of male voices. This was the realm of businessmen; a prestigious affair to which no women or common folk were invited.

Cartwright was praised throughout the event. Even his principal rival, Horsfall, was generous with his compliments though it was well known the two did not much enjoy each other's company. Horsfall considered Cartwright a foreigner with his swarthy skin and odd accent and, in Horsfall's eyes, not a man to be trusted. Cartwright believed his competitor a bombastic bully who treated his workers badly, who thought himself a kind of deity among his peers so arrogant were his manners and talk. This day was, however, reserved for smiles and praises.

"I must say, Cartwright, you're made of the stuff we all need in these times. So many of these fellows merely talk, yet do nothing at all in preparation. Your example is a prime model. I take my cue from you, Sir, and if given the opportunity I'll kill even more of the bastards myself!"

"I'd suggest you request some militia," Cartwright said.

"You and I are different men," Horsfall said. "I myself have training in the military arts. You know I have been named First Lieutenant of the Huddersfield Corps of Volunteers. Those Luddite criminals also know it. Should they come at me, they shall have their comeuppance!"

There was one slight divergence from the camaraderie. Cartwright had finished his ale when a lesser member of the clothiers approached him. John Wood offered congratulations to the man he had recently sought to destroy, then added a warning.

"I'd be careful, Mr. Cartwright," he said softly. "I've heard of some change in the outlaws' schemes. I've heard they intend t' go at the *maisters*."

"They've tried already." Cartwright took the smaller man's arm and led him between two pillars. "I don't want this bandied about but I was accosted last week by two ruffians with pistols. They tried to force me from my horse and when I would not dismount, fired upon me. Fortunately, they missed."

"Already." Wood feigned surprise. "I'd not thought them so brazen. I say, Wood, you must approach Radcliffe with your information. It could be vital."

"I will."

"Here is the magistrate now!"

The portly frame of Radcliffe took Cartwright's arm in a simultaneously gracious yet patronizing manner. He led the mill owner away ignoring the presence of Wood. His mutton chop whiskers ruffled a little as he looked up at the tall clothier. The magistrate muttered: "What were you doing speaking with that kind of man? You *do* know he is suspected of having some connection with Luddites?"

"I did not, Sir. But his conversation along with your news gives me pause."

"In what manner?" Radcliffe asked as they turned the corner.

"He has heard of increased violence in the offing."

"Threats everywhere," Cartwright said. "Gunfire in the night. Had they any training at all they'd have murdered someone by now. They almost had me."

"Really," Radcliffe responded, not particularly interested in Cartwright's tale, assuming he was speaking of Rawfolds. "I thought you made quite an account of yourself."

"But there's more."

"It must wait until later. Now, I have someone to present to you."

The ready arm of Magistrate Radcliffe led him through a winding, congratulatory route to the small dais set in the midst of the building. As it was just after noon and a sunny day, the dais was lit as if by a heavenly light, lending *gravitas* to the occasion. Ready to meet them upon the stage were a group of senior officials from the Cloth Hall. But more significant and so shocking that many attributed the perfect light to his presence: Sir John Ramsden himself, Fourth Baronet and owner of Huddersfield and the weald surrounding, stepped into the brightness which seemed meant for him.

Radcliffe quickly fell into obsequiousness as he introduced the two. He attempted to remain in the light while the ceremony took place, as though he were a part of it. To his dismay he was ignored. He was grateful only that his dear Fanny was not present to witness the slur. That an absentee blue-blood might slight him, treating him as a mere bureaucrat, Radcliffe knew would diminish him. It gave him pause. He had no idea at that very moment her faithfulness was threatened by an enemy undiscovered.

Meanwhile, the Baronet readied himself to address the throng. He was a full, frothy man dressed formally in old style blue silk from the tip of his bicorn down through his short-wasted, long tailed coat and the polished black of his buckled shoes. He wore lace at his wrists, and carried an ebony stick. The Baronet possessed sky blue eyes. His nose was broad and his lips even more so. His smile was soft and fetching and meaningless. He wore a powdered white wig.

Hardly ever was he glimpsed in the confines of his domain, preferring the civilization of London and his Parliamentary duties there. But the tide of the mutinous commoners had been turned and the man who now stood before him, William Cartwright, had been the one to accomplish that turning. True, Cartwright had complained after the battle regarding his expenses. A *gentleman*, the nobleman thought, would never have stooped. The Baronet handed a pouch full of money and a red sash to the astonished mill owner. There would be no precious speech this day to honour a beggar.

Yet apparently both Whig and Tory establishments alike had raised a sum of three thousand pounds, and requested the Baronet proffer the sum to a dumbfounded Cartwright. The mill owner nearly wept, not because he was grateful, not because it was his due, but because now his actions had been made authentic and even Elizabeth would be forced to acknowledge his rectitude.

"My understanding, Mr. Cartwright," the Baronet said, deigning to speak to the recipient, "is that it was quite a match. You are to be congratulated. How many windows were smashed?"

"More than three hundred your ... your Grace ..."

"Yes, well, this should have them swiftly back in place," the Baronet said as he turned away, accompanied by the fervent applause of the gathered multitude. He quickly departed the dais, the Cloth Hall, Market Square, Huddersfield and northern England in a gilded coach pulled by four matching greys. Duty done.

Had he known in a mere fortnight's time the sedition he had so lightly passed off would arrive with the jolt of a bullet in the epicentre of his beloved London, perhaps he would not have been so complacent.

—

Uninvited to the Cloth Hall's festivities and left home by her husband, Fanny Radcliffe spent the day strolling through Milnsbridge House's expansive gardens, enjoying the buddings of April. Wandering through a glade of buttery daffodils she found herself entering a footpath flanked high by beginning rhododendrons. She herself was blooming as well, the sun kept away by her parasol, her milky skin fairly shone and her golden ringlets tousled a little in the light breeze. Her eyes took on an azure shade. As she was alone she wore no bonnet and her dress was simple white linen with the usual high-wasted Empire silhouette. In short, she was as beautiful as the day.

This was the sight Captain Frances Raynes came upon as he rounded a corner of the garden path. He'd not expected such exquisite perfection. For a moment she actually took his breath away. And when she noticed him she too had an instant of fascination. The captain was dressed this day, not in uniform, but in civilian fashion. The fitted, single-breasted indigo tailcoat set off his tight buff breeches, silk stockings and fawn top hat, and he wore his cravat wrapped to his chin. Quickly removing his hat revealed the *Brutus* style natural hair and sideburns which offered a perfect frame for his rugged good looks. Fanny's heart felt that flutter she had so cherished since their walk on the bridge in Huddersfield.

They came together quickly, their hands touching through their gloves, her parasol and his walking stick discarded by the wayside. There was an instant of trepidation as they gazed into each other's eyes. They knew they were in private, no one at all about the gardens that day as the groundskeeper, Jackson, had driven Radcliffe into town. Yet training and manners pried them apart, though just to arms' length.

"What a wonderful surprise, Captain Raynes," Fanny exclaimed.

"But where is Milly?" Raynes replied. "I'd expected to hear her bark and so find ye the more quickly."

"Milly is being groomed today. She is in need of clipping and cleaning and whines so when it happens. The maids are ministering to her."

"So we are alone?" Raynes whispered, his words expressing so much in so little.

"We are, Sir," she replied. "Shall we take a turn among these rhododendrons or, better, just down this path is a perfect dell of daffodils!"

"Never so lovely as ye, my dear Mrs. Radcliffe." He retrieved parasol and stick, took her arm and escorted her the way she had come.

"I find comportment so stifling at times. As I said, we are alone. Please call me Fanny, or Fan if you wish."

"That would be too forward of me ..."

"Yet I just said we are alone and do not mind. Indeed, Frances, I would enjoy the informality, though I hope you do not think *me* too forward."

The sound of his name on her lavish lips, so young and full, so tempting, pleased Frances Raynes indeed. He returned the familiarity and in speaking her name lost all sense of etiquette. Had there been any thought of Anne, his wife at home in Stirling, he quickly turned it aside. Breathlessly she brought her hand once again to his arm if only to feel the cords of muscle beneath the material.

"When we walked, you recall, to the bridge in town you were wearing your cavalry attire. I thought of you then as a knight."

"Had I known, dear Fan, I'd hae worn it today, but I've come to bring reports to your ..."

"Yes." She touched his elbow. "But I find the gentleman arrived today another and much different aspect of that same knight, Frances."

He was not yet prepared to fulfil the dreams of his barracks cot, or the lonely bed in the Star Inn, for he had not thought she would return his feelings. He was a man standing on the cusp of wonder, or perhaps of mortification. He turned again down the path and walked silently toward the daffodils shining so brightly in the sun. As they arrived, she withdrew her arm and stepped away from him, her brazenness seeming to have embarrassed her.

"You must think me untrue, Captain Raynes," she said, her milky skin flushing with discomfiture, yet the blue of her eyes turned hazel.

It was too much for Raynes. He had married for duty. Anne was a woman who never smiled, never sang or laughed, never flirted. She was as military as all other things contained in Frances Raynes' life.

Here he was with an angel, perhaps his only remaining chance to grasp the fantasies so bereft in his life, yet he hesitated. What if they were discovered? Bad enough to be found alone with no chaperone or interlocutor. They would be ruined. He would be returned to Scotland, dishonourably discharged. She ... he had no idea what would happen to his dearest Fan should the old goat she'd married punish her.

"Oh, Fanny, dearest girl, I've dreamt of this since the moment we met. We are, both of us, caught within loveless liaisons. And here we are, free in this charming garden. *Untrue*, Fanny? I could nae find ye more *true* than I've dreamt!"

He took her then in his arms, feeling the smallness yet fullness of her body, and kissed her. Their lips met in what was at first a gentle touch but quickly they opened and swelled in a passion both had desired. They lived other lives in that kiss until, breathless, they broke apart, their eyes gleaming as they gazed upon one another.

"Where can we go?" Raynes asked.

"Just back here, between path and meadow, there's a small dell."

"Ye're sure?"

"I am overjoyed, Frances."

Pushing through a gap in a bank of azalea they found themselves in an intimate space. Quietly, though both knew no one was near, they touched each other, kissing new places, hands inside clothes. He tugged at her shoulders, she shrugged, allowing her sleeves to dip and her dress to drop low enough that his lips could caress her nipples. Each touch, each new revelation brought them amplified passion. Their movements became more purposeful, their clothing tumbling to the ground around them. Both exalted in those new discoveries which brought fresh passions, until he had laid her upon the ground and knelt before her.

Then he hesitated.

Frances Raynes was no innocent boy but a man with a wife and child. He knew the potential import should he enter this nubile girl; should he completely possess her.

"What is wrong?" she breathed.

"Sweet Fan, surely ye must know what could happen should we ..."

"Oh, God," she said. Unlike him, she had become thoughtless in her passion.

"I feel I cannot, my dear Fan," he said.

"I can do something," she said, looking up at him, her face flushed with ardour.

"Fan, we must stop."

"Frances, stand up."

"Of course ..." He rose, grasping at his breeches to pull them up.

"No, leave it out for me."

"I ... what are ye doing?"

She was on her knees in front of him. She had grasped him at the very root of his manhood. She brought her lips, those plump, luscious lips, to touch him. Her kiss nearly made him collapse.

"Until now," she said, looking up at him, her eyes indigo then, "I had thought this act humiliating. It is what my old husband taught me to do to help him stay ... but never mind that, now *we* shall use this for us. You've never done this, Frances?"

"Never. My wife would never ..."

"So this is for us, my knight."

19

WILLIAM HORSFALL DEPARTED the Cloth Hall in a fine fettle. Certainly the wine punch had done him no harm. Retrieving his bay gelding from rented stalls he hummed to himself the *Lillibullero* while the stable boy saddled the beast. Mounting, Horsfall guided the horse along the cobbles of Half Moon Street, a curving thoroughfare from which he could catch a wide view across the Colne valley towards Crosland Moor. He crossed the canal and set off on his journey quite unaware of what awaited him.

William Horsfall considered himself a leader of men. He had assumed control of the Ottiwells Mill from his father, Abraham, and his Uncle John. It had been he who had paired himself with the ambitious blacksmiths, Enoch and James Taylor. It was he as well who had loaned them the currency and sold them the land to build an iron works and so make their machines.

It was he had who first installed cropping machines. As a result his croppers were sacked. He had, however, heeded their potential revenge. He had armed his most trusted workers and placed them on sentry duty. He had built a castellated stone wall which commanded the frontage of his mill. His aggressive nature had even led him to purchase a small, wheeled cannon which might be used upon any who dared come against him.

In the early evening he greeted Henry Parr, a lesser owner from Marsden, who was headed in the same direction.

"Good evening, Parr! Lovely evening is it not?"

"Indeed William, it is. Would you mind some company on your way home?"

"I would welcome it. A fine celebration today ..."

"It was. Though I cannot but think a trifle provocative."

"I've a pair of loaded pistols in my saddle bag, Parr."

"I am relieved, William. I've one or two things to purchase. Can you wait for me?"

"I shall make my way toward Longroyd Bridge, then stop at the Warrener tavern a while."

"My thanks, William. Shortly then ..."

Horsfall crossed the bridge, the horse's hooves clattering on its cobbles then down the incline and past John Wood's shop. Heading west, a chorus of skylarks warbling in his ears, Horsfall felt almost giddy. It was not a mood he sensed often.

He took his time, the horse ambling along the turnpike hill until reaching the Warrener House. Outside at a table by the door, pewter mugs before them, sat two cloth hawkers. Horsfall knew them. As he turned his horse in through the picket gate he greeted them.

"Good evening Dabbs ... Lacey," he said.

The two were of a kind. Both in rough riding coats and buff breeches, their linen shirts displaying a show of their wealth. Dabbs was a fat man, his lower parts smothering the stool upon which he perched. Lacey, on the other hand, was a good looking fellow, slim and well-proportioned. He was learning his trade from the older Dabbs.

"If you see Henry Parr coming after, let him know I've gone up Crosland Moor and will take the turnpike home."

"We shall do so, Sir," Dabbs replied.

Unseen during their conversation, Thomas Smith stood behind a privy. As Horsfall departed Smith was off, running across country. He was a young man and despite his rotundity, light of foot, and so made Dungeon Wood quickly. There waited Mellor, Thorpe and Walker amid the thickness of the trees. The oak and ash were not in leaf yet but the smaller trees — the birch, sycamores and beech — were filling. Smith found the three seated on logs.

They were priming their pistols. Smith stared as Mellor loaded his formidable weapon, the long-barreled Russian pistol, with two pipe-heads of powder followed by three pistol balls. Mellor hammered the balls into slugs before ramming them down the barrel. The effect of his method, if his gun did not explode from the triple load, would be to make leaden objects which would not, as ordinary balls merely pierce, but tear out large parts of flesh with crippling wounds. He saw Thorpe do the same with a smaller load for his more conventional pistol. Walker charged his as well, though in normal fashion. Mellor told Smith to load.

"But George, you'll not use a load like that on a man?"

"I mean t' give Horsfall every bit of this," Mellor replied. "I'll let him make good his boast. Now let's be off or we'll miss him."

The men set a quick pace from the wood up across the moor. As they walked Mellor gave them his plan. It was an accomplished ambush. They arrived near the place Mellor had chosen. He halted them for a final briefing.

"He'll come up Crosland as usual. Just here are two stone gates each side of the road. He must pass by them. We'll use them for cover then step out and face him. When I shoot, wait a bit. If he's not dead, Thorpe shoots next."

"Then why are we two here?" Walker said.

"I told you. You're part of this. Now, hide yourself close t' the road."

They were wide gate posts, weathered moss green and mould black. Each could easily conceal a man, even one the size of Thorpe. There were evergreens scattered around the gate on one side of the road in a small plantation. Thorpe forced his big body into the trees, disturbing their inhabitant. Almost like a whisper, almost a prophecy, came the sound of a cuckoo. Smith heard it and shivered.

"We've no masks! 'Tis all unready," Smith said, affected by the bird's presage.

"We'll not need them this day," Thorpe replied.

Horsfall rode away from the Warrener House and turned up the trail which led onto Crosland Moor. Just as he began the ascent Henry

Parr caught sight of him in the distance. Then lost him behind the Warrener.

Horsfall steered toward the turnpike, moving up the incline he approached the gates, his thoughts far away on the soft, lovely evening. Then two men stepped into his path from behind the gate stones. Both held pistols, one of them a huge gun. For an instant Horsfall was stunned. That this should happen to him! Immediately he fell back on what he knew best: belligerence. He did not try to gallop past them; he did not try to turn around or haul his guns from their saddlebags; he simply stopped as if he owned the road.

"What is the meaning of this?" he demanded. "Get out of my path!"

He heard rustling behind him and, too late, realized the trap.

"Why, what do you think, Horsfall?" Mellor said. His eyes at that moment glittered in the afternoon light.

"I know you. Mellor! Why you young bastard, what are you up to?"

"'Tis not George Mellor you meet today, Horsfall. 'Tis a captain of those you crush under your tyrant's boot! We've come for a reckoning, *Maister* Horsfall."

The word *maister* spewed in a sneer from Mellor's lips. As he continued he accentuated the word again and again until it became more insult than title.

"So you're Luddite outlaws! And where are your cowards' disguises this day? Smith, I know you! You've come down to highway robbery now, is that it?"

"Our business is not with your purse this day, *Maister* Horsfall, though it should support a good many you've put to beggary," Mellor said.

The horse shied, feeling the animosity crackling in the air.

"Number Two," Mellor ordered, more from habit than necessity, "take his bridle!"

Thorpe stepped forward and held the horse. He did not try to gentle the animal but held its bridle like a vice. He manipulated the bit so the horse would find it too painful to move.

"Is it kidnapping?" Horsfall demanded, his voice less aggressive. Thorpe was a very commanding figure. "If it's blood money you want ..."

"Oh, it ain't your *brass*, *Maister* Horsfall; 'tis your blood we want."

Thorpe looked into Horsfall's eyes, his own eyes the pitiless stone of a killer.

"Oh God," Smith said.

"Shut your gob and raise your pistol!" Mellor shouted.

"What are you talking about, Mellor? Have you thrown in with murderers now?"

"I told you 'tis a reckoning. Your brag and swagger be known all through the West Riding. Your money pays soldiers t' guard you. Well, *Maister* Horsfall, where would your soldiers be now? What does your mouth say now when you stand face t' face with your reckoning?"

"Now listen to me, Mellor. I run my business for profit. If this is about the machines and dismissals, I'm sure we can come to some terms ..."

"And what of your mouth, *Maister* Horsfall, and the things you've been saying. Riding up t' your saddle girth in blood? Strong words, *Maister* Hors ..."

"Don't call me that! I'm no master. Look, I realize I've said some regrettable things. I'm a brash man, I know. You must understand my business was threatened! Be reasonable, Mellor!"

"Your business? And what of the lives destroyed by your business, *Maister* Horsfall?" Mellor spit the words yet again. "While you ride such a fine horse, paid for by your business no doubt, your business has driven men to their knees and their families into starvation. Dost know what that is, *Maister* Horsfall? Dost know what 'tis like t' live on your knees?"

"I'll offer a written apology! I'll negotiate terms with the workers ..."

"Too late for that *Maister* Horsfall. 'Tis time t' drop t' your knees. Get off that horse!"

"I won't," Horsfall said, all trace of wrath erased from his voice.

"George, enough ..." Walker tried to break in.

Mellor walked around the horse and grabbed Walker's shirt front, ripping it half away as he pulled the man close.

"I told you, Walker, the price of cowardice!"

"Mellor, this is insane! I'm a mill owner ..." Horsfall said.

"Shoot his horse, Walker!"

"What?"

"If he won't come down we'll bring him down! Now shoot!"

"I won't!"

"Coward!" Mellor released Walker, shoving him to the dirt, standing over him. "I know now why Jilly Banforth wouldn't have you. White feather!"

The big horse began to shift, Thorpe exerting his strength to hold it in place. Horsfall tried to kick its flanks, drive it over the cropper. Thorpe had but one reaction: As he held the horse he fired his pistol up at its rider and heard the man scream as the pistol ball struck him. Then Mellor wheeled, raised the huge pistol and he too shot Horsfall. The big gun boomed and kicked and Mellor cried out as his finger was broken by the recoil. Mellor's flattened bullets ripped up Horsfall's thigh, tearing it open on their way to his groin, throwing him with their leaden power from his horse. For a moment one foot caught in a stirrup. The panicked animal circled trying to loose itself, dragging Horsfall through the dirt. Then Smith reached in and released the foot. Horsfall lay in the road in agony.

"Up to your girth in blood, *Maister* Horsfall?" Mellor said. Thorpe hauled the horse to the side of the road where he tied its reins to a tree. Walker tried to get up but Mellor pushed him back down beside Horsfall. His eyes blazed. He shouted through Horsfall's moans.

"This is a war now. It was made so by you and your cronies the day John Buckworth, young Johnny Booth, Sam Hartley and others were killed!"

"He's mad!" Horsfall managed through his terror.

"Curate Buckworth, now he was a reasonable man! He would've heard your pleas. Men ain't machines but you've made 'em so, Horsfall! You and the other *maisters*!"

Mellor pulled a paper from his pocket. It was wrinkled and torn and had obviously been handled many times. He held it in front of Horsfall, then opened it clumsily, his broken finger swelling. He spoke, reading from the page.

"This is what a reasonable man might say: *'If this machinery is suffer'd to go on it will probably terminate with civil war, which I wish to be avoided, therefore as you are not interested by machinery and the spirit of the people appears so resolute in the cause that if some measures are not adopted and immediately, it will be attended with great destruction, and particularly those who are our greatest persecutors* ... then your name is mentioned, *Maister* Horsfall, along with others as marked for death. But you've one service left with your filthy mouth. In your mouth they will find this manifesto, the words of a *reasonable* man."

"You're a mad man!" Horsfall said, sobbing.

"No. I'm what you made me. Not a man at all. A machine. I feel nothing for you."

Thorpe had come forward, Smith joining him, Walker remained on the ground. Horsfall, in his agony, held his hands helplessly over his shattered groin. He was bleeding gouts.

"Help me ..." he said, whimpering.

"Shut your gob," Mellor answered, then rolled up the paper into a ball. "Walker, shove this in his mouth."

"George, 'tis inhuman ..."

"Thorpe, kill Walker if he won't follow orders."

Slowly Walker raised himself, mesmerized by his leader's eyes, took the paper ball and pushed it into Horsfall's mouth. The paper softened as the wounded man slobbered, but it kept him quiet. Shock was setting in. He fainted.

The sound of a horse pounding down the road just around the bend briefly panicked the group. Henry Parr had heard the boom of guns from Crosland Moor. He'd quickly set out to discover the crisis. He was unarmed but thought nothing of it. People did not shoot at people in the West Riding. Not on a public road. Not on such a soft evening. As he rounded the turn he saw four men standing over another. Blood pooled on the road. He reined in quickly. Parr was no coward but neither was he a foolish man. In a few seconds he'd recognized what had happened. Then two of the men fired their pistols at him. The roar of their combined shots startled his horse and he drew her around and kicked her flanks so she ran like the wind. Parr went for help. He knew the Queen's Bays were in Huddersfield. They would deal with these murderers.

"You've missed again!" Thorpe bellowed angrily at Smith and Walker.

"He's gone," Mellor said. "Now we've a witness!"

"What'll we do?" Walker shouted.

"We'll split up. First back t' Dungeon Wood then off in different directions!"

"Just as well," Smith said to himself. He was in shock.

"I feel sick ..." Walker turned and threw up on the roadway.

"That's the man who'll hang us," Thorpe said to Mellor, pointing down the road.

"What? I don't understand ..." Smith murmured.

"That rider was forty feet off!" Thorpe said. "You've shot rabbits that close."

"George just shot Horsfall," Smith said. "This wasn't as I thought ..."

Mellor turned on him.

"And just what did you think, Thomas? Did you think I'd not do as I said? I told you before *not* to think!"

"What's done's done. Now we've trouble ahead," Thorpe said. "We should scatter, each t' his own."

"Right then, Will, us two must go back t' Longroyd. They'll have missed us today. They must be first t' take the Oath."

"Aye. What of him?" Thorpe pointed down at Horsfall.

"Leave him as he is," Mellor replied. "He has one lesson left t' deliver."

In forty minutes a detachment of the Queen's Bays arrived, guided by Henry Parr. With them was a young surgeon named Mason Stanhope Kenny. The wounds he found were appalling: two gouges up the left thigh, one bullet in the abdomen, one in the scrotum, and one which had somehow found its way ripping across the saddle into the right thigh. He could not understand the ball of paper in the victim's mouth. He handed it to his captain.

Just before he died, in Kenny's arms, Horsfall gasped: "These are awful times, doctor."

It was all he said.

20

IT WAS HEAVY going in Dungeon Wood. The ground was a tumble of rocks, logs and uneven terrain. The air itself seemed green and thick. They moved in emotional jolts as well, fear pushing them forward while anger delayed them. Two of them had not killed. Two of them had. The situation did not bode well.

As they made their way Mellor began to have trouble. Because of his broken finger, swelling now and discolouring, he could not use one hand while lifting himself over obstacles. He struggled a while as the others impatiently waited for him.

"I'm slowing us down," Mellor said.

"Aye, that's true," Walker said.

"We'll have t' split up. Smith and you should go on t' Honley, find a pub and make sure you're seen. We'll need alibis now that horseman saw us."

"I've no money," Walker said. The man's snivelling perturbed Mellor. He pulled a pouch from a pocket. The pouch jingled softly as it changed hands.

"You'll find two shillings in there. Tom Smith look at me! What's the matter with you?"

"We killed a man, George. Killed him like a dog ..."

"Go with Walker. Take a few pints but not too much. We don't want you blathering. Ben, make sure of him."

"What about your pistol. You can't carry it. We should bury it!"

"No," Mellor said quickly. The Russian pistol was special to him. A Russian ship's captain had given it him. George's surrogate father from the time he'd joined the ship.

"Give it t' Thorpe. Now get moving!"

Smith and Walker quickly departed, glad to be out of sight of the murderers. Once away they buried their own pistols deep in the woods then found a path toward Honley.

—

Twilight found Mellor and Thorpe back at Longroyd Bridge. There were men in Wood's shop. When the two arrived Thorpe ducked into his cottage and returned with a Bible. He followed Mellor into Wood's shop.

Wood was there, but left for his living quarters upon seeing their grim faces. John Wood knew how to stay out of trouble better than most and, though there had been no news, he could tell from the visage of his step-son something significant had occurred.

"All of you," Thorpe said, "leave your work and que up here!"

The men, surprised at Thorpe's tone, set down their shears and shuffled into place. Thorpe held up the Bible.

"You all know George has been gone this day. Soon you'll know why. George is a hero in the fight against the *maisters*! I know some of you have decided not t' join us. That won't do no longer. Each of you will take Ludd's Oath now and once *twisted in*, you're bound t' be silent. Should I find any man breaks his Oath he'll find this" — he proffered the huge Russian pistol — "in his face!"

The four men remained quiet. They recognized desperation when they saw it and knew it could kill them. But Joseph Snowden, oldest man in the shop, was a singular type. He was senior and no young lout would be ordering him to do anything he did not choose.

"Taking the Oath's illegal!" he said. "It means seven years transportation! Dost think I would place myself among outlaws at my age? No, Thorpe, I'll not be taking your Oath!"

"There's no room, old Joe, for you t' refuse. Things've happened this day ..."

Snowden was accustomed to argument. He possessed that nature. He enjoyed the role. So it was with genuine shock that Snowden found Thorpe's gun muzzle grinding into his ear, the Bible crushing the other as the massive Thorpe literally took his head in hands. Thorpe squeezed hard. Snowdon's ears suffered.

"You'll do this old man, or it will be your last day."

Snowden had little choice; as did the others. He took the Luddite Oath and in swearing became a criminal in the eyes of the law, and a potential executioner of anyone who broke the Oath. But Thorpe was not done. Once finished the ritual he handed the Bible to Snowden commanding he issue the Oath to the rest. Faced with Thorpe's pistol Snowden complied.

Once finished the two young men left. Outside the shop, Mellor stopped Thorpe. It was dark and they could see each other only as shadows in the light through the windows.

"You should leave me now, Will," Mellor said. "Travel around, find what's happening, and let none see you. I must bid my mum farewell. She'll fix up this finger. We'll meet back on the moor at first light, our usual place. I've a way t' escape Raynes has never dreamt of."

That night Captain Francis Raynes was at his best. Filled with the triumph of his tryst with Fanny, the news of William Horsfall's shooting took that self-confidence and turned it to swift, sure action. He quickly dispatched his patrols. The descriptions from Henry Parr had been vague, only that there had been four against Horsfall: two of them giants and two others — one portly, one smaller and thin. He'd said they were not gentlemen. He was quite sure they had fired upon him.

Raynes crisscrossed the West Riding that night detaining anyone found out of doors, for he assumed no man would be out so late were not his business nefarious. The contents of the note retrieved from Horsfall's mouth were disseminated that night as well, along with the horrid nature of the once proud owner's death.

Prisoners were taken to Milnsbridge House and imprisoned in the vaults without Radcliffe's knowledge. Release would come only through Lloyd. Raynes despised Radcliffe for his aberrant sexual treatment of the blooming, young Fanny, despite the fact he'd enjoyed the act himself that very day. Raynes ensured his prisoners went directly to John Lloyd. He did not take them himself. He could not bear to feel Fanny's presence or even catch a glimpse of her alongside her decrepit husband.

So Lloyd and Raynes began an affiliation that night, a combination of military force and civilian fog, a collaboration of the young against their senior superiors. If anyone would defeat this rebellion it would be young men, the future in a changing age who understood change and acted ruthlessly, as the young will, leaving their seniors behind.

—

But those superiors had not been not idle. Horsfall's death, the horror of the balled paper in his mouth and the cruel nature of his wounds produced an effect on the middle classes as dramatic as George Mellor had hoped. Within hours Major Gordon and Magistrate Radcliffe had met with a sizable number of merchants and owners. They composed a memorandum to the Home Secretary, Richard Ryder, describing the desperate state of affairs in the West Riding. Thomas Atkinson, owner of Bradley Mills, was the messenger chosen to travel to London with two aims. He would describe the situation in detail and explain how he himself had been victim of a miscarried attack by Luddite criminals.

Radcliffe reworked the appeal to Ryder, placing himself in a proactive light, and sent the letter by immediate post.

Lloyd returned to his disguise and shifted his operations once more from interrogation to espionage.

When the centre collapsed.

When Prime Minister Perceval, political leader and policy maker of the British Empire ... was assassinated.

21

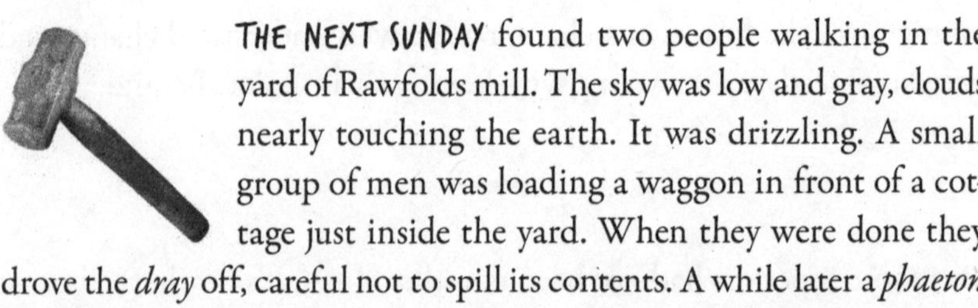

THE NEXT SUNDAY found two people walking in the yard of Rawfolds mill. The sky was low and gray, clouds nearly touching the earth. It was drizzling. A small group of men was loading a waggon in front of a cottage just inside the yard. When they were done they drove the *dray* off, careful not to spill its contents. A while later a *phaeton* appeared, the four-wheeled carriage stopping at the cottage door. A woman came out and was helped into the vehicle by its driver. The jingle of the horses' traces and rattle of the wheels slowly faded as it drove away. Soon there was only the patter of rain on turf.

They had watched the carriage disappear over a rise far up the road heading toward Huddersfield. They had watched the departure of a woman who would not allow her spirit to be broken. But they did not know that. They had simply stood, unseen, by the thorn bushes enclosing the mill yard. Each of them wore rain gear to keep out the drizzle: Mary Buckworth in a g*arrick*, or coachman's great coat, Sam Lodge wearing greased *woollen*. Mary looked up at Sam queerly.

"That was Elizabeth Cartwright," she said.

"Aye, ma'am, if you say so."

"But with so much luggage she seems to be leaving for quite some time. I wonder if someone is ill. A family member perhaps ..."

"I'm sure I don't know," Sam replied.

An uncomfortable silence followed, until Mary spoke once more.

"It's very quiet here, on a Sunday," she said softly.

"Aye, ma'am. 'Tis that."

"What was ... it like ... that day?"

"Now Mrs. Buckworth, why must you put yourself through this? 'Tis a torture for you."

"Just ... tell me, Sam."

Though they had arrived in Mary's carriage, Sam Lodge rested on his crutch and tried not to show the physical pain their walk had wrought upon him. He was now a cripple with no way of supporting his family. His family would either starve or break up as each child was put out to work and Bonnie, eventually, with them. The once big, burly Sam Lodge seemed even more reduced now. Yet his gentleness had not changed.

"Well, it was just before dawn. Quiet like, with the rustle of men and something sharp in the air; smell of fresh torches it was. A dog was barking. Then there was a bell ringing, and shouts from the mill, and George Mellor told our men t' take down the mill door. There were soldiers coming and things got hot. I hardly know how t' tell this. It was all a confusion. I saw young Booth shot. He went down over there, by that horse trough. Then all went mad. I don't recall much after that except being hit, and the pain, and your husband had me carried t' safety. If not for him, ma'am, I'd have been hard done by."

Mary listened carefully to Sam's tale, trying to solve the gaps in the story, hoping to understand the chaos of that night of which Sam, despite his presence, seemed to have so little inkling. She needed more knowledge, more clarity. She required an exactness he could not provide.

"Where ... where did John die, Sam?"

"They told me he was shot at the opening here. He wanted t' warn us that troops were coming," Sam replied, trying to offer the comprehension she seemed so much to need. Once he had spoken she walked away, wandering in a mystical manner, almost floating above the misty ground. She placed a trembling hand on a gate post, discoloured red-brown just where she touched it. She stepped forward into the gateway itself.

"It was here. I can feel it, Sam."

She could no longer hold herself up, sinking to her knees in the muck, rain drizzling around her. For a moment tears formed, but as quickly receded as she drew upon the abhorrence she'd felt since the day George Mellor had brought her dead husband home.

"And for what?" she said to herself. "A life ended. A good, gentle man who could not harm a soul."

Sam Lodge mistook her meaning.

"His death weren't in vain, Mrs. Buckworth. He's a hero now t' all the lads."

"A hero! A hero of what, Sam? Luddites? No man should die because of machines. Yet they did. Two of them mine: my husband ... and my lover ... both dead. Oh, God, I've been such a fool; such a bloody, bloody fool!"

Sam Lodge was confused. Her reference to her lover, a curate's wife, he could not quite take in. He had no idea how to respond to this staggering information.

"Ma'am?"

She was caught in the throes of her grief.

"Machines. Is that all we are? Machines to be worked then discarded? Was George in the right after all? And poor John who thought we were rational people ..."

"I'd bet you were in his last thoughts, ma'am. He loved you truly." Sam Lodge came to her, helped her up, looked into her face and tried his best to comfort a woman he could not comprehend.

"I wonder if George had the chance to tell him ..."

"I'm told George Mellor carried him off, last t' leave the field, then disappeared right after. This past fortnight I've heard nowt of George at all. Dost know, ma'am, where he be?"

"He is dead to us, Sam," she said, her eyes still staring.

"I don't think so. Some say they seen him on the Dewsbury road just after the fight. That's near your place, ain't it?"

"Take me home, Sam. I've seen enough." She sagged against him.

"Aye, ma'am. Are you alright, Mrs. Buckworth?"

"Call me Mary, Sam. I do not suit the good name of Buckworth."

"That's not so, Mrs .... Mary. You're the curate's wife."

"Oh I'm much more than that." She laughed harshly. Still in Sam's arms, her hand touched the crutch which held them both up.

"What will you do now?" she asked.

"Not much with this." He fingered his crutch. "I'm not fit for work anymore."

He felt her shiver.

"We'd best be off now," he said.

"Yes, but to your place, Sam."

"That's a long way ... Mary."

"We'll take the carriage. I want to speak with you, Sam, and with Bonnie. I have things to tell you I can tell no one else. I want to try to help you as well."

"I'm not sure how you can do that, ma'am. Still, I'll have Bonnie make us some tea. A good mug of tea and you'll feel better." He smiled tentatively.

A cup of tea. England's answer.

They began walking back the way they had come. Lodge's limp had become more distinct as the wet, the cold and the distance told on him.

"There is another way," she said, her thoughts lost on him.

"I don't know what you mean, Mary."

"George said once he wanted to be honest. I wouldn't listen to him. Things ... happened between George and me, Sam."

"What?"

"I shall be honest, Sam. Let us go to your Bonnie. I ... have things to say ..."

As they reached the opposite side of the mill pond, Mary Buckworth halted and looked back a moment. The mist closed in past the pond, shutting the yard out of sight.

"We can go now," she said, her voice fierce with anticipation.

Mellor and Thorpe left the moor, descended Penny Hill and crossed the small arch of the dog bridge warily. The moon made the turf and trees glisten after the rain. Down in the *clough* between Steel Head Lane and Penny Hill, having crossed the stream at the back of the hut, they stopped to examine Sam Lodge's place. Meagre light glimmered through the sheepskin covering its window.

The two bore rucksacks and walking sticks. They looked like bent, tired giants, worn by their efforts. They moved closer, listening for the children inside, but quickly took shelter behind a bush as they heard the rattle of some kind of carriage. A carriage did not belong here. The two looked at each other, mystified. They walked cautiously around the cottage then ducked inside.

The children were not there but someone had been only moments before. A smell of stew mixed with the fire's peat wafted through the place. A candle burned on a shard on the table. Mellor opened the door and peered outside, the door's leather hinges squawking to his push.

"Sam? Bonnie?" He raised his voice slightly. There was no reply.

"Where'd the man be?" Thorpe questioned.

"I don't know. 'Tis too late t' be scavenging."

"Or run off. Just four days; the news has spread like wildfire."

"Aye. Patrols everywhere."

"My da' told me a reward's been offered," Thorpe said glumly. "Two hundred pounds my da' said, for them who killed Horsfall."

"Two hundred?"

"Aye. 'Tis a tempting amount."

"And they waste it on us! Two hundred would put five hundred men back t' work!"

"They're frightened, George. My da' got the Leeds paper. It printed that part of Buckworth's manifesto you had Walker shove in Horsfall's mouth. You got what you wanted alright, but we're in the soup ..."

"What does that mean?"

"George, what troubles me is how it all came about. I'm no white feather, but I've thought we might have taken a better way. If we two had just quiet-like laid our heads together we'd have done for Horsfall and none would've known ..."

"Don't you see it had t' be public? The Movement will strengthen as each hears the news."

"It would be fear, George, not commitment."

"I've learned a bit from old Baines in Halifax. He told me t' divide the men in small groups, no more than five or so in each. And no contact with others. That way should one be caught the others won't be turned."

"But us? They all know us."

"We'll stay hidden. Use Sam's uncle t' get us through the tunnel, and then we're gone where none'll look. Manchester. We'll pass back and forth from there. A Movement needs leaders, Will, so old Baines says. So they've us t' direct them."

"But you've nothing organized yet."

"It takes time. And the *maisters* will keep buying machines, throwing more men out of work. Their greed works for us, Will. Their greed and our terror."

He was interrupted as laughing children opened the door. In that instant Thorpe's pistol appeared in his hand, the children squealed and went silent. The last one ran outside and quickly Sam Lodge's bulk stepped through the door. Just behind him was Bonnie.

"Sam! Bonnie!" Mellor greeted them, smiling.

The return was not what he had expected. Bonnie told the children to leave. Dutifully they obeyed her. Then she shouldered her way past her silent husband and stood before Mellor, hands on her ample hips.

"What dost want in this house?"

"We've come t' see Sam."

"He'll have no truck with Luddites no more. Get out of here, the both of you!"

At that moment Lodge seemed to straighten. He lurched from behind Bonnie and began to object: "Bonnie, these are my friends ..."

"They've come t' press you, Sam, force you back in as they're doing with others."

"Is that the way of it, George?" Sam asked. Clearly news of their work with the men at Wood's shop had travelled.

"The iron's hot now, Sam. We need faithful men t' press our strength!"

"Look at him, George!" Bonnie said, harsher than before. "A crippled man! Has he not given enough?"

"Shush, woman, this be men's business," Thorpe said.

"Shush yourself, Will Thorpe! 'Tis our house you're in and you've made this the business of everyone now. Your bloody act has brought soldiers down on us all!"

"Sam." Mellor stepped close to Lodge, grasping him by the arms. "We need you now. Your uncle's the tunnel boss at the canal. It's our best way out. We must speak with him."

"He'll have nowt t' do with you! Sam has other plans now!" Bonnie said.

"What does she mean?" Mellor's eyes flamed for an instant, piercing his friend.

"I've promised the wife and Mrs. Buckworth as well. I'm t' be her gardener. Old Grommet's near done and with this hip 'tis my only chance for work."

"That's good news, Sam. I've just this one thing left. We have need of your uncle."

"George, I told you I've promised never again t' yoke with Luddites."

"Even the man who helped you when you were down?"

"I've got t' live by my word," Sam said.

With that Mellor seemed to explode. His huge right arm encircled Sam's neck. He shifted behind the big man for balance. He had to use his left hand to produce a pistol, not the big gun, but a smaller one which he put to his friend's temple.

"We'll see about that, you traitor! Other men have gone back on their Oath. I've dealt with them. Now I'll do the same with you!"

"I've not taken the Oath, George," Lodge said through the choke hold. "I helped you at Rawfolds was all! What's happened t' you, George?"

"Happened? Happened! Why do you think I do this? I'm an outlaw! Someone had t' fight this battle! Someone had t' make the choice! I've given myself up for you, Sam, and all like you, t' do this. And now you turn your back."

"You've become just like 'em, George! Like the *maisters*! Dost reason now with a pistol? With that machine in your hand? Alright, George, if it must be it must ... shoot me now for I'll not go back on my word and I'll serve no man who compels me! Go on, use the thing. Use that machine!"

"No! Please, George!" Bonnie screamed. But it didn't matter. The eloquence of his taciturn friend, the poor man, father of four, who had given what he could with no hope of reward, produced the words Mellor needed to hear. All his pent up rage was resolved by the reasoning of a simple man. He lowered the pistol, then stepped back from Lodge.

"You can't kill 'em all, George. They're men too, confused as us. They'll listen when they've sorted it out. John Buckworth was right with that."

"And he's dead for it. I killed him!"

"More killing won't bring him back."

"Then what am I to do?"

"Escape. Get away from here."

"That's why we've come here this night."

"Alright," Sam said. Bonnie began to step in. A quick look from her husband stopped her. She knew her man. She knew when the things which had brought her to love him stood forward as they did now. As he spoke she departed a moment, returning with the children.

"I'll take you t' see my uncle. But I want you t' visit Mrs. Buckworth as well. She was here just a few minutes ago. We were seeing her off likely when you arrived."

"We heard her carriage," Mellor said flatly, his face now stone, eyes dull metal.

She had been so close.

"I know she'll help you, give money t' go where none'll find you. Build yourself a new life. You were gone once before, I recall, on the sea. You might find yourself some work as a sailor. It don't matter ... just be George Mellor again."

"That man's gone, Sam."

"That's not true. My *bairns* know you." Lodge looked at his children. "And I know you too. You're right here, George. The man who could not shoot his friend. Give me your guns and I'll bury them. Thorpe as well. Will, can't you see you must flee?"

"Aye, Sam."

The two handed their pistols, including Mellor's cherished Russian gun, to Lodge.

"You must get t' Mrs. Buckworth, George. She'll help you."'

"I'm not so sure, Sam. There are things between us."

"She told us what happened," Bonnie said. "She had to for her own sake. She needs you at least to say you forgive her."

"There's nowt t' forgive."

"She don't see that. For your own sake, and hers, you must go t' her."

"His death wasn't your fault, nor hers," Bonnie said.

"We'd best leave. We'll find another way ..." Mellor said.

"I'll take you t' my uncle," Sam said.

"Thank you, Sam."

"Live, George. Just live."

22

MELLOR REALIZED IT would not be long before he was caught. While Walker and Smith were ordinary chaps Mellor and Thorpe were exceptional, and Thorpe's size was legendary. Part of the Horsfall plan had been disappearance. So Sam Lodge took the lead that night, being familiar with the Colne Valley, Mellor and Thorpe following, each bearing a rucksack. They had not far to go, just to Marsden.

A year previous the canal had been completed linking Huddersfield with Ashton-under-Lyme in the far west. It made easy access to Manchester and other markets. At just over three miles beneath the Pennines, Standedge tunnel was both the longest and highest in all England; a feat symbolic of an age which struggled toward an uncertain future. The tunnel had taken seventeen years to build.

Before the tunnel existed, packhorses had wended across Standedge moor to the big markets. The Narrow Canal eased that journey and made it more economical. The boats, seventy feet long by seven feet wide, were hauled by horses along the tow path beside the canal. One horse could move a boat load equal to that of one hundred packhorses.

Unfortunately, the tunnel itself had been constructed to the same width as the Narrow Canal, somehow the need for a towing path having been overlooked. A conundrum most certainly when it was suggested the boats be 'legged' through the tunnel. 'Legging' meant men would lie on their backs on the roofs of the boats, place their feet on the tunnel's ceiling, and quite literally walk the boats the entire length, meeting at the other side more tow horses to continue the journey.

This, of course, required a toll. Professional *leggers* were paid one shilling sixpence for one trip through the tunnel. A boat took them on average an hour and twenty minutes. The canal boats paid their water toll by the weight in the vessels, quite lucrative for the *leggers* and the Toll Taker as well.

With no passing lanes within the canal (another engineering blunder) competition between crews grew violent until Richard Brookbank appeared. The appointed Toll Taker and Wharf Master organized specific times for the passage of boats moving one direction or the other. He'd fashioned a fine livelihood from his invention. And it was he who was related to Sam Lodge, being his uncle on his mother's side.

Richard Brookbank was not a popular man. With the powers he held and money he'd amassed, a great deal of jealousy had arisen among other men. Brookbank knew this. It did not trouble him. His family was important to him: Margaret, his wife just as stout as he, Jessie his daughter now coming of age and, though a touch portly, ready for a match to some rich merchant's son, and finally his son, Willis, heir and future comptroller of Standedge tunnel. It was odd such a narrow tunnel should produce such wide inhabitants, for Willis too was noted for his girth.

Brookbank needed for nothing and was one of those individuals for whom a little power was just enough. His decisions brooked no appeal and, apparently, there was no one to whom an appeal could be made. In Standedge, Brookbank was omniscient.

Yet he was central to Mellor's plan. Mellor and Thorpe would be looked for upon roads and turnpikes, even across the moors. But there were many men populating what they called *Stannidge*: looking for work should a crew need a *legger* or a loader at the warehouse. Some of the men might know each other but more often not, coming from both sides of the Pennines. Men the size of Mellor and Thorpe would be valued for their strength and, more important, more likely to fit in.

—

Captain Francis Raynes had learned hard lessons from his few months in the West Riding. He would require that wisdom as he scoured the countryside in search of Horsfall's murderers. More than a score had been arrested and given over to Lloyd. And yet the authorities had not captured the murderers. Word spread of their failure. General Maitland, upon further appeal by Gordon, sent increasing numbers of troops.

Meanwhile Henry Parr remained uncertain regarding just whom he had seen. John Lloyd was nearly driven to distraction by Parr's prevarication but Parr was a law-abiding owner, secure against the solicitor's methods and frightened of men who would murder.

So Lloyd went back to disguise, to tinkering from hamlet to town to roadside inn.

—

"I am afraid that is impossible, Samuel," Richard Brookbank said in his doorway, dressed in nightshirt and cap. Lodge stood with two others at his door. The three of them more than filled his alcove. His son stood behind him, round as a white linen ball. "First you awaken me at ... what time would it be?"

"'Tis sunrise, Uncle."

"Have you no timepiece, man? Of course not. You have nothing, do you? And yet you ask me to employ these two men. Not you, I note."

"I can't work, Uncle. Dost not see I'm crippled?"

"At any rate, it won't do. Take yourselves off, you men." He gazed up at the two huge beings. Better to have a barred door between his family and them. He began to back his way into the house but Willis' bulk prevented him.

"You're sure now, *Maister* Brookbank," the lad with the piercing eyes said.

"I cannot simply allow you to leg a boat through. We have crews for that."

"When does the first of them leave?"

"Well, I would have to look into my schedule. Enough! I've said *no*! Now off with you!"

"Will," the young one said calmly to the giant beside him.

A massive arm shot past Richard Brookbank and a massive hand closed around the throat of his son, hauling him bodily out through the doorway nearly capsizing Brookbank himself. His son was dangled off the ground by the huge man holding his neck. Willis' feet were kicking as those of a hanging man.

Suddenly everything had changed. Richard Brookbank, Toll Taker and Wharf Master of the famed Standedge Tunnel, accustomed to refusal, negligent to negotiation, found himself fearful and powerless as his son was shaken like a dog. The diamond eyed man glimmered at him.

"Now I'll tell you what we'll do, *Maister* Brookbank ..."

"I'm no master, Sir!" he said panicking. "I'm simply a toll ..."

"You control this tunnel?"

"Yes."

"Then we'll be off t' your office and find your schedule and put two good men upon the first boat."

"Please, put down my son! You're choking him!"

"We'll move faster with him in the air. Now come on! Sam, you're done here. Go home."

With Sam Lodge turning away, the four quick stepped to the office. Brookbank quickly lit a lantern and perused his schedule.

"I'm afraid there's a boat coming through from the west first today. You've seen the chain up on this side. We'll have to wait."

"When does it come?" the young man questioned.

"It should arrive by seven."

"That means it hasn't left yet."

"Yes, but they have right of way."

"And does your son here have so much breath left?" The man gestured at the dangling Willis. The boy was turning blue.

"I have a boat for you! Right now! It's there by the wharf. Only the two of you. I can't get more men this quickly. You'll have to start immediately. Please, let Willis down."

The big man dropped the lad. He fell like a stone in a gasping puddle.

"We'll have your signature on orders t' let us back and forth when we wish; any boat, any time. Write the orders," the smaller one said.

"I can't do that."

"We'll be taking your son, *Maister* Brookbank. He'll stay with friends of ours on the west side while we've need of your tunnel. He won't be harmed. But should you decide t' speak of this to anyone you can say farewell t' him now for you'll never see him again. After that comes your daughter. One day she'll be gone and none t' say where. Then your wife, *Maister* Brookbank. I speak with the force of Ludd's army. Dost make myself clear."

"Yes. Yes! Of course. Yes! Not a word, Sir. Nothing. But you can't take my son!"

"You know his writing. You'll receive a letter each time we pass."

"How do I know you won't simply make him write letters then murder him?"

"Because I say so."

"Of course. Yes ... Of course."

"Da'!" Willis said, wheezing.

"Don't worry, son. These men have given their word. Just be a good lad and cause no trouble. This will all be over soon will it not Mr. ..."

"Just write down Mr. Lloyd and Mr. Raynes on your order paper. Make it neat now. And your signature."

The orders finished, the boy tied, gagged, bagged and stashed in the bilge of the boat, the two men cast off and poled to tunnel entrance. Thorpe leapt ashore and, with a strength that took three men to lift it, tossed the huge chain from its clasp. Brookbank watched them disappear into the dark.

Once inside the echoing core, Mellor lit a lantern and placed it at the bow; then he and Thorpe went up top. They lay down on their backs. They lifted their feet to touch the roof of the tunnel and began to walk. After some confusion and cracking of bulwarks against the unforgiving rock, Mellor began to count aloud as he took his steps, mirrored by Thorpe. It would take them hours to get through the tunnel. On the way they would meet the boat from the west but a show of orders from Brookbank and the western boat would reverse itself.

They arrived with little commotion. Having thanked the western crew they took up the significant baggage, whose contents were obviously responsible for such uncommon orders, and carried it off on their shoulders.

They would be back. They had work to do and fear to spread and George Mellor had promised to meet a certain woman; but first they would learn more of their craft in Manchester; where riots were happening.

Terror requires training.

23

IT WAS FIVE fifteen according to his time piece. Spenser Perceval was in a hurry. His open coat fluttered behind him as he mounted the steps from Saint Margaret Street to enter the lobby of the House of Commons. He took his habitual glance upward, gazing at the Palace of Westminster. Long and heavy, soaring and solid, the building basked in the afternoon sun. A glance behind offered a view of Westminster Abbey, its great entrance now in shadow, but no building in this great city of London could match its towering majesty. On Saint Margaret, the street was clogged with the fancy barouches of arriving members. Harnessed to their elaborate carriages, the horses were as beautiful and muscular as the buildings surrounding them. He was at the centre of the British Empire, about to enter the Parliament which governed that Empire. It remained difficult to believe he himself was Prime Minister.

He had always been a humble man despite his aristocratic origins. He was slight and pale though at fifty years still fit enough. His hair was thinning and going to grey, but his brows remained dark above prominent brown eyes which gave his face a youthful appearance. His clothing beneath the great coat was conservative, as befitted a Prime Minister: black coat and breeches, black hose and black leather shoes and a glistening white, starched cravat. He carried his bicorn in one hand and returned the ticking orb beneath the folds of his coat with the other.

Due to attend the latest inquiry into the Orders in Council, he did not wish to be late. He pushed his way through the great double doors and into the crowded vestibule. He had a history of being late: even to the tardiness of his own birth.

He'd been born the son of the Earl of Egmont but unfortunately, the *second* son of a *second* marriage, making him a virtual non-entity in the noble family. After his father's death, with an allowance of only £200 a year, Perceval faced the prospect of having to make his own way in life. He chose the law.

Fortunately he discovered himself a scholar and triumphed at Lincoln's Inn. But then he'd languished, an impecunious barrister on the Midland Circuit. An insignificant man fallen in love too late, or too old, with a nobleman's younger daughter. Her father, the Honourable Sir Thomas Spenser Wilson, was against the marriage to a man without prospects. But despite her father, he and his Jane had eloped. Fortunately his family ties had protected him from the peer's wrath and the couple's love had eventually produced a family of twelve children. Early on their life had been difficult: simple lodgings over a carpet shop in Bedford Row, with but a housemaid and cook. It seemed they would live a tawdry life. Yet after several years his connections began to see him through sundry governmental positions until finally he'd achieved the King's Council and an income of £1000 a year. With relief he'd realized he could support his family in style.

His enhanced legal practice had also allowed him entry into politics. At that time, nearly all Members representing county seats were landed gentry. Too late again for Perceval to have represented his father's, and later, his eldest half-brother's seat. He'd found his own constituency in Northampton. His maturity and those speaking skills long practiced as a barrister won him the election, then he evolved until he became a valued debater for the Tory Party.

From there he had worked his way up the laborious ladder of ministerial positions until, just three years previous, he'd been elected Prime Minister by his Caucus. The exalted position, ruling the Tory Party of Great Britain, should have been an honour, the ultimate distinction for such a man as he. Yet he found it an exhausting role, particularly at a time with Bonaparte commanding the Continent, with America declaring war, with bad harvests and the troubles in the North Country.

He was a tired man this day as he crossed the stone flags of the lobby, its neo-Gothic woodwork a business of spires and arches. He caught sight of his Home Secretary, Richard Ryder, and altered direction hoping to compare notes before entering the meeting.

Thus he did not see the man seated in an obscure alcove rise and make his way through the nattering groups of Members toward him. The antechamber of the House of Commons was an echoing, vaulted hall and at this time of day congested with Members, suitors and servants. It was a hubbub of noise and activity.

He searched to find Home Secretary Ryder, caught a glimpse of him, and made his way toward him. At last he noticed the man from the alcove approach. He thought for an instant to shift sideways, join the dispute of a band of Whigs as they undoubtedly planned to take down his government, but then thought the better of it and stopped, awaiting the stranger.

The man was unpleasant looking. Not only physically ugly but possessing a scowl which foretold a quarrel. He was fumbling with something inside his coat. Perceval noticed he was unshaven and sloppy, perhaps even a working man, Perceval thought derisively.

The slovenly character advanced. Too late Perceval spotted the pistol drawn from the man's coat, its dull metal so alarming within the sanctity of this place. The assassin was a mere five feet away when his arm lifted, the pistol's hammer pulled back and Perceval shouted helplessly: "Oh my God! Murder!"

The explosion boomed throughout the lobby shattering senses as well as a life. Perceval collapsed to the floor, shot in the chest. He tried to rise but could not, his bright brown eyes questioned his assassin with an astonished, unspoken: "Why?"

Chaos surrounded the slender, bleeding body. Some ran from the lobby out to the street or down convenient hallways. Others moved quickly toward the scene. The assassin still held his pistol but did not attempt to escape. He simply returned to his alcove, walking dead-eyed past shirking groups of men and sat down again until guards appeared.

Some tried in vain to revive the Prime Minister. He remained unconscious. They carried him to an adjoining room and laid him upon a table. A surgeon arrived a few minutes later. He was too late.

Guards and Bow Street Runners were soon in the lobby, restoring order, moving all and sundry away from the scene of the crime. Lords and Members were herded like sheep, shock rendering them powerless: a condition to which few were accustomed. Then finally the facts rolled over them, almost concurrently.

The Prime Minister had been assassinated.

In Westminster, the sacred centre of the Empire.

His assailant a rough looking character who had not even tried to escape.

A fanatic. What could lead a man to this?

Many thought the assassin a Jacobin, or a Bonapartist. Others considered he might be American, thinking their former colonials audacious enough to stage this murder. But a few with knowledge of what was occurring in their north country thought instantly of other culprits.

Luddites.

The meeting grew sombre as Radcliffe finished reading aloud the letter from Home Secretary Ryder. The remains of a lunch were scattered across a deal table in his library, four other men sat at the table, listening intently. With him were Major Gordon, Solicitor Lloyd, Captain Raynes, and Colonel Campbell himself. They had been cast together, these five diverse characters, to find solutions to circumstances none had ever expected: revolution, though it was not called so yet.

"That's all they got from him?" Campbell said.

"Name, John Bellingham, no reason given other than Parliament's refusal to hear his grievances," Radcliffe responded gravely.

"He murders a Prime Minister for so little?" Lloyd said.

"Ryder seems to think otherwise. It seems to me he fears *that* gunshot might signal the start of an uprising," Radcliffe said. He'd become anxious for his own life, his once quiet district now a warren of dissent, crime and violence. It had physically taken its toll on the man.

"He's had Burdett imprisoned in the Tower," Gordon said.

"He can do that?" Lloyd said.

"Who is Burdett?" a frustrated Raynes said. His business was with Luddites, not politicians.

"Sir Frances Burdett, Baronet and MP from Formarke Hall, his family seat," Campbell said, "and a radical. He's been making speeches about reform. Locally there is a man named Ellis, a mill owner, who appears to side with him."

"You mean a Peer is taking the side of commoners?" Lloyd could hardly believe it. The world to which he aspired was turning upside down.

"But what is this Russian connection?" Lloyd sought more of the letter's meaning.

"Only that Bellingham was imprisoned there," Radcliffe said, "over some sort of shipping sabotage. It is not at all clear according to Ryder."

"Bellingham was involved with shipping in Russia?" Lloyd said.

"Some skullduggery regarding a ship led to his imprisonment there."

"In Russia. When, Sir?"

"It seems he returned to England three years ago."

"Don't we know someone local who served on a ship in Russian waters?"

"I've no idea, I'm sure," Radcliffe said, seemingly confused by Lloyd's tack.

"I think I do," Raynes said. "One of the local croppers went to Russia."

"Where did you hear that?" Gordon asked.

"I've heard it as well," Lloyd said.

"Common knowledge," Raynes said. With this piece of intelligence the two young men held the upper hand over their seniors.

"Bit of a coincidence," Campbell said.

"It is, isn't it?" Lloyd said.

"Well for heaven's sake, man, tell us!" Radcliffe said, frustrated again by the shifty Lloyd. "An uprising might truly be in the offing!"

"Ye should be safe." Raynes stared down at the older man, the captain's face filled with disdain. "Ye hae enough men around ye to protect a village."

"How dare you, Sir!" Radcliffe rose from his chair, if a little unsteadily.

"An entire troop of men I could be using pursuing these criminals," Raynes said.

"I've been threatened. Shot at. Stones through my windows!" Radcliffe could hardly contain himself. Raynes seemed not to care.

"Raynes ..." Gordon said, and was ignored. The major was now less his superior than a mere a go between. Campbell had informed Raynes that General Maitland himself was interested in Raynes' tactics. To have the eye of a General officer was never a bad thing.

"Any number of individuals in the West Riding, Sir, have had the same threats," Raynes said, continuing to address the Magistrate. "Ye are not alone, yet ye demand so much."

"That is enough, Captain Raynes," Campbell said, perplexed by the officer's behavior. "You might enlighten us upon your conjectures. What could Russia have to do with this? They have their hands full with Bonaparte if I'm not mistaken."

"Oh, it isn't Russia itself, Sir," Raynes replied. "It's the coincidence."

"Explain yourself."

"Perhaps I might offer something, Colonel," Lloyd said. "As you know, we two have been travelling the countryside. We've not heard of an uprising yet, only threats."

"And that isn't enough?" Radcliffe said. He had seated himself once more. He seemed exhausted by the energy emanating from his juniors.

"Thuggery, Sir," Lloyd replied offhandedly. It was clear he too had little regard for the magistrate simply from the tone of his voice. "But we have both ... check me if I'm wrong in this Raynes ...both heard of a fellow named Mellor who came back recently, two years I think, from Russia."

"How could a common lout earn the *brass* to get to Russia," Campbell said.

"His father disappeared," Lloyd said. "Left him penniless. He went to sea."

"Common enough," Campbell said.

"Agreed, Sir," Lloyd replied, "but it's likely he was in Russia when Bellingham was as well. Now Bellingham has assassinated Prime Minister Perceval and we've heard rumours Mellor is some kind of organizer here."

"You mean a Luddite?" Radcliffe roused himself once again.

"Frightened, Radcliffe?" Raynes said harshly.

"Then bring him in, Captain. That is your responsibility," Radcliffe said. "Give him over to Lloyd here. He and I will get to the bottom of this fellow."

"There's one problem with your order, Sir," Lloyd said.

"What would that be?" Radcliffe receded again, unsure of himself. Raynes peered at him with livid aversion.

"They can't find him," Gordon answered for Lloyd.

"Your commission is to find him," Campbell said.

"I'm sorry, Sir." Raynes' character altered as he switched glances from Radcliffe to Campbell. "As the major said, the man hae disappeared."

"Not at his place of work?"

"No, Sir. His step-father is John Wood, a small owner. He's mentioned his son might hae gone back to sea."

"Why would he do that?" Campbell said.

"We've made arrests since Horsfall's death," Radcliffe said. "Perhaps this Wood might be a guilty party."

"No one's mentioned him," Lloyd said, "in any interrogation."

"That's right." Radcliffe seemed happy to be in agreement. "We've heard nothing at all."

"But there is Russia," Gordon said, "and Bellingham."

"But no Mellor," Campbell said.

"Well this letter is enough for me. Ryder would not have written did he not suspect something in the offing. Raynes, you'll increase your patrols ..."

"I've not enough men, Sir," Raynes said quickly.

"You'll have the troops," Campbell replied. "This letter guarantees that. I shall speak personally with General Maitland. And you Mr. Lloyd ... I suggest you return to tinkering and find this Mellor fellow."

"But, Colonel, I've work to do here! Interrogations! Magistrate Radcliffe requires me!"

"You mean the methods you employ."

"I've more chance of succeeding here, Colonel! The magistrate has promised me the opportunity of prosecuting the criminals I've seized ..."

"That has yet to be determined, Lloyd," Radcliffe said. "And this Mellor talk must mean something. I agree with the colonel. You should return to spying."

"Sir! I'm known now! I could be murdered."

"As could we all," Radcliffe said.

"Yourself, Sir?" Raynes taunted Radcliffe once more, stirring Campbell.

"Mind your manners, Captain, or I'll have Major Gordon assume your command."

"I stand ready, Sir," Gordon said clearly, though clearly he would not relish the night rides of his younger officer.

"But ..." Raynes tried to speak.

"You have something further to say, Captain?"

"No, Sir. I am tired, is all. These nightly patrols ..."

"We all have our duty, Raynes. I shall report to Maitland in Buxton. And be careful, Captain. Despite your successes neither of you have produced much at all in the way of solutions. General Maitland is not a man to cross."

"Of course. Of course, Sir."

In Manchester, George Mellor discovered it was not unrest over machines causing riots, but lack of food. Manchester was a large city in the throes of turmoil. Indeed, as the masters and merchants of Lancashire imported new technologies to achieve new profits, they cast numerous labourers out of work.

Worse, the past year had been disastrous. Poor harvests had driven up the cost of food so that even the middle classes struggled and ordinary folk had begun to starve. A year before a penny would purchase three pounds of potatoes; that penny now bought just one pound. It was the same with everything: beer, bread and vegetables all nearly beyond the reach of most people.

What Mellor found as well was not the vast organizations vaunted by men like Joseph Kentworthy, John Baines or George Weightman.

There were no great strategists, no Luddite generals, no skilled combatants, no armies of rebels. There was only the starving mass.

There had been food riots; thousands of hungry people desperate for respite. Leaderless thousands. At times characters appeared to propose some new redress. They came and went, these redressers; rose and fell, fought and died, were arrested and imprisoned.

The authorities were relentless and lethal. Officers commanded live fire upon mobs almost at will. There was little for Mellor and Thorpe in Manchester, so estranged were they from these urban battles and ignorant of their leaders. They were themselves suspected of being government spies. No one knew them, their accents were wrong, and so they were threatened and forced from the city.

Discouraged, they made their way back to Diggle near the west end of Standedge tunnel. They lived in a rundown shanty: a door-less, turf roof hut with a tumbled chimney, dirt floor, and no furniture but stumps and pails. They ate what they could catch or steal, often vermin or vegetables from someone's spring garden.

They had left young Willis Brookbank with a family known to Thorpe. When they returned they took Willis back guarding the lad and watching him grow increasingly thin. They spent their nights in silence while Mellor planned and Thorpe simply sat quietly. It was one such night after a sparse meal that Thorpe finally questioned Mellor's designs. His questions were not kind.

Near the end of the conversation — the two men edgy, the Brookbank boy terrified — Thorpe struck with the most obvious question.

"What I want t' know is the point of carrying on with this."

"You've taken the Oath, Will," Mellor responded, unsure himself of a true solution.

"That's no answer. I thought we were part of something bigger. Now I'm not so sure."

"They're losing in Manchester, I admit," Mellor said, "but we must go on! I won't leave the West Riding in the lurch! I admit I was a fool. It ain't easy t' say this but I was led false by John Wood. I was his puppet. Seems the same in Manchester. What we saw were tyrants running over any who tried t' make out the truth. Dost want that in the West Riding?"

"No, George. You know how I feel."

"And I feel the same. But someone must go at these greedy *maisters* t' make them see people mean more than profits! We can make a difference in the West Riding at least. We'll put fear into the *maisters'* hearts. But from ambush. We'll not win a war against them, but we can win the battles we choose to make. We'll raise such a rumpus to make them think twice about standing against us. We'll kill if we must, as we done with Horsfall. A few more like him and we'll have them listening. But I need you, Will, t' help me raise men. What say you to that?"

"I say I think we can't fight the future, but I'm willing t' try. You told me we do this t' cobble the way for them who come after us. If that's true I'll join you though it seems hopeless."

"We'll be outlaws, Will, but not thugs. Can you recall tales of Robin Hood? He came from Nottingham way. Maybe us two can do the things he did. We'll start by stopping the criminals stealing from others in the name of Ludd. Then we can work the real business, make a difference, make things better for those coming after."

"That's our new rally cry, George." There were tears in Thorpe's eyes as he said this. They were not simply outlaws or vandals. They were the men who would re-make the future.

"'Tis time we went back under this moor t' make that difference," Mellor said.

24

AND SO IT fell out that John Lloyd, aspiring prosecuting solicitor, and Captain Francis Raynes, striving military hero, were instructed to work together by their superiors. Ironically they were the very people who would come to replace the older men; the future, one might say, overtaking the past. Their obvious targets were the murderers of William Horsfall but there was more to their mandate than a murder investigation, just as there was much more than murder involved in this uprising of commoners now called Luddites.

The two were the perfect duo to accomplish this task. Raynes was an action oriented soldier, tough and unflagging in his pursuits. His successes thus far had been hailed by his superiors even if he had failed to capture any actual leaders. Lloyd, on the other hand, was subtle and deceptive though equally as merciless as his military colleague. His disguise as a *tinker* had exposed significant events. His infamous interrogations had produced reams of information, though nothing had revealed the real leaders of the rising.

Despite their differences, the soldier a direct, handsome, charismatic Scot while the spy was more devious and a touch repulsive, the two shared certain traits. They were young. They were ambitious. They shared a duty and ruthlessness which propelled them to methods becoming notorious.

They met together in secret. They selected the Red Lion public house, a place known to serve the middle classes. The food was substantial, the atmosphere subdued and, most significant, it was not frequented by those the two were avoiding: their superiors. Both men wore merchants' clothing, their coats and breeches subdued browns and blues with equally conservative shirts and stockings. Raynes had donned a pair of spectacles to alter his look. They ate heartily and drank little. Once the meal was finished, roast of beef for both, the two lingered as though conducting negotiations over the remains of their wine. In a way, they were.

"Whichever way we look at this, Lloyd, it seems Parr is too frightened to be any use."

"Indeed. He is terrified."

"Still, shots to the groin and all. I've known men in battle who hae altered upon beholding a comrade's wounds." The smallest hint of his accent insinuated itself, embarrassing him slightly: the man who wished to be known as an officer of the British Army. Yet it was that very Scottish background and his antipathy toward his roots which made Raynes so keen to defeat the rebels.

"No facts, other than two of them were tall and two were small," Lloyd said. "I ask you ..."

"Ye may find it amusing but what are we to do?" Raynes replied sternly. He was not a man to waste his time unless it happened to be in dalliance with a certain married seductress.

"What was the first act against a mill owner?" Lloyd asked, signifying he too would treat their business seriously.

"Why Bradley Mills, of course. There were more than a fifty there."

"Yet all escaped. Now, where is the place we've derived at least some information?"

"Rawfolds. Though not enough. I do wish the two wounded captives had talked."

"Indeed, had I had but a few more hours I'd have had something from them. Did you discover anything at the scene?"

"I hae one article might be of interest, besides the usual detritus."

"Oh?"

"Ye might not like it."

"Try me."

"Alright then ... a hat. Recovered from the mill pond. It was floating so hadnae been there long when one of my men recovered it."

"Is it distinctive in any way?" Lloyd grew intrigued.

"It wasn't a labourer's, I can say that. It was a topper."

At that time only boys wore caps. All men wore hats. For informal or rough occasions the Tilbury and the Turf were popular top hats for those who could afford them, tri-corns and *rehoboams* or shovel hats were the customary headgear of commoners. They served an obvious functional purpose but to be without one was as likely as to be without shoes, both noticeable and remarkable. It was the reason Raynes had considered it evidence.

"Were you to ask around, perhaps as the *tinker* who found it, we might trace the owner," Raynes replied.

"A fine idea," Lloyd said, smiling. "I wonder was there no one that night who might have noticed a hatless man. Perhaps you with your resources might look that way."

"I shall, though as ye know I arrived late. Oh, we picked up a few suspicious characters, but it seems patchy ground."

"It is but one avenue." Lloyd smiled and waved his hands delicately in front of him as though sweeping the table of the subject. "There are others. I, for instance, have interviewed a Mr. Vickerman. He follows the reports of that fellow Baines who writes for the *Leeds Mercury*. At any rate, this Vickerman suspects John Wood, proprietor of that shop near Longroyd Bridge, might be one of these Luddites."

"An owner? What would he gain?"

"Strange, I admit. But the hat was likely an owner's?"

"Yes."

"Ah, and who works for this Wood?"

"I'm sure I hae no idea."

"One George Mellor, if you recall." Lloyd smiled. His smile was a thin, ugly leer.

"The lad who was in Russia when Bellingham was there?"

"Indeed."

"But why on earth would ye suspect him?"

"Where is he now?"

"I don't know. I'd thought, from our meeting with Radcliffe, he'd gone back to sea."

"After Rawfolds."

"Precisely. I wasnae looking for him."

"But you will now."

"Your point being?"

"He's connected somehow. And yet he's disappeared. You don't find that suspicious?"

"Not particularly." Raynes felt edgy. "Why? Hae ye heard something I should know?"

"Only that he is Wood's step-son."

"Thin," Raynes replied, unaccustomed to deduction.

"And now we have this mysterious hat which could be an owner's. But perhaps another tack." Lloyd relaxed his intensity. He took some wine. The two looked around a moment. The Red Lion was clearing out this time of day.

"I'm afraid I'm not much good at this game," Raynes said.

"I'll look into Wood," Lloyd said. "Perhaps you might try to find Mellor, in case it is *we* who are at sea and not him."

Raynes chuckled.

"I hae a second bit of information." Raynes turned to face Lloyd. "A *tich* of gossip really. I've been informed of a Corporal Barrowclough; a sergeant of mine suspects he may be a spy."

"Interesting." Lloyd folded his hands to lean closer. "In my tinker travels I've heard the same. Barrowclough, with that name he's native to the district. What reason did your sergeant give?"

"None; other than Barrowclough's local and seems overly curious, and he spoke out when Private Shepherd was given the lash for refusing orders at Rawfolds."

"Spoke out, did he?" Lloyd stroked his diminished chin. "I suggest we find this man, Raynes. If he's on that turncoat Shepherd's side he's likely a rebel. We could do worse than question him. Who knows what he'll have to say."

"I'll hae him picked up, delivered to Magistrate Radcliffe."

"I would say not at this time, Captain," Lloyd said. "The Star Inn might be a better destination."

"I understand." Raynes knew the Star and what had happened there. It did not trouble him in the least, not when dealing with traitors. "So my assignments are Barrowclough and Mellor. Yours is the search for a hatless man. It still seems very vague, Lloyd."

"Think of it as alike to your night rides, searching for trouble, ready if need be. At times you are lucky and find it, if not it is merely another night."

"Yes, I can understand that."

"Patience and diligence shall win the day." Lloyd smiled again, trying to inveigle the captain into a sense of collusion.

"One thing," Raynes said as they stood from the table. "I must hae a special constable wi' me to make an arrest on Barrowclough."

"Isn't it military business?"

"If I were to arrest him, he'd be sent to a military prison. No chance for ye—"

"—to question him. Good thinking, Raynes. Have no doubt, we shall get to the bottom of these Luddites. It may take some time but I know we'll succeed."

The meeting ended with the two men shaking hands. They agreed Lloyd would ride with Raynes that night. Lloyd paid for the dinner. At any rate the costs would come from Radcliffe's pocket. Lloyd had no trouble expensing his account with the magistrate's funds. He mentioned this to Raynes who laughed louder than he'd expected at his second small joke.

Lloyd, ever inquisitive, wondered why.

Mellor and Thorpe returned to the West Riding through Standedge Tunnel, courtesy of Richard Brookbank's letter. They left young Willis with Thorpe's friends once again, who were only too happy to be of service. Not only were they paid, they seemed to hold a grudge against

Brookbank but, of course, almost everyone did. The two did not see Brookbank himself when they came through the Marsden side. They had a boy take a note from Willis to his father but were gone before he'd received it.

At the New Inn near Marsden they found John Dean, who had lost part of a hand in the Rawfolds attack. He'd been using his hammer on the door when he was shot. They could see the scars from the searing iron applied to staunch the bleeding. He kept the hand concealed as much as he could. It was a telling wound.

He told them the Movement continued, though truncated. Attacks were less frequent and too many seemed simply criminal acts. The chaos which was now the West Riding proved dependable ground for felons, just as Mary Buckworth had foretold.

Thoughts of Mary were still painful for Mellor, yet she was rarely from his mind. She would appear in his dreams too often. Awake, he could put notions of her aside but asleep, she commanded. He was sure she still loved him and yet she had turned him away. They had caused the death of her husband, however indirectly, and both had changed as a result. He had no idea how much she had changed but he knew his own character had evolved.

Perhaps it had been his time in Manchester. He'd watched leaders rise and fall. He'd witnessed soldiers ride down women and children. Each malicious act drove him further and further from the man he had been. Other than those of Mary, his thoughts were more machinations, schemes to reap his revenge on the *maisters*. He had turned himself, indeed, into a kind of machine: conspiring with no thought of mercy against those with whom he felt himself at war. Yet he knew in Manchester it had all been done wrong. It had all been too proximate, too much based on the latest food shortages or dismissals of workers. It had led him to thinking how he would work things in his own district, a rural rather than urban scape. He recalled the advice of John Baines in Halifax.

He knew now how to create the terror he was bent on inflicting. On returning he would construct around him small groups of dedicated men. They would transform into something more deadly than anything the West Riding had known. They would be urged to employ shocking acts. Strokes of terror. Only then would change happen. Only then would authorities pause to listen. Only then would the West Riding live in real fear.

Mellor decided it was time to convert his theories to action. He had planned a diversion allowing his emergent forces more freedom of movement. After visiting Dean at Marsden, he and Thorpe moved southeast to Sheffield to start up the kinds of riots they'd seen in Manchester. These mutinies wouldn't amount to much, mostly noise and looting, but troops would be sent to restore order which would mean fewer of them patrolling the West Riding. Only then could his campaign be carried out. But first he and Thorpe had to make for Sheffield and work toward disturbance.

Along the route, they planned their actions. Yet one evening they were obstructed by an enemy neither had expected. It could not have occurred on a less likely night: the first night in June presaging summer; peaceful and serene, a nightingale's song shattered by a woman's scream.

They moved quickly toward sounds of struggle. They leapt onto a farm lane which led to a typical smallholding: a two storied, limestone house, roofline sagging, chimney rising at one end. There were lanterns in the windows yet they moved from place to place as someone passed through the house. Just beyond the house in the barn were more lights and sounds.

They ran toward the cry of a terrified woman. As they came to the barn they caught all in a glance. A man sat subdued, bleeding from his nose, his muscles straining to force release from the ropes binding him. Two other men stood over him while a third in a stall opposite was occupied hauling up the skirts of the farmer's wife. He had ripped her bodice and exposed her breasts. A wave of nausea swept George Mellor. What he'd thought as mere gossip from Dean was happening here in front of him. Just as Mary had said it would.

Thorpe's big voice boomed. That voice was enough to halt any man. The three stopped what they were doing; the one with the woman still had his breeches unbuttoned. Mellor knew him. A brute named Earl Parkin. Mellor recalled him from the Shears; a friend of Ben Walker's. Even then he had sensed the man's dubious character.

Parkin was red-haired, the hair shaved so short it was barely there, the beard a shade darker and equally thin. His ears stuck out. He had rheumy gray eyes, protruding front teeth and a compact though muscular body. He stared at Mellor while his two friends, obviously minions, stood just behind him. They were solid men, though neither as big as Mellor or Thorpe. One had grabbed a pitchfork as a weapon.

Mellor took a step toward Parkin. Though Parkin held his ground Mellor could feel fear surge in the man. His eyes widened slightly, his breathing grew quicker, his stance vaguely altered protectively; all diminutive changes which Mellor, to his wonder, observed. For an instant George Mellor paused. This was new, this perceptive ability he'd not realized he possessed. He found it made him more confident; something he'd lost after Rawfolds.

"What's this then?" Parkin said loudly, designed to scare Mellor off.

"'Tis that question I'm asking you," Mellor replied, his own voice unwavering.

"I know you!" Parkin said. "You're the cropper lad, aye? John Wood's boy. The Shears, lad! Mellor, ain't it? I was there with Ben Walker. I saw you there, with that Kentworthy fellow, the man making speeches."

"I'll ask again and you'll give me an answer."

"Doing as the man said. Finding guns for the cause."

"And you do that by taking a man's wife?"

"She's a saucy bitch," Parkin said, "scratched down my arm. Just look ..."

He began to roll up his sleeve when Mellor stopped him.

"I know you as well, Parkin. Nothing more here than robbery and rape."

"Watch yourself, Mellor. You're but a lad despite your size, and your friend there ..."

"Could beat the three of you t' pulp."

As he spoke he noticed Parkin's eyes shift.

"Turn around, Will, we've more company," Mellor said, feeling his big friend shift on his order, yet keeping contact with his back.

Thorpe uttered: "But two." Parkin swelled with the power of his numbers.

"I tell you be off! You may be stout lads but you're no match for five."

With that, the two behind Parkin stepped forward. Their eyes were hard, their bodies tensed. Yet Mellor felt no fear whatsoever. He found himself measuring the forces against him, depending on Thorpe to do the same. For an instant he recalled the panic of Rawfolds when he'd seemed so powerless to do anything but here, now, he was different.

"I'll say this once, Parkin," he spoke evenly. "You are a thief and a rogue and I mean t' make an example of you."

"Hah!" Parkin said, laughing. "I've four men with me t' take the two of you!"

"Dost recall Rawfolds?"

"I recall you lost there, lad," Parkin replied, sneering.

"Aye, but I'm beginning t' see I learned something as well."

"Get out of here, you young bastard!" Parkin shouted.

Mellor sensed the man's shout as the cue. He knew Parkin would not put himself in jeopardy so first he would face one or both of Parkin's henchmen: pitchfork and knuckles. It would have to be Knuckles first and fast so Pitchfork couldn't stick him. He wasn't worried at all about Parkin. If the lout had a knife he'd have shown it by now. He felt Thorpe nudge his back, not the touch of fear but the rub of aggression. No trouble there.

"Try me," Mellor said.

And then it all changed.

At Rawfolds events had transpired so rapidly Mellor had felt he could not keep up, take command, do anything other than what he had done: lose himself in his own frustrations and fear. Rawfolds had seen a boy used and deployed, struggling to be a leader with no training, no plan, nothing more than a child-like zeal to overcome a perceived enemy. He'd had no idea his enemy was prepared to kill. He had never seen a man die. And so it had all rolled over him. Pummelled and shocked, he had lost control and so led more men to blood. It had been the most shameful night of his life.

Yet now, as Parkin's two thugs came at him, it was as though time slowed. He could see Knuckles make the mistake of moving in faster, his big fists raised. Pitchfork had to cross Parkin to get at Mellor, so he was blocked. Knuckles moved in with a wild right windmill meant to fell Mellor. But Mellor was already two moves ahead. He leaned backward and simultaneously kicked up between the man's legs. There was a whoosh of breath but Mellor caught him before he could fall. Then Pitchfork was stabbing, trying to pierce Mellor's side. Mellor used Knuckles as a shield from the tines and impaled the man on Pitchfork's thrust. Knuckles could not even scream. All Mellor heard was a strangled "Aggh." Then he twisted the speared man pulling the pitchfork with him, throwing him to the floor.

Pitchfork, no longer armed, was helpless. With the shock of having stabbed his friend he'd let go the weapon. He just stood there as Mellor leapt forward then grabbed his neck with both hands and drove his forehead into Pitchfork's nose. Pitchfork dropped like a stone.

This all happened so quickly that Parkin had had no time to move. He was turning to run as Mellor let Pitchfork fall. Panic gave Parkin speed. Mellor would not catch him.

Suddenly a blur brushed by Mellor's right shoulder. It flew ten feet past him to connect with the back of Parkin's head. There was a dull clunk. Parkin collapsed in a heap. A wedge of firewood, Mellor could see, dropped beside him. Blood poured from the wound it had made. Thorpe had thrown it.

Time returned to normal.

Mellor turned to Thorpe. The giant's two assailants lay beside each other, blood oozing from their ears, the result of their heads having been cracked together. There was no sound in the little barn but the shallow breaths of the woman and the moans of the skewered thug. Mellor crossed to her

"Are you alright?" he asked.

She did not answer. She gathered her torn clothes about herself. She searched to find if her husband was living. Then she looked at Mellor. Her eyes were huge as they gazed upon him. Unsteadily, she stood. Mellor helped her as she tottered to her husband and removed his gag. Mellor untied him. While he did so Thorpe examined their assailants. He reported that all were still breathing. The man and wife held each other closely. What might have been catastrophic had turned extraordinary and both knew it. After a minute the husband spoke.

"I thank you, Sir, for saving us," the farmer said. "Can I help you in any way?"

"We'll borrow your waggon awhile t' take these men off. They'll not bother you again."

"You've saved my Anne ..."

"Don't say it."

"God save you, Sir, as you've saved us," the woman said.

"Who are you?" her husband asked.

George Mellor considered a moment. It dawned upon him that his work in the West Riding could not simply be terror. He had to begin, Mellor thought, this time without the influence of others. Wood, Kentworthy, Weightman and those in Manchester were either too scheming or too abstract. And they were losing.

There were people who remained as they always had: those like Sam Lodge who could not or would not, be *twisted in*. Though mostly passive, they would conspire against the authorities but would do so only if they could feel the trust they had felt before. And they needed something else: a rallying cry, a name to use so they might understand the coming tactics. While on the one hand George Mellor intended on terrifying the middle class, the merchants and even the military with his campaign, on the other he wished to bring hope to those who had none, who would know his rebels were their own folk, acting on their behalf. To begin, he had to begin again. There was only one way for him to tell the farmer who he and Thorpe were.

"Ned Ludd," he said.

And Earl Parkin heard him.

25

WILLIAM THORPE WAS not the most intelligent of men, nor the best looking, nor the most skilled. What he was, was big. Thorpe had always been big. Even as a lad he had towered over his peers. No one had ever mocked him for fear of that bulk and potency. He could lift more, push more, haul more and drink more than any two men in the West Riding and had proven it often enough. But Will Thorpe was a gentle giant, possessed of a kind nature, and among his other fine qualities was the merit of indivisible loyalty.

As a young man he had apprenticed for Charles Fisher's, a finishing shop next to John Wood's at Longroyd Bridge. Fisher had valued the lad even if his work was not quite up to standards. For Thorpe's size and strength allowed him to work longer hours than other men, a benefit to Fisher who, like Wood, lacked the resources to purchase machines.

Thorpe met George Mellor when the latter had returned from sea to become an apprentice cropper. Mellor was no small man either, though smaller and younger by several years than Thorpe. A friendly relationship evolved. Thorpe spent much of his spare time with Mellor. Often times would find them in a public house revelling in dark, strong ale conversing over their cups; that is, George would most often speak and Will would most often listen. When other men would approach their table speaking about loss of work, the *maisters'* greed, starvation and hopelessness ... George Mellor would listen to them, as would Will Thorpe. Though his knowledge was not as sophisticated, it was clear he understood what was happening to his world and what would happen if men did nothing. When William Thorpe was *twisted in* it was not as a buffoon trailing his mentor, but as an informed individual who took the Oath comprehending its meaning.

It is strange yet common how men, simply by meeting others, by choosing certain words and ways, find themselves upon paths neither dreamt of nor anticipated. Thorpe continued to follow George Mellor with that fidelity for which he was known. And Mellor returned his actions by treating him as a trusted lieutenant.

Thorpe felt himself part of something important which might change the way of the world and bring relief to those suffering from its indigence. He admired Mellor. He still did, though in a far different way ... after Rawfolds.

After that event Mellor had changed. Lad no longer, Thorpe sensed a character emerging so at odds with the friend he'd known he hardly knew how to react. The once caring, curious, charismatic George Mellor had become someone dark and dangerous. Thorpe thought it the result of the lost battle, but considered too it had something to do with the Buckworths. Being who he was, he did not speculate. He adjusted.

And then one day Mellor had disappeared, leaving Thorpe curt instructions to maintain the network they'd built. Thorpe tried, but found it beyond his powers. He kept hold of those he knew best: Ben Walker and Thomas Smith, Samuel and James Haigh, Thomas Brook and a few others.

It wasn't long before the first of the strangers had sought him out and, with knowledge of Mellor only *he* would recognize, had issued orders to a startled Will Thorpe. There was to be murder. He was to arrange it according to Mellor's directions. The victim would be William Cartwright in retribution for the Rawfolds raid.

Thorpe gave the job to Walker and Smith as directed. They failed.

That had brought Mellor back. Thorpe was even less sure of this person. The compelling leader who had once commanded with humour and grace, now treated his people as pebbles in some game of *draughts*.

The murder of Horsfall was ruthless, vicious, beyond the pale. After that the two spent their time together as exiles while Mellor studied the chaos of Manchester. Thorpe had stayed close to this new, brittle Mellor in case he might vanish once more and return as some kind of monster. Thorpe gradually, in his own way, became aware of how Mellor had transformed himself because he found himself altered as well.

The fight with Parkin's toughs had bolstered a new sense of identity in Thorpe. They had not only beaten five men, they'd done it with a controlled ferocity. It made him think how alike they'd become. When they had trussed and carted off the five, dumping them in a shallow, muddy pond with dire warnings from Mellor to end their corruption, Thorpe knew the old George Mellor had not completely vanished. There was still some sense of compassion when he chose not to kill them as Thorpe feared he might.

Though nothing in Thorpe's understanding of Mellor approached what he witnessed in Sheffield in early May. It was there he beheld a man truly transformed. A *man*, not a lad, who became a leader. The subtlety both astonished and amazed him.

—

Bare handed fighting has an ancient and storied history. The word *pugilism* comes from a mixture of Greek and Latin. By 688 B.C. boxing was a fixture in the Olympics; fighters wore leather gauntlets from the knuckles to the elbows. By 1812, however, fist fighting had regressed from its golden age to a matter of two men, usually found in the centre of a ring of other men watching, usually in or near a drinking establishment, usually with bets exchanged as they battered each other with their bare fists until one of them could not continue. There was no referee other than the drunken voices of the crowd and no *rounds* between in which the combatants might rest. Kicking, biting and gouging were not allowed; neither was hitting or grabbing below the waist. Most other things were.

At the moment Lloyd, Raynes and a squad of horsemen arrived, Corporal Harald Barrowclough was finishing his opponent with the popular *cross buttock* move, wrestling the man to the ground then falling upon him with all his huge weight after twenty minutes of brutal punishment. His opponent was a pulpy mass. He could not get up. But Barrowclough had not gone unscathed. He too had a bloody nose, a ballooned ear and two eyes nearly swollen shut.

Barrowclough was offered a tankard along with a purse of coins from the publican who had arranged the meet. He was proudly proceeding toward the bar when Lloyd stepped in front of him. Two soldiers, his barracks companions, were with him when this happened. Lloyd presented a writ for Barrowclough's arrest. The two companions thought briefly of battering the smarmy little turd who stood so cockily before them when a glimpse of an officer in the background ended that line of consideration. The officer, Raynes, stepped forward and two hefty dragoons quickly replaced Barrowclough's friends. They manacled his hands behind him, rushed him outside and threw him into the back of a double-horsed *dray* where two more soldiers chained him to its sidewalls. All of them were gone before anyone in the inebriated crowd, except perhaps the publican, could recall what had happened ... a masterpiece of seizure.

Just outside the hillside village of Golcar, Raynes signalled his troop to halt then joined John Lloyd. They spoke quietly in the light of a waxing moon, the heights of the moors stretching purple before them. They found themselves at a crossroad, though not in the physical sense.

"That was fine work, Lloyd, locating the man," Raynes said, smiling.

"Nothing really. A simple investigation turned up the man's propensity for prize fighting. From there it was a matter of questioning the locals, as a tinker, of course."

"And now we hae him."

"We do."

"I suppose we must bring him before Magistrate Radcliffe for arraignment?"

"I'd not be so quick to think so, Raynes. After all, we were tasked with the arrest of Horsfall's murderers. We have nothing yet but a suspected spy. No, I think tonight we shall ride Standedge moor, cross into Lancashire and arraign Barrowclough there. I need to question this man without Radcliffe's interference."

"Aye, the old man does get in the way." Raynes smiled once again though Lloyd had no idea why the captain felt as he did about Radcliffe. Lloyd had a great deal to gain by seeing this investigation through. He did not understand why Raynes was so co-operative, even to the point of crossing their superiors. It troubled him for he could not discover a motive.

"How long will it take?" Lloyd asked.

"With the dray we might make it by tomorrow night."

"Then let us put him on a horse."

"Hae ye had a good look at the man, Mr. Lloyd?" Raynes was concerned. Corporal Harald Barrowclough was a muscled, brutal half-man; the perfect soldier for the army but not such a perfect prisoner. Chaining him had been a fine idea. Unchaining him was not.

"On a horse, how long?" Lloyd said, ignoring Raynes' concerns.

"Riding hard, by morning."

"I see no choice," Lloyd said. "By morning Radcliffe shall be made aware of our action. We have your dragoons, as well, to watch over the hooligan."

"Then by horse it shall be. But ye must keep up, Lloyd."

"I shall. I will. It is in my interest."

Those words quite summed up John Lloyd, Solicitor.

They'd arrived in Sheffield much as they had in Manchester: friendless and unknown. Both Mellor and Thorpe walked into the bustling municipality crossing a bridge on the River Sheaf whose name had given the town one half of its name. The other half came from the Old English *feld*, meaning a forest clearing. Neither man knew it but Sheffield had existed as a place of human habitation far into the distant past. With its situation among flowing rivers to drive water wheels with their power, surrounded by hills containing *ganister* to line ovens, and iron ore to make blades, the town had become a producer of knives and other cutlery as early as the fourteenth century. In the original act of Parliament, the Company of Cutlers was given jurisdiction over: *all persons using to make Knives, Blades, Scissers, Sheeres, Sickles, Cutlery wares and all other wares and manufacture made or wrought of yron and steele, dwelling or inhabiting within the said Lordship and Liberty of Hallamshire, or within six miles compasse of the same.*

The Guild of metal producers was the most powerful faction of the town, the Guild Hall commanding the centre. It was an attractive Georgian three-story building with a delicate cornice running horizontally around the building just at its eaves. The building exuded power.

The town would have a fine future once *crucible steel* was invented but at this time in its history its many forges made Sheffield a filthy place with uncertain prospects. As the two wandered its narrow streets they noted how dark, even black, the limestone of buildings had become through constant use of the forges. There was a subtle rumble about the town, noticed only by those new to Sheffield. It was the vibration of hundreds of grindstones. Yet beneath that rumble was another tremor: the frustration of the exploited.

Mellor insisted they take time to fit in. They sought work in a foundry, their size and strength giving both men jobs, though for small pay and long hours. Mellor, Thorpe noticed, once again became his old self: gregarious, humorous, curious and attentive. For Sheffield too was suffering the effects of the war with France and Parliament's Orders in Council. Its workers were being removed from their jobs unless they accepted less pay.

In a matter of weeks Mellor was a trusted man by others who, Thorpe understood from their talk, were ready to do more than serve the Cutlers. Indeed, with Mellor's persuasions and stratagems these men became confident in their beliefs. Thorpe watched as his friend morphed from jocund companion to the steely creature existing beneath. Thorpe listened as his comrade stirred the pot of rebellion, deployed the pawns of dissent, and turned what had been a tremor into a full-fledged insurgent quake. It was masterful. It was cunning. It was George Mellor working men the way men worked machines. He produced an achievement in only three weeks which Will Thorpe would not have thought possible.

"We'll be moving along tomorrow, Will," Mellor said before they turned in. "I think soon we'll be hearing of riots in these very streets."

"I'm more'n ready t' get on, George. I don't like this place. When we first came, I thought it would be a waste of our time."

"What do you' think now?"

It took Thorpe a minute to try to gather his thoughts. He found it difficult to explain what he wanted to say. All this time he'd realized he'd been watching a leader. If he thought back to that callow lad who had once tried to command a Luddite army, he noted the difference two months had made. The man before him was a weapon of destruction in a different kind of fight. He could not find the words to elucidate it, so in the end he spoke as he normally did.

"I think you're a leader, George, though you've changed."

"And not you, Will?"

"Aye, me as well. I've learned from you, George. I've seen you take men and convince them t' do your bidding. 'Tis a bit frightening."

"'Tis for good reason, Will. When this town bursts, it will bring soldiers running from the West Riding. By then we'll be up there ourselves with little t' stop us."

"As we did with them Parkin lads."

"No, Will. This time it will be the *maisters*. We'll make them so fearful they'll start t' think twice about their bloody machines."

"But we'll not attack the machines themselves?"

"If the Parliament can pass a law giving death to us who break machines, then why not take the *maisters* with us?"

"Murder again."

"Aye. Are you with me, Will? Can I depend on you?"

Again Thorpe was lost for phrases. He wanted so much to be like George Mellor. Yet he could only be what he'd was: the wheel supporting the waggon, the anvil helping the hammer give shape, the loyal man who would never betray his friend.

"I'm with you, George. I'll not fail you."

Mellor was comforted by his friend's constancy. He thought, as well, he had done the necessary to open up his campaign. Now he could manage the West Riding with his stratagem of shock and dread. What he could not know were those forces already in movement which would shred his plans.

The two went north the next day.

—

The dragoons had ridden through the night across the moors which had brought them to Manchester and Barrowclough's arraignment in a civilian court. After that, Raynes had returned with his men to the West Riding. He gave those men the next night free. He did not take it himself. Instead he rode the countryside in search of this Mellor who had previously mattered so little.

He himself was convinced the man was innocent, the only proof of his Luddite involvement the suspicions of Vickerman regarding his stepfather and the deductions of Lloyd about Russia. What it had to do with the Horsfall affair completely eluded him. He himself thought the hatless man was the key. Find that man and *he* would lead to bigger fish.

Those thoughts and a lack of sleep made Raynes more edgy than normal. His mood drew him to contemplations of Fanny. Radcliffe had increased his guards again after the Horsfall murder and had so trapped the lovely Fan that Raynes had had the devil of a time seeing her. He knew she was not happy. Their previous couplings had proven her love and her complaints about the old lecher made it clear she despised him. If only there was a way, he thought, to find freedom together. He began to think of India. The East India Company, he'd heard, would readily accept an experienced officer and then ...

He physically shook his head. He was a realist. Fanny was a dalliance and could be nothing more. He had his own way to make in his career. He had best forget her and move on with his family, however tedious, and achieve for himself the rank he deserved. There was but one way to reach those heights: battle on the continent or the suppression, indeed the destruction, of this irksome insurrection. But he could not advance if he continued reporting up the clumsy chain of command: to Major Gordon then to Colonel Campbell who then reported to General Maitland who finally reported to the Home Secretary. No. He would have to think as John Lloyd thought; find a way to cut out the middle as the aspiring Lloyd had done with Radcliffe. Maitland, he thought should be his objective; better a general as a mentor than a major.

Still there was Fanny whose body he now contemplated. No imagination required, he smiled, as he pictured the lady in various vigorous moments of their love making: her skin near translucent, her hair golden strands, her eyes depthless blue, her actions shameless. An angel with a devil's touch, a lady with a whore's refinements, she was a soldier's dream. His dream. Until he would move on. As soldiers do. If ever this mystery of murder was resolved. If ever he ended this rebellion.

John Lloyd was back to Huddersfield in two days. He'd had Barrowclough for a day and a night. It was all he'd needed; for the tough, resilient soldier and prize fighter, the man who could take punches hard as hammers and give back as much, had broken completely under the delicate torments of Solicitor Lloyd.

Lloyd met Raynes again at the Red Lion. Once more they partook of a noonday meal. Yet this time there was no conjecture, no deduction, no guessing. Lloyd had a list. That list contained confessions extracted from Barrowclough. Lloyd admitted the corporal had been difficult, 'troublesome to take' were his words, but once the man had broken, begging for mercy, crying like a boy, his signed confession was sensational. Raynes tried to ignore the spots of dried blood on the paper as he read it.

"These are his words?" Raynes said, astonished at Lloyd's success.

"Indeed, Captain, every one."

"Ye realize this resolves everything."

"We must ascertain their truth."

"If they are true there's but one way to discover it." Raynes imagined the ramifications.

It was his turn now.

"The military," Lloyd said.

"Ye won't turn this over t' Radcliffe?"

"He and his special constables running about like headless chickens. He would make a proper mess of it."

"Ye're saying ..."

"You have done me the favour with Barrowclough of allowing a civilian arrest, so I might interrogate him. I am returning that favour. Take this to your superiors. You deserve recognition, Raynes. All I ask is to be kept to the forefront of the outcomes."

"Ye hae my word on it," Raynes said, already considering how to reach Maitland in far off Derbyshire.

Not only had Harald Barrowclough named one of Horsfall's murderers, a Luddite named Samuel Haigh, he had also told of French officers training men up on the moors of the Pennines. He also had named fifteen sites where quantities of small arms awaited the uprising of the North. Raynes was excited. Never for a moment did he consider what might have been the ravings of agony.

"I shall arrest Haigh and question him, "Lloyd said. "Meanwhile, these other matters are your line of work. Major Gordon shall be pleased."

"This information is far too significant for the major."

"You intend taking it to Campbell?"

"I intend taking it directly to Maitland."

"Another long ride, Captain Raynes." Lloyd grinned knowingly.

"It is what I do."

He paid for dinner.

26

BEFORE HE COULD travel south to see Maitland, Raynes was directed by Major Gordon to inspect local troops. Apparently General Maitland anticipated an escalation.

So it was his tour of the countryside which convinced Raynes to hurry south to Maitland. In every house he found people living in fear. All had heard of some outrage, threat, or criminal act since Horsfall's death. It placed class against class in a conflict as bitter as it was random. No one knew who would be assailed next, where it would happen or what would be its nature.

In addition to his other intelligence, Raynes took the time to write a personal letter to Maitland in case the general would not see him. In it, he explained how the Watch and Ward groups, the Voluntary Defense Associations and indeed the embedded military were, with the exception of his night riders, nearly useless since the situation had evolved into an asymmetrical struggle. In his letter he concluded: *I fear, Sir, it will be some time before we can break up this lawless band*. It was that simple, telling sentence which stirred into action the commander of all of forces posted to England's North.

—

Lieutenant General the Honourable Thomas Maitland was fifty-two years of age and very much at the height of his powers when he was appointed command. He had had an active and varied career: serving from India to the West Indies. His gentlemanly exterior and effeminate, if slightly aged, good looks concealed a complex individual who was simultaneously bawdy, alcoholic, intelligent and successful. His success was born of his Scots' acumen for understanding the military and comprehending human nature.

Following his initial appointment, Maitland had considered the situation with a certain *ennui.* Maitland was not the type who relished the discomforts of travel, particularly in the gloomy North. He decided, being the man he was, to place his headquarters in Derbyshire, in a spa-town called Buxton. He was well suited to Buxton.

Safely insulated from recent disturbances, Buxton was all the rage to those titled classes who created trends in English culture. An astute Duke of Devonshire had built a number of hotels and spas to exploit the healing properties of the area's hot springs. The town was at the beginnings of its vocation as a medicinal and fashionable centre. John Carr, the architect, had turned the place into a jewel of style. But Maitland was ahead of fashion, particularly during the spring and summer of 1811, when he moved his staff north from London to take up residence in the Great Hotel.

Certain pleasures were embraced by Maitland in Buxton. Coffee houses abounded; candle-lit dances graced the Crescent Ball Room; card assemblies assumed almost compulsive attendance; the best and most popular apothecaries and vendors came north for the season to supply the elite with their medicinal necessities. It promised to be a most worthwhile season.

Second son of the Earl of Lauderdale, Maitland possessed slight concern for the working classes of England. Indeed, other than the occasional glimpse of his infantry, he seldom dealt with anyone beneath officer status. But one thing he did care about in this dangerous time was those aristocratic peers of whom he was one and, almost as much, those wealthy merchants who served them. The murder of the Prime Minister had been solved. It had not been Luddites, apparently, but simply a man with a grudge. Still the killing of Horsfall, a manufacturer, was enough.

And then Captain Francis Raynes had appeared.

Raynes had arrived at Buxton alone, having requested from Gordon a leave of absence. Gordon, a good though perhaps naïve officer, had readily complied. Appearing at the Great Hotel, Raynes was put off by Maitland's second in command, Major General Acland.

Acland was an acerbic man who looked upon the mere captain as a usurper evading the chain of command. It was a cold meeting in which Acland relieved Raynes of his reports and told him to return to his post. Raynes informed Acland he'd been given leave and would stay in Buxton at one of the lesser hotels for a few days' rest. Acland dismissed him with a sniff, a salute and an escort out of the Hotel's premises.

It took ten hours until he was back.

Raynes was recovered by a more than courteous colonel at the small hotel in which he'd taken a room. The colonel returned him to Headquarters at the Great Hotel and, rather than waiting, Raynes was ushered through ranks of various staff officers, suffering the cuts of their envious stares, directly into the presence of Maitland.

Not, actually, the presence ... his escort left him in a room the like of which he'd never encountered. His first impression was of being transported into a white and gold Palladian world. He glanced up at a vaulted ceiling, gold wreathes offset from alabaster held in place by delicate marble columns beneath an equally enriched cornice. In the centre of the vault was a magnificent, glittering tear-drop chandelier. Upon the floor was a huge *Turkey* carpet, white with gold, but augmented by pastels of green and pink. The furniture consisted of three balloon back walnut chairs upholstered in snowy white and a gold silk damasked divan perched upon delicate chestnut legs. A small, ornate table polished to a gleam stood upon ball and claw feet between the divan and a fourth chair, this one straight backed and made of oak.

Other pieces lined the room's walls but Raynes had no time to examine them as a door opened and through it strode Major General Acland, militarily erect, accompanied by his complete contrast: a handsome older man, effeminate in a way, who carried in his hands Raynes' report and languidly took a seat upon the divan. It was clear to Raynes who this was. He snapped to attention.

"Tak' your ease, Captain." Maitland's accent gave Raynes new hope. The man was a fellow Scot. "This chair." Maitland gestured to the hard oak beside him. Acland too sat, but on an upholstered piece across the carpet from his general. Clearly Maitland wished to keep the meeting informal. He placed a leg up on the divan, his black polished riding boot glinting in the morning sun reaching in through the windows. Raynes remained rigid in his hard chair.

"Now then, Captain," Maitland said, his voice mellifluous and clear, "it seems you've travelled some distance to see me. This work you've brought is outstanding. Yet I have one question. What are you; that is you *personally* doing here?"

Raynes had anticipated the question.

"I felt the information so significant, Sir, I deemed it surpassed the normal progression of command. My superiors, General, must co-operate with civic authorities and in my opinion, that melding of military and magistracy hae created confusion in the West Riding."

"Your point, Captain?" Acland said.

"Yes, Sir. I was certain the information would create panic among those civil authorities without some direction imposed from your Headquarters."

"I see," Maitland said, smiling. "What is your opinion of Major Gordon?"

"I surely cannot speculate upon my superiors, General."

"Indeed. And yet here you are, having bypassed both the major and Colonel Campbell."

"I apologize, Sir. As ye see, this information was unearthed by a Solicitor. John Lloyd by name. He and I hae been tasked with investigating the murder of a Mr. Horsfall. Mr. Lloyd also saw this material's potential and offered me time to provide it to ye."

"This Lloyd seems a trifle ambitious," Maitland said, "as do you, Captain."

"Perhaps I hae made a mistake in coming, General." Raynes stood to attention.

"Alright, Captain. I understand your motives. Are you standing now to show respect or simply because you want out of that God awful chair?"

The laughter of his two superiors confused Francis Raynes. This was not at all as he'd foreseen it. The meeting was to have made his reputation, provided the stepping stone to his career. Now, it seemed, Maitland belittled him. He remained at attention and fixed his gaze on a Grecian vase placed serenely upon a games table opposite him.

"Captain Raynes." Maitland's voice softened. "I beg you to take a seat. No, not that one. You are not on trial here. Indeed, I commend your initiative. And, it seems, your major has no qualms in his praise of you."

"Sir?" Raynes said.

"Nothing less than the best! That is how he reports you. I've read of your tireless night rides. Major Gordon is your most enthusiastic supporter. I'm beginning to see why."

"Sir?"

"We fellow Scots must stick together, eh? You remind me, Captain, much of myself when I was your age. You may have bypassed protocol but in this case I think you might be commended. Something is brewing, Raynes. Though I think currently there is no bottom to it despite references to this General Ludd. Perhaps it *is* the French, in hiding. I am going to send you back, Captain, with additional men to search out those arms caches. While you accomplish that task your cavalry will serve as my right flank while I move on Manchester. We must quell this business swiftly."

"Thank you, Sir"

He took a seat across from Maitland; this time an upholstered one.

"Your patrols help alleviate anxieties in the West Riding. I like that. People must see us as saviours, Raynes, for what I will do in Manchester shall appear somewhat callous."

"I shall be proud to continue my work, Sir."

"Should it go as well as it has, Captain, you may find yourself filling a staff position in future. Now, why don't you stay to lunch? Do you like pigeon pie? This establishment makes the best I've encountered."

"I thank ye, Sir, and look forward to it."

"I thought you might."

—

Maitland advanced into riot torn Manchester by mid-May. His methods were brutal. Having quelled the disturbances within weeks, he left an occupation force and continued with seven thousand men on into the West Riding. Suddenly the district was smothered in soldiers: the red coats of his infantry, the flashing brass of his cavalry, the jangling harness of his artillery and the strange shapes of his rocket detachment were inspiring. They were meant to be. His purpose was less to subdue the rebels, whom he had only just begun to take seriously, than it was to reassure the frightened classes he cared for.

In more northern districts he'd committed further forces. In short order, no less than thirty-five thousand soldiers were stationed in England's north; more than the number posted with Wellesley in Portugal fighting Napoleon. Parliament could not permit even a whiff of rebellion and the Crown, more than any, felt memories of the French revolution.

Yet Maitland's forces found few places to strike for, particularly in the West Riding, the upheaval seemed a chaos. Bunches of disgruntled commoners made vicious threats, beating certain people, vandalizing their property. There seemed nothing for Maitland's forces to do but enhance Raynes' night rides, further garrison villages, and assist Radcliffe in harvesting men for interrogations.

Then, unaccountably, Sheffield blew up in a series of riots. Maitland shifted his mobile troops south. Cavalry best handled rioters so most of his horsemen were posted to Sheffield. Raynes, to his annoyance, was left once more with a paltry few.

It was Maitland's way of informing him he'd failed.

As it turned out Barrowclough's information, his wild claims brought on by the anguish of torture, were but creations of his imagination. Raynes found no weapons, no French officers, nothing. Lloyd had botched things with his brutality.

But one thing did come of Raynes' night rides, and from a surprising quarter.

By the meagre light of an old moon, its silver crescent glowing through mist, Raynes and his dragoon squadron were pressed to a slow pace across Meltham moor. They travelled with muffled harness keeping the silence of the night heath until they heard, distantly, sounds of command. Raynes ascertained the direction and after ten minutes the troop had reached a clough in the moor.

On the ridge overlooking it, they stared down at torches moving through the dark. Each of those torches represented men marching and counter-marching down in the valley. They shambled and stumbled in a confusion of movement. The man shouting commands was, from the sound of his accent, no Frenchman at all but an upland farmer who appeared to know even less than his charges. Raynes sent a section of his men south to come around the group trapping their escape while he rode north until he discovered a descent for the horses: a standard hammer and anvil manoeuvre.

Once reaching the clough's bottom the dragoons followed a stream until the valley opened out. As soon as they saw soldiers, the buffoons scattered in panic up the steep sides or down the clough's course only to be met by Raynes' anvil. For a time it was a mad house: men running helter skelter to escape, soldiers chasing them down with their horses. In the end Raynes held the captured leader and eighteen others. Their torches now in the hands of soldiers, they stood in a single line.

The captain had two of his hefty dragoons haul the leader before him. Raynes sat his horse, glaring down for effect.

"What is your name?"

"I've no name I'll give you," the man answered.

"We'll see about that," Raynes replied. He turned to his sergeant. "Sutcliffe, draw your pistol. Let's see how this fellow does with an arm shot off."

"No, Sir!" the man said. "I'm a farmer."

"It seems to me ye were training men. Ye hae military experience?"

"I was a cook in the Durham militia. But that was twenty years ago."

"Your name?"

"Sam Holmes, Sir. What's t' become of me?"

At that moment Raynes began an interrogation far more significant than the arrest itself. Perhaps he had seen something cloaked in his prisoner's face. Perhaps he'd simply been bored with the obvious. Later, when his questions led him to the true murderers, he would wonder at this strange instant, at his luck that it should happen to him seemingly from nowhere. Life was a mystery.

"Were ye at Rawfolds mill?" he asked.

"I don't know what you mean, Sir."

"Of course ye do. Sutcliffe, cock your piece."

The sergeant did so, the sound of his pistol's hammer snapping the night air metallically. Holmes tried to shy away. The pistol went to his shoulder. A ball fired that close and he would lose his arm. His face drained of colour.

"Aye, I was there," he said.

"Who led that attack?"

"I can't say. All the men used numbers t' identify themselves. It would mean my death should I hazard a guess. There's an Oath, you know."

"I won't kill ye, Holmes, but you'll hae no arm. An owner's hat was discovered at Rawfolds. What do ye know of that?" Raynes questioned, the gun pushed at the man's shoulder, for a moment there was only terrified panting, then came the astounding response.

"Alright! Alright! The hat!" Holmes cried.

"As I said." Raynes played calm, yet his stomach leapt to his throat.

"The one found in the pond! That hat was Thomas Brook's! Thomas was with the man that night who might have been the leader! I'm not sure. I know Thomas lost his hat!"

"And where is this Brook?"

"I can't be sure."

Raynes would not let him retract. He dismounted, standing face to face with the prisoner. His instincts, it proved, were correct.

"No one need hear, Holmes. Just whisper to me. Now where is Brook?"

"As I said, Sir ..."

"How would a spell in Milnsbridge House do? Ye've heard of Solicitor Lloyd."

"Not that, Sir. Please!"

"Then answer me."

"He's been keeping low since Rawfolds. He knows he was seen without his hat."

"Which of these men knows Brook? Quick now."

"I told you, Sir, I don't know nothing more!"

A nod and Sutcliffe fired. The noise drove an animal scream from Holmes but it was more terror than pain. Sutcliffe had shot past his ear. A ploy. It deafened the man while infusing shock. In the seconds before he realized he wasn't wounded he'd blurted the answer.

"Hardgrave!" Holmes sobbed. "Peter Hardgrave! He knows Brook! And John Wood too, another *maister*!"

The dragoons dropped Holmes. Raynes stepped around him, addressing the others.

"Peter Hardgrave, step forward!" Raynes commanded.

A large man did so. He seemed less fearful than Holmes. Without an escort he strode directly to Raynes. When his face was revealed by the torches his eyes were like burning coals. Raynes had no doubt that given the chance this man would kill him. Again he asked the question of Brook's whereabouts.

"Should you want t' know of Tom Brook, best ask north of here. I'll say no more."

But Raynes knew he would. He had the prisoners roped together and marched through the night to Milnsbridge House, to Lloyd. He hoped Lloyd would draw even more information using his talents but sent him a note cautioning too much torture. He wanted no repeat of Barrowclough.

That night's good fortune had reassured Raynes.

It should have.

By pure circumstance George Mellor had, that very night, arrived from Sheffield. The true terror was about to begin and the chase was already on.

Maitland's moves had produced a new sense of security. It relieved society of its anxieties and offered instead other pastimes. Indeed, the number of officers available made the social season of 1812 a tremendous success. Dozens of eligible men vied for the hands of local maids in festivities fashioned by families both to enhance their reputations and divest themselves of their marriageable daughters. Maitland encouraged them. He was a general who enjoyed a good party.

For the likes of Fanny Radcliffe, Anita Cooke, Julia Fairhead, and Maria Bronte, it was a time of pure bliss. New dresses were purchased, homes cleaned, manners dusted and foods and wines previously untasted were imported into the district. Radcliffe, as magistrate, though not a man to enjoy revelry, found himself forced both to attend and produce balls, banquets, evenings of cards and so on. Fanny, on the other hand, danced through a dream and, an added windfall, found more times to conduct her affair with the sensual and increasingly famous Captain Raynes.

Milnsbridge House was in full fettle that June. A garden party featured the best people of the West Riding. There were at least fifty ladies and gentlemen present, including several young officers and even more available damsels. They were dressed in their best, most fashionable attire: buttons gleaming, fabrics rustling, shoes and boots polished to a shine. Their smiles luminous, each and every guest was pleased to be there. They matched the liveliness of the gardens in bloom, a carpet of colours just receding as daylight faded; replaced by lanterns. If anyone noted the Stirlingshire guards placed at strategic positions, so glittering in their dress uniforms, so martial in their disciplined silence, he or she thought them merely added décor rather than essential security.

Most guests stayed on the terrace at the rear of the house, bathed in the glow emanating from its windows and perhaps, subconsciously, nearest the majority of the guards. Joseph Radcliffe had engaged a quartet who had played through the afternoon and, following their suppers, continued in fine form so the younger people might dance. If there was any discord found in this harmony it was Radcliffe himself who, after a tiring day of greeting visitors, was currently missing his vivacious wife. She, who had spent the afternoon shining with joy, the centre of attention, *doyenne* of the entire affair, had vanished somewhere. Radcliffe was disconcerted.

"Where is the girl?" he said to Wilbert Shaw, as though it were the footman's responsibility.

"I've no idea, Sir, though she may have taken a turn in the gardens. I'm sure she'll return shortly."

"She's not one to miss a dance," Radcliffe said. "Take a look, Shaw? Perhaps you might find her."

"Of course, Magistrate."

The footman sketched a slight bow. Radcliffe's suggestion had set poor Shaw upon an Odyssey. Milnsbridge's grounds were a maze of pathways. Some wended their ways past ponds and over streams, others delved into shaded woods, and still others opened into theatres of floral splendour. He mumbled to himself why it should be he and not one of the younger servants sent upon such a mission.

Deep in the woods, just by the rushing watercourse wending through Milnsbridge garden, lay an enclosed gazebo. It was occupied by Fanny Radcliffe and Francis Raynes, both dishevelled from their efforts, both sated with the outcome. They lay upon a wooden divan entwined in each other's arms. Both would have liked to remain but with the growing dark, knew they would be missed. Raynes was the first to stand, pulling up his trousers. He felt trousers made him a more modern man.

"We must return, my dear," he said softly to Fanny, his hand extending to help her rise. On this fine June evening she wore an ivory coloured dress, high-waisted to accentuate her breasts, almost translucent in moonlight, almost Grecian with its soft muslin. She straightened it once he had helped her up. When she'd finished there were tears in her eyes. He thought immediately: *Not again*. He wished to turn away, repulsed by her recent penchant for weeping, but her voice prevented him.

"I'm sorry, Francis."

"But why are you crying now, my dear?"

"Because of the old man's power over me. Do you know I have two personal guards posted with me every day now?"

"Not this day," Raynes said, smiling.

"No, today he's more worried about some silly attack ruining his party."

"I only wish I could free ye."

He rendered the words she expected.

"Why can't you? You speak of it, yet you do nothing."

"What would ye have me do, Fanny dear? Ye know I'm ..."

"You are married. I'm sick of hearing it! You once told me of India ..."

"Fan, ye know even there we'd not escape the shame."

"Shame? You call this shame, Francis?"

"Of course not, my dearest, but others would."

"Perhaps we should end this. Oh, Francis, what shall we do?"

Francis Raynes had no answer. Indeed, the thought of ending their affair was most tantalizing to him. Now he'd met Maitland, set his career upon its path and become an advisor to the general, he'd begun to wonder at his own foolishness. If he should be caught, what then? Ignominy. Court martial at least. He felt a chill run up his spine.

He had come, as well, to resent these interludes which perpetually ended in tears. His wife, Anne, did not cry, did not whimper like a child over things which could not be undone. He was weary of Fanny's blubbering protestations, her silly dreams, and her yapping dog. He grimaced to think of the risks which she, in her immaturity, discounted. It was time, he knew, to end it.

Still wondering what he could do about her, Raynes led Fanny back up the path toward the house when Shaw came into sight. Hoping the footman had noticed nothing Raynes broke away, finding another path branching off. As Shaw arrived Raynes had almost disappeared.

Almost.

"Are you well, Ma'am?" Shaw asked, carefully noting the departure.

"Of course, Shaw. I twisted my ankle up the path. Captain Raynes ... Where is he? The captain assisted me but seeing you, well, I suppose he knows I'm in good hands."

The clumsiness of her lie was an insult yet Shaw retained his customary aplomb. He was familiar with human foibles. He never forgot a single one. No telling when he could use it.

"May I take your arm, Ma'am? I'll assist you to the house. Your maid can look at the ankle."

"No, Shaw. I wish to return to the dance. My ankle has much recovered."

"Very well, Ma'am." Shaw turned and led the way.

As the silent man always in the room and ready to serve, Wilbert Shaw had overheard many morsels of information. One of those fragments was a description of Captain Raynes' responsibilities regarding the Luddites. That knowledge, coupled with what Shaw now suspected, would make interesting news for certain people who needed what help they could get. Shaw's youngest brother had been wounded at Rawfolds.

The next day he sent for his brother and told him to find Will Thorpe, a boyhood friend of Shaw's who had also been at Rawfolds. The two had been called Wil and Will in their early years in Wakefield. Shaw, a slight but schooled lad, had gone into service; Thorpe, big and muscular, became a cropper. Shaw knew Thorpe had a friend named George Mellor ... that very same Mellor who'd been mentioned in the meeting at Milnsbridge House earlier in spring.

27

MESSAGE FROM THE Leicester secretary of the local committee for Watch and Ward, to The Right Honourable Richard Ryder, Home Secretary:

Sir:

I have been informed that a Mr. Trantham Hosier of Nottn was shot on Monday night at his own door, report says that on Saturday last he docked his hands twopence per pair and told them to tell Ned Ludd. How true this may be I know not, certain it is that this is not a proper time to irritate the public mind by gross insult. The Parliamentary Committee examining the Bill regarding the capitol penalty for machine breaking should consider this murder in its deliberations. More masters are likely to be targeted if the legislation is not rescinded.

Message delivered.

—

They began the way he'd been taught by Baines. Once back in the West Riding, Mellor and Thorpe went separate ways in order to cover more territory, meeting every week to compare notes. Each would recruit those *twisted in* previously and therefore most likely to be trusted. They stayed north of the High Peak district, going only as far south as Glossop in the west and Holmfirth to the south east. They stayed away from Barnsley thinking it too close to Sheffield and the troops there. Then they would retreat through the canal back to Diggle, avoiding roving patrols.

They had even recruited young Willis Brookbank who, away from the influence of his father, had lost weight and become an ally. He continued writing letters to his father informing of his health, though he chose not return home. He remained on the Diggle side where he'd met a girl who would not have met with his father's approval, but certainly did his.

In the West Riding the men recruited were confined to small groups. This was an asymmetrical insurgence; the few against the many. Their strikes would be mere pinpricks though with enough of them, and those accomplished successfully, they would be lethal.

They left the common people alone but the middle classes were prey to them: merchants, small masters, minor officials and at times when opportunity presented, those of the more elite classes occasionally left unguarded. The coinage they purloined was, of course, to keep them fed and equipped.

Forays were made against those seeking profit from penury. One after another the swindlers were brought into line. Should illegal gangs interfere they were dealt with harshly. Men were crippled, others disfigured. The banditry stopped, but not the Luddites. That fear which Mellor had sought to instill began once more to infect the wealthy, while helping the poor and out of work.

Robin Hood indeed.

Next they went after authority figures: special constables, Watch and Ward chiefs, and then even land owners, magistrates and army officers. They employed missives which would inform their victims they'd become targets. That was the terror. No one knew when and where the strikes would next come.

—

Solomon Law had come a long way to meet two strangers from Huddersfield. The descriptions provided by Thorpe had been accurate. John Kinder was a tall, thin weaver and Joseph Fisher, from his solid build, a cropper. Both men had glanced up when Law entered the Shears, expecting him. They had received his description from Mellor. Law had been a soldier once, having fought in Egypt against Napoleon.

This act upon which he was engaged would employ Law's particular experience. They ate their suppers and waited for dark, then left and made their way to Huddersfield Cloth Hall. This night they would make a symbol of it.

"Did you bring the powder?" Law asked of Kinder, once they had arrived.

"Aye. And Joe here has the fuse."

"Good then. Give me both and gather some kindling t' burn once this goes up."

The men did as ordered while Law assembled his explosive. He was ready when the two had returned with wooden pallets they'd found in the market. They piled them around the back entrance to the Cloth Hall. The powder would blow the doors and the resulting fire would catch what materials remained in the hall.

Law's flint and steel lit the fuse. The men walked away into shadows. They waited until a huge *whompf* filled the night. They could see fire burning. Fortunately for the Cloth Hall, the fire caught on the pallets but burned itself out. The powder had not blown the door. Still ...

Message delivered.

—

Longley Old Hall, once the Manor of Almondbury, had been purchased during the Civil War and since been home to the Ramsden family; though none were living there now. When the West Riding's troubles increased it had been offered to General Maitland. With the need to depart his treasured Buxton in order to more closely command his forces, Maitland had moved in and Longley became headquarters. Even in summer it was a musty edifice. After Buxton, Maitland loathed the place. But while there, he poured his every endeavour into ending the series of actions infecting the West Riding on the heels of Sheffield's sudden riots.

Tempers were high that day in Longley Old Hall's library. Lloyd and Raynes had circumvented their seniors having reported directly to Maitland. Clearly Raynes had ignored the chain of command but Lloyd too had overstepped his place by not informing Radcliffe of Barrowclough's revelations. The older men were outraged though their juniors were not at all contrite despite the fact that their information had proven useless.

"So you are telling me, Raynes, you've found *nothing* out on the moors?" Maitland maintained a cool calm amidst the ire of the others. "There have been no weapons caches, no French officers?"

"Unfortunately, Sir, that is correct. Mr. Lloyd's findings hae proven false."

"You yourself, Captain, approved of them," Lloyd said.

To Maitland, he did not seem as trustworthy as Raynes apparently thought him to be. Maitland made a mental note to be wary of this little man with the scheming mind.

"You've achieved no results in all this time!" Radcliffe said, his face turning to purple, jowls shaking.

Maitland worried about apoplexy.

"That is not true, Sir," Lloyd said. "What of my work on Bradley Mills ..."

"Ah yes, and your *tinkering* about the countryside! You wanted control of this investigation, Lloyd, and I allowed it. Where has it got us? I was not even informed of this erroneous intelligence! I assure you, should I have been, I would have seen its irrationality and saved Captain Raynes days of wild goose chase!"

"Which Captain Raynes fully deserved," Major Gordon said. "General, he and Lloyd have deliberately conspired to evade their responsibilities to their superiors in pursuit of personal glory!"

"I agree, Major," Campbell said gruffly. "Though I believe it is your duty, Major, to anticipate incorrect conduct among your officers."

"You have a suggestion, Colonel, to mitigate this situation?" Maitland asked.

"Captain Raynes should be broken to ranks, General! There is no place in the King's army for the likes of him!"

"Sir, if I may ..." Raynes said.

"You may not, Sir!" Campbell said, stridently. "You shall speak to a superior officer only when spoken to, or have you forgotten *that* protocol as well!"

Maitland, who was enjoying himself watching this quarrel of minions, decided to allow its continuance. He had his own plan for these men, but required them to possess clear heads when he presented it. The current release of emotion might accomplish his needs without his interference. Maitland, though he loved indolence, was an experienced man who knew how and when to manipulate.

"I should like to hear the captain's explanation, Colonel," he said. "It was I, after all, who sanctioned his actions, thinking him a prodigy. Go ahead, Raynes."

"Sir!" Raynes stood to rigid attention. "I admit I should not hae overstepped my place and taken this information to ye, but it seemed so convincing at the time. I believed Mr. Lloyd, Sir, and was fooled as much as anyone."

"That is not exactly true," Lloyd said in his unctuous voice; always soft, always greasy. "When the captain and I compared notes, he agreed with my conclusions. How was I to know Barrowclough was a liar?"

"He lied because you tortured him!" Radcliffe shouted.

The man was near to a fit.

"I employed methods you have sanctioned," Lloyd said.

"I believe Captain Raynes was speaking." Maitland dismissed the hopes of the nasty little man by stopping his argument. "We have already heard of your failings, Lloyd."

"I can only appeal to ye, General," Raynes said, "with my record of achievement. It was I who created the flying squadrons which hae prevented more damage. It was *my* work every night, and much of it at my private expense, to search out and curtail the rebels. And I hae placed myself in personal danger in order to quell what I've come across."

"You've betrayed us, Raynes," Gordon said sorrowfully. Unlike Campbell, beneath his military exterior he was a kind man who valued his captain's efforts, though he did feel troubled the man in whom he'd placed his trust would dupe him.

"Gentlemen," Maitland said, "the enemy is not us, but Luddites. Let us sit, take some tea, and settle ourselves. I want no more accusations. There are certain objectives which must be achieved and only we, working together, can facilitate them."

"I see no need for the inclusion of underlings in this meeting," Radcliffe said, still shaking.

"Nevertheless, Magistrate, these men have been closest to the action and vigorous in their investigations. We need their perceptions."

"Lloyd is a scoundrel, General!" Radcliffe said.

"I shall brook no more of this, Radcliffe!" Maitland raised his voice slightly, subtracting Radcliffe's title to get the man's attention. "Am I being perfectly clear?"

Silence, a pause, Radcliffe grasped a chair to remain upright.

"Indeed, Sir," he answered, then sat down heavily.

"Good then."

Thomas Smith had always been accurate with firearms. From his youth hunting rabbits he'd learned the skill. Often his kill was the only food for the stock pot bubbling in the family cottage. His father had injured himself at millwork and was crippled. Thomas, as he grew older, had tried to take his father's place. That was when he'd met George Mellor. That was why he now peered through a hedge into the parlour window of Patrick Bronte.

Smith had nothing against the curate but his orders were clear. Bronte was no friend to the Movement. Smith was to frighten the curate who had been boasting lately of witnessing men marching to Rawfolds mill. Mellor, Smith surmised, wanted to show up Bronte for what he was: a loud mouthed weakling.

Smith saw Bronte through the window, entering his parlour. He carried a large book, likely his Bible. Smith primed his weapon. He aimed, not at the curate but at the lamp Bronte had set upon a table. His shot would not kill the man but it might start a fire by smashing the lamp.

Just as he took aim, the hammer pulled back, finger squeezing the trigger, he caught a glimpse of a second figure. It was too late. His action already in motion, the gun fired. The ball smashed through leaded glass and into the oil lamp, the lamp exploding in flames. He saw then the figure was a woman. Bronte's wife.

He could hear her scream. The table cloth caught fire, then the Bible which Bronte had dropped. Smith had not intended burning down their house. A maid entered with a bucket. She sloshed water over the fiery table. The room went dark ... a small glow from embers. Thomas Smith backed out of the hedge and departed.

Message delivered.

—

"Now take your seats," Maitland said, having eased the charged mood in the room. "I have proposals to offer in the wake of our recent failure. We need to co-operate, gentlemen, to render the West Riding under our control. As it stands that is not the case."

"General," Lloyd said, "it seems they have all gone to ground. I hear little."

"And my rides hae turned up nothing of late, Sir," Raynes said.

"The prisoners are not talking," Radcliffe said.

"And yet I have heard on my travels," Campbell said, "of new atrocities. They operate in small groups. If anything, they are *more* organized."

"It seems none of us has an answer," Radcliffe said.

"And so we must find one," Maitland said.

"Our sources have dried up," Lloyd said.

"Then we shall create new ones!" Maitland said, smiling. It was always positive when a general officer possessed stratagems beyond his subordinates. "But first some luncheon." He signalled vaguely to his servant.

—

Special constable Elvin Wilkinson was a good sized man. He enjoyed the power his size and rank offered him. People lived in fear of Wilkinson. How often was he tendered a free mug of ale at the nearby King's Head? How frequently at market was his wife provided choice cuts of beef, bags of vegetables, even the occasional trinket? And all Wilkinson had to do was employ his power. He did so with relish. Should a man threaten him personally the penalty would be prison or transportation: assault of an officer of the law. Wilkinson was content with that, with his life, with his modicum of power.

Thus, it did not occur to him that the young man before him would do anything other than passively surrender. He'd demanded the man's name. It was not given. When Wilkinson attempted an arrest, the man rounded on him. Wilkinson had his club ready. He struck the youth, but the cudgel seemed to bounce off him. Then fists came at Wilkinson. The first stunned him into blind, shocked submission, the next hammered him into a whimpering lump. There was a boot to his gut. He lost his air. He thought he would die. Yet he could hear a voice above him.

"You are finished, Elvin my lad, with your bullying. Dost hear me? You'll no longer be a constable, by command of General Ludd. Tomorrow you'll meet Radcliffe and resign. No more law for you, Elvin, or I'll be back and not so gentle. Dost hear? Stop up your tears and be sure t' take what I've told you t' him, when you resign."

Message delivered.

Luncheon complete, litter cleared away, both Campbell and Maitland stood at the end of the table. Maitland's minions, now filled with baked pigeon and chine of mutton as well as two delicacies of artichoke and French beans, were in brighter spirits, though it was hard to tell with Lloyd.

"As I mentioned, gentlemen," Maitland said, "if indeed we have no intelligence then we must make our own from what we have learned. Let us put our heads together and arrive at a list, a dossier shall we say, of potential suspects and sympathizers to Luddism. What say you, Sirs?"

Their anger assuaged by the sharing of food, each man had a great deal to say. They sounded like a gaggle of geese honking names upon names of men. Maitland could not help secretly feel they mimicked the style of the Inquisition of so many years before.

"A man named James Starkey," Lloyd said, "told me not two weeks ago of a plot to blow up Cartwright's mill. It turned out to be false, though I could not but note the man seemed to believe it. I've heard too of a younger man named John Dean and had him traced. He seems connected."

"There's a fellow named Solomon Law," Raynes said, not to be outdone. "Former soldier. Seen in Huddersfield the night of the Cloth Hall incendiary."

"And what of John Wood from Longroyd?" Radcliffe said. "I hear more and more often of activity up that way."

"I agree with you," Campbell said. "Around Dungeon Wood where Horsfall was killed. Let me think now: a John Kinder, another named Benjamin Walker, then Wood's step-son, George Mellor. Joe Mellor, a cousin, has a house near there as well."

"Of course! Fisher's shop!" Lloyd said. "Let me see, there was a man named Schofield, and another, huge man whose name I cannot recall ..."

"I have another," Raynes said, "A fellow named Brook. Small owner. He lost a hat, I believe, at Rawfolds and may have been a leader. Lloyd and I have been trying to find him."

"There are more as well, "Lloyd said. "John Baines of Halifax, his son Zachariah, one Thomas Smith, and a low life by the name of Sam Lodge."

"I have a roll of rogues as well!" Radcliffe said, not to be outdone.

"We must list these names while they still remain fresh," Maitland said. "We must not confuse them. Corporal! Pen, ink and paper. Lloyd, perhaps you would do the honours."

"Of course, General." The solicitor was accomplished at creating documents and even better at organizing them. Within an hour a list was scribbled. Within a week, a cloth bound, alphabetically indexed book was produced by Lloyd.

—

"One final piece of business, gentlemen," Maitland said.

"What might that be?" Radcliffe asked.

"A way to make this dossier work for us," the general said. "I am about to propose something radical, gentlemen," Maitland paused for effect. "I believe it is time we invoked an official pardon. Do you understand? A pardon for those who reject their Oaths. I believe they call it being *twisted in*. I propose we *untwist* any who appear before us voluntarily, offering them a script ascribing to such and paying each a guinea."

"That would have a strong effect," Major Gordon said.

"But there will be retaliations," Lloyd said. "This type of action could stir the Ludds to further aggression."

"Yes, but against their own people, don't you see?" Maitland said. He had thought this through carefully. "And if they do they shall turn those people against them. If they've nowhere to hide, we shall have them!"

"Splendid, General!" Raynes said.

"There is something else, however," Maitland said, "I should like to discuss with you Lloyd and you as well Radcliffe — your methods of interrogation." Maitland turned sombre. "It seems you may have broken the law by holding men without regard for *habeas corpus*."

Lloyd said nothing. Radcliffe as well. They knew they had stretched the rule of law.

Radcliffe recovered with a lighter note: "We shall be seen as *merciful*, as Vicar Roberson would say."

"By the by, where has that man got to?" Major Gordon inquired.

He still had no inkling what had happened at the Star Inn.

"He's begun building a boys' school beside Healds Hall, his Vicarage," Radcliffe said.

"I haven't seen him since before Rawfolds. Are you sure he's not ill?" Gordon said.

"In a way," John Lloyd said. "He was a soft man even for a vicar."

Message delivered.

28

THE MEETING COMPLETED, the men gathered their belongings. Raynes donned dragoons' overalls. He would be escorting Lloyd to Halifax and Colonel Campbell to his former headquarters in Leeds. Having delivered his charges Raynes would continue his quest in search of George Mellor, who seemed nothing less than a ghost. He was impatient to depart.

Radcliffe lingered, looking forward to supper with General Maitland. The magistrate and his wife were being given most regal treatment by Maitland who had caught a glimpse of Fanny. Maitland was a connoisseur of foods, wines and women and, from what he had seen, Mrs. Radcliffe was worthy of his attention.

As Gordon left the library, he was accosted by Acland. In a few moments Major Gordon, pale as a corpse, walked slowly, though erect and dignified, down the hallway leading to one of Longley's more discreet exits. From there he would begin his journey home. Though not demoted, he had been informed his command was finished. He had proven ineffectual and was to be given work in supply, in Scotland, far from war or rebellion.

Major James Gordon departed the field without complaint and lived the rest of his life happily. He found peace in a simpler world.

The others would find no such measure.

—

As he departed, Raynes caught sight of Fanny. She did not notice him. She was busy inspecting a new *curricle*: the two wheeled gig all the rage among her set. It was a sporty vehicle, perfect for excursions to town; the latest present from her generous husband.

Over time, Raynes had developed certain negative feelings toward his once lovely Fan. She too, he could tell, had become disenchanted. It had sickened him, as well, to be sharing her with an old man.

He had work to do now: important work which would lead to promotion. Clearly, despite his brief dressing down from Maitland, he was valued. Raynes had a bright future. He decided in that instant he would no longer dawdle with the magistrate's wife.

—

On the road Raynes rode beside Lloyd as the two conferred on tactics.

"Tell me again, Lloyd, why Halifax?" Raynes asked.

He'd had little time to speak with his partner the past few days.

"Barrowclough's confession."

Lloyd was furious at Raynes' desertion upon the Barrowclough failure.

"But surely ye know he was lying," Raynes said.

"Just before he broke down he named names: Charles Milnes, John Baines and his son, Zachariah, from Halifax."

"What of Brook, the lost hat? Should I arrest him?"

"I am beyond that. I know John Baines has delivered the Oath. He is a Ludd leader."

Lloyd's intensity excited Raynes. Finally there was progress. He hoped for a way to include himself, steal some success; be noticed.

"These men are killers. Ye'll need a guard. My dragoons ..."

"I've my own arrangements. Your soldiers are much too obvious. This time I've hired a bodyguard. I've used him before. His name is M'Donald."

"Sturdy man?"

"Good in a corner. What of your search for Mellor?"

Lloyd had put him off. Raynes was disappointed.

"Nothing thus far, I'm afraid. I shall find Brook."

"This Halifax business takes precedence."

"I salute your daring. Be sure you're careful."

"Do I detect a note of concern, Captain?"

It was as if he could read Raynes' mind. The two had come to depend on each other. Both clearly knew they used each other for their own ambitions.

As the sun set the squadron trotted through the greens and golds of the fields around them. Then gray twilight faded the colours. An evening star blinked in the east. With only brief rests for the horses, the squadron made good time. When they neared Halifax, Raynes steered his troop and the colonel toward Leeds while the slight, dark shadow which was John Lloyd vanished into the night. Raynes reflected a while on the man. So obnoxious in so many ways, so ugly in person and mannerisms, so vicious as an interrogator; yet John Lloyd was an enterprising partner. In the normal state of affairs Raynes would have despised him, yet he found he admired Lloyd's skills.

Raynes dropped back to join Colonel Campbell and his aide, Lieutenant Sutherland. The colonel was in a good mood, enjoying himself. His horse was a fine Irish gelding. His attire was civilian: rust breeches and a grey hacking jacket. The colonel was a devoted hunter. He had ridden with the Quorn, the Cottesmore, the Belvoir, and the Pytchley hunts, though there were others in Yorkshire where, it was said, the practice of the hunt had actually begun.

It was said Arthur Wellesley did not like Campbell, finding him common and ill mannered. Sutherland, Raynes had heard, was a different story: educated, mannered, noble. The lad should have been in Portugal. Wellesley had even requested him. His family, however, was overprotective of a beloved son and had preferred his posting to England's north, far from Napoleon's guns.

"A good squadron, Captain!" Campbell said. "Fine order!"

"They're good men, Sir," Raynes replied.

"I should like to see them afield!"

"I'm afraid this night we must stay to the turnpike, Colonel. We've orders to hae ye home to Leeds before dawn."

"At this pace you shall. This gelding I ride, a superior animal."

"I'm happy ye like him, Sir. He is my personal mount. His name is Topper."

"I thought not a regular army horse. Is the mare you ride yours as well?"

"She is. I keep a small stable though none to match yours!"

"Your horses equal your tactics," Campbell said, then turned just a little sour. "I'm surprised to find such a talent not swept up by Wellesley. He has an insatiable greed for fine officers; am I not right there, Sutherland!"

"The captain's tactics are outstanding," Sutherland said, smiling, wishing to sway his superior away from thoughts of his nemesis. "How do you do it, Captain?"

"They would not come to us, Sir. I found it best if we went at them. Force the issue."

"Riding moors at night. Dangerous work."

"Small works compared to true war," Raynes replied.

"Any war is true war," Sutherland remarked. "Men die in even the smallest."

"And it seems our hero, General Wellesley, has made his war larger," Campbell said. "Have you heard, Raynes, his recent victories in Spain? It seems the bugger can fight despite his effeminate nature. And he doesn't mind blood. Heavy losses. He'll be needing new officers at the rate he's running through them."

"I would welcome the opportunity," Raynes said, meaning it.

"Keep at this the way you are and you'll be with him all the more quickly, and likely promoted to major at that!"

Campbell gave his horse a leg and cantered forward, tired of a war he himself would not fight. Sutherland took his place beside Raynes. As loud as Campbell had been, Giles Sutherland's voice was soothing. He was the appeasing presence to counter Campbell's bluntness. He appeared relaxed, almost careless in attitude. It was ironic, Raynes would later recall.

"The colonel too would like to be in Spain," Sutherland said gesturing toward Campbell. "But his character prevents it. He and Wellesley are not friendly."

"You know Wellesley?" Raynes asked.

"Acquaintance of the family," Sutherland replied. He did not do so boastfully but simply stated the fact to an envious Raynes. "Though my family thinks him a touch foolhardy. And that is why I am here."

"In a small war," Raynes said, "if, despite what ye say, ye could even call it that. More a confusion of sheep. These Ludds know nothing. They mill about until someone makes up his mind to do something. Then they all follow. They're best at running away. I've seldom seen a hundred men vanish like ghosts in the night. They're very good at that."

"Apparently, so are the Spanish," Sutherland said. "They call that tactic their *guerilla*, their little war, so I'm told. Quite effective."

"These criminals are not the Spanish, Lieutenant," Raynes replied sharply, "and their flights are not tactics but panic."

"Yet people seem terrified of them. I've been with the colonel throughout his inspection. It seems these Luddites strike with precision. Have we no idea who is behind it?"

"The man who just left us in Halifax is close to arresting one of their leaders. When I return to Huddersfield I too will make arrests. These are criminals, Sutherland; they're not soldiers. They vandalize their own country. And why? They fear the future, is all. They cannot face a new world!"

"The world is new each day," the Lieutenant replied.

Raynes said nothing further but spurred his horse and caught up with Campbell, a man more to his taste. He could not help but wonder why General Wellesley had asked for young Sutherland. He could not understand the boy's mind at all.

—

It was three o'clock in the morning when they noticed it. South, off the turnpike near the village of Birstall, they observed a ruby glow in the darkness. It was a strange sight. The weather had changed and low hanging clouds amplified it. The dragoons knew what it was, they'd seen it often enough. Campbell had not. He asked Raynes.

"I say, Captain, what is that light to the south?"

"Some sort of fire, Sir," Raynes replied.

"But the size of it, man ... local celebration?"

"More like a conflagration, Colonel. That's no bonfire but someone's buildings."

"In the village?"

"No, Sir. The village is sou-west of us. That'll be a manufactory."

"Burning?"

"Luddites," Raynes said.

"We must apprehend them!" the Colonel shouted. "I shall see your men afield after all!"

"No sense in that, Sir," Raynes said.

"This is your chance, Captain!" The Colonel's blood was up.

A hunt. A hunt for men.

"With the glow so bright the fire is in full flame. The Ludds don't stay to watch."

"I could order you, Raynes."

"As I say, Colonel, despite my desire to ride them down by now they shall all hae vanished."

"I'd thought you a different man from the tales I'd heard," Campbell said harshly.

"I am not reckless, Sir. It would waste my horses and men."

—

They arrived before dawn, the horses' breathing forming the bass notes for the high pitch of skylarks as they entered Leeds, slowing now with daybreak traffic in the town,. Iron horseshoes on cobbles echoed through the streets. At this time of morning the sun, blocked by buildings, offered only a half-light. They headed for Woodhouse Park Hall, Campbell's headquarters.

The Colonel had originally been sent to Leeds, with a robust number of troops, because it was considered an epicentre of Luddism. There had once been reason to think this. Tales of the old *Black Lamp*, a secret society, had their origins here. There had even been an early version of a union, called *Working Meckanics*. The sharpest conflicts, and the earliest, had occurred in Leeds.

As dawn cracked a thin line beneath low clouds, Raynes left his charges at the door of their stable and took his men off to their billet, hoping to avoid the coming rain. The sun disappeared as it rose, gone in the gray mass of cloud in the sky.

So it was gloomy when Campbell and Sutherland handed their horses to their grooms and headed toward their quarters. Their brief journey took only moments, the path winding through a short hawthorn maze, but this morning was not to be normal.

"Good man, that Raynes," Campbell said. The night ride had softened his temperament.

"Indeed, Sir," Sutherland replied. "I thought him rather ingenious."

"His tactics you mean."

"You'll find tactics here as well," a gruff voice said.

Quickly Sutherland stepped in front of Campbell to face a huge man straddling the path. The man wore a mask and a nondescript hat. Campbell turned back for the barns but found himself blocked by another masked man. The two were trapped.

"Who are you?" Sutherland said.

"As if you don't know," the big man said.

"I am sure I do not," Sutherland said. His hand went to his sword hilt. Neither he nor Campbell wore a firearm. The big man, however, pulled out a pistol. Pointing the pistol directly at Sutherland he fired, the ball smashing through the young man's chest. He was dead before he hit the ground.

Campbell, facing the other man, found the felon failing to draw his pistol. The gun's hammer had jammed on his belt. It gave Campbell time to save himself. He ran pell-mell into the hawthorn, diving through the branches, scratching and piercing and one thick limb broke his collar bone. His opponent, finally with his gun in hand, fired into the bushes. The hedge saved Campbell. The shot ricocheted off its thick branches.

Campbell shouted for his guards from inside the hedge.

It started to rain.

Mellor and Thorpe knew they would be captured, the colonel's bellows leading his men to them. Both turned and ran the maze well. They'd been told of its twists and turns by a stable lad. They also knew of a hollow with a low, narrow entrance in the thick shrubbery. They ducked in there, waited for running soldiers to pass, then were out of the maze and running toward the forest on its west side.

It started to pour.

The soldiers found Campbell, surrounding him, awaiting another assault. They shuffled like a huge crab as they carried him quickly toward a portico. Other soldiers found Giles Sutherland. He lay on the ground the way he had fallen: arms flung out, one leg bent strangely. They picked him up to carry him to the barn. As they did, one of the soldiers found an object beside him. It was a scroll. The ink was seeping from the rain. The corporal gave the letter to his sergeant at the stables. The sergeant read it.

Dear Cambell,

By now thou'rt dead and this message for your betters. You wanted a war now you have one, but not the one you thot. This is a terror. A little war not like the french but of your own makinge. This will not stoppe before them machines stoppe. Redressers forever amen.

Ned Luud, Clerk

Message delivered.

Sutherland was lain upon some straw, his eyes closed with tuppence pieces, a long way from his loving family; a long way from the risks of a *real* war.

The rain became a deluge, nearly opaque, a white-gray sheet forcing men to shield their eyes. It covered Mellor's and Thorpe's escape. They rode to an inn just by the Leeds Bridge. For five hundred years the old Leeds Bridge was the main crossing point over the river Aire. It was supposed to have been guarded but at that moment the sentries were eating a welcomed breakfast out of the rain. They would pay for deserting their posts ... a crime in all wars.

Even small wars.

Even wars which are not wars at all.

29

MARY BUCKWORTH WATCHED her maid, Nellie Mosby, in the process of ironing. Mary sat by the window, book in hand though her mind was elsewhere. It was raining but the day before had been bright and breezy and allowed a good laundering. Now the tubs, coarse soap and washboard were neatly stacked away in the shed by the scullery door. The clothes were tumbled in baskets beneath the big kitchen table; the same table her husband had lain upon the night she had washed his body, the night her affair with George Mellor had ended. Those dark thoughts were seldom far from her mind. Her hand briefly caressed the miniature *Enoch*.

Nellie, using cast iron tongs, gingerly removed hot coals from the fireplace. She placed each into the base of the *box iron* she used. She closed the hinged lid pierced with air holes, then carefully carried the instrument to the table. Reaching under the table, she pulled up a bed sheet, sprinkled a dash of water upon it, took up the iron and went to work. She hummed a good Methodist hymn as she laboured. Work was good for the soul, the parson had said and the harder the work the more benefits, so Nellie was happy.

The curate's widow was not. Two nights past she'd received a note she'd recognized as George Mellor's. It had begged her to allow him to meet her. It had asked her to leave her *Enoch* in the scullery window as a sign.

Mary Buckworth was a clever woman. Since she'd cast him out she'd heard little of George; but he was back and it was not only the note which informed her. She recognized the signs of the man who had altered before her eyes the night he'd brought her dead husband home. She could read his *messages* of the past months. He had told her he would give the owners what they had bestowed upon him. Murder for their machines.

Mary had heard all the explanations for Luddites from Whig intellects: the wars wasting England's manhood, blocking its trade, reducing its assets. She had experienced along with all others two years of bad harvest reducing so many to near starvation. And she was aware of the new technologies pursued by those callous *maisters* who sought to economize labour and increase their profits.

The true reason, she'd decided, for Luddites was the changing times and with them the recognition by commonplace people of a notion of what was *fair* and *unfair*, of what, quite simply, *ought to be*. Inside that ambiguity, in the face of overwhelming odds, people stood their ground as much as they dared or, like George Mellor, fought ferociously back for a better future.

It was just then, looking out at rain through the glass, Mary decided to place her small *Enoch* in her window that night.

—

It was late evening when Fanny Radcliffe journeyed home from her market day. She sat beside her driver, Harrison, in the yellow-wheeled curricle. It was a showy vehicle matching the character of its owner. The latest in fashion, the fastest of buggies, its two wheels almost as tall as she, Fanny was proud to be seen in it. The matched pair of greys, over which the driver snapped his crop as he hurried his lady home, were proving skittish having been stabled too long through the shopping day.

She was sure Joseph would be angry with her. He had told her it was not safe on the roads at this time of day. She was learning the truth of her husband's words. The twilight concealed the ruts and runnels of the muddy roadway making the ride uncomfortable. She should not have stayed in town quite so late but the Tuesday market had turned lively, with three new vendors which she and her lady friends felt should not be missed, and the rain had delayed her departure.

They were nearing Milnsbridge House, just rounding a curve in a murky wood, Harrison slowing the horses so the tall wheels of the curricle would keep steady, when the first of the women appeared by the roadside. She seemed almost a sylph from the shadows. Harrison hustled the horses past but Fanny regarded her with curiosity for she noted the woman was unnaturally large. She had a mob cap perched on her head and wore a dull beige dress seeming too small for her. Fanny thought the woman very plain, repulsive even, with her heavy jaw and large shoulders.

And then there was another woman dragging a tree branch across the roadway in front of them. Fanny wondered why she would do such a thing. She too seemed big. She too wore an unsightly mob cap and a blue dress. On closer inspection Fanny noted this woman wore boots.

Harrison slowed the horses. Fanny glanced at him. His face was pale. He began to turn the horses about but suddenly there were two more women standing in the midst of the roadway, each holding a pistol. Harrison hauled the horses to a stop. They breathed heavily in the quiet evening surrounded by horrid wood nymphs.

"What dost want?" Harrison said hoarsely.

"For you t' get down from that carrick!" one of the women said, her voice a man's. Fanny was confused by the commands, the dresses, the dark, the menace of this encounter.

"I'll do no such thing," Harrison replied.

"Then you'll be a dead man," came the answer from behind. The blue dress had climbed onto the outsized leaf springs at the gig's rear. His breath stank of drink as he spoke. He shoved poor Harrison out of the vehicle. Fanny heard her driver grunt as he struck ground. He wheezed as the beige dressed man kicked him, taking his breath. Summoning her courage Fanny tried to make herself sound like an older, less frightened, woman.

"Do you know who I am, you bully?"

"No ma'am. We're only looking for what you carry."

"Who are you? And why are you costumed like women?"

"Why we're the wives of Ned Ludd! Have you not heard of us?" The beige dress, now standing over Harrison, answered with a laugh.

The other two had grabbed the horses' bridles.

"What do you want?"

"Only what you have."

"You mean to rob me? You are highwaymen?"

"Not at all, just brides of Ludd needing some help t' live," the blue dressed man said as he climbed down beside her. It brought laughter from the other men-women and a quick comment from the one in beige.

"Ain't that just right, Earl!"

He reached to the floor of the curricle and pulled up parcels of merchandise. He tossed them down to the beige dressed man.

"I am the wife of Magistrate Joseph Radcliffe, you ruffian," Fanny said, hoping her husband's name would be enough to stop the plunder.

"Are you now? Well that's peculiar, ain't I right, lads!"

One of the cross dressers holding a horse heard something around the curve. He seemed alarmed. He let go the horse and ran quickly toward the noise, then back again.

"Somebody coming, Earl," he said nervously. "Sounds like a waggon."

"Then meet it!" the woman named Earl snarled.

A waggon appeared abruptly from out of the dim. It was a hayrick, empty now, returning from market. It was driven as well by a woman. But she was truly a woman, Fanny could see. She recognized Matilda Wood. She recalled Mrs. Wood from the spring gathering at Milnsbridge House. She recalled as well that Mrs. Wood was the one who had hurt poor Milly. It hardly mattered now.

"Please, Mrs. Wood!" Fanny cried, "These men a stealing from me. They've hurt my driver. Ride on to my home and find my husband's soldiers!"

Mathilda Wood did not drive on. She stopped her cart opposite Fanny, glanced knowingly at the men around her, and smiled.

"And if I do that, Mrs. Radcliffe, what do you think these men'll do t' me?"

"They are criminals!" Fanny screamed.

"Now'd be the time for a good big dog t' take these men on. Where's your Milly? That mutt'd protect you, would she not?"

"I am being robbed! Please!"

"You'll notice, Mrs. Radcliffe, that in certain places your name serves no purpose. Don't hurt her, you men! She's a delicate creature," Mathilda said loudly, then a quick "Hup!" to her horse and her dray passed on, edging around the branch blocking part of the road.

The felons in dresses said nothing, nor did they try to stop her.

"What are you doing?" A tearful Fanny twisted to watch her go, only to have her hands grasped and removed of rings and bracelets by the blue dressed ruffian.

"We don't rob them who have nothing," he said harshly. "Now you'll behave or worse'll come of this."

Up close the man's breath was the least of her concerns. She could see him clearly now, his reddish beard stubbling his chin. One ear protruded from the mob cap as though reluctant to be enclosed. He had rheumy gray eyes and protruding front teeth which gave him the look of a ferret. His was a cruel, alarming face.

"Yes. Yes. Of course." Fanny's false courage collapsed.

She gasped as she felt the man's hands upon her, searching her person for further treasures. His hands moved over her body like spiders. Once he touched her breast; fingers pinching her nipple. Her breath stopped. The ugly man sniggered. She thought of rape. These four bearded women. She could never live with the shame. She would take arsenic, throw herself from a bridge, an appalling end to a once lovely life.

"That's fine now, ma'am." The blue dress took her reticule and with it the remainder of her money but made no further attempt to molest her.

She was sobbing. The man climbed down from the curricle while the beige dress took his foot off of Harrison. Harrison climbed into the vehicle, his face sickly pale in the dark. The other men turned the horses back the way they'd been going, then let go their bridles and stepped aside. The blue dress spoke.

"You've a ripe young body, my girl," he said, "and I would've taken more time with you were it not for Mrs. Wood. You should be grateful she happened by."

Fanny continued weeping. It was as if he had done what he'd threatened. She could not look up. She could only cry and remember the insult of Mathilda Wood which had made it all worse. She'd forgotten her own insults from the past. Mathilda had not.

"Driver!" the blue dress commanded, "get on home now. You'll have t' move the branch first. Then slow and easy. We don't want t' jar the lovely Mrs. Radcliffe, now do we?"

And with that the four melted into the dark. Harrison lit the curricle's lanterns. His hands shook as he used his flint and tinderbox. He knew how close they had come to calamity. He had heard the name *Earl*. There was only one man of that name he knew: a dangerous, malicious character. By the time he had pulled the branch off the roadway, mounted the curricle and got the horses underway Mrs. Radcliffe had stopped her weeping. She sat as still as death, staring straight ahead, robbed of her pride. They reached Milnsbridge House, with Harrison turning into the gate, when the jingle of a cavalry troop announced itself. Harrison noted they were dragoons with the famed Captain Raynes riding lead. They were passing when Harrison waved Raynes over. He greeted Harrison and tipped his shako to the lady. Then, once she realized she was safely home and surrounded by soldiers, Fanny shattered once more into tears.

"Mrs. Radcliffe, what is wrong?" the captain asked, rather coldly.

She could not answer, struck dumb by realization. To tell this man what had happened, to dishonour herself even more *with him* was unthinkable. She thought once again of the blue dressed man's hands on her body.

"'It was robbery, Captain," Harrison said. "My lady's not well. They were rough men."

"Where?" Raynes asked.

"Just back up the road. In the wood where the path curves. Dressed like women. Called themselves Ned Ludd's brides."

"Luddites?"

"I don't think so, Sir. The one of them called another Earl. Most likely Earl Parkin and his bunch. They aren't Ludd's men; just thieves and rapers."

His final words brought wails from Fanny.

"Oh hell," Raynes said. "They ... they didn't touch Mrs. Radcliffe?"

"Only t' find what she carried. John Wood's wife came by from the market. Nothing for her t' do but warn 'em she knew who they were. That stopped 'em doing anything more."

"But we passed her on the road. She said nothing at all!"

Harrison leaned out of the vehicle. He whispered to Raynes.

"Might be bad blood or something between her and Mrs. Radcliffe."

"She was part of it then," Raynes said.

"No, Sir. She put a stop t' what might have happened."

Raynes rode round the rear of the curricle and touched Fanny's shaking shoulder. The familiar softness aroused him despite himself. He pushed away the flash of memory: his hands on her naked shoulders in another place and she in a far different mood.

"Mrs. Radcliffe, are you hurt in any way?"

"He ... he insulted my person!" she said, bereft of any decorum.

"I'm afraid I don't take your meaning. Your driver just said ..."

"He placed his filthy hands upon me! He said awful things!"

Raynes realized he'd get nothing useful from Fanny. He had not realized how plain she could look when in distress: her nose dripping, her eyes red, her face drawn and colourless. It made it easier to turn away and once again question her driver.

"Do you know which way they might have gone?"

"No, Sir. Just back into the wood. I'll bet they're up Crosland moor by this time."

"My thanks, Mister ..."

"Just Harrison, Sir."

Harrison tugged a forelock.

"Well done of you, Harrison, to have the man's name. We'll find him."

"And what of *me*!" Fanny screamed at Raynes. "I want that man killed, Francis! Shot down like a dog!"

"Please Mrs. Radcliffe," Raynes said, nervous the tormented girl would let loose some intimacy in front of his men.

"He deserves to die! How can you live knowing he has offended me?"

"He will be captured, madam. He shall be brought to trial, I assure you. Do you truly wish what happened tonight to be known any further afield? Think of the gossip."

That brought more tears from Fanny, though her raised hand signified acquiescence.

"Best get yourself to your bed, madam. You've had a difficult night."

His words, ill chosen, brought her to a wail once more.

"You! Where were you when I needed you? You are no more than a braggart soldier! That's all you are! I never want to set eyes upon you again! You should have been there! You should have ..."

With her insult delivered, she dissolved into lamentation. There could be no response from Raynes but her words sealed the pact he had made with himself. Never again would he trifle with women. They were far too hazardous. Far too unstable. Far, far too threatening when it suited them. Raynes signalled his sergeant and the troop thundered off toward Crosland moor in the hope of catching the criminals.

He did not realize how close he was to apprehending his real prey.

—

With Nellie safely sent home, Mary sat once again in her scullery. A cup of tea, her third since midnight, steamed before her. Why, she wondered, was so much of her life measured in the time it took to make and drink cup after cup of tea? Her upbringing had made tea the drink of choice in both houses, her father's and her husband's, though for different reasons. Mary's life as a manufacturer's daughter with a mother who wished only the best for her family, as well as the best reputation, had introduced *China tea* into their home. Then as a curate's wife, though wine was allowed, Curate Buckworth had selected tea as the beverage for church social gatherings and other such events. With the rise of the Methodist movement pushing its puritanical Wesleyan theology, John Buckworth had decided to show the Church of England as equal to, and even surpassing in character, its more strident competitor. His wife, of course, followed suit.

The tea steaming, she pushed her chair away, stood and paced the floor. A single candle lit the room. The candle sat on a window ledge. Hanging from the window's lock was the tiny *Enoch* signaling her consent.

She was no longer the curate's wife. Now she was a victim of tragedy. There was great sympathy for the widow but widows enjoy a lesser place than women married to respected men. She had been allowed her grief and put her affairs in order. Eventually, however, she was informed through increasingly less subtle letters that Dewsbury required a new curate, and *that* curate required the residence. Once even old Vicar Roberson had visited: solicitous to her grief, considerate of her needs, yet wondering about her plans for the future.

There was, of course, a widow's pension, though it was small. Most widows were older than she and could make do. At any rate her dowry provided an annual stipend which far exceeded her husband's salary.

The plan had formed after John Buckworth's death and endured even when she had cast out George Mellor. She could not help it. Whatever she was doing, even at the burial of her husband, even as the first earth clattered onto his casket, she could not keep herself from thoughts of George. She had loved two men, each for different reasons, and knew now her folly. But her emotions for the living man could not help but swell no matter how guilty she felt or how altered he had become.

They belonged to two classes, as separate as if they were foreigners to each other. Society would not abide their disregard for its unspoken rules. To be with a man such as George, particularly after John, would be thought the height of betrayal. She and Mellor would be banished for their shocking behaviour. It would follow them wherever in Britain they chose to live. Even her father would disown her.

So her plan had formed ever more hastily with the nudges for her to leave the rectory, with her mounting feelings once more for George, and with the money she possessed in plenty. She would convince George this night. She would use every ploy, each part of his love for her to force him to see things her way. Her mind was near bursting with anticipation.

She returned to her tea, cooled now, and sipped. The aroma settled her. She was calm when she heard the soft tap at the window. Had she known how close to the truth she was, how her plans would come to such an ironic conclusion, she would never have answered.

—

It took little more than an hour to ride them down. A few soldiers dismounted and entered the woods while the remainder skirted its flanks. They eventually came to the road heading up Crosland moor when Raynes had an idea. He wondered where a gang of robbers would go to celebrate their loot and came up with the answer quite quickly. Just down the road was the Warrener House. Keeping his men concealed he rode to the rear of the inn and entered. A few sharp questions revealed Earl Parkin and company were within, drinking away their ill-gotten gains, no longer dressed as women.

Within a few moments the inn was surrounded. Raynes' sergeant and three dragoons entered the front door, pistols drawn. The Parkin group were up and out the back like hares. It was a joke how amazed they were at meeting a ring of dragoons where they'd sought to make their escape. A few of the troopers could not help but laugh.

The men were manacled. The next day, Raynes made clear, they would be questioned at Milnsbridge House by the very man whose wife they had molested. That news threw the group into panic. They claimed not to know her, they blamed each other, they even tried to have Harrison tied into the conspiracy saying he had lusted after the girl and would have had her there in that *carrick* had they not prevented the act.

Raynes mentioned the girl would surely select from a group the man who had touched her. That brought Earl Parkin upright, requesting a word. Raynes accepted. He had been wounded by Fanny's insults. He wanted this credit in particular, not only to best her old husband but to have the spoiled wife beholden to him. Perhaps one final grateful act before they parted. She was so good at what she did, the thing other decent women would not, what Ann would not; just one last time.

"Right then, Parkin." He swung down from his saddle. "I wish a statement from ye. The facts of what happened. The location of Mrs. Radcliffe's belongings. Quick now, for ye know what's in store tomorrow."

"Aye, Captain," Parkin whispered so his men would not hear. "I can give you that. But what if I told you I know such news as would set me free?"

"I doubt that possible, Parkin."

"Then I'll just tell Radcliffe. I know, despite his wife, when he hears me he'll let me off."

"Tell me."

"Grab me and pull me behind the horses," Parkin said. "I can't have my men hear."

Raynes quickly obliged. He hauled Parkin into the dark outside the ring of dragoons as though he were about to beat the man. Once in shadow he backed him against a tree.

"Alright. What is it ye hae to say?"

"I'll need your promise t' set me free. You can have the others for all I care."

"You're in no position to barter. State your case."

Parkin paused a moment, then nodded his head. His voice dropped even lower.

"I know you've been chasing through the moors these last nights looking for Luddites. Have you found any lately?"

"Stop your gamesmanship, Parkin."

"I know why you can't find 'em. They're hid so deep they don't even know each other. But all of them are being run by one man. I know who that man is."

"Alright." Raynes tried to keep his voice calm. "Tell me."

"Should I tell you I'll be in the *shite*. I'll need protection."

"Ye shall hae it. Now speak."

Parkin paused again for effect. Raynes shifted, his ear tuned to hear the news he had worked so hard for so many months to attain.

"The man's name is George Mellor."

Raynes was stunned by John Lloyd's powers of deduction. That the solicitor could associate such a man as Mellor through the thinnest of clues ... the Russian connection with Bellingham, the suspicion regarding his step-father, the simple fact he'd disappeared after Rawfolds ... Raynes found a new respect for his partner in that moment.

"That is not news to me," Raynes replied, trying to learn more.

"And dost know he's back from where he went after Cartwright's place?"

"Do ye know where he is?"

"I must have a promise."

"If ye know his location."

"I'll speak true, Captain. I don't."

"Then why are we bargaining?"

"I know how t' find him."

"Tell me and I'll find him myself."

"The man you must see'll take one look at you and be off like a racehorse."

"I have other agents. Not soldiers."

"But strangers t' this man. He won't talk with strangers. 'Tis the Oath is why."

"Yet he'll speak with ye?"

"Aye. We were friends once. I know his da'."

"What is his name and where shall we find him?"

"Name's John Dean. He lives in Marsden."

"And how will we know from this Dean where we'll find Mellor?"

"He's twisted in."

"I beg your pardon?"

"The Oath. He's taken the Oath! The man's a Luddite. 'Tis sure he'll know where his boss stays."

"Alright, Parkin. If this is true you'll be protected. If it's lies, ye'll get the gallows."

"'Tis all true what I say, Sir. I know when I'm beat, and I've no love for Mellor."

Raynes could hardly believe it. At last a chance at the illusive Ludd leader! Though he did not much trust the tales of Parkin, he wanted to apprehend Mellor if only for Lloyd's gratitude.

And as he considered this, his partner was miles away on what Raynes now thought was a false path. The arrest of Baines was nothing when Raynes knew the identity of the true Luddite commander. Still there was also the man who had lost his hat. Lloyd was on that track just as was Raynes.

When their paths converged they would have their success.

It was much closer than Raynes thought.

30

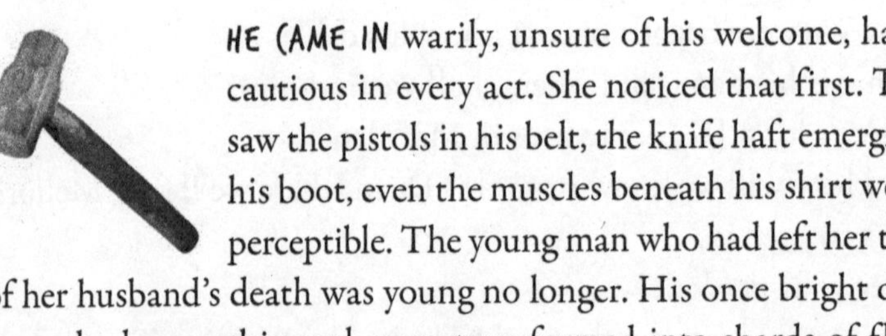

HE CAME IN warily, unsure of his welcome, habitually cautious in every act. She noticed that first. Then she saw the pistols in his belt, the knife haft emerging from his boot, even the muscles beneath his shirt were more perceptible. The young man who had left her the night of her husband's death was young no longer. His once bright diamond eyes, the keys to his soul, were transformed into shards of flint. His formerly youthful face had become a visage of lines, each line a worry or a plan. And yet he had written her, begging to see her.

"Hello, Mary," he said softly.

There was something in his voice which had not been there before: a terse callousness. She decided if her plan were to work she must break him down, make him hers again. It seemed the only way was to match, for the moment, his reticent nature.

"Why did you write? Why have you come?" she asked curtly.

"I wondered if you were well."

"I am as you see."

"Then you haven't changed your mind."

"About what?"

"Us."

She saw his shoulders sag. He placed his hand on the door's handle, preparing to leave. "Wait!" she cried, nearly bursting with her impatience.

"Why?"

"I ... I love you, George," she said softly.

He paused, then came to her, embracing her, turning her head up to touch her lips in a lingering, loving kiss. She could feel the tension flow out of him. She could feel in that kiss once again the man she had come to love. Part of him, at least, had returned.

When the kiss ended, he held her so close she could hear his heart beating, hear the ragged breaths of a man weeping. She had not expected tears. They melted her. Then he stopped and held her at arms' length. His eyes shimmered briefly once more, then the spark twinkled out and he released her. She did not want release. She felt herself so proximate, so relishing his presence. She reached for his hands if only to touch him.

"I told you once, Mary, I'd come for you and no man would care. I was wrong, I know now, but I couldn't stay away. I love you, Mary. Since we parted I've done as I said. I've made myself into something stronger; a leader now, not a child pretending to something."

"I know. I've kept up with the news. People talk. They're afraid."

"Not all the actions were mine. There's many a gang of thieves about now. We do our best t' make them suffer."

"But don't you understand you cause the chaos which allows these criminals their way? I told you once you had them in your ranks and you wouldn't listen. Listen now, George. You've frightened everyone. People don't sleep. Children have nightmares. You're affecting more than just owners and the authorities. There is a spirit of terror over this land ..."

"Have you forgotten Rawfolds? I've seen worse in Manchester. Someone must go against these bloody tyrants."

"I don't want to argue, George, not now. It's been so long. Please just hold me."

She knew she must be very careful not to wake that desperate character she'd glimpsed or he would transform to iron. Iron has no feeling. She found it curious he could not recognize he'd become the same as the tyrants he cursed.

As she softened she felt him relax. She kissed him and despite his transformation she could still feel his passion. But he ended the kiss. He had come for more than love.

"I wanted t' say I know now we'd never be accepted. Society's too set in its ways t' change. But I can't help loving you, Mary."

"Then what can we do, George?"

"I think you should leave here and forget me. There's talk of you moving soon ... a new curate coming ..."

"I must leave here shortly, at least by October but what I truly want, what I wish more than anything else, is for you to come with me."

"You know what would happen. You knew before me. We'd be tainted no matter where we went. I came back t' tell you I understand that."

"That's not true." She had not been expecting logic from him. "I've money, George, of my own. Enough to get us away to where no one would know us."

"There's no place ..."

"There is! Since you've been gone I've made a plan. I've been very thorough and found a way to carry it through."

"What kind of plan?"

She thought she detected hope in his voice. She saw his eyes flicker for just an instant.

"We cannot go to Europe because of the war, nor America for the same reason, but there is a place we might start anew."

"I know of none."

"You went to sea, spent time in Russia. Surely you admit there are such places."

"News always travels, Mary."

"But I know a place where it would not matter, a land so new it needs people. We would be welcomed!"

"Alright, Mary. Tell me of this place."

"It's called York, a town in Upper Canada close to the frontier. I believe people go there to start again. I've read of a place called Sand Hills purchased from the natives by a Colonel Beasley. We could buy a tract of land. We could build our lives out of a wilderness. All we need do is find passage. If we could reach Liverpool ..."

He said nothing but turned away. He sat down at the table his head in his hands shielding his face from the candle light. She had no idea what he was thinking, deciding to say nothing further. She had to maintain a balance of logic and love simultaneously. Only that fusion would reach his core.

When he finally spoke she heard in his voice an overwhelming sadness.

"York," he said. "Why dost think they called it York, over there? Dost think it's not filled with English owners just like the ones here? I said news travels. *York*, of all places."

"Then we'll find another place, George," she said.

He remained seated not looking at her.

"We could cross the frontier into America."

"Dost wish me to give up my honour? Desert the men I've *twisted in*? You told me yourself, Mary, we've made a difference here in the West Riding. If we don't make things right, who will?"

"Then you won't come with me?"

He rose slowly and turned to her.

"No, lass. I came t' say goodbye proper, not like it was when John died. I wanted you t' remember me as a good man no matter what you might hear. I'm going t' do what's necessary: make a path for those who come after. I've told you all this, I just wanted t' say it one last time."

"You'll lose, George. You'll be caught and declared a traitor. They'll hang you!"

"Still, Mary, I must carry on. I wish it were different."

His sense of quiet desperation, his acceptance of what he considered inevitable welled inside Mary. She recalled his vision of their lives as little boats fighting a current. She felt the depth of her love for him then. She could not help herself. All her attempts at manipulation had been defeated at the hands of his honesty and her feeling now of such complete loss gave her license to kiss him one final time. When he tried to break away she intensified her kiss, allowing all that dwelt inside her to flow into to him through their touch, her kiss, their need for each other. He held her and then carried her through to the sitting room where by moonlight the two gave themselves to each other.

—

John M'Donald was drunk. It was not an unusual state for the man but, drunk or sober, he signified safety for John Lloyd. With powerful limbs and a trunk like an ox, with a hard edged, scarred face and thick primitive forehead, no one would call him handsome. But make him angry and one would find oneself down in the dirt being kicked into broken bones.

Lloyd had met M'Donald in Stockport when the former had been a solicitor there. M'Donald was always in some kind of trouble. Lloyd realized if he could make the man somehow beholden to him, he would have a dependable, dangerous bodyguard. Lloyd had taken steps and M'Donald had responded. Indeed, when Lloyd departed from his *tinkering,* he'd left many accoutrements with M'Donald knowing they would be safe upon his return. And when he did use his skills as a spy, M'Donald would often be his driver and sometime assistant.

The big man could hold his ale well. It was difficult for most to distinguish when he had been drinking, but Lloyd was careful to notice. Now the man leaned heavily against the wall which shadowed them. Lloyd said nothing about the drinking. M'Donald was a thin-skinned man and would brook no affront. Instead Lloyd looked about, investigating his surroundings.

The Piece Hall in Halifax was a huge building, thus called because weavers took their *pieces*, or lengths of cloth, to the hall to be sold. It was identifiable because it was actually four long buildings constructed in a square. The three-storied colonnaded structures were massive, and advertised their purpose (as if no one knew) with a dramatic weathervane in the shape of a sheep. At this time of evening, with the sun nearly gone, it served as sufficient cover for the two men who kept to its eastern shadows.

Just after the supper hour, they departed the Piece Hall and made their way to the Saint Crispin Inn for a meeting with Charles Milnes. If Milnes would talk he might lead them to the reputed leader whom Barrowclough had claimed to be John Baines.

The Saint Crispin Inn took its name from the patron saint of shoemakers but it also was a known hotbed of revolt. Constructed in the old style, it was comprised of multiple rooms and therefore was a splendid environment for two strangers to remain anonymous.

They entered an ancient white-washed room, smoky and low beamed, filled with wooden booths lining the walls. Two larger round tables sat in the middle. They chose a booth where they saw Milnes waiting. Lloyd had contacted the man at his home and, as usual, had convinced Milnes he would be better off away from his family with the matters he would be discussing.

Milnes too had been drinking, though not for pleasure.

The two sat down opposite him, M'Donald on the outside. He ordered more ale.

"Well Milnes," Lloyd said without preamble, "we know you to be a friend of Samuel Haigh given us through the testimony of Corporal Barrowclough. The question is, where is he?"

"I've no idea," Milnes said, a little the worse for the drink.

"Produce him or be arrested for sedition. You were at Rawfolds with him were you not? You know he murdered Horsfall!"

"No, Sir!" Milnes replied unsteadily. "I knew Sam was at Rawfolds but I wasn't! I can only tell you the truth. Sam Haigh'd not hurt a fly. He's no murderer."

"Careful, Milnes," Lloyd said, "we have information ..."

"Then 'tis wrong!" Milnes said, slamming his tankard down on the table. "I don't know this Barrowclough, but I do know he's lied."

"Then what is the truth?"

"I'll say this ..." Milnes looked out into the room, then lowered his voice. "I know from Sam telling me, one of the leaders at Rawfolds. He must have been for he's a *maister* as well. Thomas Brook went along that night. In the fight he fell into the mill pond and lost his hat ..."

"His hat, you say," Lloyd said coolly, masking his elation at this corroboration of evidence.

"Aye. He tried t' get Mellor t' help him find it."

"Mellor? George Mellor?" Lloyd said a little too quickly. "He was there?"

"There? Without him nowt would've happened. Anyway, he gave Thomas over t' Ben Walker and they got away. Ben Walker talked t' Brook while they were running off. He claimed t' be a Ludd officer."

"Where is this Mellor?"

"I don't know. He disappeared after Rawfolds. Probably dead."

"Then where is Walker?"

"As t' that, Mr. Lloyd, you'll have t' ask old John Baines."

Lloyd tried to stay calm, pursing his lips, folding his hands on the scarred, blackened table, speaking softly yet insistently. But Milnes feared the thought of offering more. After some minutes of coaxing, Lloyd turned a different page.

"You seem to know a great deal you're *not* telling. I think it is time our Mr. M'Donald here took you out into the alley."

One look at the grinning M'Donald and Milnes turned pale. As he took up his mug once again Lloyd noted the man's hand was shaking. In that vulnerable instant Lloyd struck.

"Milnes, I wish to see Baines. I know he lives in here in Halifax and I know you know where he is. Take me to him immediately or ..." Lloyd nodded toward M'Donald.

"I don't have t' take you anywhere, Sir!" Milnes replied quickly. He was terrified. "John Baines spends his evenings here, upstairs. But you won't get t' him."

"You note my companion ..." Lloyd said.

"Aye, but they'll be gone the second they see a man of your ilk. They've many bolt holes from this pub."

Milnes formed his own plan in that moment. He looked into the reptilian eyes of Lloyd.

"If I took Mr. M'Donald upstairs to see Baines I might say he'd asked t' be twisted in ..."

"You mean given the Oath?" Lloyd was elated.

"Aye. John Baines delivers the Oath. Let me take Mr. M'Donald with me. You should stay here though. You don't fit in."

Lloyd turned to M'Donald. The big man had finished his second tankard. His beady eyes peered from beneath the primordial brow.

"John," he spoke carefully, "I've not asked before but I'd like you to play act. Go with this man, pretend to be a cropper, and ask to be twisted in, that is, given the Oath. Then ask this Baines where your cousin, Ben Walker, might be. Say nothing of Mellor. The man's a ghost and there must be a reason. Walker only. Say you want to celebrate your

Oath-taking with him. Get Baines to tell you where Walker is. Don't threaten him, John, or our business is up. I'd not expected this or I wouldn't ask you. Can you do it?"

"Aye. I can. I'm in the mood," he said, grinning.

"No threats. No fisticuffs no matter what they might say."

"I'm but a cropper." M'Donald grinned wider. "I wouldn't hurt a fly."

"Good man," Lloyd said.

"We should go," said Milnes, rising from his seat. They disappeared from the room, both weaving a little as they took the stairs. They were eyed closely by men who sat at the base of the staircase. Lloyd watched them leave then ordered a saddle of lamb. The other men in the room ignored him once the hulking M'Donald was gone.

They had no idea they'd been joined by a Judas.

—

Francis Raynes and Earl Parkin had been riding all day to reach Marsden. This was the place, according to Parkin, where they would find John Dean and thus some clue to George Mellor's location. Raynes had brought no soldiers with them and dressed in civilian attire. He was nothing now but a gentleman, likely the son of an owner by the look of his horse and his expensive waistcoat and tails. Parkin was along to identify Dean. He was Raynes' last resort. Raynes needed to find Mellor.

Parkin guided him to the New Inn. It was the kind of hostelry a gentleman such as Raynes portrayed might stop for a night. Its public house was roomy and clean, its ale superb and the clientele a mix of merchants and artisans. The two sat at a table awaiting the late afternoon when the New's customary clientele would arrive. John Dean was one of the first.

Parkin called him over. Dean came warily. He knew Parkin and did not trust the man, but *because* he knew him he accepted a drink and sat down to be introduced.

"Johnny, lad, I'd like you t' meet a friend of mine."

"Have you taken t' gentlemen now then, Earl," Dean replied with a smile.

"Just so, lad. This gentleman's named Francis Raynes. Maybe you've heard of him?"

Dean pushed back the chair to escape but was stopped by Raynes' calm voice.

"I would nae do that, Mr. Dean," Raynes said. "I've a pistol beneath this table levelled right at you. Ye'd be gelded. Why don't ye stay and answer some questions?"

"I don't know anything!" Dean said.

"I look at that hand of yours. It seems ye've had the wounds burned to close them."

"'Twas a work accident!"

"I'm a soldier, Mr. Dean. I know a wound when I see one. How did ye get yours?"

"If I tell you what'll happen t' me?"

"Why nothing, if ye give me what I need. If not, I should imagine Huddersfield gaol."

"What dost want?"

"Ye got that wound at Rawfolds, did ye not? Ye were there."

It took a moment. Raynes noted Dean glancing around the room. They sat in its midst and no one seemed to pay any attention. Dean knew he was trapped. With the pistol trained on him attempt to escape was unthinkable.

"Aye," he answered.

"And who led that attack?"

"I'm not sure. It was all done with numbers. No names used, everyone in disguise."

"It wouldn't hae been George Mellor, would it?"

"How ..." Dean's face fell. He looked as though Raynes had indeed just shot him.

"Where is he now?"

"I don't know."

"If ye listen carefully, Mr. Dean, ye'll hear the click of my pistol's hammer. Simple to claim ye tried to escape."

"Earl?" Dean pleaded.

"I'm trapped just as you are, Johnny. Captain Raynes is a serious man. I'd tell him the truth were I you. He'll offer protection. Best take it."

"Go ahead, Mr. Dean. Where is George Mellor?"

"Honest, Sir, I can't tell you. Him an' Thorpe ..."

"That would be William Thorpe of Fisher's shop?"

"Aye. They came t' visit me a while back. They wanted news of the West Riding. I know they spend most of their time over here, but they've a place at the other end of Standedge Tunnel. They go there when things get hot."

"How do I know you're not lying?"

"Ask the Tunnel *Maister*, Brookbank."

"I intend to. Why would he be involved?"

"He's Sam Lodge's cousin, and Lodge is a friend of Mellor's."

"Are they there now?"

"I don't know! If they want me they come here. I'm almost sure, though, they haven't been back through the tunnel of late. They'd have stopped for a drink and a talk. If they find out about this meeting, Captain, they'll kill me, friends or not."

"You'll be protected, Dean. I'll see to it. Now, we'll stand up together, I'll state quite clearly to the room that you're under arrest and we'll leave. Until I have Mellor you'll be kept in custody, or perhaps a while longer so you may testify. Am I clear?"

"Aye."

As they rose to depart Raynes was good for his word, vociferous and officious and with pistol in hand, enough to keep every man seated. As they reached their horses, Parsons and Dean riding double, Raynes had a thought.

"By the way, Mr. Dean. Who is this Sam Lodge ye spoke of?"

—

Mellor and Thorpe came together in a shepherd's hut deep in Ramsden Clough, southeast of Holmfirth. A huge gorge, it possessed the value of near invisibility; as well, there was no possible approach without discovery. They were careful now in all they did. They travelled apart, met covertly, and commanded with detailed attention.

It had been a hot August day and the climb down was gruelling. The stony paths winding in switchbacks gave way to long grass with a hint of blue amidst harebell verges. Lapwings, or *Peewits* to the locals, had finished nesting and now skimmed low in their sunset flight making that distinctive onomatopoeic cry for which they are named. The grass was straw-like with the August dry. They reached the bottom in twilight, the only sound a soft breeze whispering. They shared their oatcake and cheese.

Thorpe had been in Huddersfield to report on troops coming north. The more the terror spread the more the military seemed to think it could be smothered beneath their scarlet, but with Mellor's strategy it was like trying to catch flies with a blanket.

Mellor had stayed north in Leeds to stir up more conflict then moved south to make his farewell to Mary in Dewsbury. After their meal and a brief conference, Thorpe rolled himself in a blanket while Mellor would spend the first half of the night on watch.

It was not easy to be alone with his thoughts. At first they were joyous remembrances of Mary's passion. Then, however, came reflections of the desperation within both of them. His feelings for her were as strong as ever. He wanted to leave for Canada but knew he could not. He'd modified his strategy and had to remain to see it carried out.

His plan now was to murder soldiers: on duty, off, drunk or sober, from all regiments from whatever rank. They would be found shot to death, or with their throats slit. And more owners would begin to die. Mary would come to hate him. He'd become aware she did not understand the world beyond her theories. She would never comprehend greed. He did. He had seen it in killing to protect machines, or in the beatings of women and children who simply wanted food.

Mary would be leaving in early October with the new curate's arrival. He doubted she would try the new world. She would realize a lone woman would not be allowed that kind of freedom. More likely she would return to her father and keep his house; keep her passion locked inside the primness expected of a dead curate's wife. He wished it could have been different. He wished they could have made the trip to this Sand Hills she'd told him of, purchased land, worked it with the vigour of their youth, had children, watched them grow, become respected in some tiny hamlet. Was it so much to ask?

He sighed aloud.

Neither of them could desert their values and he could not choose to run and hide when the men he had organized could not. He thought a moment of Sam Lodge, so stricken by society. Change had trampled him like a herd of horses. The future was thoughtless. It could not be stopped, but it could be shaped, and that was Mellor's incentive. The future altered each day, determined by the past. A single day's action might influence it. He could not change the world but he could, if careful and cunning, make it a better place for those who would live in that unknown future.

Then perhaps a Mary Buckworth could travel to new lands without a man to constrain her. Then perhaps a Sam Lodge would be judged by his character rather than his class. Then perhaps people would not kill to protect the machines which stole their humanity. His thoughts grew too heavy. He was only twenty-three years of age. And yet here he was deep in a clough pursued by relentless authorities and all because he might alter a *single day* in the life of the world.

—

It was two hours before M'Donald and Milnes returned, so drunk they could hardly stand. Lloyd was incensed. He forced the two out of the pub then commanded both to duck their heads in a horse trough. For a horrific second M'Donald started to turn on him, eyes like blades, then he stumbled and fell. In the end Lloyd doused both with buckets of water. Sputtering and swearing they started to begin to make sense as Lloyd questioned them. All of his work depended on what he heard from these two.

"Where have you been all this time?" he demanded.

"With Baines. He gave us fine ale!" Milnes said.

"Aye. A good man," M'Donald said.

"What happened?"

"I was given the Oath. Now I'm a Luddite," M'Donald said. He was so bleary-eyed he could hardly see.

"Baines administered it?"

"Whaaat'?" M'Donald said, slurring. Milnes was sharper.

"Aye, he did," Milnes sat down, collapsed really in a realization which literally took his feet from beneath him. "What the hell have I done?"

Lloyd knew Milnes had just recognized the consequence of his actions.

"I'll have Baines arrested," Lloyd said.

"Are you daft, man?" Milnes stopped up Lloyd's triumphant thoughts.

"How so?"

"There's at least twenty men up there. You must wait for troops. 'Tis the only way."

"Did he say anything of Mellor? Where he might be?"

"He said nowt, except he told us Ben Walker wasn't t' be trusted."

"Benjamin Walker? Baines knows where he is?"

"Walker used t' be Mellor's companion 'til Mellor disappeared."

"This Walker ...

"He's about. Maybe in Huddersfield, or Longroyd Bridge."

"Of course."

"Whaaat?" M'Donald came around just in time to misunderstand.

"I'll be riding tonight to Huddersfield," Lloyd said. "The two of you can find a barn. You couldn't ride without killing yourselves. Take the horse. Stable it and sleep beside it. In the morning ride for Radcliffe's house. I shall be there."

"What about my pay?" M'Donald said.

"You drank it."

John Lloyd mounted his horse and was gone.

Closer.

31

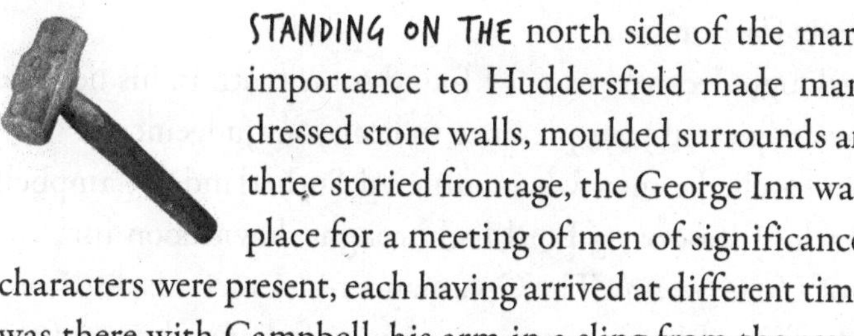

STANDING ON THE north side of the marketplace, its importance to Huddersfield made manifest by its dressed stone walls, moulded surrounds and imposing three storied frontage, the George Inn was the perfect place for a meeting of men of significance. The usual characters were present, each having arrived at different times. Maitland was there with Campbell, his arm in a sling from the assassination attempt, and Radcliffe came later cursing the stairs as his gout was troubling him. Last to arrive were Lloyd and Raynes.

They gathered in a private room: a no nonsense space for privileged businessmen with its thick walls and heavy oak door. A fire burned away the cool of the late August evening. The furniture was substantial but with none of the opulent delicacy of private homes. The chairs comfortable enough to seat the prominent posteriors of the wealthy. The remains of a meal littered the table and, with the port passed round, the summit began with Raynes. He stood, toasted the King, and got down to business.

"Gentlemen, we thank ye for agreeing to this meeting."

"What about my situation?" Radcliffe said. He was a traumatized man at this point: his reputation threatened, his house vandalized, even his wife assaulted upon the road. "If they will attack Colonel Campbell as they have done, what will become of me?"

"You, Sir, and your family are protected." Raynes could scarcely keep the rancour from his voice. Though he no longer cared for Fanny, he knew old Radcliffe for a coward and a cuckhold. "Next you'll be asking the general here to make camp in your garden."

"Captain," Maitland said, "I suggest you get on with what brought us here.'

"Sir!" Raynes replied. Maitland was the one man in the room immune to insult. Raynes knew this night would prove either the end of his career or a new beginning. "Solicitor Lloyd and I hae been active in our investigations ..."

"Not active enough," Radcliffe said. "Things have altered for the worse! More robbery and arson, more acts of terror."

He turned to Lloyd, the man he realized was a threat to his status. Lloyd was ready for him.

"Barrowclough deceived us but I found some truth in his lies," he said. "We have requested your presence to hear your judgements."

"Did you catch the man who murdered Sutherland?" Campbell said. The death of the young Lord had brought down upon him the indignation of *Horse Guards*. The Commander-in-Chief was disturbed and worse, the fury of Baron Gower, a grieving father and peer of the Realm, was threatening to have Campbell court-martialed. The colonel's reputation had been mortally wounded at Leeds.

"We hae not, Sir," Raynes said, "though we believe we know the man who ordered the assassination. He was targeting you."

"I know I was the target! There was a note. But who would those men have been?"

"Colonel, the captain and I have been busy," Lloyd said. "After our last meeting you recall I rode with you as far as Halifax where, with a servant, I was able to have my man administered the Luddite Oath. I now know the identity of one of their leaders, a man named John Baines. He has no suspicion of my knowledge and is being monitored as we speak."

"Bring him in then!" Radcliffe said. "Leave him to me at Milnsbridge."

"I think not yet, Sir," Lloyd said. "There are other fish to fry. Captain Raynes, I believe it your turn."

"Thank ye, John," Raynes said, smiling. Lloyd may have been one of the nastiest men Raynes had come across, but he was also most valuable in the circumstances.

"Who ordered the attack that killed Sutherland?" Campbell again asked.

"In a moment, Colonel," Lloyd said. "How can you judge our information if you insist upon not attending it?"

Lloyd's voice, for the first time rose to a new authority with a suddenness which dazed Campbell. The colonel did not reply.

"As I was about to say," Raynes said, "after my journey to Halifax and Leeds, I returned to this area continuing my patrols. One night I arrested the very man who had robbed and nearly raped Mrs. Radcliffe." Raynes could not help but augment Radcliffe's humiliation with a touch of hyperbole. "Before I could take him to Milnsbridge House the man, his name is Parkin, informed me he had the knowledge to lead me to someone significant; someone who knew the Ludd leader organizing this terror."

"Rape, did you say ..." a fragile Radcliffe said.

"And did he?" Campbell asked.

Maitland ignored both Campbell's and Radcliffe's agendas. This, to the General, was real progress.

"Indeed, Sir. Parkin took me to a fellow named John Dean in Marsden."

"This Dean is the murderer?" Campbell said.

"He is not, Colonel. But he has long been friends with a man named George Mellor."

"The one we spoke of in our last conference?" Maitland's quick mind, concealed beneath his hedonism, startled the group.

This was a far different man than the *flimsy rake* who had appeared from Buxton. Maitland had come to know he was up against an unpredictable and dangerous enemy. It had meant his undivided attention and focus. Never a man to underestimate a situation, he gave this rebellion his full concentration.

"The very one, Sir," Lloyd said.

"Have you this man in custody?" Maitland asked.

"No, General," Raynes responded. "The man is a phantom. According to Parkin and Dean he organizes the West Riding's terror attacks.

Parkin also mentioned a man named Sam Lodge who might know where Mellor hides. I hae yet to visit him."

"I would do so quickly, Captain Raynes," Maitland said. "I would also suggest, Magistrate Radcliffe, to rid ourselves of the terror you fear, that you make more arrests."

"I've been doing that very thing," Radcliffe said.

"We must be more aggressive. I speak now of random arrests under martial law. Cast a net wide enough and this Mellor may be caught up. Arrest Baines as well, Lloyd. Arrest enough and the rest will wither."

"I understand your logic, General," Lloyd responded, "but there is a flaw to it."

"Really?" said Maitland coldly. "How so?"

"Mass arrests must occur simultaneously and with enough men to succeed; otherwise, the organizers will vanish."

"You miss my point, Solicitor," the general said. "I said *random*, not mass arrests."

"But that is illegal, Sir." Radcliffe was worried his powers were being stripped from him.

"It seems *you* forget, Magistrate Radcliffe," Lloyd said, "since Horsfall's murder the West Riding has been regulated by *martial law*."

It was time to remove an impediment. Radcliffe had intruded too often. Lloyd had finally had enough.

"That is why," Maitland said, "these young prodigies here were enabled to work together. Are you losing your memory, Radcliffe?"

Radcliffe was no match for Maitland. He sat defeated and silent.

"If I may, Sir," Lloyd said, "might I remind you of your earlier notion? It was significant at the time, and of even more consequence now."

"Being?" Maitland asked.

"Luddites recanting their Oaths, being *untwisted*, as you said."

"Official pardons? Yes, I did say that."

"Random arrests would provoke the public whereas a pardon, accompanied by a *guinea* payment in reward, would accomplish much more. It would split the opposition. Those not recanting and still on our list could then be arrested through quick, direct means."

"Who pays for this?" Radcliffe asked.

"Why you do, Radcliffe!" Maitland said. "The pardon shall be in your name as magistrate therefore employing your currency, or I should say that of the West Riding. Oh, don't worry, old boy, if this works you shall be reimbursed."

"By whom?"

"Viscount Sidmouth, our *new* Home Secretary. It is he to whom I now report and he has strong control of Parliament, particularly after Perceval's murder."

"General, the West Riding cannot dole out the amounts you anticipate. I expect many will recant whether they've taken the Oath or not. Times are hard, Sir, as you know. They shall come for the *brass*, as they say, Luddite or not."

"Tell me, Sir, as magistrate would you rather keep the money along with the terror, or spend the one to end the other? I suggest you return to your treasury in order to produce the funds. *Now*, Radcliffe, if you please!"

Lloyd smiled across the table at Raynes. Radcliffe rose and shuffled out. He was beaten. A frail old man down, rendered helpless, no longer a power of any concern. They had worked their manoeuvres well.

"I want a hand in making arrests," Campbell said.

It was clear what he meant by his words. Certain Luddite killers would not reach a cell.

"That shall not happen, Campbell, "Maitland said. "You're in enough trouble as is; allowing a Peer to be murdered. You have a great deal to answer for."

"Sir," came the gruff, crushed reply, and another part of the younger men's scheme took shape; a second piece in the game reduced.

"Meanwhile," Raynes said, "Solicitor Lloyd, with a squadron of dragoons, shall travel to Halifax and hae this Baines arrested, then on to a small manufacturer named Thomas Brook. We're sure he was at the Rawfolds affair. I myself am after a man named Benjamin Walker. Apparently, he was with Brook at Rawfolds according to Mr. Lloyd's information which this time appears impeccable. Then I'll act on my knowledge regarding Lodge. He might know something of Mellor. I'll hae him tomorrow."

"What about the Sutherland murder?" Campbell roused himself again, shoving his chair back and rising, once more disrupting proceedings ... as Raynes had anticipated. He had omitted Sutherland's murder on purpose.

"Campbell!" Maitland said. "I've had enough of your outbursts. I am ordering you to conduct an immediate *personal* inspection of all troops throughout the West Riding! Your work now is to ensure our regiments shall be ready to cast our net when the time comes. I should say you have several weeks of hard riding in front of you."

"Yes, Sir." Campbell stood to attention.

"When you are finished report to me. You shall no longer be required at these meetings."

"But ..."

"You should have known you had insurrection on your hands? Your men, for God's sake, were unprepared! You have your orders and this time they will be performed with acumen."

"Travel the entire West Riding again?" Campbell said.

Raynes nearly snickered but covered his delight with a sneeze.

"Your role, Colonel, is to carry out my orders!"

"Yes, Sir."

"You shall start today with Radcliffe, visiting Milnsbridge House for the funds we require. You should join him. *Now*!"

Campbell saluted, his hands shaking as he gathered his belongings. He maintained a military posture though the shuffle of his boots imparted a different meaning.

Second old man down.

The young men smiled at each other. The world was turning as it should. The game was playing out perfectly.

Checkmate.

Thomas Brook's home was also his mill. His operation in Lockwood was small, much like John Wood's. Brook too had known he'd be driven from business by the import of machines but unlike Wood, Brook's principles led him to stand with the men who rose up for their rights. Thus he had joined the attack on Cartwright's mill.

Yet the violence at Rawfolds had so confused Brook he'd panicked. That night had turned Brook's world as topsy-turvy as it could possibly be. Nothing made sense to him after that. After the battle, the confusion and losing his hat, Mellor had sent Brook with Walker to Brook's mill. Through the next day Walker had slept in a loft, departing the following night. Brook, sleepless, had carried on, re-assuring his wife all was well, that he might be a little under the weather from a long night at the pub. She'd accepted it, though she'd asked him what he'd done with his hat.

Days passed, laced with worry about that hat, but when weeks followed days Thomas Brook began to relax. Perhaps the hat had sunk to the bottom of the pond. Perhaps someone had found it and kept it for his own. It was, after all, a costly item. So as time passed Brook tried to focus on keeping his mill. He'd kept his head down, minded his business and hoped the tumult would pass.

He thought himself safe.

Thus the dawn knock upon his door, the alarm of his wife and children and then all which happened afterward, simply dumfounded him. Two men, one huge and swarthy, the other slight and sweaty, came down upon him like a lightning bolt. He was punched, seized, manacled and hustled into a tinker's van where a hood was placed over his head. He begged for mercy. For that he received another blow which broke his nose and knocked him unconscious. When he awakened the bag was gone, his nightshirt was stained with blood, and he found himself manacled to a chair in a whitewashed vault.

The space was small. It might have been a store room. It was empty now but for him. He had no shoes. His feet were cold. He stared straight ahead at the windowless door. Even should he try shouting he doubted he would be heard. He tried once, his voice rattling around the vaulted ceiling. His nose began to bleed again. He breathed through his mouth because of his nose. His throat became dry. He could not move out of the chair and, even if he could, there was no water to slake his thirst. He began to cry.

He stayed seated in the white room a long time. The door never opened. He pissed and shat himself in that chair. He wept again as despair took him. He wondered if this was to be his tomb, if he would be buried alive, left to die, become bones; become dust.

When the door finally opened he welcomed it until he saw those who entered; the same two who'd abducted him, each holding a cloth to his nose to ward off the stench which had become Thomas Brook. The big one carried a foot stool. He set it in front of Brook. He signified Brook should raise his feet and place them on the stool. Clearly he did not want to touch Brook. The smaller man held a straight-backed chair which he set down beside Brook. He offered a cup from which Brook might sip. Blessed water. It restored him briefly. He placed his feet on the stool as instructed. They were so cold he could hardly feel them.

In a quick motion the big man produced a rope and in two fast loops bound Brook's feet to the stool. Brook cried out in disbelief. The rest of the water was thrown in his face. The ferocity terrified him. Brook knew his tormentor.

Solicitor John Lloyd was Magistrate Radcliffe's retainer. Brook had seen him during the meeting at Milnsbridge: a fetching, fawning, oily sycophant. All Thomas Brook could feel now was horror of a man who seemed more serpent than human: his eyes slits, his slick skin glowing. What he said to Brook need not have been spoken yet he seemed to relish his power.

"Thomas Brook of Lockwood, you are under arrest for riot and insurrection."

"I'm ... sorry ..."

Lloyd scowled.

"You admit to your crimes?"

"Wha ... what will you do with me?"

"That shall be left to justice in the form of Magistrate Radcliffe or perhaps, if you are not co-operative, a Judge of the York Assizes."

"I'll co-operate, Mr. Lloyd. Tell me what I must do?"

"M'Donald?"

Lloyd glanced toward the big man. Upon hearing his name his hand dived into his coat and withdrew a crumpled object. He handed it to Lloyd. Lloyd held it up.

"This is yours, I gather?"

It was his hat.

"Aye, Sir. I lost it."

"When?"

"I'm ... I'm not sure. It was so long ago ..."

"I warn you, Brook, this is not the worst you'll experience should you choose to lie."

"I lost it! I lost it at Cartwright's place. I was visiting ..."

"Visiting was it?" Lloyd sneered.

"I'm sure. Yes. His wife baked bread ..."

"M'Donald!"

Lloyd's voice transformed from unctuous to imperious. The big man stepped forward again, his hand reaching into his coat withdrawing a thick, black leather strap. Before Brook could react M'Donald had swung the strap with all his huge force and struck the soles of Brook's feet. The slap echoed around the vaulted room accompanied by a scream ripped from Brook's throat. M'Donald struck again. Brook's feet, once cold, burned with pain; from numb to burning in two quick strokes. The strap was a tongue of fire.

"Once more, M'Donald, to make clear the message ..." Lloyd said quietly yet audibly beneath Brook's shrieks.

"No! No! Please ...."

The strap struck his feet with a heavy smack pushing his wails to the squeals of a beast, barely human: pleading, weeping, shocked, stupefied. It took some time for Brook to find his humanity, or what was left of it. Lloyd sat sated as a cat. Only his hands ... opening, closing ... indicated his passion. When Brook's eyes finally focused he began again.

"You were there the night Rawfolds was attacked. Don't deny it. Your hat tells the truth. We have evidence enough to have you transported. What I want from you is the names of the men who were with you that night."

"There were hundreds! How could I know?"

"M'Donald."

"Oh God no! Please. No more!"

"The names."

"They all had numbers. They wore disguises."

"With whom did you escape?"

"I ran off by myself."

"Your wife says you arrived home with a man."

"You have my wife? Is she here? Oh God help me! What have you done to her?"

"Who was the man?"

"You won't harm her?"

"M'Donald."

The strap thundered into his psyche. His bowels let loose. He felt fire in his feet and wet heat on his buttocks. Shame.

"Waaaalker!" he screamed.

This man had his wife; had her in his power.

"Who did you say? I can't understand you."

"Ben Walker. Benjamin Walker."

"Of Longroyd Bridge?"

"Yes."

"Where is he presently?"

"I don't know. Please. I've given you what you wish!"

"You haven't yet begun. Who led the attack?"

"He's from Longroyd too ..."

Brook tried to evade.

"M'Donald."

"It was George Mellor!" Brook shouted, trying desperately to avoid the strap.

"And where is this Mellor?"

"Oh Lord, I don't know. He's not been seen since Rawfolds!"

"You are a Luddite. He is your leader. You must know ..."

"I'm not! I swear! I've not taken the Oath! I went to Rawfolds to help ruin Cartwright the way he's ruining me! Please! Where is Susan?"

"Safe enough if you co-operate."

"I can't help you with things I don't know. Get to Walker. He'll know. He hates Mellor! Or find Sam Lodge. He lives down near Slaithwaite! Please."

"M'Donald."

"Nooooo!"

The strap thrashed him again. Blood spattered from the soles of his feet.

"Just a reminder, Brook," Lloyd said. "We'll be off now, give you a chance to think. The stool, M'Donald."

Brook's feet were untied, the stool swept away and carried from the room. At the door Lloyd turned and smirked before closing it.

Something else had been swept away in that cold white room.

All that was left was pain, shame and desolation; trying vainly to keep its feet in the air.

—

Raynes had trouble finding the place: so out of the way and so decrepit it appeared abandoned. Smoke curled from the chimney, however. The smoke was what had attracted him. Raynes and two of his men dismounted. He signalled them to the rear of the dwelling. The rest remained mounted ready to chase a runner. Raynes knocked on the cracked wood door.

A woman answered. She was big boned yet reduced through hunger and hardship. Her once red hair had gone mostly grey. Her face was a story of worry, her hands callused from menial work. Her eyes, however, were a stunning green. They should have shone. Instead they were dull and within them he noted a tinge of fear.

"You are Mrs. Lodge, wife of Samuel Lodge?"

"And if I am?"

"Where is your husband?"

A burly man appeared behind her. He had rounded shoulders and close cropped hair. Rather than the panic he'd expected, Raynes felt only a sense of loss emanate from the man. He would not resist.

"I'm the one you want. Bonnie, get the kids out of the house."

The woman retreated, Lodge held open the door and immediately four tattered urchins filed out and away. They were silent, terrified, yet engrossed by Raynes' glittering uniform.

"You'll be Captain Raynes," Lodge said. "Step inside, Sir."

Raynes entered. The place was humble. The home of a pauper.

Raynes removed his riding gloves holding them in one hand: the picture of authority.

"Mr. Lodge, ye're acquainted with George Mellor, yes?"

"He knows him, aye," the woman said.

"I am not addressing you, madam. Hold your tongue. Now Lodge, where is Mellor?"

"I don't know, Captain. He moves 'round. Once every while he stops in."

"He must live somewhere?"

"He's never told me."

"Mr. Lodge, I can place ye under arrest ..."

"No, Sir, you can't! My Sam's done nothing but mind his business," Bonnie Lodge said.

Raynes realized the woman, for all her beaten down looks, was a creature who would defend her family to the death. He tried another path.

"Madam, I asked ye to stay quiet. Do so. Now, Mr. Lodge, if ye know Mellor then ye'll know his friends. Give me their names."

"I ... I won't," the beefy fellow replied. The door's leather hinges creaked. Raynes saw his sergeant's silhouette against the light.

"Sorry for the disturbance, Sir. Private Dayle happened t' follow the children. They went down by the stream."

Raynes felt a tension between the couple.

"What is out there?" he asked.

"'Tis where they play is all," Mrs. Lodge replied, but her voice was shaky.

"I should like to see this area, Sergeant. Remain with the wife. Lodge, come with me."

The two left the house and turned toward the stream. Raynes saw the children sitting not on the grass but on gravel beside the stream. They appeared frightened. He felt Lodge check for an instant but the big fellow seemed to collapse within and carried on toward the gravel patch.

"Sir, if I'm arrested what happens t' Bonnie and my kids?"

"Nothing, Mr. Lodge, if ye co-operate."

There was a pause: the children gaping up at their father, their father gazing down.

"Young Zack, go on back t' the house and get the shovel," Lodge said.

The oldest boy rose and did as told.

Two soldiers returned with him. One took the shovel.

"Should my man dig in this gravel, Mr. Lodge?"

"Aye. Kids, off with you now!"

The children moved, though not far. The soldier began to dig. It did not take long. Within five minutes his shovel struck something other than gravel. The second dragoon swept away the loose stone revealing three pistols, one of them a huge gun. Raynes, recalling Horsfall's wounds, knew instantly what he'd discovered. His heart jumped. To control himself he took the large pistol from the soldier and washed it clean in the stream. He examined it carefully. There was writing embossed upon the grip. It was in an odd language, the characters unfamiliar to him.

"You're under arrest, Lodge. For murder."

"No, Sir. I but hid the guns."

"Whose are they?"

"I won't say."

"Ye be a Luddite."

"I've taken no Oath. But I'll not go back on my friends."

"Sergeant, shackle him. If not murder, Lodge, you're arrested for concealing evidence and therefore abetting a fugitive. I hope this friendship was worthwhile."

Sam Lodge was fettered and led to a waiting spare horse amidst the troop of dragoons. As they put him on the horse he looked sorrowfully at his wife and children huddled by the doorway of his home. The children were crying. Bonnie's green eyes shot fire. He recalled what she'd said to him about Luddites and Mellor. He had made his choice then. As usual, Bonnie had been right.

That fact helped neither of them as he was taken away.

32

THE AUTUMN OF 1812 was cold and dreary, the green of birch trees turning to yellow with days marked by magical flights of swallows as they swirled together in their formations, the flocks nearly touching the ground before swooping upward again into heavy grey skies. They were beautiful in their synchronicity but they signalled another storm.

That fall heavy rains came often. They bore down upon crops and what they did not crush, they rotted. The cost of food went up again and people began to go hungry. It would be a long, cold, even fatal winter for some. Without support, besides that contributed by parish churches and Methodist assemblies, there would be starvation. People began to know a despair beyond their fears of both Luddites and Government. They tried to stay out of the way of the heedless crossfire.

Then things changed.

Word finally spread through handbills and town criers of the *Pardon of Illegal Oaths.* There was a *guinea*, twenty one shillings, to close the deal. It seemed too good to be true so it took time before men trickled down from the villages to towns such as Stockport, Sheffield, or Huddersfield. As others watched from a safe remove they noted no man was arrested and each came away with the promised *brass.* Those who took the golden guinea did so at substantial risk. The Oath was a thing to be feared. Retribution became ferocious.

Lloyd and Raynes had been lying in wait as foxes anticipating their prey: those who did not take the pardon. They chose their timing carefully. On a Sunday when most men were at home, indeed more than usual as it was raining that day, they struck. The captain's dragoons captured scores of suspects bringing them directly to Huddersfield gaol to be processed by Solicitor Lloyd. Fear, Raynes advised, should be Maitland's policy after the Pardons; more fear than that instilled by Luddites.

Lloyd took to riding with Raynes. Lloyd's dossier of names was a great help. John Baines, John Kinder and John Wood were captured; indeed, every *John, Dick and Harry* remotely connected to the list was brought in for questioning. Because the Lancaster Assizes had proven too merciful upon the suspected rebels, as too had the Nottingham Assizes under Justice Bayley, Lloyd insisted the prisoners be taken to York. These actions were barely legal yet little did the middle class care, for the terror began to abate. And Lloyd increased his influence: from the West Riding to the greater theatre at York, leaving Radcliffe in his wake.

And just at the end of their campaign, Raynes and Lloyd swept into their net one very curious fish: Ben Walker. This prisoner required special treatment. Lloyd altered tactics and took him to the vault in Milnsbridge House.

Close indeed.

With the hope of pardon and peace came a sense of relief as both sides stood down. As Lloyd's and Raynes' reputations grew, those of Mellor and Thorpe diminished. They found themselves camping in desolate places when barns, sheds and cellars were denied them. They ate sparingly when less food was provided and even risked further acrimony by stealing from gardens, though by this time most of what was still in the ground had become mildewed. Finally they slaughtered an ewe, a crime punishable by death but "might as well be hung for a sheep as a lamb," quoted Thorpe. They knew by now they were outlaws indeed.

Mellor's plots became increasingly vicious until Will Thorpe prevailed. They had to remove themselves, Thorpe realized, before Mellor pushed things out of control. A return through Standedge Tunnel to their cottage at Diggle was the best they could do until things settled. They were on their way toward Marsden, just coming down off Meltham moor's rugged ground, when they clashed.

"I've it in my head t' get hold of Ben Walker again, Will," Mellor said.

"He's no man t' trust, George. He's jealous of you. Has been since you met."

"I cannot understand him."

"He's not loyal, George. He's just frightened of you."

"Then the better for me to speak with him."

"Times are dangerous, George. I think we're right t' high tail t' Diggle. Raynes and Lloyd have the upper hand: the Pardons."

"Their bribes won't keep once they've had their way!"

"Nothing new in that," Thorpe said. "People have short memories."

"They know we fight for them? They know we're winning! That's why these Pardons have been invented. They're desperate measures. We're finally making them change their ways, Will! What's happened that people can't see? "

"Most are desperate this year. A guinea'll go a long way this winter."

"Will, you're my right hand!" Mellor clasped his friend's massive shoulder.

"Then let that hand shepherd you! Look what's come against us! Dost hear yourself, George?" Thorpe stopped walking.

"You sound angry, Will." Mellor faced his friend.

"Maitland's offering pardons! You've won. But that's not enough. Now you want t' control the same folk you came t' rescue. And why is that? George, you're becoming more like the *maisters* each day."

Mellor didn't respond. At first Thorpe thought his friend in a sulk, something he'd never known him to do, then he thought again. George was not angry, he realized, as he noted his friend's glance toward him. Once they reached level ground near the weir marking Marsden's outskirts, Mellor waited for Thorpe to join him.

"So dost think I'm a felon now, Will?"

Thorpe feared his friend's resentment, then unexpectedly witnessed a rare sight these latter days. Those eyes, diamond eyes, sparkled again for an instant as Mellor smiled. Thorpe knew then he'd done right to tell the truth.

"So the reason you're steering us back t' Diggle is me?" Mellor tapped his chest.

"Lad, you know I love you."

"I do, Will. I've fooled myself with my plots. 'Tis time for us both t' rest a bit, take that pride of mine and temper it."

"Just forget Walker," Thorpe said, pleased that though they were dangerous men, they were not savages. They were not felons. They were fighters against tyranny. Yet both needed respite. Facing overwhelming odds not even Mellor's drive could endure.

Thorpe had no idea how right he was.

—

They approached the canal as they normally did, stopping by the pub to visit John Dean. Once they discovered Dean had been arrested, the news made them wary as they approached Standedge Tunnel. Their custom had been to arrive in the night, sleep in the warehouse and at first light show Brookbank's permission to *leg* a freight boat.

They found room in the warehouse easily enough but spoke sparingly with the *leggers*, quietly making space amidst bales of cloth, bedding themselves down for the night. Each took his turn on watch. In the very early morning George Mellor noticed a man rise and slink into the pre-dawn darkness. It put him on edge.

At dawn they found the first boat going through and presented their papers to the overman. They boarded but noticed three new *leggers* manning the boat; men they didn't recognize. As the boat entered the tunnel, with only torch light to see by, they could hear the *pad pad* of the *leggers'* boots upon the tunnel ceiling and feel the push of the vessel as it made its way deeper into the dark. Shadows flickered along the walls. They waited, knowing something was different. Then two men appeared from below: one of them as big as Thorpe, the other was Richard Brookbank himself. He held a pistol.

"Stop the boat!" he shouted and instantly the vessel slowed.

Fortunately, Thorpe and Mellor had remained in the stern so the other three *leggers* assembling on the roof were visible in the torch light. Five men, perhaps two of them armed. Richard Brookbank was seeking revenge.

"What dost want, Richard?" Mellor asked warily.

"My son," Brookbank demanded.

"He's at the other end. A cottage in Diggle."

"I've been there!" Brookbank said. "I've seen what you've done to him! He won't return home! He lusts after some trollop he met through you!"

"The sweet girl who cleans for us? No, Richard, that grew of itself. Your lad's in love."

"You've taken my boy! You've changed him! Now I'll take you. Two thousand pounds reward! That might entice Willis back and if not, shall provide my daughter a healthy dowry. She shall marry a title."

"You know we won't go easy," Thorpe said.

"I think five to two are very strong odds," Brookbank replied. He'd forgotten he faced two killers. It takes a hard, desperate man to kill another. Mellor and Thorpe were veterans.

"Look here, Richard, we can bargain on this. I've *brass* t' pay you. And I can have a talk with Willis. He'll listen t' me." Mellor spoke soothingly, reaching into his coat.

Brookbank brought up the pistol.

"Wait now, Richard, don't point that gun! I'm only getting the notes from my pocket."

Mellor pulled out papers. In the flickering torch light they would look like pound notes. Mellor gestured, Thorpe took a subtle step closer.

"'Tis yours, Richard, for the trouble we've caused. Take it, man!"

Mellor had gambled. It took but a moment until Brookbank's greed got the best of him. He stepped forward. The instant their fingers touched Mellor dropped the notes. As Brookbank bent to retrieve them Mellor grabbed him, spinning him around into Thorpe's arms. The gun fired as Thorpe took hold, the sound of its shot echoing like thunder through the tunnel, damping the ears of every man there.

So when Brookbank ordered his attack his deafened men could not hear him. Mellor tossed Brookbank out of the boat. Thorpe too moved quickly. Pistol held by its barrel he ran at the big man smashing the gun's butt against his opponent's head. The man went down like a felled tree. The three on the roof looked at each other in wonder. Before they could move two were shot at by Mellor, a pair of pistols from his belt in an instant. Smoke. Booming thunder. The men panicked. They scampered forward and leapt into the water. The encounter had taken five minutes: four to bluster, one to wound and maim.

When his hearing returned, Mellor heard splashing. The men overboard were hugging the boat. There was nowhere to go. He asked Thorpe to get on the roof to start *legging* but something seemed wrong. Thorpe had thumped down on a bale, his face contorted.

"I can't do it, George. He shot hit me when I grabbed the gun."

"Where Will?"

"My side. Burns like the devil."

"We've got t' go back then. A surgeon in Marsden. I'll get us moving. Can you keep watch against them boarding us?"

"Aye," Thorpe said, hauling his own pistols from his belt. He moved slowly and gingerly, clearly in pain. Mellor went up to the roof and literally ran the boat back to Standedge.

—

Ben Walker was terrified. Unlike other prisoners sent to Huddersfield gaol, he'd been trussed and placed in a wagon and when night fell he'd been taken along a road he knew well ... the route to Milnsbridge House. Lloyd had sat with the driver up front. When they'd arrived Walker was removed from the waggon and pulled along a gravel path into an echoing, stone-flagged hallway. He was chained to a chair, then left to his thoughts in a white vaulted room.

He was frantic when the door opened and Lloyd entered along with an almost primeval character. Walker knew the man was there for one reason: to hurt him. Ben Walker had always feared pain. His was a special soul, he thought, set apart somehow from the rest. If he was not as large or handsome as others he made up for that with his wit and his song. But he could not face pain. He'd already made up his mind to that.

Lloyd carried a small ladder-back chair which he placed beside Walker's. He sat. His face was unctuous, his lank hair hung down in clumps. He smiled at Walker. His smile was awful, more grimace than grin. Walker knew he would hang for Horsfall's murder. He tried to establish a connection with Lloyd, grinning in return. Lloyd turned and looked at the huge bloke with whom he'd entered. He gestured.

The animal had a stool. He placed it in front of Walker. Lloyd instructed Walker to place his feet on the stool.

"No, Sir! I won't!"

"You shall do as you're told or suffer worse consequences," Lloyd said.

"This big bastard's going t' beat me!"

"Not if you tell me now what I wish. Show him the instrument, M'Donald."

M'Donald produced a strap. Black ... darker black along its edges from blood stains, it came to an arrowhead point. It was three feet long and almost half an inch thick. When it swung in the still air it looked like an awful black snake. It took little imagination to comprehend what it could do.

"What do you want? Anything!"

"Names?" Lloyd said, grinning.

Walker gave them. Gave them all. Gave some who had never done anything in case the first weren't enough. Lloyd wrote each down in his book. The belt dangled, ever present.

"Very good, Walker! I was told you could sing. I had no idea so well."

"What dost mean?"

"I've heard other birds, Walker. They've told me you sang a lovely song at a meeting a few months past in a public house called The Shears. Is that correct?"

"The Shears?"

"M'Donald," Lloyd said softly.

Walker saw the strap rise.

"Aye! I know! 'Twas the meeting just after Rawfolds!"

"Very good, Walker. It seems we have a great deal to discuss. Would you like some water? You'll be talking a while ..."

With the offer of water Walker was released from his terror. He began to calculate. In the back of his mind, as they always were, thoughts of George Mellor welled. Walker remembered sweet Jilly and her choice. He recalled Mellor's sharp orders to stop his roughness with prisoners. He even evoked those eyes which seemed always to glitter and laugh at him. He knew then precisely what he must do.

"Mr. Lloyd, Sir ... I don't need long t' tell you what needs t' be told. You're after *Maister* Horsfall's killer. Am I right?"

"And what do you know of that?"

"There's a two thousand pound reward, I've heard."

"That depends on the information."

"George Mellor shot him with a big Russian gun, and Will Thorpe shot him as well!"

"How could you know that?"

"About the reward," Walker said.

"Continue!" The strap rose higher in M'Donald's hand.

"I know because I was with 'em! Me and Tom Smith! But 'twas all Thorpe and Mellor! After they shot him a rider came down the road. Saw the four of us. You must know that much!"

There was a moment, an instant of stasis.

"M'Donald," Lloyd said, "lay down your strap and remove this man's manacles. Mr. Walker, Ben is your Christian name is it not? You shall provide King's evidence in court once we have those two in custody."

"'It would mean my death," Walker said. He had already determined the only way to avoid imprisonment, transportation and even the noose was to tell everything. He knew he needed Lloyd to protect him. He knew as well he'd found his chance to return George Mellor's abuses.

"I shall have you safeguarded, and rewarded, but I require more detailed information."

"Anything, Sir."

Walker massaged his wrists where the metal had bitten.

"Where are they now? Thorpe and Mellor?"

"I can't say, Sir. They move 'round so much."

"They must have places to hide?"

"I heard one time, it was Thorpe talking, about the *Stannidge* tunnel. That's all I heard."

"I see. Mr. Walker, I am deputizing you as one of my special constables. You shall ride with myself and Captain Raynes until we find these men."

"I'll ride with you, Sir, though I don't know how t' ride a horse." He could think of no safer place than amidst a troop of dragoons.

"A curricle then, so you can keep up, with a driver and guard to protect you."

"Aye, Sir. I'll do what I'm told."

There was a knock at the door. Conversation stopped. M'Donald opened it. He signalled Lloyd. Lloyd went to the door exchanging words with the man outside. When he turned back to Walker he was grinning.

"It seems your reward may come sooner than later, Mr. Walker. Mellor and Thorpe have been seen at Standedge. We leave momentarily. As soon as Raynes assembles his squadron."

"*Must* I go with you?" Walker, now facing the fact of meeting Mellor, had begun to transform to his craven self once again.

"I've no idea what either man looks like so, yes, you must come to identify them."

With his shoes back on, he walked down the long hall in Milnsbridge's cellar. That walk would take him to a life he would, every day for the rest of it, come to regret.

Mellor kicked the boat through the tunnel's mouth into the pool by the docks. As soon as they'd cleared the outlet he heard shouting from the stern. It was Brookbank screaming orders to arrest the felons on board. The moment they touched the wharf Mellor helped Thorpe over the gunwales. They struggled down the tow path to Marsden's south side. They knew of a surgeon there.

Once on land and a safe distance from the hijackers, Brookbank berated them with the strident voice of the afflicted. Mellor heard him shout something about a man sent for the cavalry; doubtless the one who had sneaked out of the warehouse in early morning.

So Mellor knew there was little time before Raynes or someone like him would arrive. He urged Thorpe, despite the wound, to press on. They struggled through back lanes until they came to the surgeon's home. His name was Barnes; a slight, studious man. He opened his door to the two huge characters who pushed their way past him into his home.

"What is the meaning of this?" Barnes said.

"This man's been shot," Mellor replied. "He needs help."

"Why was he shot?" Barnes asked.

"That's none of your concern. I need him patched right quick."

"How do I know you're not villains chased by the law?"

The answer was simple. His guns empty of shot and useless, Mellor drew a knife, the kind used for killing and dressing game. Surgeon Barnes paled.

"Now!" Mellor ordered.

"Follow me. My surgery ..."

Once in the surgery Barnes lifted Thorpe's shirt. Thorpe remained standing. The surgeon examined the wound. Blood welled as he probed. Thorpe groaned.

"Yes, I see," Barnes said. "Lay him on the table. On his stomach. The ball has lodged by his lower rib. I must remove it, then clean the wound."

"Do it quick," Mellor said. "We've little time."

"I do not know your name, Sir, but by your behaviour I know you for an outlaw," the surgeon said, his round glasses had slipped down his nose.

He pushed them back into place. He was a spare, ascetic type who, after his initial shock, was not a man to panic.

"If you want him to live I must do as I've said. The ball in itself is simple, but when it entered the body it took part of his shirt with it. His shirt looks none too clean. If I do not ensure the wound is dirt-free, he will succumb to infection. Now put that knife down and assist me."

It was finished in half an hour. Thorpe was on his feet, bandaged around his middle and, having been given some laudanum to quell the pain of the ball's removal, seemed comfortable.

Mellor thanked the surgeon.

"Do not thank me, Sir," Barnes said. "I have done this under duress! Be assured when you depart I shall attend the local Justice. Now leave my premises and do not return!"

Mellor should have killed him but the man had done nothing other than help. Still, he knew the surgeon would do as he said, so using Barnes' own supply of bandage he wrapped the man like a mummy, carried him to his bed and rolled him under it, then returned to Thorpe.

Mellor opened the front door. The canal was a hundred yards down the slope. He spied the first redcoats on the other side of the valley. Cavalry. Brookbank had not been blustering. The horsemen rode toward Standedge Tunnel. Fortunately their direction gave him and Thorpe time to find cover.

Thorpe by this time was able to move at a fair pace, his pain masked by the drug. The two wended their way up the slopes to Binn moor making south, keeping the canal between them and their pursuers. Somehow they had to evade cavalry until dark. Their only hope was that the surgeon would not be discovered too soon for, once he was, it would be clear which bank they were on.

They struggled up over the rugged ground, staying to the path. Thorpe once again began to bleed. They slowed, but both knew they fought time and distance. Once seen, they would have little chance. At this time of year the heather was dense and purple and tall. It concealed them until they reached the summit of the moor. In an hour they achieved the height of the Rocking Stone, a prominent feature on the ridge line, and got behind it. They turned and, in the distance just at the edge of the moor, observed scarlet again. They knew an officer would have a glass quartering the ground in search of them. The glass flashed as it caught the sun.

Thorpe needed rest. He was weak. He insisted Mellor go on without him but Mellor returned his request with a shrug.

"What good would that do me? If I move they'll spy me out anyway."

"But they know it was us. They must know we'd head south."

"No, Will. They'll think we'll go t' ground in Marsden. First they must search the village and, when they find the surgeon, start looking further."

"But they know I was wounded. There's blood in the boat. Won't that take 'em right t' the surgeon?"

"I think I shot two men, you clubbed another. Whose t' say the blood's yours?"

"Brookbank watched us. Saw you help me."

"Can you move, Will?"

"Aye. I know we must."

"We'll crawl a bit. We'll keep this stone between us and them. We'll go down south east then head t' Holmbridge and try for some food and a place t' rest. If not there, then on t' Ramsden Clough. We've supplies still there."

"That's quite a piece, George. I'm not sure I'll make it."

"If I have t' carry you, we'll get there!"

"Carry me?" Thorpe looked at Mellor, then laughed aloud. "I don't think so! I was last carried when I was but six years old."

"Then I'll drag you," Mellor said, laughing in return.

"Look west there," Thorpe said. "Cloud. Maybe we'll have a mist. We need something more than we've had this day."

"Aye. I've another thought. We'll spend a day or two at Ramsden Clough, then we'll strike north."

"Why there? Why not south t' the High Peaks."

"Up there how are we t' get food? Winter's coming, lad. I've a friend, as you know, in Dewsbury. If she's not gone she might help us."

"Mary Buckworth."

"The same."

"Dewsbury's a long stretch, George."

"Hasn't it always been?"

33

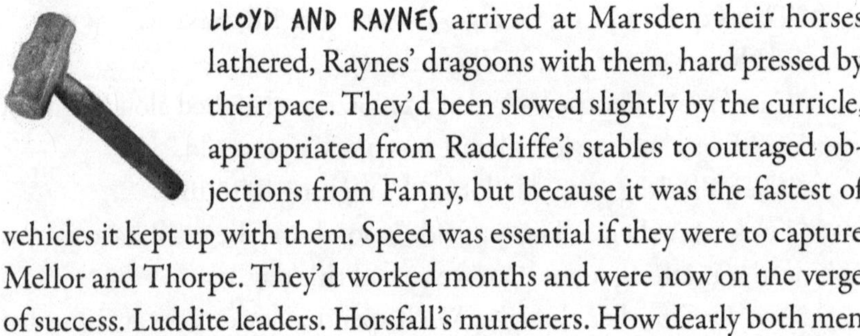

LLOYD AND RAYNES arrived at Marsden their horses lathered, Raynes' dragoons with them, hard pressed by their pace. They'd been slowed slightly by the curricle, appropriated from Radcliffe's stables to outraged objections from Fanny, but because it was the fastest of vehicles it kept up with them. Speed was essential if they were to capture Mellor and Thorpe. They'd worked months and were now on the verge of success. Luddite leaders. Horsfall's murderers. How dearly both men wanted this.

In Standedge they quickly found Brookbank at home. He was filling himself with hot tea and, covered by a thick coverlet, still shivering from his waterborne stint. The formidable tunnel official appeared more a fat, wet rat than the character of whom they'd heard, though his anger provided a detailed description of the botched arrest.

"You mean to say, Mr. Brookbank, that with five of you against only two, you were unable to apprehend them?" Lloyd said.

"I'd no idea they were so dangerous!"

"Why were they on the boat in the first place? And what have they been doing these past months?" Lloyd said. "You understand, Sir, your reputation and your position are threatened by your behaviour."

"They took my son!" Brookbank said. His *position*! "They've kept him captive in Diggle threatening to kill the boy should I not co-operate!"

"You might have come to us, Sir," Lloyd said. "We possess both the men and the skills to have rescued your son. You, Mr. Brookbank, have made a gross miscalculation!"

"What can I say? Have some mercy, Sir! What would you have done?"

"As I told you." Lloyd snubbed Brookbank as he turned to Raynes. "Perhaps you might send some men over Standedge moor. If they were headed that way they must have been trying for Diggle; hopefully they'll continue."

"Immediately," Raynes replied, then turned on his own to Brookbank. "Ye said one of them was wounded?"

"Yes, Captain. I'm sure of it. I fired my pistol directly at him!"

"That would mean they required a surgeon," Lloyd said. "Have you any in Marsden?"

"Surgeon Barnes, Sir! Up the hill south of the canal," Brookbank replied. Happy to be off the solicitor's hook.

"Gi'e me a man to show mine his house," Raynes commanded.

It was not long before the searchers returned having found the surgeon beneath his bed. "So they went south," Raynes told Lloyd who had joined them.

"Binn moor," Brookbank said. "That makes no sense. Surely they'll swing west. There's nothing south of here: Wessenden, Meltham, the High Peaks ... dangerous moors ..."

"I agree," Raynes said. "Because ye last saw 'em moving south doesn't mean they kept that course."

"With a man wounded, they could *not* go up the Pennines!" Brookbank said.

"Very well," Lloyd said. "Raynes, how soon until we've additional troops?"

"Not long," Raynes replied. "Good roads to Marsden. The trouble will be the moors. My men must keep to the paths. I don't want a horse sucked into a bog nor a chap injured should the ground collapse."

"That can happen? I know of peat bogs but ..." Brookbank said.

"I've spent months on those moors, Mr. Brookbank, and lost men to them."

"Can you move on them, the criminals, now, Raynes?" Lloyd said.

So close. So close to their prey.

"I'll order it, John," Raynes answered, "but only reconnaissance. I'll not have understrength units engage them."

"They are but two!" Brookbank said.

"Who dispatched five of ye!" Raynes replied.

"Amateurs," Lloyd said.

"Four to a detachment," Raynes said. "I want them as much as ye, John, but I must be wary for my men's sake."

"Please then, Francis, get on with it!" Lloyd used the familiar as Raynes had done to bolster their partnership. He wanted these two. He knew their capture would give him their prosecution and his own enhanced reputation.

Men were sent off in several directions. One group led its horses to the edge of Binn moor. The men rode up through heather and bracken toward the moor's the highest point: a group of scattered stones.

They carefully stayed to the path wending its way in that direction. When they'd reached the top the officer scoped the far side of the moor, dropping steeply to the south. One of his dragoons approached. He carried a sprig of heather. Handing it up to his Lieutenant the man simply said: "Blood trail, Sir."

—

They went south once clear of the stones. They went deeper out into Wessenden Head moor, deeper than they'd ever gone. They had to get back to Ramsden Clough but the route was rugged and unknown to them. Thorpe's wish had come true, however. Mist had descended and a light rain joined with it, blowing *moor grime.* It concealed them but made the trek harder. Nothing was familiar. The mist concealed landmarks.

They were lucky then to come upon a shepherd's hut. The man was within, a peat fire heating the tiny stone room, filling it with an acrid aroma. When Mellor hailed him the man poked his head out. His appearance, to those unfamiliar with the high moors, might have seemed alarming for the shepherd spent most of his time living rough. His beard was a thick russet bush, his hair a mixed rust and gray and quite long down his back. He had piercing hazel eyes beneath thick brows and his skin was the bronzed tan of those who spent their lives out of doors. He was a thick man: his body square, his clothing sheepskin, his hands gnarled and scarred. Yet he smiled and signalled them in.

Three big men within the tiny stone hut made it crowded. Still, they were out of the rain, The heat seemed to help Thorpe. He curled his great bulk on the dirt floor and tried to sleep. Mellor asked the shepherd his name.

"Hezekiah Hardgrave, they call me," he said, his voice all gravel.

"Where's your home?" Mellor asked.

"I stay out of the towns. I don't like it there since the soldiers."

"What of the soldiers?"

"I'm told they hold the south flank against Ludd brigands."

"And what do you think of Luddites, Hezekiah?"

"'Tis nowt t' me. I keep t' my work. I said, didn't I? I don't like towns."

"But you know these moors?"

"Like the back of my hand."

"Hezekiah, I'm going t' ask you a favour."

"I thought ye might, seein' that big chap seems hurt."

"We're Luddites being chased. We're bent on Ramsden Clough but we're lost."

"Why you're not lost, friend. You're just by Dean Clough, near Wessenden Head. But Ramsden Clough ... now that's a rough crossin'. 'Tis coarse land and the way's blocked by Holme Moss."

"Peat bogs?"

"Aye. And I see you don't have staffs t' find pulpy places."

"We weren't prepared."

"I don't see you makin' Ramsden Clough. Not alone." Hardgrave shook his head.

"Would you guide us?"

"That depends."

"On what?"

"Hast *brass*?"

"Aye. A guinea. Would that do?"

"Aye. I'll take you tomorrow."

"Hezekiah, it must be tonight."

"I told you, 'tis dangerous! Not even I travel at night."

"Two guineas"

"What? Show 'em!"

Mellor retrieved the last of his funds from a pocket. The coins glinted. Hardgrave's eyes nearly popped from beneath his heavy brows.

"So?" Mellor asked.

"It won't be easy, but I'll help. And I don't want it known."

"Of course. The same for us. We can't be seen."

"Let your man sleep. I'll cook some supper, then we'll be off. I'll take the *brass* now."

"One now. The other at the end."

"You might be dead before that. Sunk in a bog. Drowned in a *beck*."

"'That bad up here?"

"As I said."

—

After four hours and the onset of showers Lloyd and Raynes began to lose hope. They remained in the Brookbank house awaiting news. Lloyd became edgy. He ordered Ben Walker escorted into the house. When Walker arrived Lloyd wasted no time. In Brookbank's parlour he ordered M'Donald to beat the man until he told the truth. M'Donald took one kick. It snapped a rib.

"Nooooo!" Walker cried. "Stop! Please! Please! I told you all I know!"

"Then tell me something you don't know!" Lloyd screamed.

So close, now so far once again.

"What do you mean?" Walker asked.

"Speculate, man!"

"What?"

"Where would they go if not over Standedge moor? Think!"

"I'm not sure he knows, John," Raynes said.

"He'll know something!" Lloyd said.

"No! No!" Walker shouted. "How far would your soldiers have gone?"

"Miles on the roads. Not so far on the moors," Raynes replied.

"Then 'tis the moors. South. Likely Holmbridge for shelter."

"Anyone harbouring those men knows the penalty," Lloyd said. "It will not be a home. Where else?"

"There's shepherd's shelters up there."

"They've no food." Lloyd turned to the captain. "Raynes, how far south did your men reach? I mean those on Binn moor."

"It was Saunders. He's only just back. He took his men up to the stone crest, found a blood trail, and then lost it going south."

"So they went south. Where would they hide if they went that way?"

"The best place is Ramsden Clough," Walker said. "Horses can't get up there and I've seen your men, they don't like t' walk."

"Where is this place?" Lloyd asked.

"Directly south of Holmbridge," Raynes said. "We'll hae to take the roads. The moors up there are too dangerous."

"Then we'll move on Ramsden Clough."

"It's growing dark, Lloyd," Raynes said. "My men hae been out all day."

"Do you want these two or not!" Lloyd shouted.

"Mr. Lloyd, ye're frustrated, I know, but if ye dare speak to me in such a tone again I'll have ye returned to Milnsbridge House to join Magistrate Radcliffe. Is this clear to ye, Sir?"

Lloyd knew he'd overstepped. He shifted quickly to the sycophantic character he assumed the moment he sensed a threat. Not just his voice but his mannerisms, his physicality, transformed. He would have made a fine actor.

"Of course, Captain Raynes. I am sorry, Sir, to have insulted you. Please, Sir, be aware of how long you and I have pursued these men and to have had them so close and now to have lost them ... well, I am a fool to bewail the situation and cause affront to yourself, Sir. Please accept my apology and excuse my behaviour."

"I too want these men, Lloyd. We'll leave directly but my men must hae food and must care for their horses. A night ride lies ahead!"

—

The trek was far worse than Mellor had thought could be possible. In the dark, in the rain, in the fog they followed Hezekiah Hardgrave as they took the narrow paths concealed by wet drooping heather. Often Hardgrave was reduced to a pace at a time, ever probing with his staff, finding solid ground. There were times when Mellor or Thorpe would step off a track and feel their feet sucked into peaty muck. It was dreadful.

They moved south, the rain coming slantwise into their flanks, up and down steep slopes until they reached what appeared a flat area at the base of a cliff. Here Hardgrave stopped.

"What's wrong?" Mellor asked. Thorpe simply sank to the ground to regain his strength.

"'Tis Holme moss," Hardgrave said, as if he'd said all necessary.

"A problem?" Mellor asked.

"I'd thought we were further east. I don't like this moor. Soft soil and millstone beneath."

"Then we should move east," Mellor said.

"No, lad. Do that and you're into the peat."

"So we follow this cliff."

"Aye. 'Twill take us t' Twizzle Head moss. That's right above Ramsden Clough. But I don't rightly know the way from here."

"We must try. My friend's nearly finished."

"Get him up, but stay back a bit. Should I start t' sink you must come up slow, grab my staff and pull me out. Come up slow, mind!"

In the end Hardgrave did not sink. He died when the ground collapsed beneath him, the stone undermined by rain water flowing down the cliff side. He had not even had time to scream. Mellor and Thorpe dared not move forward. The ground was giving way closer to them. They retreated. For a quarter hour they waited in case Hezekiah Hardgrave might climb out of a chasm and once again lead them. It was useless, both knew. Their only choice was to move east despite Hardgrave's warnings. Mellor led, testing the ground with each step. It was a tortuous journey. Slow as mud. Every step was planned. It took hours to travel but a short distance. As it grew light, the rain was still falling, though the mist had lifted.

After their hours of cautious walking Mellor spotted a landmark:

a jumble of rock marking the head of Ramsden Clough, its small stream now in spate roaring down the valley. They made their way on familiar yet rugged ground, to the stand of ash which served as their refuge. They had left some food there, oatcake and dried pork, which they wolfed down until they realized it was all they had. They saved some for the further journey they knew they would have to make.

They had no idea how soon.

Francis Raynes, flanked by ten dragoons, made his way up the difficult vale called Ramsden. The rain had stopped but the stream flooded dangerously. They moved slowly, carefully; not only was the terrain perilous but the men they sought to arrest were equally so.

They had ridden the dark hours of morning through rain and fog until Holmbridge. There they'd appropriated a guide to take them to Ramsden Clough. Raynes left men with the horses then took his best soldiers on foot up the clough. It was difficult: the ground wet, rocky and treacherous enough that two men were injured to the point they could not continue.

Now Raynes approached a small stand of trees hanging on the hillside. He thought he detected movement. He signalled his men to cover, then continued on his own into the wood. His sight had been true. Two men were struggling uphill through the trees. One seemed hurt, the other aiding him. Raynes pushed forward. He did not think to call for his men. He could see his quarry clearly now having gained on them. Only twenty yards. They were both big men, one extraordinarily so. But it was the other: muscular, auburn haired, who turned toward him. Raynes fired. The ball struck the young man. Raynes could see him knocked down by its force. And then, to his complete surprise the fellow rose again. The ball had but creased him. Blood welled from a line across his chest.

Then the two were up out of the trees and gone past the edge of the clough. Raynes followed but slipped. His ankle twisted. He shouted for his men. It took them some time to locate him then pursue the fugitives. He was carried back down the valley. When his men returned they told him they'd found no trace but a campsite.

Raynes cursed. Now it would be fox and hound against men who knew the land.

Still, there was Walker. And Lloyd. He was a fox if any man were.

—

Mellor and Thorpe awoke from sleep still utterly sapped. Their constant dodging through the past days, as they'd made toward Dewsbury, had drained their strength. They wondered at Raynes' tenacity. Wherever they went he was soon there as well. Neither man understood how their opponents could so anticipate their evasions. Had it not been for more bad weather they were sure they would have been taken. The mist was their friend, the rain their ally.

Even in Dewsbury, its lanes empty but for runnels of rainwater gouging into the gravel roadways, it took them a long, cautious interval to approach the Buckworth vicarage. At the verge of the graveyard they observed the house warily.

They saw lights within. Occasionally, men would exit the scullery doorway to load a wrapped bale into a covered waggon. Mellor realized Mary was moving out but clearly the weather was holding her up. As evening wore on the men departed taking Nellie, Mary's maid, with them. Mellor glimpsed Mary once or twice through windows, a lamp in her hand.

He helped Thorpe across the cemetery, through the headstones toward the house. Even as he knocked, the door was opened and Mary was pulling him into the kitchen. Then suddenly, and in front of Will Thorpe, Mary grasped his head, brought it down to hers and kissed him. The kiss was loving and anxious and long.

"Where have you been?" she asked, fear in her voice.

Thorpe, meanwhile, sat heavily his head resting on the table. Mary glanced toward him.

"He's wounded. Shot last week ..." Mellor said.

"Yes, I know."

"How?"

"It's been all around, shouted by criers ... why did you take so long to come here? You had to know I would shelter you."

"We tried. Raynes and his men seemed t' know our every move. 'Tis been a close chase these many days and Thorpe can't move quick."

"You must leave the country, George. You've no choice now. They know what you've done and claim even more dreadful things."

In that instant, Mary advising him, George Mellor envisioned his long, complicated journey. He found within himself finally a glimmer of comprehension. He was *not* vengeance. He was *not* a machine. He would not, could not, change history. He was simply George Mellor: twenty-three years old, caught inside history as everyone else.

"You must understand, Mary, how it takes a man. The commitment. Once you're in it, 'tis cruel and pitiless. I told you before I thought I was making things better until Will here showed me what I'd truly become."

"I tried as well, but you wouldn't listen," she said softly.

"Aye. It was me who has done this t' myself. I've no one t' blame."

"They published John's manifesto," Mary said. "Yet it wasn't his anymore. I know, I worked on it. Who changed it, George? Who added those horrid threats?"

"I don't know, Mary. I've not read it either. Weightman maybe. John Baines? I put it in Horsfall's mouth as ordered. I thought it was John's."

"You didn't read it?"

"No. I'm sorry, Mary. I was blind with rage."

"What's done is done," she declared firmly. He realized then she was stronger than him. He had been wrong and now, at the weakest point of his life, she nurtured him.

"We must get you out of the country. Can you make Liverpool and take passage?"

"I'm not sure."

"England isn't safe, nor Scotland. Oh, Lord, you're exhausted. You'll stay the night. I'll have money for you in the morning."

"Seems you're moving out."

"They won't be back tomorrow. They've another job before mine."

"But Nellie?"

"She has a new position. She must start tomorrow. George, it's safe here."

"There's no place safe. Our being here puts you in peril. I'm a murderer, Mary, a machine wrecker, a Luddite; some even call me a terror maker."

"And am I any better? I have nothing left, George. Oh, I own this baggage around me but I've nothing left. I've destroyed it all. I am the Luddite of my own life. Can you understand? We, both of us, have only one option. We must make a new life so some day we might forgive ourselves. Something good must come of this, George, otherwise John's death, the deaths of so many, will have been worthless! You speak of your crimes but look at mine: I loved two men. I had not the courage to choose. I thought only of myself."

"I was the same. I used John and you."

"Perhaps together we can rebuild our lives."

"Mary, dost mean what I think?"

"I've told you of Upper Canada, the place called Sand Hills. I've money enough for passage, to purchase a plot. That is, if you'll still have me ..." She lowered her eyes.

"Mary, I don't know what t' say."

"Just kiss me."

Their kiss was interrupted by Thorpe.

"I'm sorry, Missus ..."

She turned reluctantly from Mellor to face the big man.

"Will, you'll be coming as well."

"I need t' see my mum and da'. I know I must leave but I'll at least say goodbye."

"You can barely stand, man," Mellor said. "I know they live close, but how'll you ever make Wakefield?"

"He can use my carriage," Mary said. "Are you sure of this, William? It's very dangerous, and dangerous too for your family."

"I can't just disappear without them knowing."

"You look too weak."

"I've been going days now with George. I'll make it."

"Then I'll find you my driver's hat and cloak. You'll be less obvious;

just a man on his way to fetch his master. George, dear, will you harness the horse?"

"I will. Where's your driver?"

"He's gone as well; taken a position as a footman. Once he and Nellie understood I wasn't intending to return to father" — she laughed bitterly — "both asked for references. I gave them very good ones."

It took little time to send off Will Thorpe. Mellor saw him away with the promise of a return before morning, then went back to the house. He found Mary wearing a linen shift, cut low, his tiny *Enoch* on its delicate chain at her throat. She took his breath away.

"If you're too tired ..." she said, sighing, "this can wait."

"I thought I was 'til now. You're a lovely sight, Mary."

First she removed his clothing, then washed him, cleansing his abrasions, pausing a moment to study the fresh scar, a red sear across his chest. Then she led him through the packed bales and boxes into her parlour. There, on a mattress upon the floor, they made love. This time it was not desperate but delicate, discovering again the delights they had once shared and lost. This time there was neither guilt nor remorse but the joining of their bodies in the one safe place left to them. This time was a linking of souls in harmony and a peace neither had ever experienced.

Together, for part of a night, they made a new world.

34

THEY AWOKE TO pounding on the back door. George was up quickly and dressing until Mary stayed him. She donned a robe and put a mob cap on her head. She would look to whomever was at the door as though she'd been sleeping ... alone. She pushed George to the stairs leading up to the bedrooms, then turned for the scullery. The day was beginning, still raining, as Will Thorpe pushed past Mary through the doorway. His look was grim.

"Where's George?" he asked with urgency.

"He's upstairs. I thought you ..."

"I'm here, Will!" Mellor entered the kitchen.

"George! Thank Christ!" Thorpe cried.

"What's the matter?"

"Walker's turned on us. That's why they've been on us since Ramsden Clough! I heard Sam Lodge was arrested. They found the guns at his house."

"Shite!"

"Aye. And they were waiting for me. Had me too but I got free. That's when I got a look at Walker. We must get away, George, back t' the moors, even south t' High Peaks! Missus Buckworth, I'm sorry ..."

His apology was interrupted when a horse neighed outside. A moment passed then came muffled voices from the front, then a hammering on the door, and a shout.

"We know ye're there, Thorpe!"

"That's Raynes!" Thorpe whispered. "How would he ..."

"Walker," Mellor said bluntly, his voice like steel. That his miniscule enemy might have deduced his connection with Mary incensed him. Given the chance, he would kill the man. He realized then he *could* murder not for political, but personal reasons. It no longer mattered. They had found him. They would arrest him. Mary's voice jarred him.

"Out the back, both of you," she said. "Get past the graveyard and through the hedge. I'll delay them."

"Right," Thorpe said. "We'll tie you so Raynes won't think you helped us."

"Take rope from that bale there," Mary replied.

George Mellor opened the kitchen door. He peered out. No one to be seen. Raynes had not had time to flank them. The beating on the front door continued, then a rattle as someone tried the lock. Mellor held the back door open but did not move.

"George, what are you doing?" Mary asked.

When he looked at her any light in his eyes had vanished. He seemed much older than his true age and tired, not physically so much as worn down by the months of pressure. From the moment he'd chosen to lead, or, he thought bitterly, had it chosen for him, it had never let up. He could not escape. He could never escape. The authorities would be relentless. He had threatened their standing, their very culture, and that act alone had terrified them and made him a marked man: never to be forgiven, or forgotten. He realized he had indeed stumbled into a place in the history of his beloved West Riding. It seemed now he would be forced to see that history to its end. He straightened himself. His voice was unwavering.

"I'll be running no longer, Mary."

"George! For Heaven's sake, you must ..."

"'Tis time I faced what I've done."

"They'll hang you!" Mary cried.

"George, we've time t' escape!" Will glanced through the doorway. "Come on, lad!"

"Then do it. And take Mary with you."

"No, George!" she said.

Shoulders slammed against the front door. It would be mere moments before they were flanked at the rear of the house.

"If you're found you'll be treated as Sam," Mellor said to Mary. "You'll be arrested."

"George, I love you!"

"If you do, show me. Escape."

"We'll face this together."

"No, Mary. This isn't your part. I'll cause no more harm in my life. Will, take her with you. Wait, get her cloak. Where is it?"

"I won't tell you," Mary said. Mellor picked a shawl from a rack.

"Wear this. 'Tis raining. I'll not have you die of consumption!"

"I won't wear it."

"Fine. Take it, Will, and her with it. Do it now, man!"

Without question big Will Thorpe grasped Mary up and carried her out the door. His wound meant nothing in the rush of escape. He'd been told to get away, take this woman with him, by the man who had always meant best for him.

"Leave me alone!" she cried, struggling within his grip, his arm like an iron band around her. "William, I want to stay with him!"

Thorpe kept going. He talked softly as he walked. The girl was light as a feather.

"Can ye not see he loves you? You must come with me, Mary."

"Where?" she said, crying. "Where can you possibly go?"

"I've a place for us now; later on we'll part ways and I'll go where they'll never expect."

"To the High Peaks. You said ..."

"I've a different thought now. I've a friend named Wil Shaw, the footman at Radcliffe's. He'll hide me in the very place where this Lloyd bastard tortures his prisoners. Most like they'll take George there. When that happens, I'll be there t' help him."

"Milnsbridge House? You'd have no chance!"

"I've no chance now but at least I have hope!"

When they were through the hedge out of sight of the house, Mellor shut the kitchen door, quickly crossed the room and stopped in the parlour's archway. He pulled a huge sideboard only a man of his strength could move across the hallway. He wanted no one thinking about a back door. The front door splintered as it was smashed in. Captain Raynes entered with two armed dragoons, each taking aim at Mellor. Behind the soldiers Walker skulked in. He could not look at Mellor. Raynes, pistol in hand, pointed at Mellor but spoke to Walker.

"Is this the man?"

"No. He ain't Will Thorpe."

"I've seen this man at Ramsden Clough," Raynes stared at Mellor.

"You're right, Captain. My name's George Mellor."

"Then ye're under arrest, Mellor, in the name of the King. Resist and I'll shoot!"

"I'll not resist," Mellor said.

"Where are the others?" Raynes demanded.

"I came here and saw the place being moved out. When all went off t' their suppers I broke in t' rob this house. I needed food and shelter from the rain."

"That's not what Walker has told us. Where is Thorpe?"

"He was wounded. I left him. He wanted t' get home. I told him he was wrong."

"Thorpe was in Wakefield. His parents' house was being watched. We had him. He escaped. He drove a carriage! Walker told us he would come here!"

"I've not seen him."

Raynes turned to his men.

"Sergeant, shackle this man! You two, search the house. Every room. Every cranny!"

"Not necessary, lads," Mellor said as he was manacled. The dragoons marched past him, heedless of his words. Walker attempted to leave but was halted by Raynes.

"Ye'll remain here, Walker! I'll need ye to identify Thorpe."

"He's not here, Captain," Mellor said, then turned to look at Walker and, with leaden eyes, spoke to his nemesis.

"Why Ben?"

It took a moment for Walker to salvage what remained of his integrity beneath the hard look of Mellor's once magical eyes. He'd feared this moment the instant he'd turned, and now it had arrived. Despite his antipathy toward Mellor, Walker found himself not so much afraid as ashamed. It seemed he'd just realized the consequences his actions would deliver upon him in future. He would be hated in the West Riding. His voice was a bleat, a snivel.

"They arrested me, George. They were going t' blame Horsfall's murder on me."

"And the reward?" Mellor said.

"I'm no Judas, George," Walker said. He'd expected worse. Instead, Mellor was strangely mild.

"Then you've done right, Ben. I hold no grudge. Take the *brass* but not for yourself. Give it t' them who need it. Otherwise 'tis all for nowt."

"I ... I will, George," Walker said weakly, though he had no intention of following through. "I'm sorry."

"Me as well, Ben. I was hard on you in past. I can't blame you for this."

The two soldiers returned.

"Nothing, Captain," the corporal said. "House be empty as he said. The scullery's full of bales and boxes. Looks t' me they're moving; all packed up."

"This is Mrs. Buckworth's home. Where is she, Mellor?"

"I told you, Captain, she went off with the others before I broke in."

"I'll hae Dewsbury searched in the morning. If she isn't found ..."

"I've told you the truth."

"And ye've not seen, Thorpe? We followed him! Does he hae her with him?"

"He was wounded, I told you. Slowed me down."

"Typical. Desert a loyal follower once he's no further use," Raynes said. He had the sense of this man, he thought.

"You don't know me," Mellor said, lowering his head.

"A matter of time," Raynes said. "Thorpe will be caught as the others. And now ye'll be taken to Milnsbridge House to meet Solicitor Lloyd and from there to Huddersfield gaol. Ye'll join your cronies. Yet I think we've found the best prize in ye!"

"Is that what I am, Captain? A prize?"

"A criminal, Mellor. Ye've wreaked terror amidst the West Riding and led us a bloody chase. But your day is done! We'll see how ye do with our Mr. Lloyd. He's a knack for eliciting information from such as the likes of ye. Ye've seen the last of your freedom, Mellor, and done the last of your crimes!"

"No matter what you think, Captain, I am a man just as you. Perhaps in more than one way." Mellor smiled disconcertingly. "Perhaps it wouldn't turn out so well for you t' have me meet your Solicitor Lloyd. Who knows what I might say in torment? Who knows what I know of certain soldiers and fancy ladies?"

Raynes felt a chill down his back. Was it possible this man knew of Fanny? To gain time he grasped an upended chair, turned and sat upon it, glaring at the shackled Mellor.

"Ye admit to being a Luddite leader?"

"I do." Mellor played along with the pretense he recognized Raynes was creating.

"And to the murder of William Horsfall?"

"That's why you've been chasing me, is it not?"

"I think, with these admissions, ye should be taken to prison at York. Solicitor Lloyd'll visit ye there. Ye're far too dangerous for Milnsbridge House or Huddersfield gaol."

"Aye. T' you I am," Mellor replied.

"I've no idea what ye mean," Raynes said. "But I suggest ye stay quiet! Or would ye prefer a hood o'er your head all the way to York?"

"I'll mind my business and keep all to myself," Mellor said.

The two had come to an understanding.

"Very good. Sergeant, ready the men."

"Sir, they've been up all night ..."

"Do as I order! We leave immediately!"

"What about Thorpe, Sir?"

"We've other squadrons searching. He's wounded and shouldn't get far; a matter of time."

He was going too far with his justification. He needed to eliminate any question of his unusual orders. Raynes signalled the sergeant to his side.

"Ye'll remain here with two men in case Mrs. Buckworth returns.

We wouldn't want her to come unawares on the ruined door to her house. If she doesn't return, the three of ye are to comb Dewsbury for news. I've no idea whether Mellor is telling the truth, but if not and Thorpe indeed has her, she'll slow him.

"Aye, Sir."

Raynes was elated. He had secured the confession of a Luddite leader and murderer. He knew it would lead to promotion and even a possible choice of station. He would choose Spain and Wellesley, a way to get past this morass and into active service. Raynes knew Lloyd would be furious at his betrayal. Still, he had too much to lose should Mellor indeed know what he'd implied. He began to think as Lloyd would: ahead.

"I'll take Walker with me as a witness," he said. "Any man suspected of being Will Thorpe is to be arrested and taken to York. Walker can identify him there."

"Should you not send Walker t' Mr. Lloyd, Sir? Let him know what's happening?"

"A little more time'll make no difference. Besides, both Walker and Mellor require a guard and I've divided this squadron enough. Let's be about it, Sergeant!"

His orders were issued forcefully. For the first time in his life having faced, so often, extraordinary odds in pursuit of his duty, Francis Raynes now felt the strange emotion of fear beneath his elation. He knew precisely why Mellor had proved such a dangerous opponent. He was someone who understood other men's foibles. Raynes wondered how one so young could come to possess such a terrible talent ... the very same as John Lloyd.

Raynes found himself in another conundrum. All the way to York he considered which he should be most concerned with: George Mellor's blackmail or John Lloyd's vengeance.

The ride was a long one.

In the drizzling grey morning two observers scrutinized the activities at the Buckworth manse. From the heights of the Norman style bell tower, it's crenellated top customary in Anglican churches, Will and Mary watched a squadron of soldiers ride off with George Mellor in their midst. His hands were manacled behind him, his horse being led. Nearby an unshackled Walker was a passenger in a curricle. Yet rather than riding west to Huddersfield the group went east. When they were gone, Thorpe was on his feet.

"I'll take a look 'round the house. 'Tis best t' get you home before the movers come."

"I'll go with you," Mary said. Watching her lover taken away, she had tried to suppress her tears. Now she simply wanted warm clothes and a place to mourn.

"No, ma'am!" Thorpe said sharply. "We both heard George. He don't want you suspected of helping us."

"But surely they've gone, Will. We just saw them leave."

"Best be certain, ma'am."

"Why would he do that? Why would George just give in?"

"Raynes and his men have followed us for a week. He's had Walker with him and the man's like a dog with a bone. George stalled them so we'd be away safe. Dost not see he's done this for you?"

"They'll hang him!" Mary was crying, her eyes like a sea. Her plans, dreams, her lover ... all dead.

"Aye, that's sure," Thorpe said.

"You've never trusted me, have you, Will? So long ago ... Mr. Wood's shop at Longroyd Bridge, you were the first to object."

"Aye, I did. I was wrong, I'm not ashamed t' admit. You've been a treasure t' us with your writing. And I know as well the *brass* you gave them needing it. I'm truly sorry, ma'am, for my feelings then."

He left her and took the stairs down through the belfry. Once outside the church his demeanour altered. He physically hunched and slowed his pace as he reached the hedge by the graveyard. He studied the back door then moved stealthily, from headstone to headstone, until he was at the scullery window. Peering in, he noted signs of a search: a table upturned, bales shifted, a sideboard pushed back from the pantry door. Otherwise, the place seemed empty. His hand was on the door's latch when a voice from behind froze him in place.

"Raise your hands, Thorpe, or die where you stand!"

The voice was accompanied by the clack of a pistol's hammer. Thorpe raised his hands.

"Mosby! Shaw! Get out here!" the voice barked. "You can turn 'round now, Thorpe."

Thorpe turned. He faced a sergeant, the man's pistol trained unswervingly upon him.

"So you must truly be Thorpe t' turn when ordered. You heard me call you by name." The sergeant smiled. "I was looking 'round and found horse and carriage still hitched in the shed; the very one you were driving in Wakefield. I knew you'd been here. Did you not think the Captain would leave a guard?"

"Why? House was empty."

"Where's Missus Buckworth?"

"Who's she?"

"You're from Wakefield and don't know Curate Buckworth's widow?"

"I've not been in Wakefield for years. I went t' see my mum. I'm wounded, Sergeant. I needed help and the only place I could go was home."

"You've led us a merry chase, Thorpe."

"Me and George Mellor."

"Where's he?" the sergeant asked, trying to gain an advantage. If Thorpe lied about Mellor he'd be lying about other things as well.

"Don't know that neither. We parted ways. I told you, I needed help."

"Yet here you are in the very place we seized him."

"You have George?" Thorpe said, acting surprised. He had to convince this sergeant or Mary would become suspect.

"You'll be pleased t' know," the sergeant said, "Mellor was here. You've just missed him. Come t' rob the place same as you, it seems. He's gone now t' York with Captain Raynes. I think we'll do the same with you!"

By this time the two dragoons had appeared from the scullery. They tied Thorpe's hands behind him. The four walked through the drizzle to the carriage house where three horses belonging to the dragoons were stalled. They mounted Thorpe on the carriage horse. It was not long before they were on their way east. The sergeant was in a hurry. Having captured Will Thorpe he dearly desired credit from Raynes. He'd completely forgotten Mary.

Mary watched them depart. She remained in the belfry an hour or so: listening, watching, then descended. It was a reasonable time for a woman who had slept elsewhere to return to meet her movers. Thankful for the shawl to dress her, she made sure to walk around the church and approach the house from the road. She entered her parlour and paused a moment to recall her night with George Mellor. In the scullery, where she'd last seen him, she sank to the floor, her hand grasping the tiny *Enoch* on the chain around her neck. His gift. Symbol of his love. She sat silent.

Empty, as her house.

—

When Raynes had not returned by the next day, John Lloyd suspected the worst. So John Lloyd did what he did best: made sure he was ahead of the game. Lloyd proceeded to Sergeant Mook, the man charged with Radcliffe's protection and demanded four soldiers. Such was the power of Lloyd's intensity that Mook instantly complied.

Ordering the footman, Shaw, to have Radcliffe's coach harnessed, Lloyd loaded himself and his guards into it. Over Harrison's objections he too was ordered to mount to his box and drive *post-haste* to Huddersfield. Once there Lloyd stopped to gather his constables. The entire troupe rushed to Longroyd Bridge. They invaded John Wood's shop arresting every man there.

Within a day an inmate broke. His name was Snowden. He was brought to the white room by M'Donald where, rather than the strap, he received a heaping plate of food and some ale to loosen his tongue. Once he'd eaten his fill he talked. They sat in the ladder back chairs: Lloyd's bright with polish, Snowden's darkened by blood.

"I know George Mellor, Sir," he said.

"I realize that, you fool!" Lloyd said. "Did Mellor force you to take an Oath?"

"Aye, Sir, he did," Snowden spoke strongly. Lloyd had hit a nerve.

"Only you?"

"He and Thorpe came in one night. They were carrying guns ..."

"Pistols?"

"Aye, and a Bible. George had a busted finger."

"Was the owner there, Mellor's father?"

"John Wood? No, Sir. He's a *maister.* He don't do much real work anymore."

"Never mind that. Return to Mellor."

"They'd done something bad, that's certain, and they wanted t' make sure we couldn't peach. Thorpe held the Bible and told us all were t' swear the Oath."

"The Luddite Oath?"

He was so close now, so very close he could feel it.

"Taking the Oath's not legal, I told 'em. I'm no outlaw, Mr. Lloyd, but they had guns. In the end all were forced t' swear."

"Ha!" Lloyd exclaimed, the pleasure of this discovery nearly unbearable after his months of inquisition. He had it now. There was no stronger evidence. Add this to Walker's tale of murder and Mellor was finished!

He had M'Donald take Snowden out and then, notebook on his lap, John Lloyd rubbed his hands together with glee. If Raynes were able to capture Mellor, Lloyd had the means to hang him. There was little doubt in his mind he would be given the post of Chief Prosecutor! He saw his future in front of him. It was auspicious.

—

The next days involved examining others in light of Lloyd's knowledge, then collating the information. All that week Lloyd ordered so many arrested that Huddersfield gaol was bursting. Many were transferred to York. An alarmed Home Office contacted Maitland.

Maitland himself sought a meeting with Radcliffe and told him the Home Office was, in fact, losing track of the number of charges laid in the West Riding. The Right Honourable John Hiley Addington,

Under-Secretary of State, wrote to Radcliffe. He implored the magistrate to quell the confusion he had triggered in Whitehall. Radcliffe was ordered to create a list of the felons sent for trial.

Radcliffe, of course, passed this work to that definitive creator of lists, his assistant John Lloyd. Lloyd gladly accepted. With growing familiarity of all parts of the case Lloyd felt more bound to be designated Crown Prosecutor. Yet where was Raynes? It had been ten days since he'd chased after Mellor and nothing heard since. Without Mellor there was no case, and without that case, Radcliffe would be incensed. Once more the Solicitor planned ahead. He wrote Beckett at the Home Office regarding his superior.

Meanwhile that superior, as well, had been busy. Though the magistrate had submitted Lloyd's lists, claiming them as his own, responses to his missives became increasingly cold. Viscount Sidmouth was Home Secretary now. With Perceval having been assassinated the career of the commoner, Ryder, had ended. Lord Liverpool, the new Tory Prime Minister, had made sweeping changes placing the government, as he felt it should be, in the hands of the elite.

Still Radcliffe insisted *he* should be named Chief Prosecutor and perhaps afterward given a *Baronetage*. Lord Sidmouth possessed a much different perspective. Sidmouth, ironically, had acquired news regarding Radcliffe's shortcomings from Permanent Under-Secretary Beckett. Beckett had received the letters from Lloyd, enumerating Radcliffe's panics, errors and illnesses during the year of the Luddites. There was even some mention of a flippant wife.

—

As Lloyd scribbled away one night by lamplight, the names of informers and witnesses, he paused to reflect upon the year. He did not think in his usual, logical fashion but allowed images of events to unfold, *extempore* as it were, in a sprawling vista.

He recalled the Rawfolds attack. He remembered Raynes' brilliant tactics of night raids ... the anxiety of the middle class and even the nobility ... the radicalism of Edward Baines with his *Leeds Mercury* ...

the difficult time he'd spent as a *tinker* ... the meeting with Maitland creating the dossier ... and finally the break in the case: Walker.

More images flowed. There was blustering Horsfall murdered, the Russian pistol and George Mellor ... Barrowclough flickered in and after him Brook's missing hat ... Brookbank's tale of kidnapping ... Haigh, Cartwright, the oily Earl Parkin, and a careless John Dean ... even the carter named Zebulon Stirk who had told of a night of horror and burning wagons and the names of Mellor and Walker. It was a long and satisfying vision.

He was so very, very close, he thought. He could almost touch his ambition.

He wondered again about Raynes. He had always thought of Raynes as his weapon. Now, if Mellor were caught, he would no longer need the captain. Again he began to plan ahead yet another man's fall from grace.

He had no idea his weapon had turned ... upon him.

•

35

WINTER CAME EARLY and hard. It blew down upon the West Riding in sheets of icy rain. Trees were stripped of their leaves, the meagre harvest frozen in the ground. The songbirds of summer had long departed, the skeins of geese gone, and up on the high moors shepherds brought their sheep down to more sheltered cloughs. Storms made travel arduous and at times even dangerous. Yet still, there were migrations.

Mary Buckworth had sent her effects off, not to her father in Nottingham but to be stored in a warehouse in Liverpool. She had kept one case with some clothing. She stayed on at the house. She had no plan, only the knowledge that she would be forced to depart when the next curate appeared. So she kept to the scullery, mourning her loss at the window watching the sleet smash against the glass, holding her miniature *Enoch*.

It seemed she had lost her capacity to exist in a human way. Though she would eat a little and drink tea to stay warm, she hardly slept. Her thoughts roiled wildly but in the end condensed to one option: that somehow she must see George Mellor at York. She had no idea how to accomplish this, a woman entering a men's prison would be forbidden, but knew she must gather allies and find a way to achieve her goal.

One day, little different from others, she began.

The smithy and stable were stepped on a curling uphill street; the rear of the building part of the hillside. Its double doors were closed, the blacksmith's blaze heating the place as he moved about gathering tools. Bill Atkinson was a big man in his middle years. The work he'd done had made him as hard as the iron he wrought. Yet he was a mild man as certain to chuck children's chins as he was to offer an ale to a friend. He knew Mary Buckworth.

When she entered his shop she brought the cold with her. She looked pale and wan. He felt sorry for her, a widow at such a young age. Following inquiries about his family and his business, she got to her point.

"Bill, I was hoping to rent a horse."

"You have one, Mrs. Buckworth."

"No longer, Bill. The mare was taken by soldiers."

"Damn 'em! Oh, excuse me ma'am, my language I mean. Just last week they took the men from Huddersfield gaol and marched 'em t' York. Can you imagine? In that wicked cold weather?"

"All of them?" Mary asked.

"Aye. All the Ludds men. The usual fellas, the drunks and thieves, they're still in Huddersfield."

"About renting? I still have my carriage."

"Will you be going far?"

"No. Just the other side of Huddersfield but walking is out of the question."

"Aye, that's sure on days like this. Expect you'll be gone long?"

"Perhaps a night or two. An old friend to visit before I depart."

"You'll be going back t' Nottingham then?"

"I don't think so, Bill. It depends on my friend."

"I see. None of my business. Right then! I'll have the boy bring a mare over."

"Would you have him harness her?"

"Of course, Mrs. Buckworth."

"And the rental?" Mary asked.

"Oh, nowt for you, ma'am, for just the two days."

"I'll have her back Wednesday afternoon. But you must have your rent!"

They argued amicably back a forth until he would accept a fair price. When she gave him the coins she added extra, for the boy who would harness, she said; for his trouble.

She drove her own carriage. She'd learned the skill years past as a girl. With her case in the boot and reins in hand chucking the horse onward, she took the least travelled roads to avoid prying eyes. From Dewsbury north of Huddersfield she journeyed, then turned southwest to her destination. The rural back roads were frozen hard but had fewer ruts from traffic. Half a day had passed when she rounded Penny Hill and came upon Steel Head Lane and the cottage beside the stream. She stopped by the narrow stone bridge arching over the stream, tied the horse to a convenient tree, gave her a feedbag, and walked across.

Smoke drifted from its crumbling chimney. The turf roof had sagged even more since her last visit. It glistened with spicules of ice. Despite the sunshine the cold kept the children inside. They had few winter clothes and would venture out only upon some errand. She knocked on the door. It rattled on its hinges. One of the children opened it.

Inside were the others: Bonnie at her usual spot stirring the cook pot upon the hob. The children sat at the table playing with pieces of wood which looked like soldiers set in formation. Peat smoke suffused the room. For a moment Mary's eyes watered until she became accustomed. They greeted each other. Mary started in quickly.

"Bonnie, I've heard the Luddite prisoners have been moved to York from Huddersfield."

Bonnie's response was unusual. She seemed overwhelmed, beaten down by all which had happened. She had been a *Cassandra* foretelling the awful future when Sam first went off to the Shears Inn. She had frightened herself with her prognostications. When she spoke now it was in a low voice, as though the children should not hear, in case she might utter another divination.

"I hear near nowt out here. When?"

"Last week. You knew about George?"

"Aye. That news made its way even t' this place. So if they moved Sam and the others, it must mean a trial's coming."

"I'm sure of it. Bonnie, I've some money ..."

Bonnie stirred the pot, considering the younger woman's meaning. When she understood Mary's words, she was startled. She set her ladle in the pot and slowly turned, disbelieving.

"You're asking me t' go with you t' York?

"I am. I must see George. I hope you might also see Sam."

"What of my kids?"

"I'll pay for their care. Choose any place."

"'Tis a prison, Mary. They'll not allow women in, you must know!"

"I *will* find a way, Bonnie, and take you with me!"

"Why me, Mary? Dost forget my man was put away for hiding your man's guns."

"Please, Bonnie. I can't travel without a companion."

"I see. You're in need of a maid or some such."

"Only as a ruse. I can pay you, Bonnie, as I'll pay for the children. A hard winter is coming. You'll have money for food."

"You've said enough, Mary." Bonnie gazed into her eyes. "You're right, I do need the *brass* for winter, but I'll do this for *you*. How long will we be gone?"

"I'm not sure. It depends how quickly I can find a way to see George. We can travel by coach: the Dewsbury mail coach to Leeds, then from Leeds to York."

"Have you any notion where we might stay?"

"I do. It's a very good inn. John was often called to York Minster on Church business. I got along well with the proprietor. I'm sure he knows John has died and I'll tell him I've come as a pilgrim to pray at the cathedral."

"With me as your maid?"

"I'm sorry, but it would make sense to him."

"When do we leave?"

"Tomorrow ... as soon as you see your children safe. I've a carriage waiting, we'll drive back to Dewsbury. I don't wish to rush you, Bonnie, but I feel I must be there very soon."

"Samuel!" Bonnie turned to the table; a gangly lad stood up. "Hike over t' Mosby's. Ask Lyla if she'll have you for meals. I expect you t' care for the other three. Tell Missus Mosby I've *brass* t' pay."

"I can give it you now," Mary said. She dug into her *reticule* and withdrew some coins. "Would ten bob be sufficient?"

"Far too much! Dear Lyla'd faint dead away!"

"None the less, Bonnie, I wish to make certain the children are safe and secure."

"Alright, Mary, but you should mind your money."

The boy was out the door with her last word, his hand gripped tightly around the coins. He had never in his life carried, or even seen, so much money.

"You believe she'll accept?" Mary asked.

"For ten bob? Oh, aye, you can be sure."

"Can you pack? Now?"

"Why the haste, Mary?"

"A feeling is all. They'll put George on trial as soon as they can. I think they'll make him an example. I need to see him, Bonnie. I'll not have him dying thinking he'll be forgotten."

"I'll get my shawl and a few other bits."

George Mellor knew the season had changed. In his interior windowless cell, behind an iron-studded door, the whitewashed walls grew colder as did the slate floors. He was given no extra blankets so shivered in the one he possessed. He had no idea how long he'd been here since being brought by Raynes and glimpsing his future abode.

A limestone U-shaped building, darkened by the driving rain, it looked foreboding, a palace of inhuman justice. It was three stories high with a central cupola and clock. The new *Union Jack*, a mere twelve years in existence, hung limply from its pole above the cupola. There were walls and a rusting iron fence surrounding the building. One side of the U was a courthouse, an efficient walk from the cells; the other side held women prisoners. The centre section was a Debtors' Prison, the place where men remained confined until they made good on their obligations. They lived on the second floor. The third floor, with windows unbarred, was for Prison Administration. But below, on the first floor, half buried into the ground, its windows heavily barred, was the part to which he was bound. It imprisoned felons, men considered too dangerous to be housed any other way. The building existed to incarcerate humans. It was neat, orderly and awful.

A great iron door creaked open. Manacled still, given a number which was his cell and told the rules of the prison, he was escorted proficiently to that cell by tough, experienced warders. Lanterns provided some light making swaying shadows on whitewashed walls; low arches separated cell doors painted black against white. George Mellor missed the world's sights, smells and sounds and now would not see them again until his warders allowed.

The key had rattled in his cell's lock. His warders removed his fetters. His world was now a rectangular cubicle, windowless but for a barred transom on his door. It offered the room slight illumination. He had not thought he could quite manage darkness. He'd been given a hammock, blanket and towel, spoon and cup. His cell had a stool and a chamber pot. The room was limed, the white walls protected from prisoners' scratchings by directions designating severe punishment for that offence. For a fool who scrawled graffiti there would be the whipping post.

George Mellor had fought his own darkness that day and the next and the next. He spent his time wondering about his plight for he knew he was a dead man. In his lifetime he had lost a father, travelled the seas, worked in cropping shops, been with women, fought with men, allowed his life to run without any real goal and finally, when he'd found a purpose, it had turned out to be archaic. Society was changing. He wondered were there any seers who knew how things would change? Or wouldn't?

One day he was visited by a Solicitor John Lloyd. Mellor knew of him but not by sight. A glance at the man and Mellor disliked him. He was pale and eerie. A white rat, he spoke in soft hisses. His eyes were opaque. He was accompanied by a warder. He seemed to have wanted someone else with him, insisting vociferously when they entered.

"And why should not Mr. M'Donald be with me? He is my assistant."

"No idea, Sir," the warder said carelessly. He could not be intimidated.

"I shall speak with your superiors!"

"Do so, Sir. I follow the Warder's instruction."

"Will you leave us at least?"

"Afraid I can't do that, Sir. This be a dangerous man. That's why he's locked up here. And you don't look much in the way of sturdy. This man'd kill you in a trice. No, Sir, my instructions are t' remain with the prisoner."

Lloyd turned to Mellor, removing a small book from his jacket pocket and a pencil from another. There was nowhere for him to sit but the stool which George Mellor refused to give up. He would not stand like a peasant before this excuse for a man. The warder, looking at both, said nothing. Neither did he offer another seat. Mellor smiled his thanks, the warder nodded.

"My name is Lloyd, Mr. Mellor. I've come to ask a few questions."

"I've none t' answer." The half smile left Mellor's face in an instant.

"I understand you've confessed your murders to Captain Raynes."

"Who told you that? Raynes and his lackeys are making it up. I said nowt."

Lloyd stood before Mellor, completely lost for words. He'd expected a martyr. He'd found a fighter. It took him a moment to recover.

"He informed me *that* was the reason he'd brought you here."

"Instead of to you? I've heard of you. I prefer this place."

"How could you know anything of me?"

"Ben Walker."

"He turned on you! Gave you up for money! You trust his word?"

"Against yours? Aye."

"Don't play the fool with me, Mellor."

"Done your work on me, have you? Been at that strap again? Got some new information?"

"Unless you provide me the names of your co-conspirators you shall hang."

"What dost mean? I've done nowt!"

"I possess a list, Mellor! A list of your crimes and outrages! I have the names of a hundred people! Do you understand? Your life rests in my hands!"

"Oh, I see. You're the prosecutor."

"A prosecutor has not been named," Lloyd replied, though Mellor caught the desire glinting in his eyes. He now had the man's weakness; something to use.

"Then why are you here? It won't be a common joker like you t' be named prosecutor, I'm sure! None of these smarmy nobles trust you."

Lloyd could hardly speak. The insults had speared him. He sputtered on.

"I … I have proof of the … Horsfall murder! One of your mates has informed on you!"

"As you said. Ben Walker," Mellor replied flatly. "That man'd peach on his mother for *brass*. Now as you see, I'm busy here."

"You shall answer my questions!" Lloyd shrieked. His nose was running.

"Walter." Mellor faced the warder calmly. "Take this man out before I hurt him."

The warder smiled. He'd seen it *all* down here but this was a new one. This one he'd tell the lads at The Black Bull when his shift ended. The tale would ensure him one or two pints. He crossed his arms but didn't move.

"George, don't be a fool. I can't have you harming the solicitor," he replied.

"You can't threaten me!" Lloyd said, quite unaccustomed to felons refracting his interrogation. He was the one who should be in charge. If only M'Donald were here. A hand grasped his arm. The warder.

"What are you doing? Unhand me!"

"I'm keeping you safe, Sir. You heard Mellor's threat. Get out now, Sir. Do as I say or I'll be the one reporting you!"

Mellor chose that moment to stand. He towered over the slight solicitor. Lloyd twisted like a frightened dog expecting a blow. Lloyd left the cell in a confused flurry. Walter smiled at Mellor as he left, put a finger to his nose, and then closed the cell door.

The last thing Lloyd heard was Mellor's laughter.

36

To Viscount Sidmouth,
my Lord

YOUR LORDSHIP IS *already apprized of the great number of Prisoners in York Castle, on charges emanating from the combination & system, now commonly denominated Ludditism: your Lordship is likewise aware what a great length of time, this description of crime has prevail'd, & gone uncheck'd, because unpunish'd.*

These considerations have long made All, who are witnesses of what is passing, most anxious, that whenever any cases can be brought home against the persons charged, that they should be brought to trial as early as possible, every one considering the conviction of some of the Offenders, as positively necessary for the restoration of tranquillity in these parts, & for the safety of the peaceable Inhabitants — this is not the opinion of the last-mention'd description of person alone, but equally so the body of the Magistrates, & particularly of those most actively engaged in attempting to suppress this combination — I am empower'd to stick it likewise, as the decided opinion of Gen: Maitland, with whom I have most recently corresponded on this point, & who joins with the

Magistrates in opinion, that it is most desirable that the Trial of these persons should not be delay'd a day, whenever any of them cannot be brought to conviction —

Offenders under this system, may be class'd under four different heads — 1st Murderers & Terrorists — 2d — Destroyers of machinery — 3d Housebreakers for Arms, or mere plunder — 4th Twisters-in, or the administrators of Oaths —

Under the first class, come the Murderers of Horsfall, against whom, I am given to understand, the evidence is most complete — likely to become much more strong, if confidence can be inspired into the witness —

2d Class — the attack on Cartwrights mill — evidence agst some of the parties, said to be strong — other cases of this class, evidence said to be strong.

of the 3d Class I know little — of the 4th, I believe there are not more than two cases, both from Barnsley — one of which I believe, will be brought home —

But it is wasting time to attempt entering into particulars, the whole body of evidence in all the various cases being before your Lordship. From that body of evidence the Att & Solr Genl will select such cases & such only, as afford reasonable ground for supposing acquittals will not be consequence — Undoubtedly if among these cases, none are to be selected, which promise a moral certainty that conviction must ensue, it would be very inexpedient, because it would prove most mischievous to have an extraordinary Assizes held: it would stamp the system as invulnerable; the dangerous consequences of which, under the certain pressure of scarcity, no one can estimate. In urging therefore the consideration of a Special Comn, I do it, in the full confidence, that it will not be granted, but upon the decided conviction of the Law Officers, that some of the cases cannot fail to be brought home to the some of the Parties accused — On that presumption, but on that only, I state it to be the opinion of Gen: Maitland, the Magistrates, most actively engaged in this business, & my own, that early Trial will conduce, & is essential to tranquillizing these parts: they will not be secure, untill exemplary punishment has been inflicted, & great must be the danger, considering the pressure of the times, should nothing be done before the Lent Assizes.

I have [etc]Wentworth Fitzwilliam

—

The Luddite faction had been curtailed. Indeed, those men who had accepted the amnesty had also decided to return to work where available. Maitland had known most people had not been involved other than to supply or conceal. They had done what they'd felt was right.

The first crack of what was to become a social divide appeared in the north. Before this time, master and worker had shared in the pride of the quality of their *woollen* trade, until new technologies and an ancient nemesis, the markets, had changed. A term yet unknown, *The Industrial Revolution*, was now open to beginning. None, of course, could peer into the future though one man, from experience, possessed an inkling of what was to come.

Lieutenant General the Honourable Thomas Maitland with his second, Major General Wroth Acland, stood before a hot fire. Wind and rain once again peppered Milnsbridge library's windows. The two awaited the meeting Maitland had called to finish the business of the West Riding. He swore to Acland, in quite shocking terms, this would be the last time he would have to visit this back country quagmire.

Yet of any involved, Maitland had analyzed the social unrest of the district impeccably. He had advised Lord Fitzwilliam to send correspondence to Viscount Sidmouth to bring about action resolving the differences in the region. Then he himself had written Sidmouth regarding his own solutions and found strong support from the Home Secretary. He had, after all, facilitated an end to what so many thought might become civil war.

He was a hero now to the Lords of Whitehall and with that power possessed the weight to act as he thought necessary. Armed with Fitzwilliam's letter, he was comfortable with what he was about to do. With Colonel Campbell still on his endless tour of the troops, Maitland's three remaining minions entered. It was clear each had come to abhor the others despite, or perhaps because of, what they'd been through.

Radcliffe came into his library hobbling on two canes. He appeared every bit his sixty-eight years: feeble, fat, gouty and flatulent. The white mutton chop whiskers lining his round, ruddy face were thinner now, as was his head going bald. Still, his rheumy eyes as he regarded Maitland told the tale of his ambition. Chief Prosecutor and Baronet were his aims for himself, Maitland had heard from Lord Sidmouth, and Maitland knew too he was about to quash both.

Solicitor Lloyd and Captain Raynes followed, clearly in the midst of a bitter argument. Maitland had heard of their acrimony: Mellor's capture and the resulting, competing attempts by both men to further themselves, like crows over carrion, had put them at odds. Lloyd's normally pallid face was flushed into rosy patches. He carried one shoulder higher than the other, walking like a man about to be struck from behind. Raynes carried himself in a martial manner: his arrogance obvious, yet his nagging self-doubt keeping him just a step behind Lloyd.

One without the other, Maitland contemplated, would have failed. Somehow they had created an extraordinary enterprise: Lloyd's intuition and Raynes' skills in action meshing like gears in a mill. More than any, these two had brought down the Luddites in the West Riding. But their methods had been self-serving, even viciously brutal and if brought to light would devastate Maitland's plans for the prosecution.

"Gentlemen," Maitland said, smiling coldly, "I've brought us together to resolve certain imminent matters. I, for one, shall be pleased to be finished this business."

"Of course you'll be staying the night," Radcliffe said, his tumescent ambition already rising. Naturally, some supper and brandy with Maitland would smooth his way, along with a sparkle of flirt from Fanny.

"I shall not," Maitland replied. "I am staying with the Earl Fitzwilliam. I've come by coach this time, Radcliffe, having expected your offer."

"Should we not be celebrating, Sir?" Radcliffe said. Maitland ignored him.

"It is true you've accomplished your duties, gentlemen, and for that I congratulate you. Unfortunately, it is your actions and intentions which I must address here."

"I hae done as ordered, Sir!" Raynes said, standing to attention as he did.

"Sit down, Captain," Maitland said. "I'll get to you soon enough."

"Sir?"

"Sit down!" Acland, who stood behind the three, shouted. Raynes crumpled.

"I have letters here from which I intend reading segments," Maitland said. "Though you have been at the centre of things, it seems you've had slight inclination to look past yourselves to the problems burgeoning from your behaviour."

"General," Lloyd said, "I do not take your meaning."

"You shall momentarily, Solicitor Lloyd." The use of the pallid man's title illustrating the meeting would remain formal. "We shall begin with General Acland. These are my written instructions to him as he takes command when I depart. I've been offered a post in the Mediterranean. Time to fight a true war though I believe old Boney is on the run now from the Russians."

Acland produced a note and read crisply; the meaning of the instructions made clear by his sharp military tone. None could misunderstand the note's implications.

> *Let us have no quarrel with the country, which will be infallibly the case without the utmost caution observed, as the general disposition here is a feeling of fear, that render the military necessary, but at the same time there exists a feeling of detestation against us that makes its appearance ever in the middle of the fears.*

Maitland made sure that each apprehended his meaning. These three, after all, had been misrepresenting each other for months.

"The common people distrust the army for the manner in which certain troops have behaved. I blame that on Gordon and Campbell who both should have had more control. They pay their price now with their new assignments."

"But General." Raynes rose once more from his chair. "My own patrols have been *quite* disciplined. They dealt only with the guilty."

"And who, in fact, *were* the guilty, Captain? Men on a moor marching about playing soldier? A gathering of people in front of a mill to protest a manufacturer's methods? To you they *all* seemed guilty! I do not doubt your tactics, Raynes, nor your men, but *you* personally. That is the nub of what brings me here! Did you, or did you not, operate against Magistrate Radcliffe's instruction by arresting Mellor and, rather than take him to Milnsbridge House, convey him to York Castle gaol?"

"Sir. The man had confessed! There was no need for the magistrate!"

"It seems so to you. Yet Magistrate Radcliffe represents the law. You represent the military *without* the powers to arrest citizens of the Realm. At other times you and Solicitor Lloyd had arranged for special constables to accompany you but on this chase, lasting a full week, mind you, you neglected to bring a single one! You have no idea the trouble you've caused. Mellor has denied his confession. Lloyd here could extract nothing from him. Thus it comes down to your word and those of your subordinates, against his. That is not evidence in a court of law, Raynes; that is but the action of an overly ambitious officer!"

"That's not true!" Raynes said. "My men heard him!"

"And no one else has, since you brought him to York! Can you not see, you fool, your behaviour has placed our prosecution of an important insurgent at risk?"

"I hae done my duty, General," Raynes replied bravely.

"No, Captain Raynes, you have overstepped. *Twice.* Once is forgivable, a second time means defiance, or stupidity. You came to me once before, you recall, behind the backs of your superiors with what you considered significant information. I warned you then you'd upended the proper channels but it seems you chose to ignore *me* as well! You took Mellor to York in order to receive accolades and promotion! Don't bother disputing the point. It is obvious. The reward for that is quite simple, Captain: a military one. You shall retain your present rank and be assigned as one of *my* staff at my next posting. And I shall have my eyes upon you."

"Why, General Maitland, I'm not sure I take your meaning."

Raynes was stunned. No promotion at all, placed under the auspices of a superior who had just disparaged him, told he would be observed like a raw recruit ... Raynes found himself bereft of response.

"Despite your tactics, which seem inspired until one examines the Spanish *guerillas* against the French, and despite your personal courage, you are *not* a man to be trusted."

An overt reply would have Raynes cashiered. He was forced to accept Maitland's decision. He would no longer advance. He would remain in place. He would become an embittered man stuck within the rigidity of his rank.

"Yes, Sir. Thank you, Sir," he said as he slumped to his seat.

"But there is more, gentlemen," Maitland said. "Though you seem to think this hubbub has been stopped, it has not, and shall not in the near future. Here is a part of my note to the Home Secretary.

> *So long as the price of manufacturing labour is so low, and that of provisions so high, we must still contemplate with a considerable degree of anxiety the result of the present winter.*

"What I mean by this is that hunger drives people to desperation. I've informed Lord Sidmouth that troops must remain here in low profile, in barracks outside the towns in case another rising occurs. The Luddites are finished. Privation has not. A watch must be kept through this winter and that, Radcliffe, is your bailiwick." Maitland's words were biting.

Radcliffe, with Maitland's wrath turned against him, could not register an objection. He could not rise, he could not speak, his jowls ruffling, not a word left his mouth before Maitland was on him.

"*Sixty-four* prisoners from the West Riding! Over a hundred in all overcrowding York prison, but *sixty-four* from this pitiful backwater! Have you any idea how Whitehall has taken your list of felons? Why, Radcliffe, you've denuded this region of its best men! What, indeed, have you actually done? Without Lloyd's work, nothing! You've blustered and blamed and chaired silly meetings! Worse, Sir, you have broken the law! You know as well as I that men have been imprisoned counter to writ of *habeas corpus*! Shame on you, Sir! Your zeal has turned to animosity. Your objectivity to prejudice. Yet, until a change can be affected your work must continue, overseeing Lord Fitzwilliam's holdings. *Baronet* indeed."

"But ..." Radcliffe said.

"I suggest you take no time to thank me, Radcliffe, for my favour ..."

"You have no right ..." Radcliffe objected with the only phrase he was sure of. No military man had entitlement to dictate to his office.

"For if it came to light the things you have permitted these past months in the *name* of the law," Maitland said, "I doubt you'd much longer hold your position, or any position at all. The Home Secretary supports me in this, as I said, as will Lord Fitzwilliam when he is apprised. Your reward, Sir, is to keep your position!"

There was a moment of absolute silence in the library. Two men's careers, their very lives, had been reduced by General Maitland in a few minutes from expectation to ashes. The old magistrate shifted uncomfortably in his chair.

"I see," Radcliffe said.

"Now to you, Solicitor Lloyd." Maitland's eyes bore into Lloyd's. The younger man actually cringed. He stood, through a kind of ingrained education, a recalcitrant schoolboy about to take his strokes. He was hardly ready for what came next.

"My communications with Lord Sidmouth have included a suggestion for a necessary show trial to undercut thoughts of a Luddite recurrence. I said to him," he peered down at his notes:

> *If we make good our cases at the ensuing York Assizes and do not attempt too much, I think the spirit of the late combinations will be completely broken.*

"I agree absolutely with your estimations, Sir," Lloyd said. Perhaps with the others out of the way his own was cleared.

"Solicitor Lloyd, you have made much of this coming prosecution possible with your doggedness, your deductions, and your will to find the heart of this workmen's mutiny."

"Why thank you, General," Lloyd said.

"More thanks," Maitland said. "I hadn't finished. I'd meant to finish with your methods. *Inquisition* might be the best word. You think I am not aware of your tortures? How could you amass this many names for this many crimes but through agony! Your M'Donald has been arrested for assault, on my advice, by Justice Bayley of Nottingham. Don't quibble, I've had your thug conveyed there. I wish I could do the same with you. Unfortunately, I cannot, for no one knows more of these Luddites, their stratagems and crimes than you. *Not* to avail ourselves of your knowledge would place our prosecution in jeopardy."

"I am ready, Sir, for your instruction," Lloyd said, unsure which way to turn.

"Of course you are. You are *infamous* for following instruction. You are expecting to be named Chief Prosecutor in the coming trials. Am I correct in my assumption?"

"Only if you find me suitable, Sir."

"Whether I do or do not, the position has already been decided. The prosecution's case shall be led by Mr. J. A. Park, a noted barrister whose skills in the courtroom have already won him a considerable reputation. Indeed I find you completely *unsuitable*, Mr. Lloyd."

"But what of *my* work, *my* skills?" Lloyd said.

"What skills?" Maitland asked. "Those of a country solicitor? Or those of a secret Inquisitor? How you could believe, knowing what you've done, that we could have you in a position of responsibility is quite beyond me! Lloyd, you are a criminal; as much as those you have written up in your infamous dossier! Were it my choice, I would have you flogged!"

Maitland's voice, for the first time raised to a bellow, drove Lloyd into his chair and terminated all pretense. It took a moment for the general to compose himself. He had risen from his own chair and his hand had actually moved to his sword hilt. He stared down at John Lloyd, the pallid solicitor cringing before him, as a man would regard a toad.

"You shall have your reward Lloyd, as have Raynes and Radcliffe. You shall be named part of the prosecution performing as an *assisting attorney*. You shall organize your information so Park might make use of it. You'll be paired with another attorney named Jonas Allison, a man accustomed to working with Park and whose responsibility is simply to keep you in place. You will *never* speak to the court; only to your superior. Should you attempt another of your little conspiracies you shall be relieved of your position and face removal from the bar-at-law. You've a high opinion of yourself, Lloyd. Your letters to the Home Office slurring Magistrate Radcliffe were read with some interest. Did you really think you had earned the privilege of communicating with Secretary Beckett? He had, before your scurvy little notes, no knowledge of you whatsoever. Indeed, *no one* of any import knows of you and that is as it should be. You are scum, Lloyd, and once these trials end I hope to see you finished as well."

Tears ran from John Lloyd's eyes. He sniffled. Maitland threw him a handkerchief as though it were a piece of trash, and watched carelessly as Lloyd shrank into his chair. Then Maitland himself sat down. He'd delivered his rulings but had something of even more import.

"Did any of you actually believe your actions would bring you acclaim? Indeed, the three of you seem to think yourselves *saviours* of the Realm. Yet the Realm never needed saving. This will appear in history as a minor anomaly in an otherwise glittering record of democracy. After your deaths no one will hear of you. Once these trials are finished no one will remember these Luddites. England is currently winning two wars, its economy is changing for the better, and it possesses an Empire which spans the globe. *That* is what history remembers, you fools. That, and a man named Arthur Wellesley. He is the stuff of history.

"I *will* inform you that Whitehall has taken notice of our rural mutiny. As the Lent Assizes begin January Eighth a Special Commission has been established. It begins January second and will bring to the court *only* Luddites. Justice Bayley shall not sit the Bench. Gentlemen, you seem surprised. His earlier judgements in Lancashire proved too moderate. I recall you yourself, Radcliffe, being livid about it. For that reason two different judges, neither lenient, have been appointed: Sir

Alexander Thomson and Sir Simon Le Blanc. I'm sure you've heard of both.

"I wish you each to note everything I have said here today has been sanctioned by our superiors even to the King's and the Regent's advisors. The ends of your work were appreciated I'll give you that; though the means to those ends have most certainly left much to be desired. The Lord Chancellor wishes no further embarrassment resulting from your joint actions, for which reason you have each been rewarded fittingly."

Maitland looked across to Acland. He donned his coat and strode to the door where he delivered his final words.

"Goodbye, gentlemen. I cannot say it has been a pleasure."

37

THE COMMON ROAD coach was a convenient method of conveying travellers across England. It was most often drawn by four horses guided by a driver and secured by a guard seated at the rear. The coach could carry, with baggage atop, a maximum of six inside passengers and, for less money, four more outside: one seated by the driver and three crammed just behind them in *the baskets*.

Mary and Bonnie purchased their fares. It was a fine, well-kept coach. There were no glass panes in its windows but the proprietor had supplied ample blankets and warm bricks to provide some comfort for passengers.

They were lucky as well in their choice of the day which was fine, cool and clear. It seemed a Thursday was not busy on the run to York. Only two other inside passengers would join them. One turned out to be a Mr. Hurst: a plump, jolly vendor in dry goods from Dewsbury on his way to Leeds to purchase merchandise and a Mr. Ackroyd who was more subdued. He was a tall, thin man whose legs had trouble fitting comfortably into the well between seats. The men and the women sat opposite. Through most of the journey Ackroyd read his *Leeds Mercury*. Hurst, however, was a willing conversationalist.

All four were bundled in thick clothing having been warned of the absent glass. The ladies were each in *woollen* cloaks purchased by Mary from Mr. Hurst's shop the day previous. Mary wore a high, though warm bonnet while Bonnie had a *calash* mob cap, more suited to the servant's role she now played. Hurst was bundled in scarf, trousers and a heavy frock coat in navy colour while Ackroyd, obviously a man of means, wore a triple *Cape Coat* made of dark wool with brass buttons, fully lined in a polished cotton.

They left Dewsbury and travelled the turnpike to Leeds, a smooth and well conserved road, the coach moving efficiently as the passengers introduced each other and engaged in polite talk. Along the road they noted numbers of red coats marching. Mary asked why. Ackroyd, who seemed an authority on such things, lowered his newspaper.

"The soldiers are being moved outside the towns, Mrs. Buckworth."

"But why, Mr. Ackroyd?"

"It seems with the Luddite threat reduced, their general wants them out of the way. They haven't been popular with people, you know ... billeted and all that. But soldiers will be soldiers, madam, and they've lacked discipline here: drinking, theft, worse things. Thus, the move from towns to barracks. They shall be less nuisance to merchants."

"I'll agree t' that, Mr. Ackroyd," Hurst said. "I've had my troubles ... several thefts."

"I see," Mary replied. At that moment Mary noted the nature of humans to suppress evil in their lives. That these two characters could so easily brush aside the Luddite offensive of the past year made her think George's efforts, though not ineffective, too handily forgotten. Now a great many soldiers were on the move. She wondered how George had been so able to evade them for so long. She wondered as well what it all had been for; upon hearing the careless discussion regarding Luddites.

After Leeds came the rougher road to York. All the bumping and swaying seemed to put Mr. Ackroyd to sleep. Hurst had left them in Leeds and so the two women looked out their windows and, huddled in their blankets, watched the rolling countryside pass. By this time the trees had lost their leaves though there still remained elder and hawthorn foliage along the roadside hedges and, in the distance, copses of evergreen on the flanks of brown hills.

After a while they heard the far off *bleat* of a huntsman's horn signalling a fox had broken cover. For the next while they could distinguish different calls as the Master of Hounds directed his *Field* of hunters following the pack in chase of the fox.

"Oh, Mary ... I see him! The fox!"

"Where?" Mary leaned to her left, peering out the window.

And there he was. A small but unmistakable orange-red with a white tipped tail, crossing the road, the hounds baying far behind him. As they travelled further they caught glimpses of the pack, and once or twice of the *Field* on their sleek, expensive horses following their harried Master. Akroyd had awakened and gave them a knowing account of the hunt's progress, clearly having participated in former days.

As he explained the inevitability of its death at the jaws of the dogs, the little fox appeared unexpectedly passing in front of them. He was going the opposite way to the *Field*, and the dogs. Mary could hear them fade into the distance. It was the same fox. She could tell by the touch of white on his tail. He trotted unhurriedly across the road as they rounded a curve on Mary's side of the coach. Mary put her head out the window to keep sight of him. He had thrown the pack. There would be no death today, Mary smiled. Her smile faded as she thought of George having been that fox run to ground. Now he would face the jaws of the hounds who would kill him.

For a few seconds tears welled. Bonnie noticed. She produced a handkerchief from her bag and offered it, mentioning cold air was not good for the eyes and Mary should keep her face inside the coach. Mary wiped her eyes and thought of ways she might free George Mellor from the dogs of the law. She knew she could not. Her only hope was to see him, if even briefly, as she had the fox on the road; just to be able to look upon him and bid him farewell.

They came upon York in the late afternoon.

The Romans knew it as Eboracum. To the Saxons it was Eoforwick. The Vikings who came as invaders but stayed on to settle called it Jorvik.

Situated at the confluence of the Ouse and Foss rivers, the city lay on both sides of those watercourses. Eventually the Normans had built a castle and York had become a northern stronghold. As time passed its perplexing maze of narrow streets changed little within its walls and eventually those walls, unrequired, were partly dismantled. What remained were remnants like old broken teeth along with the ruin of the central keep. York's significance faded with the battles at Culloden and Falkirk and Scottish threat was quelled.

Yet located at a pivotal point in north England, York maintained its status despite its decline. It provided a convenient place for both markets and justice. In 1812 it possessed a population of twenty some thousand, not counting the hundreds more who entered on market days. As well, the demands of the gentry living in and around York helped determine the city's economy. The horse races and the assizes still attracted them but those who wished York to develop as Leeds, Manchester, or Nottingham had done were disappointed. There was little in the way of manufacture. There was, however, York Minster.

Home of the Church of England's Archdeacon, the once Catholic cathedral had taken more than two hundred years to construct. It was an incredible gothic structure towering over the city. It commanded nearly every view from the streets, its nave's high tower almost never out of sight from anyone who cared to look up. It had become the northern focus of the Church of England and welcomed not only church officials, but pilgrims from near and far.

It was Mary's excuse for coming to York. She had been here before with John, but now was arriving to live a lie. Having lost her husband and home she had come, ostensibly, to fling herself upon the mercies of Mother Church. That was what she'd told people in Dewsbury, the men in the coach, and finally the publican of the inn where she and Bonnie had descended the coach at the end of its route.

The Starre Inn, all yellowed walls and beamed ceilings, was dim and smoky inside its mullioned windows. Though he heard her account, Bill Parker, the Starre's publican, made it clear she and Bonnie would not be welcome.

"Don't matter, ma'am. Your maid and you can't stay."

"But I did with my husband when he was alive. He was a curate, I remind you."

"That was man and wife. I've no problem there, but the two of you staying? Dost know what things are like with men drinking in the tap room. Any idea what kind of women come here? I'm sorry to say — "

"Just one night, I beg you, Sir. I'm sorry, Mr. Parker. I've not been to York in years. The streets are a maze. I have no idea where I might find bed and board. The coach dropped us here so we thought, naturally, this would be our accommodation."

"Look Mrs. Buckworth, I know a place not far from here and a lad who'll take you. Just down t' Newgate Market. Right close t' All Saints — "

"All Saints, High Ousegate? I've been there with my husband!"

"Good then. Now Mrs. Flesher's a good woman who runs a respectable house. You'll receive fine, clean rooms and nourishing food. Once in a while when the wind's wrong there's the smell of the Shambles, the butchers' market, but it don't happen often. Being honest, ma'am, 'tis the best place for you!"

"It seems a fine alternative, Mr. Parker."

"Might I summon a sedan chair for you and a cart for your baggage?"

"We can walk, Mr. Parker. If you'll have two men carry our cases?"

"Of course, ma'am.

And then it was outside into bedlam: narrow streets stinking of horse manure, of sweat, beer, piss and slops, of the shouts and curses of draymen and artisans. There was constant noise and movement through narrow byways and *snickleways*, narrow covered passages which led to nefarious destinations. It was almost too much for Bonnie who, despite her hardiness, had never been to a city and so never subjected to such an assault upon her senses. Mary tried to keep a sense of bearing by looking for street signs. There were few. She noted the street they walked was called Daveygate. It was wider than most, and smelled better. They passed Market Street.

A waggon, overloaded, was trying to moved forward, then reverse, at the confluence of a narrow lane and the street. They got past it just before its barrels tumbled, rolling and rumbling across the cobbles. And finally they turned past a gateway, through a dim carriage tunnel and into a yard which, surprisingly, possessed real beauty. It was sunny and quiet. A tabby cat with three kittens relaxed upon an upended barrel. Their escort knocked at a substantial door. The mayhem of the streets seemed suddenly distant.

A woman answered. From her apparel she appeared well bred: a green cotton gown woven with fine stripes and printed with small floral sprays; Empire style, of course. She was middle aged and tended slightly to plump: her cheeks chubby and ruddy. She smiled warmly down upon the worn travellers and quickly ushered them inside. They introduced themselves as they removed cloaks and bonnets. Mrs. Flesher was more than hospitable. While their baggage was carried upstairs she sat Mary and Bonnie in a cozy parlour on two *bergeres* before a glowing fireplace. At once Mary felt she could relax though, glancing across to Bonnie, she could sense her friend overwhelmed. Still, Bonnie mimicked Mary's manners respectably.

"You'll be staying how long?" Mrs. Flesher asked, handing them a plate of apple cakes.

"I'm not sure, Mrs. Flesher," Mary said. "It could be a few weeks. You see my ..." She went into her story of her husband's death, her impoverishment, her pursuit of the clemency of the church. She noted Mrs. Flesher's eyebrows rise upon hearing the word 'impoverished.'

"Please don't fret about imbursement, Mrs. Flesher," Mary said as she retrieved a small sack from her reticule. She opened it and promptly offered the landlady two *guinea* coins. Mrs. Flesher seemed relieved knowing her lodgers possessed the *necessary*.

"You'll be attending the Minster, then," she said. "I'm sure someone there can help."

"I do hope so," Mary said. "My husband was once a lay-canon at the Parish Church of All Saints before he became a curate. It is nearby, is it not?"

"Why it's just around the corner! High Ousegate. A few minutes' walk takes you there."

"Perhaps tomorrow, then. It's getting on now and we've had a long ride."

"We must see to your supper immediately, then get you settled in! You are in a much safer place than the Starre, Mrs. Buckworth, particularly if you'll be staying some time."

"I'm sure we've been fortunate to have been referred, Mrs. Flesher."

Mary went to bed that night filled with hope.

—

He could have ordered his sergeant to deliver the documents to Radcliffe at Milnsbridge House, but decided the thing to do would be to present them himself and, more meaningfully, make a noble farewell to Fanny. She would remember him as a gallant officer and magnanimous lover. Others, it seemed, could not wait to see the back of him. The final meeting in the library had been devastating. Maitland had outfoxed them all and then taken credit for their work.

Francis Raynes would be moving on, his *reward* more a reprimand. The fact he'd been offered no promotion had left him stupefied. After what he'd accomplished in this campaign he felt cheated. To have been degraded for simply omitting the chain of command when he'd felt it necessary ... how had it been put? *You have overstepped. Twice. Once is forgivable, a second time means defiance, or stupidity.* Maitland might as well have flogged him. And then the final insult as though he were some recalcitrant schoolboy ... *you shall retain your present rank but be assigned as one of my staff at my next posting. And I shall have my eyes upon you.*

It was all so insufferable!

Still, there was one element from which he drew satisfaction regarding his sojourn in the West Riding. He approached Fanny's drawing room following a stiff-backed, shuffling servant. He'd been told Radcliffe and his wife were at cards. It was precisely what he had not wanted. She would not be alone. He'd wanted to impress her upon the event of his leaving. He'd wished to stride into her presence: the military gallant, the scourge of the Luddites, the scarlet Captain of the Stirlingshire Militia, all busy with papers for her addled old husband and gracious enough to acknowledge her with a brief, ironic farewell. And perhaps, had they found a moment alone, a last kiss? Her lips were so full, soft and moist.

They were wonders, those lips.

But as in war, and as in love, each and every tactic had gone amiss. The servant announced him while standing in the centre of the doorway so Raynes had to edge around him to enter. Then, instead of the feeble old Radcliffe he'd seen after Maitland's dressing down, Raynes found a man in high spirits. Radcliffe sat at a card table around which were Fanny, with her back to Raynes, joined by Curate Bronte and his wife, Maria. The group had obviously enjoyed supper and was now at *whist* and wine. Raynes came forward to stand beside Radcliffe. The magistrate was miffed at his presence.

"What is it, Captain?" he said shortly. No introductions, no offers of a beverage, nothing but the voice of a man receiving a subordinate. Looking down at Fanny, Raynes glimpsed silken breasts in her low cut gown and experienced an instant of loss. Her lips were pursed as she studied her cards.

Before reporting to his next post he'd been given home leave. He would return to his dour wife, Anne. Anne's lips were thin and taught, as was her character. The daughter of a major general, Anne was perhaps more military than Raynes himself. Whatever she was, she was not Fanny Radcliffe. Raynes fought for the right words; something vaguely scathing.

"Papers from General Maitland, Sir," he managed to say, stiff and subservient. Fanny would not look at him. She was using this moment to dismiss *him*!

His plan was in shambles.

"Leave them on the settee," Radcliffe said.

Fanny played a card. Her partner, Bronte, laughed with delight. Raynes at that moment wanted to kill him. Who was he to share any intimacy with her?

Her lips.

Blue eyes that changed to azure with passion.

Alabaster breasts.

Diverted by Fanny's behaviour, Raynes found himself mute. There would be no soft, noble farewells, no last kiss, no tears. He retreated over the carpet, cerise and emerald offsetting the pastel green walls. There was a fire in the marble hearth. The marble was white with pink veins. Like blood. In his ears was a roaring the like of which occurred just before his climax. He stuttered to a stop and turned. He tried to say something trite or droll. She did not even deign to look over her soft white shoulder at his departure.

Her shoulders.

She was beautiful. Her blonde hair was up in a wispy *chignon* exposing the grace and length of her neck. He remembered kissing her throat.

Her throat.

He remembered her throat would make moaning sounds that drove him to ecstasies.

And her lips.

Raynes left the room with the servant shuffling after him.

It had been as though he did not exist.

"I recall our walk one day last spring, I think, with Captain Raynes," Maria said when he had departed. "A pleasant day at any rate. We'd had tea in Huddersfield. We met him outside The George and walked to the bridge where the rivers join. I thought him a charming man."

"I thought him rather full of himself," her husband said.

"Really?" Fanny replied. "I hardly remember."

38

ALL SAINTS PAVEMENT was indeed but a few steps along High Ousegate. Mary and Bonnie made their way to the church after breakfast. As usual, the street hummed with activity but because they knew their destination, neither woman was quite as flustered as when they had first arrived in York. Indeed, they could see the church not far off, its almost lace-like tower floating atop the limestone structure. It was a beautiful, simple church. The original cruciform plan had been lost amid additions across the years until now it possessed a rectangular look. The simplicity belied its significance. Named All Saints Pavement because it stood on the first paved street in York, the church, unlike the Minster, served several parishes within the city. Indeed, John Buckworth had attended here to learn from veteran parish priests. The place was not unfamiliar to Mary.

They found the church empty and as cold inside as the winter without. Both women kept their cloaks wrapped around them. Bonnie, who had never seen the interior of an Anglican church, was astounded by its beauty. Up the centre aisle was a burgundy runner with polished oak pews on either side. The ceiling, as her eyes scanned above the arches, seemed almost a sky. It was the colour of sky. Behind the altar was a stunning, stained glass window. All the other windows but this one were clear glass, providing the church illumination by natural light.

"Tis so beautiful," the country woman said.

"A lovely place," Mary said, "though nothing like the grandeur of the Minster."

"I should like t' see that," Bonnie said.

Bonnie had grown up a Wesleyan Methodist. She was accustomed to plain halls with nothing more than a simple cross. She felt All Saints Pavement, despite its minimalism, somewhat pagan. Still, she could not stop admiring it. Mary took a pew, kneeled on the bar and pretended to begin her prayers. Bonnie had never seen a *kneeler* before. She felt a strange uneasiness at her friend's apparent self-effacement and looked away. It was then she discovered another penitent, a man dressed in black. Neither woman had seen him as he'd been ensconced in a *box pew* and, until this moment, concealed by its aisle wall. As he stood and opened the pew's half-door, Bonnie thought she'd seen him before. She tapped Mary lightly and pointed.

He wore black. He was a large man, older, though possessed of broad shoulders and a large girth. Yet as he walked down the aisle he seemed hunched to make himself less prominent. As he came closer, unconscious to their presence, Bonnie noticed his skin was pallid and his eyes self-absorbed. His face drooped with jowls. He seemed a man who had suffered.

Mary stepped from her pew and stood in his path.

"Reverend Roberson?" she said. This was not the commanding figure she had known as her husband's vicar.

"Why, Mrs. Buckworth. I'd heard you had moved."

The former robust, room-filling voice was diminished as well.

"I don't live here, Vicar. I've come to visit a friend. But why are you here?"

"Ah, Mrs. Buckworth, I am no longer a vicar. I felt unworthy given my part in events of this year."

"I don't understand."

"Mrs. Buckworth ... may I call you Mary?"

"Of course."

"Thank you. And my name is Hammond."

"This is my companion, Mrs. Bonnie Lodge."

"Mrs. Lodge."

"I'm Bonnie t' my friends, Sir."

"She is here in York for the same reason as mine," Mary said.

"Not regarding your late husband?"

"No. Another ... person."

"Perhaps we might sit. I've the use of a *box pew* of some friends. That way we might face each other rather than sit in a line."

"Are you in ill health, Hammond?" Mary asked.

"I have felt better. Tiring days. But my school for boys is nearly complete."

"Why that's wonderful!" Mary stepped through the waist-high door of the box. The three took their seats, Roberson against the wall half-facing Bonnie and Mary.

"Have you any boys, Bonnie?" he asked.

"Aye, I've three."

"Perhaps they might attend my school."

"No, Sir. I'd never afford it."

"There is no cost. I have done this deed with boys such as yours in mind."

"Why is that?"

"Let me say I hardly deserve to speak with you, Bonnie. At one time I would have shunned you. My calling was lost through ambition and vainglory. You see, I thought your people the enemy. You are Methodist?"

"Aye."

"The past years since John and Charles Wesley wended their ways across England have had much effect. Many decided to leave the Anglican fold and join the Methodists. That change has happened most often among common folk and has created concern for the Church of England. As I mentioned, I thought Methodism at odds with my Church. I considered the Luddite rising a Methodist rising as well. Thus I grew to believe their repression a kind of crusade in which I came to picture myself as a warrior-priest."

"Whatever would give you that idea, Reverend?" Mary said.

"I inhabited the circles of the gentry, merchants and masters. I could not see — as I did not care to look at — common people being thrown out of work with no charity. I did not understand their plight. Most of them were Methodist. Thus my error."

"We are all Christians, Hammond," Mary said, "though sinners as well."

"You mean yourself, Mary? The worse sinner is the hypocrite who sits in this box with you. I supported the wealthy, the titled, anyone who could further my ambitions. I went along with their disregard for the common class. They did not question what I was doing despite its hypocrisy and I did not question myself. It turns out I witnessed the brutal underside of the government's campaign; indeed I was part of it. I and a man named Lloyd ..."

"You need say no more, Reverend," Bonnie exclaimed. "All know of Solicitor Lloyd."

"Yes, but unlike you I had the chance to stop him. I was there when he allowed a boy to die. No, that is prevarication ... when he *killed* a boy, and another fellow."

"You mean young Johnny Booth and Sam Hartley?"

"I do. I was quite full of myself until then, Mary. I'd forgotten in my foolish pride that Our Lord was also tortured and killed. I'd lost the golden rule. And while it happened ... I was there while it happened ... I stood by and did nothing. Oh, I offered one slight belch of Christianity, but not enough to deserve my calling."

"That then is why you've built your school?" Mary said.

"It is. I intend now on building a church nearby. My departed Phoebe's inheritance has been spent on the school. I am out of money. So I've come requesting funds from the Archbishop. The cornerstone is already laid on a knoll in sight of Healds Hall. I hope to glance out my window each day and see it, above me across the river, a remembrance of my weakness. The school is my penance, the church shall be my benchmark."

It was the humility of his confession which opened an avenue for Mary. This meeting in All Saints Pavement was truly God's work, she thought. She recognized Roberson's redeemed faith which prodded her to return his confidences. She had not felt this since childhood. She spoke openly, honestly, as a child would.

"Reverend, I too have lost The Lord. It is only now I feel I can appeal for your help."

"What is it, Mary? Of course I'll help you."

"I am ... with child." She raised her hand to prevent his blessings. "The child is not John's. I am an adulteress."

For a moment Hammond Roberson was struck dumb. That this paragon of the Faith, this wife of a near martyr, this woman with whom he'd so often shared company should admit to such a horrendous act staggered him. Then he recalled his own sins. He took her hands in his.

"How can I help you, my dear?"

"It involves Bonnie's husband Sam and my ... my lover ... George Mellor ..."

"Mellor?" he said, shocked to his core.

"Yes. They are both in York castle prison. We've come here to try to see them. I don't expect you to understand, Reverend ..."

"You'll never be admitted. Two women? York gaol?"

"That is why I kneel here now," she said as she sank to her knees before him, still holding his hands, "and beseech you to help us. If you were to visit them as their minister, we might have a chance to be included."

"I ... I don't know what to say. I can't believe you would ..."

"Believe it, Hammond. I admit it. I carry his child."

"Oh, Lord," Roberson said.

"If you find my sin too horrid, if you will not help me, please don't include Bonnie. Her *true* husband is confined. She loves him deeply and wishes to see him. Hammond, her Sam will be transported. He concealed weapons from the authorities. She will never see him again."

"Oh, my dear Mary, please do not think me the bombastic fool I once was. Of course I'll help you. I shall make arrangements this very day. I must state my case as a charity and myself as your priest. There may be a chance ... though I've resigned my position as vicar I retain some friends with influence."

"We would be grateful, Hammond," Mary whispered, tears filling her eyes.

"Aye, Sir, we would," Bonnie said. She had witnessed an overwhelming courage and charity from two tortured souls in this Church called

All Saints. She thought those Saints must all be gathered above in that sky-like ceiling to create such a moment. For the rest of her life she would never forget it.

"It seems we might yet seek forgiveness from Our Lord," Roberson said.

"But you must forgive yourselves as well," Bonnie said.

All the Saints in the ceiling would have applauded.

He was merely a spectator amid the powerful characters in his office that morning. The military was represented by Lieutenant-General Maitland along with his second in command, Major General Acland. The government was embodied in Permanent Under-Secretary John Beckett. The Prosecuting Counsel was epitomized by Barrister J.A. Park with his two assistants, Solicitors Alison and Lloyd. The Lord Mayor of York, Thomas Smith, was somewhat in awe of these men who so easily dominated the room.

The office was stuffy, heated by the fire fed each half hour by servants who entered through a side door, stoked the flames, and departed without a word. It was a plain, working office. The furniture was basic and unadorned: Two oak tables faced each other across a brief carpeted space. Because of the room's large window, though outside was grey, enough light entered.

Maitland stared out the window absently watching bundled pedestrians cross the square. Flowing snow drifted like ice snakes slithering across the square's cobbles. He turned to the men in the room.

"I think the Ludds can be broken. With that in mind, these Special Commissions must show some mercy to those who were sheep led by wolves. I believe Mr. Lloyd has a list, Mr. Park, several of whom you may dismiss from the charges they face."

Park, a corpulent, soft individual with a doughy face beneath mutton chop whiskers, nodded knowingly and accepted the dossier from Lloyd, who had been reduced to a mere note taker beneath the hawk-eyed auspices of Jonas Alison. Lloyd resented each moment: cheated of his reward and rendered little more than a servant.

Park rode Lloyd hard to produce each and every note he had written in the past year, and ensured that Alison, his straight-laced, angular assistant, would serve as Lloyd's jockey. With the whip of seniority and an intimacy with the prosecutor enough to keep Lloyd's scheming at bay, Alison's sharp legal eyes confirmed nothing was omitted. Park had been warned of Lloyd's ways.

"I see only seven men listed here for acquittal," he said. Surely there must be more who might be discharged? Alison, take a look at Lloyd's list. We cannot prosecute one hundred men!"

"However, gentlemen," Beckett said, "I assure you of the Home Secretary's support. We have two no-nonsense judges. These Special Commissions are meant for the general populace. There will have to be hangings, and transportations."

"Rest assured, Mr. Beckett, the charges prepared for several of these criminals will most certainly lead to their executions," Park said.

"In particular," Maitland said, "Horsfall's murderers. Who are they?"

John Lloyd rose to speak but was prevented by Alison before he could utter a word.

"One George Mellor, one William Thorpe and one Thomas Smith! All three are indicted."

"They are the most likely to provoke riot," Maitland said. "I understand we have no confessions from them?"

"That is correct, General," Beckett replied. "You recall Captain Raynes captured two of them and said he had heard a confession. Since then Mellor has recanted, saying Raynes and his men had invented his words. Of the other two: Thorpe remains silent and Smith denies all!"

"We have his co-conspirator," Alison said, "one Benjamin Walker, in custody. My understanding is he was part of the four involved."

"Yes, of course," Maitland said, "he took the Crown's reward."

"The defense could use that to throw doubt on his testimony," Park said.

"Who is named as defense attorney?" Beckett asked.

"Henry Brougham has accepted," Park answered.

"Not the same fellow with aims toward reforming Parliament? The radical?"

"The very one," Park said. "He was employed through another Parliamentary reformer. We believe him to be a friend to Mellor. Thomas Ellis is his name. But I think Brougham's ambitions shall weaken rather than support the defense."

"We need a confession!" Maitland said.

"Allow him visitors," Beckett said, "then listen in. Give him the opportunity to communicate with anyone not incarcerated."

"I shall put Mr. Lloyd on him," Park said. "He has experience in that sort of thing."

"I shall be happy to be of service." Lloyd perked up from his gloom. A chance at George Mellor was all he would need to pull himself from the depths where Maitland had dropped him.

"I think not in this situation," Beckett said. "Maitland, you are with me on this?"

"I am," Maitland said, glaring at the solicitor. "As I've said, Mr. Park, Solicitor Lloyd has somewhat taken the law into his own hands this past year. We cannot afford more scandal, particularly with Mellor whom people seem to admire."

"No Mr. Lloyd," Park said as he wrote down the general's instructions.

"Now we must discuss security," the general said.

On cue, Acland rose from his seat. His voice bespoke the resilient soldier.

"We currently have one regiment of Regulars camped just outside the city and, to keep order, several troops of Militia within. We are taking no chances with the populace. I've created a ring of troops around us and only those with good reason shall enter."

"That's excellent, Acland," Maitland said. "It seems we are set for the trial's duration, but another problem has not been addressed."

"All seems well in hand," Beckett said, "what other difficulty do you see?"

"You were not present when two of these Ludds" — Maitland glanced sharply at Lloyd — "died in an action and had to be buried. The people, though peaceful, appeared in great numbers to honour the first one. They literally lined the road to his grave. Worried about the second, we buried him in secret. So how do we publicly hang these high profile felons, then prevent them from becoming martyrs?"

"Heavens, this is a conundrum," Park said.

"A quick, secret burial, as you mentioned," Beckett said.

"That won't happen again," Maitland said. "We fooled them once in the West Riding. We'll not do so twice. A grave means a martyr. There must be other ways to dispose of the bodies!"

"Sir," Acland said. "There is a surgeon of my acquaintance in Leeds who, for financial recompense, will travel to York, collect the bodies and dissect them in the name of medicine."

"Good God!" the Lord Mayor exclaimed. This was a league he cared not to join and a room he would rather not, at present, inhabit.

"You're sure of this man?" Beckett asked.

"Last week Mr. Hobhouse arrived here for that purpose," Acland said.

Everyone in the room was shocked, even Maitland. Hobhouse was a significant man, responsible for government budgetary matters.

"The Treasury fellow, *that* Hobhouse?" Maitland asked.

"Indeed, Sir. He approved the sum requested by the surgeon," Acland said.

"You didn't inform me," Maitland said.

"You were absent, Sir. Nothing was certain until yesterday. I left it to today's meeting."

"I see." Maitland's colour faded from the bright ruddiness of temper. "Good work once again, Acland. Gentlemen, it seems we have our solution."

"Not quite, General," Park said. "There is the security of the courtroom itself. I shall depose witnesses for the Grand Jury. I wish to ensure nothing emotional is staged for effect."

"What can you mean?" Maitland asked.

"Let us return to Thomas Ellis. This is a dealer in a respectable profession who possesses a substantial reputation. He appears to be organizing a defense beside Brougham's which might include witnesses who will offer good references to the men under indictment."

"This man can do that?" Maitland said, going purple again.

"Ellis seems to have chosen to side with the Ludds. I've no idea why."

"Arrest Ellis!" Maitland said.

"For what, General?" Beckett said. "He favours Parliamentary Reform but we cannot dictate his beliefs. He is simply availing himself of the rights of our justice system."

"The man might ruin our Commissions!" Maitland said.

Justice.

39

HAVING BEEN A prison for seven hundred years, York Castle gaol had seen its share of tears. As they entered the bowels of the lower level, the felon's dungeon, Mary fought back her own. The gloom of the place once the outer door closed, the pungent odours of so many men, the groans and plaints of the inmates, and knowing the free spirit of George Mellor was confined within this murky netherworld, almost made her break down.

"This is such a frightful place," she whispered to Bonnie, grasping her hand for solace.

"'Tis a cold, hard place for the likes of Sam and George. But we must be strong for 'em, lass. We can't let 'em worry over us."

"This way, ladies." Hammond Roberson led them to a scarred wood table. A huge man seated behind it was clearly, from the ring of keys on his belt, the prison's turnkey. When he spoke to them the stink of ale and other ingestions emitted from his mouth in the form of a halitosis, bringing Mary's kerchief to her face.

"Now, what's all this then?" he said, grinning, his teeth stained and broken.

"My name is Reverend Hammond Roberson, Sir. Are you not in the custom of standing when ladies are present?"

The man did not move.

"Depends on the ladies, don't it!" he said.

Hammond Roberson still possessed backbone when required. Though much reduced he could still produce, if only briefly, the vociferous character which had made him a vicar in the first place. His voice rang out in the turnkey's hallway, filling it with his demand.

"I shall suffer neither insult nor innuendo from such as you, Sir, particularly toward these ladies! I have an appointment with Mr. Wharton, the prison warder. I shall not be inhibited by one of his lackeys! Any more nonsense and you shall rue the day! Now, get up from that chair and conduct us to Mr. Wharton!"

Without another word the turnkey rose from his chair, his head brushing the whitewashed ceiling, and led the three to a closed door behind him. He opened the door and stood aside allowing their passage. When they had entered he closed the door, with a murmured curse, behind them.

They found themselves in a bright office. The windows contained no bars. The room's wooden floor and clean white walls were so contrasting the murk they'd departed they could hardly believe they were in the same building. Behind a desk and rising to greet them was Josiah Wharton, the warder. He was a corpulent, middle aged fellow who appeared for all the world as a merchant or well-to-do publican until one caught a glimpse of pale eyes beneath his grey bushes of eyebrows. Those eyes held no light. Even as he smiled, extending his hand in greeting, his voice a trifle pretentious, his eyes never changed. This was a perilous individual who, at the moment, seemed in a helpful mood.

"I welcome you ladies and Reverend Hammond to York castle prison. Reverend, may I have the pleasure?" He indicated Mary and Bonnie.

"This is Mrs. Bonnie Lodge, the wife of one of your prisoners. She has a small gift for you and, as I am here to minister to him, she wished to accompany me on my visit."

"Rather unorthodox, Reverend. We seldom have women here."

Bonnie handed the man a small box.

"Please, Sir, open it," she said softly.

Within was a silver plate watch, paid for with Mary's money, insisted upon by Roberson who knew from certain circles just what bribes would work in this place. He added a packet of pound notes to the gift.

"For the prisoner's upkeep and other needs," he said. All prisoners were required to pay for their *lodging* while incarcerated. The minimum was offered those who could not provide payment. That minimum usually meant slow starvation.

"And this is Mrs. Mary Buckworth," Roberson said, "widow of my recent curate at Dewsbury, the Reverend John Buckworth. She knows a fellow named Mellor whom you hold here. Apparently he gardened for her and she wishes to cheer him."

"George is his name!" Mary blurted. Roberson subtly touched her gloved hand.

"That is *prisoner* George Mellor, Mrs. Buckworth," Wharton responded. His rheumy eyes turned upon Mary. "Prisoner Mellor is in the condemned cells. No visitors."

"I wish, Mr. Wharton, to offer him comfort." Mary somehow found strength to stand up to those dead eyes. "I have heard your wife admires tea sets. In the box the Reverend holds is a small token of my appreciation: a Sterling silver collection from one grateful lady to another."

The poise with which Mary delivered her bribe surprised Wharton. First, it was not meant directly for him and second, its great value and her gracious approach rendered him helpless. Even his eyes seemed to soften. His thin lips parted in what passed for a smile.

"My wife would thank you, Mrs. Buckworth, as do I. We shall make an exception with prisoner Mellor, just for you. There is a place we often use. I'll have it cleared and the prisoners escorted there. It is called *The Petitions*. Normally each day my wards, the inmates, gather to make requests or be ministered to. It is comfortable enough, though I'm afraid you'll find it rather stark."

He opened his office door and stepped through to the turnkey's vestibule. The three could hear him issue instructions.

"What a horrible man," Mary said. "Thank you, Hammond, for your advice on these *gifts* and the money for George and Sam."

"It is unfortunate," Roberson replied. "There has been some effort to bring about reform though it has yet to bear fruit."

"The man's a monster!" Bonnie exclaimed, for the first time losing her fear of the place.

"Nevertheless," Roberson replied, "upset him at your peril. He is a veritable monarch down here. Quiet now, he's returning."

Wharton entered and crossed the room to stand by a second door. As were all doors in the gaol, it was of solid oak planking with iron studs and bands for increased security. It was painted black. He remained beside it, holding his hands together behind his back as he spoke.

"Now as to prisoners Mellor and Lodge, there are certain rules which must be obeyed for your own safety and the good of the prisoners. You must not upset the prisoners in any way. Should that happen, the interviews will be terminated. Is this clear to you, ladies?"

"It is," Mary replied.

"This is no place for the gentle sex, ladies," he said lasciviously.

"I have brought them at their request," Roberson said. A part of the arrangement he'd made to allow the inclusion of Mary and Bonnie was to attempt to overhear a confession from Mellor regarding the Horsfall murder. He could tell Mary nothing of this. He had not wanted, after John Lloyd, to be forced to choose sides. Yet now he found himself on *both* sides.

"The turnkey shall accompany you and remain in the room for your safety. 'Tis a short walk to *The Petitions*. The prisoners are not to talk with each other. You should take seats on opposite sides of the room. Reverend, you may move from one place to the other. Now, you might be shocked at the prisoners' appearance. They've had no benefactors until now and might seem a trifle gaunt. Please do not register alarm."

With that he knocked on the door. A jangle of keys and a rasp of the lock answered him. The door opened and there, once again, stood the massive turnkey. He was a different man in the presence of the warder: obsequious, deferential, seeming just a bit smaller. They brushed by him into the hallway. It was lit with lanterns though still very dim. They walked a short distance to a room with barred windows facing into the hall, and two other windows, heavily grilled, allowing light in from outside. There were benches against the walls. Bonnie went to one side of the room, Mary to the other.

"Are these seats correct?" Mary asked.

"Aye, ma'am. I don't see why the two of you'd choose t' come here. Maybe you'd like t' tell me why?"

By this time Mary had had enough of the turnkey's patronizing. She advanced upon the man. Roberson tried to intervene. In a corner, Bonnie noted, a rat scurried under a bench. Then Mary opened her broadside upon the astonished turnkey.

"If I thought it at all any of your business I would tell you! But as it is not, and as you are prying into the lives of two law abiding women — visitors, Sir, not inmates, I believe it best you stay to *your* business and leave us to *ours*! Is *that* clear, gaoler?"

Bonnie smiled and winked at Mary.

"Aye, ma'am. Aye. I just do my job ..."

"May I take my seat again then, without further questions?"

"Aye. Just mind the rules."

"We certainly shall."

After a few minutes Sam appeared from behind a wall which obviously concealed a passage. His big frame was reduced. He'd lost weight. His clothing was rags, his hair long and unkempt as the beard he now bore. For an instant Bonnie did not recognize him. Then it came in a rush and her eyes filled with tears, though she said nothing.

"Prisoner Lodge!" the escort said harshly. The turnkey pointed soundlessly to Bonnie and Sam was taken to her. She touched his hand.

"No touching!" the turnkey shouted, recovered from Mary's attack.

Roberson joined them. He spent a few moments in prayer with them, then left them to their own devices. He hovered near Mary and made it a point to look away but kept his ears tuned.

"Prisoner Mellor!" another voice declared. Having rounded another wall from a different direction, George stood with his escort. He had the same look as Sam, even his muscular body was reduced and his eyes seemed mere pebbles in his bearded faced. He was filthy and, unlike Sam, shackled both feet and hands. Mary fought to maintain her composure. She looked once again at the turnkey, gesturing to the chains.

"These ... is this necessary?"

"Ma'am?" the turnkey responded, wringing out his own moment of triumph.

"The shackles ..."

"Oh, Aye! Prisoner Mellor's a condemned man, soon t' go t' trial for murder. The shackles be for your own protection, and the other inmates."

By this time George Mellor had shuffled over and sat opposite her. He was the shell of the man she had loved. She lowered her voice to a whisper so the turnkey could not overhear.

"Oh my God ... George."

"Calm yourself, Mary. He'll end this now if you don't."

"Yes. I understand. Yes."

"They treat me alright, Mary. This is for show. I don't wear chains all day."

"Are you well?"

"Good enough. I share a cell now with Thorpe and Smith. We're t' go t' trial together. Can Thorpe be connected t' you?"

"He went back to my house after we saw you leave. He was arrested. I wasn't with him."

"Good. He was worried."

"What will you do?" she asked. She could not help staring at the emaciated remains of a once vibrant man. She wondered had they killed his spirit as well?

"Dost know there will be a Special Commission?" he said.

"There are rumours, George."

"They're true. The three of us are t' go first. But I've not met with my attorney and I've things he must know. I've something here for you, Mary. Wait 'til their backs are turned."

He produced a crumple of paper, filthy and creased into a ball. She took it and quickly had it up her sleeve. No one noticed, they thought, but Roberson with his back turned had heard the scrunch of paper.

"Try t' get it t' Tom Ellis. He should be in town by now."

"How shall I find him?"

"Go t' the court today. Ask t' see my defense. He should be with them."

"Alright. Is this important?"

"Aye. I hope t' free some of these men. Most of 'em are innocent."

"How is it? Here?"

"I mind my business. I've had time t' think, Mary. There's a priest from the Minster who came t' see me. He's helped me understand things; deep things I'd not thought through before."

She perceived an odd passion within him.

"I love you, George."

"I wish I could touch you, Mary."

"George, I've something to tell you. Something very important ..."

She was ready to give him her news, felt the moment right as he revealed his love for her even in this horrid place; but he was not ready to hear her. His mind was filled with something else. He interrupted her intimacy with his own intense force.

"Mary, I've something as well. This priest I mentioned ... we've talked hours ... I know now why I've acted as I have."

"Where is he now? What was his name?" She could only follow Mellor's lead.

"I don't know, Mary. He never told me. But I'd like you to hear me out."

"Of course, George. Go on."

Her news would wait. He was brimming with new-found wisdom, perhaps even hope. Whoever the priest had been he had had an explicit effect. As it was, when Mellor spoke his extraordinary thoughts, she was astonished. She had not expected the kind of penetrating philosophy, or rather prediction, which came from the man she thought she knew. She had heard rifts of it before, the beginnings of beliefs, but nothing to match the remarkable ideas or strange premonitions she heard from him now.

"I recall back when my da' left us and I went off t' sea. I saw many places, Mary, but mostly Russia. Have you any idea what Russia is like? I saw there a cluster of elites; people who seemed t' think they owned everything and by everything I mean even *people*. Called them *serfs* but they were slaves. What I mean is these few people *owned* all the rest, like they were property. 'Twas a land of bondage.

"Then I returned here and saw the beginnings of the same thing; though here 'twas the *maisters* and merchants with this thing they called their factory system. I don't understand how good Englishmen could turn out like Russians. While they say they move forward, the *maisters* and such actually try t' go back in time, t' make us all peasants like the old days. Now they've a new means t' make this happen. I mean their machines. I know I've said this before, but this man, the priest; he gave it a name. 'Tis called *tekhnologia*."

"I know that word," Mary said. "It's from the Greek."

"Aye. So where'll this *tekhnologia* take us? I've seen *maisters* kill for their precious machines as though a man were worth less than a gadget. Yet Cartwright, and so many like him breed their factory system, their form of *tekhnologia*, forcing people into mills, timetabling even when they eat and sleep!"

"They use women and children now, George," she said. She wanted so much to be part of his thoughts, *inside* his thoughts, understanding him.

"Aye. They were starting that up just last year. Now, I suppose, with none t' oppose them they'll make their system work a bit smoother. But what does that do to us? Makes us serfs. Peasants. Beasts! Is that all we're meant t' be? Even our Parliament has ruled slavery is inhuman. Yet they keep on ruling in favour of the *maisters* and their machines and manufactories! Isn't that slavery as well?

"I don't want a society where we're measured *only* by our worth. Is that all we strive for? Hast our old England become like Russia? Don't these Russians know someday their serfs will rise as we tried to rise? If we're not careful this ... *tekhnologia* is going t' overcome all of us: commoners, merchants, *maisters* and gentry. Someday we'll have machines doing *all* our work for us. We'll think the machines so important we can't live without them! But what if they gain a mindfulness of their own. What if they learn t' think? I know this sounds cracked but they could outgrow us. 'Tis sure t' happen if we keep on as we are! They'll take over our society and we'll have no choice but t' serve them! Imagine, Mary! Us serving machines!"

"Oh, George," Mary said, obviously distressed. "Who is this priest? Are these his ideas?"

"We talked it through together. Once, it seems a lifetime now, I told you my way t' fight back was t' be a machine. I was a bit mad back then, I'll admit. Now I know I'm no machine. No one can be. We're human. We've feelings, and needs, and dreams! 'Tis a war, Mary, right now, against our oppressors! But in the end it won't be so much us against them, but against the machines themselves!

"So I'll plead *Not Guilty.* A soldier in war is not guilty, and this war is against *tekhnologia* and those who control it. It ain't so much against the future as their version of it. I'm not guilty so long as the *maisters* think they can own the earth. Imagine, Mary, they make a law that says breaking machines means a death sentence. What kind of men do that? They don't realize they're making a future where none but machines will rule! If we don't manage these machines and ourselves who make them, if we don't marry what we make with who we are ... then we'll *all* become nowt but slaves!"

He stopped talking then, exhausted by this stream of wild thoughts, predictions and prophecies. He leaned against the white wall, letting the back of his head touch its coolness. He closed his eyes, stone eyes once diamonds. Mary could do little but wonder. She resolved she must meet this priest from the Minster. She asked his name once again. Instead Mellor continued.

"I fathom no one'll ever remember me. I'm but a simple man from the West Riding. Yet this Special Commission is meant t' put me out of the way. Dead and forgotten. For a time I worried on that. But the Minster priest helped me. I know now I'm a soldier, not an outlaw. I know my death just might pave the way for others t' rise up and dispute the future. The future ain't certain, Mary. We can change it." He paused. "Just not now."

He finished, his head drooping. What had brought him to this? She had the answer to heal him, she hoped.

"George, you won't be forgotten."

"I'm alone, Mary. All of us are."

"I'm not alone. I've come here with someone for you."

"What dost mean?"

"George. I've come here with your child."

"What?"

"Before you were captured. We made a child, my love."

"Mary, a child ..."

"You will be remembered. I'll make sure of it. I carry your baby, George, and when he or she grows I'll give *this* as a present for coming of age. You *will* be remembered."

She produced the tiny *Enoch* from her breast.

His eyes sparked one final time ... with his tears.

When their visits ended they were escorted to Wharton's office. Wharton prevented Roberson from passing. There was an instant when both men seemed frozen. Then, with a nod and a whisper from Roberson, Wharton turned and detained Mary.

Roberson escorted Bonnie out but on his way he turned, a look of anguish upon his face.

"I'm sorry, Mary. This was the only way they would let you see him."

"I don't understand, Hammond," she said.

"I must speak with you, madam," Wharton said, his pale eyes swept over her.

"Regarding what, Sir?" she asked tremulously.

"During your interview with prisoner Mellor you accepted something from him."

"I have no idea what you mean, Mr. Wharton," she tried to deflect him.

"Madam, please do not force me to place you under arrest."

"This is how you terrorize people? What you've done to George?"

"Please give me the paper. You know what I mean. Do not make me take it."

She saw little sense in prolonging the inevitable. Having heard George's thoughts she began to find much not so hard to believe.

Deliberations from a gaol cell. Apocalypse from the condemned.

She gave up the letter.

When it reached Lord Sidmouth, having passed through the hands of Maitland, Park, Lloyd (for recording) and Beckett, the letter revealed nothing the Home Secretary did not know already. It merely confirmed Mellor was the reputed leader of the Yorkshire West Riding's Luddites and, though young, he was relatively educated and therefore dangerous.

Yet its contents surprised him in spite of his expectations. Mellor had listed thirty nine of his fellow prisoners, asking Ellis to appeal somehow to Parliament to reprieve them as they had committed no crimes. Sidmouth was perplexed.

Thomas Ellis was detained and investigated. The letter was examined for cyphers. Despite Mellor's appeal, his own right to provide a legal defence for his friend, and his radical Parliamentary beliefs, nothing in the letter could condemn Ellis.

He was released.

Mellor had also asked Ellis, in a personal aside, to reassure his cousin Joe that he held no fear of his impending judgement. In a sentence he summed up his feelings:

> *Remember a soul is of more value than work or gould.*

To anyone's knowledge, it was not a code.

40

THE DUNGEON DOOR clanked shut behind them, finished by the snick of the lock. Bonnie glanced at Mary. The latter was pale as a ghost. Bonnie had no idea what had occurred between Mellor and Mary within *The Petitions*. She hoped it wasn't as bad as what she and Sam had suffered though but from the look of her friend she thought the worst. She felt she should try to help her but Reverend Roberson was beside Mary, taking her arm as they walked past the Court Building. It frowned down upon them, its grey pitted stone and rectangular windows hard and blockish and accusing. Scarlet uniformed soldiers marched across the windswept, winter lawns. Bonnie felt thankful for the cold of the day and the sun; both made her feel stronger.

As usual, Sam had done little talking until she'd coaxed him. He'd already recognized his fate. Transportation. After Roberson's prayer he had asked the reverend where he'd be sent.

"The name of the land is *Terra Australis*," Roberson answered. "It used to be called New Holland but recently the Royal Society has insisted upon a more scientific name. I have heard the penal colony itself is called New South Wales. My understanding is it takes months to sail there. Mind you, I've not followed this subject ..."

"'Course not, Reverend. Why should you?" Sam said. "At any rate I've been told it will be the rest of my life. Better than hanging, I guess."

"Anything's better than being dead, Sam." Bonnie's strong surface had begun to fracture. She fought to keep her strength for her man.

"I'd best be off to see to Mrs. Buckworth," Roberson said. "For you it is transportation. For Mellor, I fear, it is the worst. Bless you both, and may some good come of your suffering."

After that they spoke of the children. Sam wished to have seen them one last time. He relied instead upon Bonnie's descriptions. They'd prattled on together as though for a while they were somehow free and unencumbered.

At one point George Mellor raised his voice. He was speaking fervently to Mary who listened, unmoving, to whatever it was had worked him up. They could not help but overhear. When George quieted, however, Bonnie and Sam had lost their warm place. Sam cried.

"You were right, my Bonnie," he said. "You said I'd come t' no good with them men and you were right. Look at me now. I've lost all I hold dear just t' keep my pride."

If ever a man was an innocent, Bonnie thought, her man was. He had only kindness and caring within him and, if once his vanity had stepped in his way, he would pay for that now. She wanted to hold him but the turnkey had already warned them. She'd not wanted their time to end yet, inevitably, it had. She'd noticed Mary rising and had taken her cue.

"Sam, I must leave you now. I wish t' God you could come with me. I'll say this: never worry about the children. They may be poor but they'll have good lives and I'll make sure they remember you in their prayers."

"I recall when I first saw you, Bonnie," he said, voice trembling. "'Twas you singing that time just outside the King's Head that made me come close. Then I saw your crown of red hair and thought: *How's a man t' get that girl*? But I did. And now, I've lost you."

"I love you, big Sam," she said.

"I'm dead t' you now, dear Bonnie. Find a good man and marry, for the children."

"I couldn't do that, Sam."

"'Tis my wish, Bonnie. What's done's done. The children shouldn't have t' suffer."

"'Time!" the turnkey said. Sam rose to his feet, silent now, looking at her. It was his eyes which said farewell. She watched him leave then turned to find Mary and Roberson waiting. Everything after had seemed a blur as Roberson left Mary alone with the warder, pulling Bonnie out the door. They had waited until a white-faced Mary had joined them and then they were out in the cold and the sun. Bonnie stopped and turned to the prison.

"Goodbye, Sam," she whispered.

Mary said they would go to York Minster. Roberson wanted to start his funding and Mary said something about finding a priest. Bonnie didn't care. She was drained from her final moments with Sam and thoughts of her children. Without money she would hire herself out, she hoped, to one of the new factory mills. Ottiwells was hiring, she'd heard: women and children only. Perhaps she could get work there as well.

They caught a cart for hire which took them along the river Ouse, the vehicle winding its way between buildings and the shoreline, then up wider streets with markets and taverns and churches. Roberson ordered the driver to make for the square at the West Door of the cathedral. The building was a mountain. So high and wide in the afternoon sunlight, its windows glistened like ice. It took Bonnie's breath away. It seemed so like bare cliffs up on the high moors in winter. They got down from the cart, then Mary asked her to follow. They were going to enter the mountain!

—

Mary Buckworth had hoped somehow her meeting with George would lessen the pain of her loss. The oppressive confinement of the gaol had dispelled that notion. Worse was George having accepted his fate. The shock of seeing her once robust lover reduced to gauntness and strange divinations was almost the end of her. She had tried to follow his winding logic but the weird incantations he'd weaved had evaded her. She was sure his fear of aloneness along with the prompts of this Minster priest had driven him near to insanity.

Mary, however, was not the type to long remain helpless. She employed the cart ride to compose herself. She focused on how she would find this mysterious priest who preached such tempestuous futures as she had heard from George. Her friends took her disposition as distress and said little during their ride across York.

When they arrived she saw Bonnie's wonder at the colossal Minster but quickly left her companions behind and entered the massive West Door. Ignoring the Great West Window she turned left to the North Aisle then passed through a small, side doorway just at the North Transept and found herself amidst the manicured lawns and winter-bare trees of the Liberty of Saint Peter. Several inhabitants stopped in their tracks to stare at her, surprised at a woman among them. Finally one of them stood in her path. When she tried to dodge past he moved to prevent her.

"What would you be doing here, madam?" he asked, by his attire an Archdeacon. He was a tall man, with thick grey hair and a neatly trimmed beard. He possessed a long face and his eyes contained a dove grey softness which made him appear rather gentle.

"I must find someone," Mary answered, concerned with reaching the Archbishop's lodgings. He would know of a rogue priest if any did here.

"You've no right here, madam, without invitation. I suggest you return to the Minster."

"I have every right!" Mary said. "I am the widow of a curate of the Church and have need to see the Archbishop."

"He is not here," the man stated, but Mary was used to the fabrications of priests.

"A likely story."

"Please, madam, sit with me here, on this bench." His fingertips touched her elbow and, despite herself, she obeyed. She wanted to get to the Archbishop's residence but the man's soft eyes settled her nerves.

"You seem agitated," he said. "Perhaps I might help. The Archbishop truly *is* absent but why do you seek him?"

"I need to know the name of a priest."

"As you are aware, we have quite a number here," he said, smiling.

"A priest who visits the inmates at York castle prison! Surely not all do that!"

"No. But there are several. If men ever needed God's word it is those."

"Do you know all their names? The priests?"

"Why?" he asked.

"One of them has visited, and more than once I might add, a man named George Mellor. He is an inmate to be tried for murder," Mary said, her voice hardening. "But this priest has tangled his thoughts. Indeed, no priest I've ever heard would allow such thoughts."

"I would not admonish a priest," the Archdeacon replied. "What is your name, Madam?"

"Buckworth. Widow of Curate John Buckworth."

"Ah," the Archdeacon said more softly. "Mary Buckworth. Indeed, I thought I knew you. I was sorry to hear of your husband's passing. Do you not remember me at all?"

"No."

"I recall you and your husband quite clearly. He was a gentle soul. You are a bold one."

"What does that mean?" She would not be patronized.

"I think you know," the Archdeacon said, smiling. "He was good for you, Mary."

"How would you know anything about us?"

"When he was a postulant, before his posting at All Saints Pavement, I was his mentor. When he married, I was to have been your officiating priest but became ill and could not attend. I am truly sorry for that."

"That's all very fine but what of the priest I am seeking?"

"Of the several who visit the prison, a number have left for their parishes. It is Advent after all and they are required. What was the name of the inmate?"

"George Mellor."

"How long has he been incarcerated?"

"Two months now. For murder."

"Prison can alter a man. It can be a brutal place and bring hopelessness. It might have led your friend into a world removed from his own. Perhaps it is his own way of escape?"

"Now you accuse my George of delusion!" Mary stood up, ready to walk away.

"Don't you? Is that not why you are here seeking the priest who counselled him? Please, Mrs. Buckworth, sit down."

She composed herself and sat once again.

"This man was close to you," the Archdeacon said. "A brother, perhaps?"

"You do not wish to know, believe me."

"Not a brother then ... an intimate."

"That is the polite form," Mary said.

"Have you considered the person perplexed might actually be you?"

Mary shook her head.

"Please, let me finish. Your George is to be tried for murder, you say. Perhaps this fact has dazed you. After all, how can a man be capable of loving yet at the same time of murder?"

"Have you not heard at all of Luddites?"

"Indeed. He is one of them?"

"Here in your gilded cage, you could have no idea; nor could your interfering priest!"

"I'm sure the priest meant well. They are accustomed to counselling those in need."

"If this priest did serve as a counsellor you'd have heard of him. He gave George bizarre ideas of the future ... *tekhnologia* ... men fighting machines for survival ... why, it's appalling!"

"Did he help your George at all?"

"George has justified his actions. He shall plead not guilty. He thinks his murder of a mill owner the same as a soldier killing an enemy. He says he did it for us, for humanity."

"These are George's thoughts or those of the priest?"

"I cannot tell where one leaves off and the other begins!"

"I'll not patronize you, madam. I'm afraid we both know mankind is imperfect. Perhaps you did not hear him in quite the manner he intended."

"You take me for a fool?"

"I seek to help you."

"I love him. I don't want him to die."

"Are you alone in the city?"

"No. I've a friend with me; a woman whose husband is in gaol as well, and a former vicar from the West Riding."

"Former vicar? West Riding. Not Hammond Roberson?"

"You know of him?"

"He is coming to see me regarding church funding. Apparently he has spent all his own wealth on a boy's school out there."

"He is here, Archdeacon. I left the two of them at the West Door."

"Why is he with you?"

"It would take too long to explain."

"Could it be he used his ministry to achieve your entrance to the prison?"

The whirlwind of emotions this chance meeting raised in Mary unnerved her. She sat quietly a moment, trying to say precisely what she meant. It was all so very complicated. She resorted to the simple truth.

"I am a sinner," she said.

"As am I."

"I loved two men. I sinned with one and beguiled the other. Now one is dead and the other condemned. What kind of woman does that? What creature could find herself so self-centred that others would suffer for her arrogance?"

"The same one who has realized it. The one who atones even now."

"I carry the child of the man who is *not* my husband!"

The Archdeacon paused to take in this admission knowing how much it had cost her to say. His eyes were a grey sea.

"Was your child conceived through love?"

"Yes. Oh, yes. But George will be hanged! The child shall have no father."

"But you ... you might give this child love abundant. Offer your child what you have lost. The love of two men *and* your own."

"How can I? Think what I've done to create this child. I am an adulteress."

"I'll not be him who casts the first stone."

"Others will."

"You must forgive yourself, Mary. You must live your life the best way you know."

"But my love has been selfish!" she said, almost keening in grief.

"If you know that much then you know you can change. Without forgiveness what kind of life will your child be able to live? Try to calm yourself, Mary. We do not have to talk."

They sat silently then upon the bench, the cold winds of December somewhat subsided within the closeness of the Minster Quarter. Still there were gusts to remind them of the world outside. Above them was the ancient tree, its branches clicking amid those gusts, and above it a bright sky, wispy with high thin cloud. Around them endured the beauty of the Minster: its towers reaching heavenward, its gargoyles chuckling at all beneath, its buttresses arching to support its immense stone body. Here, in the Minster's private quarter, holly bushes lit winter-bare gardens with emerald leaves and bright berries. Somewhere behind them, neither turned to look, a shovel dug into the earth. They heard its distant crushing and the throw of its burden. The shovel's rhythm became an intonation, the backdrop to their thoughts. After a while it ended and then only the wind and the clicking branches remained.

"I shall give him, or her, all the love I possess," Mary whispered, transformed.

"In my experience, one cannot love another without loving oneself."

"So I must forgive myself."

"Blame is so easy."

"George will die. John is already dead."

"Yet you are alive with new life inside you."

The Archdeacon paused, pulling his scarf a bit tighter. It was growing colder, Mary noticed. She stood, the Archdeacon stood with her.

"I came here seeking a recalcitrant priest," she said.

"And you found one."

"You? An Archdeacon?"

"I stood in your way."

"No. You gave me the chance to think."

"Of yourself?"

"Of myself, George, and John. And what I must do."

"Love your child."

"Yes."

"I think when you become a mother the truth of love shall appear clear to you."

"What is *your* name, Archdeacon?"

"Do I need have one? If so, it is the same as he who counselled your George."

"Yes. George has forgiven himself, though I fear not the world."

"That is more difficult."

"Yes. Do you believe mankind will always make war on itself?"

"We always seem to find a foe."

"Where will it lead us?"

"God knows, Mary. I don't."

"I should find my friends. They'll worry."

"I'll stay here a while. Why not send Hammond Roberson to me."

"He truly needs his church."

"It is never ours, it is always God's."

"I think, Archdeacon, after what has happened this year in the West Riding, Hammond Roberson needs God as much as me."

—

Stepping in through the north transept door Mary arrived back inside the Minster. It was not much warmer inside the cathedral though without the wind, more comfortable. She found Roberson and Bonnie in the midst of the crossing of nave and transepts, beneath the tracery dome far above, with their backs to her as they gazed at the famous Rose window. Roberson was holding forth.

"So you recall, Mrs. Lodge, the south transept there holds that window, what is locally known as *The Heart of Yorkshire*. Note if you will its design, so wonderfully complementing the Great West Window and if you will turn about, note the delicacy of the Five Sisters Window." Then noticing Mary: "Oh, Mrs. Buckworth, you've returned! I did not wish to leave Mrs. Lodge on her own. We've been having a tour, have we not, Bonnie!"

"Aye, Sir, that we have," Bonnie said, her eyes pools of wonder as she observed the gargantuan interior. "I've never seen such as this."

"But where did you go, Mrs. Buckworth?" Roberson asked. "It has been near an hour. We wondered had you got lost somewhere."

"In a manner of speaking, Hammond. But now I am found and you have an Archdeacon awaiting you in the north garden. Just follow the path out the transept door. He is sitting on a bench beneath a tree."

"I shall, Mary. And my thanks. I recall your departed husband took his training here."

"Yes, but now please find the Archdeacon. It is not so warm out and you don't want to keep him waiting."

"Of course," Roberson said, striding off upon his business.

Mary turned to Bonnie and took her hands in hers. She spoke to her as she would a sister.

"Bonnie, I've made some decisions. I want you to hear them so you too can choose."

"Aye, Mary, where were you?"

"I was drowning in my melancholy after seeing George, and I wonder if you do not feel the same. I'm sorry I left you. It was selfish."

"I don't feel the best if that's what you mean."

"I'll not remain here, in York I mean. I have no wish to see George die. He knows the verdict is already set and he will be hanged."

"Leave York?" Bonnie was bewildered.

"Do you think you'll be able to see Sam again?"

"He'd not want me t' see him," she said, close to tears. "He told me t' find a new life for the children."

"Then do as he bids, come with me."

"Where are you going, Mary?"

"Across the sea. There's land to be had over there and a new life."

"I can't leave my kids."

"I've money enough for passage for all. Together we can help each other, give each other and our children strength."

"What do you mean, lass?"

"I mean I'll not see George's child brought up in the horrid place England's become. I want our child to have a new world, and your children too, and us for that matter. We can be gone tomorrow if you agree.

A coach to the West Riding where we'll gather your flock, then we'll make Liverpool and from there by ship to our freedom. What say you, dear?"

"With my kids? All of 'em?"

"Of course. We'll go to another York, in Upper Canada. I'm told it's a bustling place where we can establish a household."

"It would be what Sam wants. We've nothing here."

"Nothing but regret. I had a talk with someone who allowed me to look at myself."

"You're changed, lass. I can see it."

"For my child. For yours. We must give them their futures."

"I'm ready, Mary. I'll not mourn my man. He wouldn't want it."

"We'll be off to Mrs. Flesher's to pack. Reverend Roberson is likely to be busy a while. I think he'll receive funding for his church. I'll write a letter of thanks to him and have it posted from Mrs. Flesher's, addressed to the Minster. I'm sure he'll stay here."

"A new life," Bonnie said, both hope and regret in her voice. As the two walked together down the nave, the sound of their footsteps echoed urgently in the vast space of York Minster. They were walking toward a new world.

41

HAMMOND ROBERSON RECEIVED the funding for his church. Because the procedures took so much time to arrange, Roberson decided to remain over Christmas in York. He lived within the *The Liberty of Saint Peter* reviewing with the experts at hand the details of construction.

Meanwhile, he attended Christmas rites at York Minster. The ceremony in Church of England parishes varied, though most services were traditionally called *low mass*. In essence, it meant the priest alone was the celebrant. But on certain occasions, Christmas and Easter in particular and most certainly in York Minster, the ceremony of *high mass* was performed. This mass included chanting by postulants and hymns by the choir, the usage of incense and the most colourful purples, whites and golds of the Bishops' Eucharistic robes. Bishops, in this case, would act as priests as the mass was conducted by the most Reverend Archbishop of York, The Honourable Edward Venables-Vernon, that Christmas of 1812. It was a show of church majesty in celebration.

Illuminated by a thousand candles York Minster on Christmas Eve was awash in celestial light. Its stained glass windows reflected the candles' luminosity in heavenly colours while stone pillars and arches were splashed with glimmering light and subtle shadow. The cathedral soared into upper darkness but at the ground floor hundreds of worshippers stood in the light. Roberson bathed his soul in the smells, sounds and rituals of this sacred ceremony.

So overwhelmed was he by the celebration that he resolved to succour a new congregation: the men who were to stand trial as Luddites. He would atone to those men he'd once hunted by serving them in their hour of need.

—

On a freezing Saturday, January 2, 1813, notably but one day after the New Year, when none without purpose deserted their cozy abodes, the Special Judicial Commissions regarding the Luddites began at the York castle court. It was a short day involving selection of jurors.

Hammond Roberson ensured he would sit in the visitors' gallery. He wished to make himself visible, as a support for the men who would stand trial, and so wore his clerical blacks with white collar.

The courtroom was large and high ceilinged, coated in dark panelled wood. It was a rich, judicial chamber. There was a *dock* for the prisoners which faced a witness box. There were tables for a court recorder, the clerks, the prosecution and the defense. There were galleries for both the jury and spectators. Finally, towering over all, was the *Bench* where Their Worships sat: directing proceedings. The judges and attorneys were stark in their black robes and white cotton *bands*, each wearing a horsehair *bench wig*. By the time he was seated Roberson was somewhat daunted by it all.

On Monday January 4 the court's two judges, Sir Alexander Thomson, Baron of the Exchequer and Sir Simon Le Blanc, Justice of the Court of King's Bench, *charged* the Commissions' Grand Jury of twenty three men, most of noble birth or wealthy demeanour. It happened, Roberson noted, that one of the jurors was Joseph Radcliffe. The Magistrate's presence gave Roberson a sense of how the Commissions would go. That the man who most hated, and was most hated by the Luddites, should sit on the Grand Jury as if he were somehow impartial, attested to prejudice at work.

Justice indeed.

On Tuesday January 5 the first trial was that of four men for *burglariously breaking the dwelling house of Samuel Moxon at Whitley Upper and stealing sundry articles.* Thomson began the proceedings with a verbal assault upon those facing the jury. He was in no way dispassionate for at that time any person brought before the court was ascertained guilty. The men pled not guilty. After just ten minutes' deliberation the jury returned with a decision of guilty upon each of the four. Three were sentenced to transportation, though one was pardoned for not having blacked his face. It came clear to Roberson what these Commissions were meant to accomplish.

Court resumed the next day, Wednesday January 6, with the trial of three men for the murder of William Horsfall. Conveniently, indictments had already been brought by Magistrate Radcliffe from the West Riding of Yorkshire, where the crime had occurred. The men charged were Thomas Smith, William Thorpe and George Mellor. All pled not guilty.

> *(The records of these proceedings remain. They are long, complex and at times filled with preposterous euphuisms. Still, they resemble a trial in the way in which each side tried to outwit the other, confuse the jury, attack the defendants and so on. Mr. Park, Chief Prosecutor, produced evidence regarding times of day, sightings of the defendants, the natures of certain guns fired, clothing worn, a wounded finger, and in particular the eyewitness account of Mr. Henry Parr along with the testimony of the fourth felon, Benjamin Walker, pardoned and rewarded for having given the others up.)*

Mr. Park had some difficulty understanding the Yorkshire dialect during testimony. This created a certain hilarity until laughter was barred by His Worship Sir Alexander Thomson. His Worship Justice Le Blanc summed up the case for the prosecution, in a more palatable accent, for the discernment of Thomson and certain baronets serving on the jury. They did not hear the *common tongue* much in their circles.

For the defense, Mr. Brougham said not a word to counter the prosecution's case. Mr. Brougham was more interested in holding his seat in Parliament and a number of jury members could help him. There were witnesses called, however, to disprove the prosecution. Sadly, these various and sundry testimonies contradicted one another, the witnesses obfuscating their own evidence. They were overawed and had not been prepared.

The jury retired to return within the half hour finding all three men guilty. The Clerk of Arraigns asked, as customary, if each defendant had anything to say so that *death* might not be pronounced upon them.

They responded thus:

Mellor: "I have nothing to say, only I am not guilty."

Thorpe: "I am not guilty, Sir; evidence has been given false against me; that I declare."

Smith: "Not guilty, Sir."

A few moments passed as the *Bench* conferred. Then their Worships sentenced each man to execution by hanging. Justice Le Blanc followed up by adding an extraordinary instruction. The hangings were to be carried out within *two* days: on Friday morning, January 8.

There were muffled cheers in the courtroom from the gallery of invited guests. The shackled condemned were led away. Smith was crying.

Roberson was appalled.

—

That evening Reverend Hammond Roberson was refused admission to York castle gaol. He was informed he must register now with the military authorities in order to visit any Luddites and those in particular who were condemned. He spent the next day answering questions and filling out forms at Colonel Campbell's headquarters. With Maitland gone Campbell had resumed command. At one point the colonel emerged, noted Roberson, remembered him, and crossed the busy room to have a word.

"You are Vicar Roberson, if I recall," Campbell said.

"No longer a vicar, Colonel. I've resigned that position."

"What would make you do that, Sir?" the Colonel asked.

"It was a question of faith."

"Hmpf. I see." the Colonel was uncomfortable. Not the type of man predisposed to self-examination, he could not comprehend Roberson's point. "You remain a priest, I see, from your clerical clothing."

"Indeed. I have chosen to try to help these men in the gaol. Three are condemned and I feel they would benefit from my presence. Your administration makes it difficult."

"You have no idea, Reverend, of General Maitland's orders?"

"I'm afraid not, Colonel."

"Did you know the scaffold was built at the back wall of the castle? It is an enclosed yet public space. People shall be permitted to witness the executions but they will be rigourously controlled. Word of the hangings has travelled. Maitland suspects a substantial crowd. He's made it clear they are to be shown a lesson. Do you know anything of hanging?"

"I do not, Sir. I should like to know now. I intend to be with those men on the scaffold."

"You do? But why?"

"I'll not trouble you, Colonel, with my own spiritual weakness. Suffice to say, I am a priest and those men will need me tomorrow. What of this hanging you think I should know?"

Campbell's voice dropped to an undertone. He sounded comically conspiratorial, but he was deadly serious. It did not take Roberson long to understand why.

"Rather than the *long drop* which usually breaks a man's neck with the fall, Maitland has ordered a *short drop*. Once the trapdoors open the condemned shall fall only the length of their bodies. They will strangle to death, likely ten minutes of suffering. The cruel thing is Maitland's further orders to remove the scaffold's front panel so these men shall be *seen* in their death throes. Can you imagine? Even Curry, the hangman, doesn't like it. It shan't be a pretty sight, Reverend."

"This is Maitland's lesson?"

"Precisely. Still, we are ready. Two troops of dragoons will be drawn up before the gallows to prevent any rescue attempt. Infantry shall be placed on either flank to shoot into the crowd if ordered. Cavalry shall be stationed at the rear to break up what's left."

"Why that's abominable!" Roberson said. "Is this Maitland so ruthless he would have soldiers kill innocent people?"

"It won't come to that, Reverend."

"Why ever not? These people shall be sympathizers, no doubt."

"Of a movement which no longer exists? Of an insurrection entirely defeated? Those sympathizers, as you call them, have eyes. They'll see our positions. We don't intend hiding. They'll not be given the chance to riot."

"What of afterward, in the streets?"

"Soldiers will be on patrol. For this month, at least, York shall live under martial law."

"From your tone you don't seem to appreciate the general's plans?"

"I would rather be fighting the French. I can, however, help you somewhat, Reverend. I'll provide you a pass. It will allow you access to the condemned cells if you wish."

"I do."

"Then consider it done."

—

The night was quiet in York castle prison. Hammond Roberson was allowed in, his pass from Campbell sufficient. Still, the basket he carried was thoroughly searched. He was closely escorted through dingy corridors. The cell door was opened by one of the warders. Roberson passed in and with a slight shiver heard the sound of iron against iron as the barred door was closed behind him. He registered the rasp of the lock. He was alone with three murderers.

Thorpe and Smith sat together. Clearly the big man had been comforting Smith. Mellor, across the cell, sat leaning against a white wall with eyes closed. At first Roberson thought him asleep, but his eyes opened and the Reverend realized the man was immersed in thought.

Roberson opened his basket: meat, cheese, bread and ale. Thorpe and Smith took the food gladly, the food breaking the anguish of their wait. Mellor closed his eyes again in refusal.

"You should take some food, Mr. Mellor," Roberson said, but

received no reply. They sat unspeaking for half an hour until the two had finished their repast. Thomas Smith began to weep. Big Will Thorpe put his arms around him once again, patting his back. Thorpe seemed to have no thought for himself. He looked over at Roberson.

"Smith cries, Reverend, for the wrong done him. Dost know he's innocent? 'Twas me and George forced him to come with us."

"I'm sorry to hear that, Mr. Thorpe."

A dark, dismal voice emanated from across the cell. It was eerie, wraithlike, and came in a harsh whisper. George Mellor spoke.

"Vicar Roberson! Why are you here? Have you been sent t' get a confession? I'm not guilty if you must know."

"I am no vicar, Mr. Mellor. Would it trouble you if I used your Christian name?"

"Don't matter much now."

"But you see, it is I who want to confess. Will you hear me?"

"What's this then?" Mellor said.

"I deeply regret my conduct, George. It was sinful. I'd become a zealot. I thought I was fighting Methodism. I thought I was fighting rebels. I forgot as a Christian I should not have been fighting at all."

"Aye. I've been sinful as well, but not in the way you think. I wronged my Mary but I'm no murderer. I'm a soldier fighting a righteous war."

"If you believe that, then I shall accept it," Roberson said, keeping his voice as low as Mellor's, trying to hold the bond between them.

"What of Mary? Have you news?" Mellor asked.

"She's left the city. I had a note from her. She and Mrs. Lodge are leaving, she says, for a place called Upper Canada."

"Aye, Sand Hills."

"You do not wish her here?"

"T' see me hang? Better, what she's doing."

"Did you love her?"

"I do still."

"Do you wish to pray?"

"No, Vicar ..."

"As I said, George, I'm no long a vicar."

"But you're still a priest?"

"I hope a better priest than I was a vicar."

"I'm not a religious man."

"That may be but He has you in His light."

"Dost mean that same god who turns men into *maisters* and *maisters* to tyrants?"

"God gives us free will."

"I've no use for him."

"I understand."

"And I have no confession!" Mellor suddenly said, their intimacy gone in a flash of his temper. He rose to his feet, overwrought.

"I don't wish one, George."

His outburst had cost Mellor physically. He reached for the wall to support himself, missed and collapsed, his face ashen. Thorpe was instantly at his side lying him on his back. The big man was their rock. For quite some time he watched over Mellor. Roberson began to think the man dead, the result of a stroke. He'd been incarcerated for months then gone through the hell of his trial. Perhaps he had died of his own sanction rather than wait for a noose.

Then his eyelids fluttered open.

"Take some ale, George." Thorpe offered the flask. "You've had nowt t' drink all day. Please, George."

Mellor acquiesced. He sipped slowly. He looked once again at Roberson. He seemed to have regained some calm as a result of his faint.

"Reverend, this struggle won't go away so long as men stand on top of others. The living can choose t' fight but those not born yet, what chance have they? The ones who come after, our children and theirs. I speak of them. I fought for the future."

—

York had always had its own hangman appointed from the inmate population. In 1813 John Curry officiated. He was known as *Mutton* Curry because he'd twice been convicted of sheep stealing. On the second occasion, while awaiting transportation, the post of hangman came vacant and he had accepted it. He was regretting it now.

All was ready. He'd measured the rope (reluctantly) for the *short drop* as ordered. He'd oiled the trap doors' hinges and made sure the pin would drop all three men at once. He'd ensured the steps leading up to the scaffold were secure and (again reluctantly) removed the front panel from that scaffold. Now, as he stood on the roughhewn pine deck on a bright winter's morning, he gazed at a crowd. Surrounding the host were regiments of redcoats. Below him, two squadrons of dragoons. The soldiers were anxious.

The men to be executed were guilty of murder, a *clergyable* offence. They would, therefore, not have the privilege of clergy beside them upon the scaffold. Roberson, who had spent the night with them, had been forced to accept a seat just below. He insisted it be where the men could see him. Two large dragoons were stationed at the base of the steps to stop him, or anyone else, from climbing; except those meant to climb and fall.

The condemned appeared in shackles, their hands bound behind them, their feet shuffling in the small ugly steps their chains would allow. Each was accompanied by a warder, each was clad in a newly washed *woollen* shirt. It took some time for them to mount the steps because of their shackles. The crowd caught sight of them as they climbed. There were murmurs which quickly succumbed to an awful silence.

Once on the deck the three stood in line. Curry heard the priest invite them to prayer. All three dropped to their knees, bowed their heads, and prayed aloud simultaneously so none could understand any one of them. After five minutes Curry received the nod from Campbell, moving him from one man to the next, helping them up and placing the nooses around their necks. The first, Smith, on the left of the scaffold, was a slight man; the second, Thorpe, in the middle was a giant who made Curry thankful he'd chosen a thicker rope; the third man, Mellor, on the right, was big enough but what made Curry pause was the man's strange, icy eyes. With that hesitation, Mellor pushed Curry's hand away. The dragoons began mounting the steps. In a voice loud enough to be heard by the crowd Mellor spoke.

"Some of my enemies may be here. If there be, I freely forgive them, and all the world, and I hope the world will forgive me."

Curry quickly moved to haul him back, but not quickly enough for the cleric below who said softly: "God forgives, George."

This brought Mellor down to one knee. In an intimate voice he looked at the priest and said something which Curry, who was behind him, missed. Curry was troubled by Mellor's actions. He knew he could lose his position if he lost control. He finally got the man's noose around his neck, a *dirk* ready in his belt should there be further problems.

There were none. Curry made his way to the pin, waited for the next nod, and pulled. The traps yawned, the men dropped. The crowd moaned. Dragoons' blunderbusses rose to the ready. But nothing happened other than the horror of three men twisting and kicking as they strangled to death. It took the smallest man longest to die but all struggled to their ends. Then there was only the smell of shit and the squeaking of ropes as the three dead men dangled. The men swung ten more minutes, by Curry's timepiece, to ensure they were dead.

When it ended, the dragoons walked their horses forward in line, forcing people back. They effected a methodical exit taking only a quarter hour, the crowd herded away like sheep.

A few officials remained below the scaffold, among them Roberson and Campbell, as Curry's underlings cut the men down. John Lloyd scurried up, his movements crablike. He had the right to be there as he had served with the prosecution. Roberson recoiled from him. Lloyd watched as the dead were placed in pine boxes, then carried off by workers from York hospital.

Lloyd knew the fate of those bodies: anatomical dissection. Yet he was the only person, in thousands, who smiled that day. Then he turned to Roberson.

"I've a question, Sir, if you don't mind," he said, hissing in the only way he knew. "Did you perhaps hear what George Mellor said there at the end?"

"What do you think it was?" Roberson replied.

"I thought I heard: 'God forgive my Ludd ways,' after you told him 'God forgives'. Is that how you heard it?"

Sometimes the lie, though a sin, is not.

It was what Hammond Roberson thought as he lied to John Lloyd.

"He wasn't clear, Mr. Lloyd. I didn't hear him."
God forgive my adultery was what he'd heard.
He was sure he'd heard the truth.

—

When the bodies were taken away, the crowd dispersed and soldiers sent on patrol; when the men officiating had departed and the hangman himself had finished his duties and gone, there was one thing left which commanded that trampled field. It overlooked all, yet saw nothing, for it was inanimate. It seemed everyone had missed the irony of its part in the proceedings.

Though it was rudimentary in nature, one of the earliest of its kind ... it was a machine.

A gallows.

EPILOGUE

THE TALLY AT York, when completed, had seen no equal in the history of English law. Within two weeks, of the more than one hundred imprisoned in York castle prison, sixty-six men had been charged to appear before the Commissions. Of those men, seventeen were hanged and seven transported, seventeen more were held pending bail, a further fifteen were discharged and seven were acquitted. One other was indicted for misdemeanor and tried at the next Assizes.

At the end of 1813 with Napoleon hurtled back in defeat, with the war against America a standoff, with the termination of the Orders in Council and with fine, full harvests that fall, the mood of the country shifted. Markets picked up and *woollens* and cottons in record quantities were churned out by the new factory system. This sudden economic surge was, of course, illusory.

By 1817, with the return of soldiers from the European war coupled with surging mechanization, the job market was flooded. It made some men wealthy and starved or emigrated far more. Conditions in mills and factories deteriorated beyond belief. By 1830 the *Leeds Mercury* gave a description of the conditions which kept the cloth industry profitable.

It spoke of children ... "*who are compelled not by the car-whip of the negro slave driver but the dread of the equally appalling thong or strap of the overlooker, to hasten half-dressed, but not half-fed, to those magazines of British Infantile Slavery — the Worsted Mills in the town and neighbourhood of Bradford ...*"

A few years later a man named Friedrich Engels observed the stinking streams, the wasted nature, and the subjugated work force of what was then beginning to be called the Industrial Revolution. He, like George Mellor, had been to Russia and found slight difference between the cultures. In 1848 he co-authored *The Communist Manifesto* with Karl Marx.

Invention is embedded in civilization and the technology produced by that invention is, invariably, irreversible. There are consequences to invention, however; most powerful those of social consequence when new technology is introduced. Yet technology too is fleeting as it succumbs to invention. The past can be glimpsed in the faded remains of ruins, antiques and memorabilia. It rises and falls in waves. It twists and reflects as a Mobius strip, inevitable yet never the same.

The same may be said of humans.

Mary Buckworth and Bonnie Lodge immigrated to York (now Toronto, Canada). Bonnie remarried and remained in York but Mary was unable to purchase land at Sand Hills. Instead, she moved to a nearby village named Galt, now called Cambridge, Ontario. Colonel Beagles' land was bought by Mennonites from Pennsylvania. Sand Hills is now named Waterloo, in the province of Ontario.

Mary had a son. She named him Mellor George Jonathan Buckworth. True to her word, she gave him her *Enoch* as a symbol of coming of age. That tradition carried on through the Buckworth family for generations. Mel Buckworth, in 2012 ironically, was working in manufacturing in the city of Waterloo the day he was permanently laid off to be replaced by a robotic assembler. He was wearing that family heirloom around his neck. He had no idea what it meant. He only knew, at age fifty-seven, his prospects for work were virtually nil.

But that is another story.

Sam Lodge was transported to New South Wales, Australia. He never again saw his wife or children.

Benjamin Walker was mistrusted for his betrayal of the Luddites and his acceptance of the reward. He lived a miserable life, despised by all. In the end, having lost his money, he was reduced to begging on the streets of Huddersfield.

Joseph Radcliffe was made a baronet in 1813. He died five years later, due to ill health, unable to enjoy the esteem he had sought. His wealthy widow, Fanny, married again quite successfully, to a Viscount.

John Lloyd's employment was terminated directly following the Special Commissions. He was ordered to leave York immediately without reward other than his wages. Radcliffe rejected him upon his return to the West Riding. Nothing is known of him after that. His dossier of Luddite suspects, however, exists to this day.

Thomas Maitland departed Yorkshire at the earliest opportunity. He was rendered a baronet and became Governor of Malta, then Commander-in-Chief of the Mediterranean and finally High Commissioner of the Ionian Islands.

Francis Raynes was struck by illness due to his efforts in Yorkshire. After some time at home in Scotland he reached London to find Maitland already departed. He had no resources to follow and never saw Maitland again. Reduced to the paucity of half-pay, he spent the next years writing petulant letters demanding reward for his work. He was ignored.

Hammond Roberson, the uncompromising cleric who was so altered by events, died at age eighty-four. His gravestone was no different from any other: two feet six inches high in a small plot of grass, identical to its neighbours. He had ensured this by instructing it so in his Will.

Following the Commissions and the hangings, the West Riding settled into passivity. After years of investigation it was decided that, other than a few locals in Lancashire, Cheshire, Derbyshire, Nottinghamshire and Yorkshire, there had never been a true leader in the risings of the Luddites.

There was only legend.

"Ned Lud did tha'!"

SOURCES

Baines, Edward, H. Fisher, R. Fisher & P. Jackson. *History of the Cotton Manufacture in Great Britain* (1835)

Brooke, Alan & Lesley Kipling. *Liberty or Death*. Huddersfield Local Historical Society (1988)

Brooke, Iris. *Illustrated Handbook of Western European Costume*. Dover Publications (2003)

Bronte, Charlotte. *Shirley*. Penguin Classics (2006)

Emsley, Clive. *British Society and the French Wars 1793–1815*. Macmillan (1979)

Halevy, Elie. *A History of the English People in 1815, Volume 1*. Ark Paperbacks (1987)

Landranger 110, Sheffield & Huddersfield Area, Ordnance Survey

Proceedings at York Special Commission, January 1813, Gurney, Harvard University Library

Reid, Robert. *Land of Lost Content*. Sphere Books Ltd. (1986)

Sharp, Robert. *The Diary of Robert Sharp of South Cave: Life in a Yorkshire Village 1812-1837*. Oxford University Press (1997)

Thomis, M. & P. Holt. *Threats of Revolution in Britain 1789–1848*. Macmillan (1977)

Thompson, E.P. *The Making of the English Working Class*. Penguin Books (1981)

ACKNOWLEDGEMENTS

My thanks and deepest appreciation to Alan Brooke, Pam Brooke, and Ann Herd ... my guides and mentors in England.

The Huddersfield Historical Society for their kind introductions.

Michael Mirolla, Anna van Valkenberg, Diane Eastham and David Moratto for their parts in making this a much improved book.

Not to mention ... Our departed companions: Meme and Aodahn.

And, of course, to my wife and loving partner, Susan, without whom none of this would have happened.

ABOUT THE AUTHOR

Brian Van Norman is the author of two previous novels: *The Betrayal Path* (Amazon) and *Immortal Water* (Guernica Editions). He is currently at work writing a sequel to *Against the Machine*.

Once a teacher, theatre director and adjudicator, Brian Van Norman left those worlds to travel with his wife, Susan, and take up writing as a full time pursuit. He has journeyed to every continent and sailed nearly every sea on the planet. His base is Waterloo, Ontario, Canada though he is seldom found there.